Nina Singh lives just outsid
her husband, children, and a
Yorkie. After several years i.
she finally followed the advice of family and
friends to 'give the writing a go, already'. She's
oh-so-happy she did. When not at her keyboard
she likes to spend time on the tennis court or golf
course. Or immersed in a good read.

Australian author **Ally Blake** loves reading and
strong coffee, porch swings and dappled sunshine,
beautiful notebooks and soft, dark pencils. Her
inquisitive, rumbustious, spectacular children are
her exquisite delight, and she adores writing love
stories so much she'd write them even if nobody
read them. No wonder, then, having sold over four
million copies of her romance novels worldwide,
Ally is living her bliss. Find out more about Ally's
books at allyblake.com.

TWO WEEKS TO TEMPT THE TYCOON

NINA SINGH

FAKE ENGAGEMENT WITH THE BILLIONAIRE

ALLY BLAKE

MILLS & BOON

First published in Great Britain 2023
by Mills & Boon, an imprint of HarperCollins*Publishers* Ltd,
1 London Bridge Street, London, SE1 9GF

www.harpercollins.co.uk

HarperCollins*Publishers*, Macken House, 39/40 Mayor Street Upper, Dublin 1, D01 C9W8, Ireland

Two Weeks to Tempt the Tycoon © 2023 Nilay Nina Singh

Fake Engagement with the Billionaire © 2023 Ally Blake

ISBN: 978-0-263-30645-3

05/23

TWO WEEKS
TO TEMPT
THE TYCOON

NINA SINGH

MILLS & BOON

To all those with the grace and heart to forgive.

CHAPTER ONE

THERE WAS SOMEONE else here in the house with her. Maybe more than one someone.

Marni Payton's heart slammed against her chest as she shut the wooden door behind her. It had been unlocked. This was so not the welcome she'd been expecting after a long, turbulent flight and an exhausting day of travel.

But she had a more pressing matter at the moment.

Nella had warned her there might be squatters at the villa this time of year. She'd said they were usually harmless. Older kids, mostly, who were looking for a place to party. Teenagers trying to get away from under the watchful eyes of strict parents.

Which, on the surface, did sound harmless enough. Or at least it had when Nella had explained it to her a month ago, while offering Marni the use of her beachside villa in Capri for two weeks before she and her husband would need it back.

Now, however, the knowledge did little to calm Marni down. Shaking with fear, she stood in the middle of the foyer, listening to the sounds coming from upstairs. What if it wasn't a bunch of kids up there? What if the house was being robbed? Or she was about to be attacked?

Marni stepped backward, readying to flee the house, her gaze still locked to the top of the stairs. She reached for the cell phone in her back pocket to call the authorities. In her fear and panic, she yanked it out too jerkily and dropped it to the tile floor. It fell with a loud crashing sound and she watched in horror as the case popped off and the screen shattered.

So much for calling for help. The taxi that had driven her to the house was long gone. She was on her own. Marni froze in her spot, unable to move or so much as breathe.

Had the intruders heard her dropping her phone? Were they scrambling down right now to come hurt her?

Squeak. Squeak. Squeak.

Oh, God. That was definitely a sound she recognized—the unmistakable noise of the springs in a bed. Whoever was up there was using the very bed she'd be sleeping in! Marni could just guess what they were doing. A wave of indignation rose in her chest. The audacity to break into a house and then do…that! She was as sympathetic as anyone to lovesick teens, but this was miles and miles too far.

It was high time to put a stop to it.

Marni pushed aside her fear in favor of outrage. Plus, they were definitely naked. She had the element of surprise on her side. She'd just go up there, demand they get their clothes on and vacate the premises ASAP. Marni bounded up the stairs before she could change her mind. When she reached the closed bedroom door, she gave a quick knock then covered her eyes before pushing it open. Some things she didn't need to see.

"I won't tell your parents if you both get dressed and leave right now," she said. It was an empty threat. She had no idea who their parents might be or where they lived. "Right now," she repeated.

No answer. Maybe they didn't understand English.

She repeated the bluff in broken Italian. Still nothing. And she didn't hear any scuffling about either.

Of all the nerve. Were they seriously just going to ignore her? At least the squeaking had stopped.

Marni cleared her throat, beginning to speak louder this time. "Listen, I'm going to give you exactly sixty seconds to gather your clothes and get out of this house!"

"Dio!" A sharp male voice exploded in her ears. Definitely not the voice of a teenager. A string of sharp Italian curse words followed.

Nope. That was no kid.

In fact, the voice sounded all too familiar. Marni's blood turned to ice in her veins. It couldn't be. But the next word she heard only confirmed that indeed it could.

"*Gattina?* Is that you?"

Oh, no. There was only one person who ever called her that. But how? Why? With great reluctance, Marni lowered her palm from her eyes and fearfully opened her lids. She immediately wanted to squeeze them shut again.

She'd been so wrong. There was no couple on the bed. Just one solitary man. To her horror, he happened to be Gio Santino. Her best friend Nella's brother. The same man she'd had a crush on for most of her life.

Well, at least she'd been right about one thing: the intruder was indeed naked.

His usual nightmare had taken quite a surprising turn. Rubbing his eyes, Gio blinked away the grogginess of interrupted sleep and tried to focus on the figure standing at the door.

Yep, it was definitely her. Marni Payton stood staring at him in shock, wide-eyed, her mouth agape. What in the world was she doing here at his sister's villa in Capri? Marni lived in Boston.

"What are you doing here?" they both asked in unison.

Gio knew what his answer to that question was. He'd been trying to get some much-needed sleep. The insomnia and nightmares were wreaking havoc on him. Not to mention the throbbing pain in his leg and torso.

Marni blinked rapidly before attempting to speak. "Nella said I could stay here. For two weeks. I just arrived."

Huh. Gio ran a hand down his face. "That's funny. Because her husband told me the same thing. That I was welcome to the villa whenever I needed."

Marni swallowed. "Well, clearly there's been some kind of misunderstanding."

"Clearly." He was tempted to throttle Antonella the next time he saw her. As much as he loved her, his sister had always been scattered and disorganized. He didn't know how her new husband dealt with it, for God's sake.

Gio sighed wearily. "Look, we're not going to solve this now." Not that he knew exactly how they *would* solve it at any other time. Other than looking for a hotel room for himself at the earliest opportunity. Which was not going to be easy. Capri was busy with tourists and vacationers this time of year. What a pain.

He was so tired of pain.

"Why don't we go downstairs and talk about this," he offered.

Marni didn't answer for several seconds. He was about to repeat the question when he noticed her gaze traveling from his face, past his shoulders, down his chest. Then lower.

She cleared her throat before speaking. "Yeah. Sure. We could do that. But do you mind getting dressed first?"

Gio flinched. He totally forgot that he'd climbed into bed completely nude. Much too tired to do more than peel off his gritty clothes before collapsing under the covers. To his horror, he saw the bedsheet and blanket had moved lower below his waist and barely sat on his hips. Reflexively, he yanked the sheet up to below his chest.

"Sure. I can do that," he answered.

"Great. I'll see you in a few," Marni replied, turning on her heel. She shut the door firmly behind her.

Gio leaned back against the pillows and threw his arm over his face. Great. Just great. Not only had his chance at some rest and recuperation just been soundly ruined, he'd almost flashed his younger sister's dearest friend.

Why did she have to be here? Now of all times? Was nothing going to go his way this year? Guessing he already knew the answer to that question, Gio begrudgingly tossed the covers aside and stood. Pulling his suitcase open, he grabbed a pair of sweats and a T-shirt then made his way down the stairs.

Marni was bent down in the doorway when he got to the first floor. In spite of himself and despite the circumstances, he found himself appreciating the view. The sight of Marni's rounded hips had his mind traveling to places it had no business going.

Whatever she was doing, she was distracted enough that she seemed unaware of him. Hopefully, she hadn't noticed just how long it had taken him to get dressed and get down here. Everything took longer to do these days. Something the doctors kept reminding he'd better get used to.

"What are you doing?" he asked Marni's back.

She straightened and turned to face him, holding

something in her hand that might have resembled a cell phone at some point in time.

"I was a little startled when I heard noises upstairs. I panicked and dropped my phone." She held up the object in question and shrugged.

"Noises? What noises?"

"The bed, you were making of lot of racket up there." She pointed to the ceiling. "For someone who was sleeping…" She drifted off and a blush of color rose in her cheeks, her bright hazel eyes grew wide. As if she was embarrassed.

Gio held his hands up, offended and slightly amused at her insinuation. "Marni, it's not like that."

She shook her head, growing redder. "Oh! Of course. Whatever you say. Um… Not that there'd be anything wrong or to be embarrassed about. If that was what you were…doing." She faltered on the last word.

Gio couldn't help chuckling. "Thanks. I guess." What exactly was he thanking her for? "The truth is, I haven't been sleeping well. Lots of tossing and turning. That's if I'm lucky enough to fall asleep in the first place."

She looked unsure of what to say. Best to change the subject. "So you're here on vacation?" he asked.

Marni looked away, but not before he caught a shadow dance across her eyes. "Something like that," she answered.

Huh. He'd thought it was a casual question. But Marni clearly didn't want to talk about what exactly she was doing here, halfway across the world from her home. That suited him just fine. He didn't really want to get into his own reasons for being here either.

She finally returned his gaze. "Gio. If I'd known you

were going to be here, I would have made other arrangements."

"I'd say the same. But we're both here now." The question was, what were they going to do about it?

She glanced around her. "I mean, the place is rather roomy."

Maybe. But there was still only one finished bedroom. And only the one bed. Nella and Alex had never gotten around to furnishing the entire house, having recently purchased it. Gio glanced past the foyer to the sitting area. It looked comfortable enough, but the furniture was hardly ample. He didn't think he'd be able to endure sleeping on the small love seat in the living room. The shape he was in at the moment, his body simply couldn't handle it.

And he wasn't going to ask Marni to sleep there. Old-fashioned or not, his masculine pride simply wouldn't allow it. Which lead to another complication. There was no way he was going to explain to Marni why he wouldn't be able to do the chivalrous thing and sleep on the couch.

"I would call around to see about available hotel rooms, but..." She simply held up her shattered phone to complete the sentence.

"I don't think you'd find one anyway. Places around here are booked months in advance." He rammed his hand through his hair in frustration. "Look. We're not going to solve this now," he repeated. "Why don't you go freshen up and I'll throw a snack together. I don't know about you, but I could use a bite."

As if in answer, her stomach reacted with a low grumble. Gio had to chuckle again. For as long as she and his sister had been friends, she'd always managed to make him laugh. He couldn't even remember the last time he'd laughed since the accident. Marni had been here only a few minutes and he'd already chuckled twice.

Despite the awkward circumstances they found themselves in.

By the time Marni made it back downstairs, Gio had thrown together a rather enticing tray of snacks and munchies, if he did say so himself. He'd loaded the fridge and pantry when he'd gotten here three days ago—it was a rare instance of him planning ahead.

If only he'd lived his life being a better planner. He might be in better physical shape right now, without the throbbing pain in his side and the pronounced limp in his gait. A limp he would have to somehow try to hide now that Marni was here.

He got an appreciative sigh from her when she entered the kitchen and eyed the food tray.

"Wow. You threw together a charcuterie board," she said, then added, "I'm impressed."

A what now? "Uh, thanks, I guess. If you mean the tray of cubed cheese, tapenade, meat and grapes. Where I come from, we call it antipasto."

She smiled wide. "Whatever you want to call it, sure beats the dry granola bars I have stashed in my purse. A man of many talents. Who knew?"

Considering they'd been acquainted for most of their lives through his younger sister, he wasn't sure if he felt slighted by that.

When was the last time he'd seen Marni? Had to have been the holidays last year. He studied her now. She looked different, more mature.

And she smelled good. Some kind of spicy, citrus scent that lingered in the air. Her cheeks had filled in. He remembered her face being much more angular. In fact, she'd filled in all over. Marni was definitely curvier than he remembered, bringing to mind images of starlets from the Hollywood of old. The likes of Sofia Loren or Gina Lollobrigida. The changes looked good on her. *Marni* looked good.

And why in the world would he notice a thing like that? Gio gave himself a mental shake. Maybe his head injury wasn't as healed as he'd hoped. He had no business sniffing around his sister's best friend or waxing poetic about her curves. This was little *gattina*, for heaven's sake. "Little kitten." He couldn't even remember when he'd first given her the nickname. They'd been kids, and she'd reminded him of a kitten because she was always so playful and constantly underfoot.

She pointed to the kettle sitting by the side of the island. "Mind if I make some tea? If I know Nella, she's got some high-quality black leaf sitting around here somewhere."

He'd been about to suggest one of the bottles of high-end Chianti he'd discovered in the wine rack by the bar but tea would work. In fact, it might be better to keep sober around her given the wayward thoughts that kept popping in his head.

"Sounds good."

"I was thinking of getting ahold of Nella," she said, filling the silver kettle with water and setting it on the stove. "To ask her if there's a friend in town who might happen to have a room."

"Good idea," he answered. Better than anything he'd been able to come up with.

"As much as I hate to bother her and Alex on their romantic trip to Paris."

"They'll have to forgive us for the intrusion."

She nodded. "I would have done it already except I have no phone." She looked at him expectedly.

Gio popped a mozzarella ball into his mouth. "Yeah, it's really too bad that it shattered like that." He really did feel bad about scaring her so badly. He should find a way to apologize. Though it was hard to say sorry about something you weren't even aware was happening at the time.

"So…uh…could you maybe do it?" Marni asked.

Gio gave his head a shake. Of course! How daft could he be? What was wrong with him? Why couldn't he suddenly think straight around a woman he'd known practically his whole life?

Had to be the lack of sleep. It was wreaking havoc on his mental faculties. He pulled his phone out of his back pocket and clicked on his sister's name. Straight to voice mail. Not surprising. "No answer," he told Marni after leaving Nella a brief message he could only hope she would check in a timely fashion. "I'll try Alex next."

His brother-in-law's phone didn't even have the option to leave a voice mail. Gio just got the "unavailable" message. He shook his head at Marni's unvoiced question.

"Sorry. Can't reach him either."

Marni's face fell, her lips forming a thin line. She was really worried. A tinge of guilt tugged in his chest. She'd be kicking back and relaxing right now with a working phone if it wasn't for him. He couldn't seem to do anything right these days.

The dejected expression on her face tore at him. Gio had a crazy urge to go to her and gather her in his arms. Lucky for him, the kettle started screeching before he could do anything so foolish. Marni silently went to brew the tea, the look on her face not easing in the least.

"We'll figure this out," he reassured her. "In the meantime, it's not so bad being here with me, is it?"

But Marni only silently smiled in answer. Whatever she was hoping to get out of this trip, it was clear Gio's presence was going to be a hindrance. His guilt grew.

Within moments, Marni had found two ceramic mugs, had brewed the tea and had a steaming mug sitting in front of them both.

"We'll try Nella and Alex again in a bit."

"Something tells me they're not going to answer their phones anytime soon." Her voice was low and forlorn.

"Then we'll make do for now and start fresh tomorrow. And first thing in the morning, we'll head into town and see about replacing that phone."

If he'd thought that was going to cheer her up at all, he was sorely disappointed. Marni barely reacted to the offer. In fact, she appeared to be deep in thought, staring at the steam rising from her mug. For as excited as she'd seemed about the food, so far she'd barely taken a bite. Yep, Gio had inadvertently ruined Marni Payton's vacation.

Nothing he could do about it now. They just had to coexist for the next few hours until he could figure out a plan of action.

And as far as sleeping arrangements for the night, heaven only knew what they would do.

Marni lay awake staring into the darkness. It had all been too much to hope for. Was a two-week reprieve too much to ask for from the universe? All she'd wanted from this trip was to get away for a few days and lick her proverbial wounds. Just a chance to leave the past behind and focus on herself in quiet solitude in what she'd thought would be her friend's abandoned villa on the Italian coast. No such luck. Because enter one Gio Santino.

What was he doing here in Italy, anyway? He had a major corporation to run. Santino Foods was headquartered in the North End in Boston.

As CEO of Santino Foods, Gio rarely took time off. Even after a car accident last year, he'd barely given himself time away. Last she'd heard from Nella, he was putting off the therapy and the appointments recommended for a full recovery.

Regardless of his reason for being here, now Marni would have to find alternate arrangements. And she would have to be the one to leave. First of all, Gio had gotten here first. He was already settled while she hadn't even unpacked yet. Not to mention, his blood sibling actually owned the house. Marni and Nella had been friends for years—but blood trumped friendship.

Bad enough she'd kicked him out of the bed for the night. Gio had insisted. He'd told her he was having problems sleeping as it was. Now he was lying on a pile of cushions they'd taken off the couches downstairs and turned into a makeshift mattress on the floor of one of the empty rooms. Try as she might, Marni hadn't been able to convince him to take the real bed instead of her. Not surprising. She'd known the argument was futile from the beginning because Gio wasn't wired that way.

What a mess.

But none of this was her fault. She'd been planning this trip for weeks. Since the day she'd walked away from Ander for good, Marni knew she'd have to get far away from her ex. At least for the short term. Being anywhere near him right after the breakup was a recipe for disaster.

She could only imagine what Ander's thoughts on her

current predicament might be. First, he'd tell her that he'd told her so. He'd remind her how little she was capable of without his guidance. That it was no wonder she'd messed up the very first thing she'd tried to do without him by her side.

Worst of all, Ander had plenty of contacts who were all too willing to print and air his version of events. It was why she'd had to get away, to find refuge in an entirely different country.

Marni sniffled away a tear and threw her forearm over her eyes. She refused to believe that Ander might be right about her. He liked to think she was useless and incompetent without him. That was just his narcissism. Being out from under his thumb and getting far away from him was the best thing Marni could have done for herself. Something she should have done much sooner.

As soon as she figured out her living situation for the next couple of weeks, everything would fall into place.

A loud shriek cut through the darkness. Marni bolted up in bed, disoriented and alarmed. She'd been closer to falling asleep than she thought. The loud noise sent her pulse rocketing.

Gio. Something was terribly wrong with him. Had someone broken in, after all? Was he struggling with an intruder right at this very moment?

Marni scrambled out of bed and ran to his room, grabbing a heavy vase off the bureau along the way. Her heart pounding, she threw open his door. Relief surged through her when she saw no one else was in there with him. But Gio was far from okay. A small sliver of moonlight from the open window illuminated just enough of the room to allow her to see him thrashing about on the cushions, his cries of anguish echoed off the walls. Whatever nightmare he was having seemed to be torturing him in his sleep. Marni rushed over to his side and dropped to her knees.

"Gio. Wake up," she cried. "You have to wake up."

Nothing. He hadn't even heard her. The thrashing didn't let up, his cries continued jarring the night air.

"Gio! It's me!" she yelled out, louder this time. She reached for his shoulders to give him a shake.

Big mistake. Gio didn't awaken but she'd managed to startle him in his sleep. His arms thrust out and he grabbed her by the arms, yanked her down. She landed on top of his chest, their legs intertwined.

Marni's vision went dark, her voice stuck in her throat. Scramble as she might, she couldn't get out of Gio's grip.

Panic and fear surged through her until she thought she'd completely lost her breath. Images rushed through her mind—all the times Ander had grabbed her arm just a little too roughly. The times he'd been frustrated with her when they were running late and given her a nudge just hard enough to be considered a push. The many moments she'd wondered if and when he'd go too far.

Steady. Ander wasn't here. This was Gio. And he would never hurt her. He was just having a nightmare.

The more she fought, the harder Gio held her. Marni forced herself to go still and take several deep breaths. It seemed to work. Gio's grasp loosened just enough for her to roll out of his reach.

Several moments passed while she tried to regain a steady breath. Gio finally grew quiet, she was debating whether to simply stand and leave the room, when his eyes fluttered open. His gaze cast about the room, his dark brown eyes growing wide when they found her.

"Marni?"

She could only nod in response.

"What are you doing here?"

"I heard you…thought you might be hurt. Or someone might be here…" She couldn't seem to make her mind communicate with her mouth.

Gio's face tightened as he put the scenario together. Even in the dark, she could see the horror flood his features. He stood and rubbed a hand down his face. "Marni. I'm so sorry. I never meant to scare you. Again."

In two strides he'd reached the wall and flipped on the light switch. Soft yellow light flooded the room. Gio wore only pajama bottoms, hung low on his hips. Bare chested, she could see the hardened contours of his muscles.

So not the time to be noticing such a thing.

But she noticed something else. It was rather hard to miss. A large angry scar ran down the side of his torso down to his hip. It looked fresh and red.

Nella hadn't told her much about his accident. Though, truth be told, Marni had been too preoccupied with the emotional toll of her relationship with Ander to really pay attention. But judging by Gio's physical scars, the accident had been more serious than Marni had known.

No wonder Gio was having nightmares.

CHAPTER TWO

GIO WASN'T IN the house when she awoke the next morning. Marni had to wonder if he'd even managed to get back to sleep or if he even wanted to, given what awaited him in dreamland.

When he'd mentioned yesterday that he had trouble sleeping, she'd had no idea how violent his slumber could get. It certainly explained the squeaking she'd heard upon arrival at the house.

What exactly happened to him? The tabloids and gossip websites had moved past reporting on the story pretty quickly. The high-profile divorce of a Hollywood power couple had taken over the news feeds right around the same time. Nella didn't give away much either when Marni asked. There was a while a few months back where Nella looked particularly distracted. Worried, even. Marni hadn't wanted to pry at the time. She knew Gio and his sister were quite close. But she also knew both siblings could be withdrawn and very private.

She gave her head a brisk shake. It was too much to think about first thing in the morning after a restless night. She made her way to the kitchen for some much-needed caffeine.

A scrap of paper sitting on the counter caught her eye. Gio had left her a note.

Gone for a walk on the beach. Let's talk when I get back.

Fine by her. They had a lot to discuss. Like exactly what the plan was if neither of them could find another place to stay.

The sound of a standard ringtone shrilling behind her cut through her thoughts. Gio had left his phone behind. The sound reminded her that her own phone sat in the bottom of the rubbish bin in several pieces. She sighed with frustration. Yet another thing to deal with and fix.

Marni glanced at the screen. Nella! As if her thoughts from a few minutes ago had conjured her. Finally.

But Gio wasn't here. Marni raced to the small window above the sink to see if he was at all nearby. They both desperately needed to talk to his sister.

No sign of him.

Marni swore under her breath then rushed to pick up the call. Gio wouldn't mind if she answered his phone. Just this once. Not in this case. Before she could change her mind, she answered.

"Hey, Nella."

Several silent pauses followed. Marni could just picture the confusion on her friend's face about a thousand miles away as she tried to figure out what was what.

Nella sounded just as confused as she'd imagined when she finally spoke. "Marni? Is that you? I thought I dialed my brother."

"It is. I mean, you did."

Far from clearing anything up, Marni's response was a jumbled mess. She took a deep breath to try again. "Yeah, it's me. But you dialed right. This is your brother's phone. He's just out right now. So I didn't think he'd mind if I answered."

That wouldn't do much to clarify things either.

Nella spoke before she could try again at another lame attempt. "Marni, what's going on? Why are you answering my brother's phone? Where are you two and what are you doing together?"

Marni scrambled for the right words. Where exactly to begin? "Well, it's a funny story actually." Except it really wasn't.

"Tell me," Nella prodded.

"See, I decided to take you up on your offer to stay at your house in Capri for the next two weeks."

"Good," Nella said immediately. "You need it."

"Right. Well, I got here last night and, to my surprise—"

Nella cut her off before she could finish. "Let me guess, Gio was already there when you arrived."

"Bingo."

Marni heard a low whistle from the other end of the line. "He's had a key since we've owned the place, with a standing offer to use it as he wished when we aren't there. Though I can't recall the last time he's actually taken us up on it."

Just her typical lousy luck, then. "I see."

"I'm really sorry, Marni. I had no idea what he planned—he's supposed to be in Chicago."

"Chicago?" As far as she knew, Santino Foods had no presence in Illinois.

Nella cleared her throat. "Never mind, the point is I

would have warned you if I had any clue that he might show."

"No need to apologize. This is your house. And he's your brother."

"And you're my dearest friend."

"It wasn't your mistake," Marni reassured.

"Still, I know how much you could use a getaway. And my brother is sort of hard to ignore."

That was an understatement. Gio was larger than life. Handsome, charming, with a sharp sense of humor. He'd always had a large personality.

Nella was still talking. "But I tried to call you last night. You didn't answer."

"Yeah, that's the other thing. I sort of destroyed my phone when I got to the villa. But that's a story for another day."

Marni cringed as the words left her mouth. Anyone but her best friend would probably deem her daft or clumsy. Or both. She'd arrived at an already occupied house and then promptly smashed her phone.

"Huh. I'd definitely like to hear it."

"Right. Well, now we're figuring out where I might move out to. If you have any suggestions."

"Move out? Why would you move out? The villa is huge."

When she put it that way, Marni was hard-pressed to come up with an answer. But she just couldn't imagine herself staying here when Gio was close by. Plus, there was the whole matter of the accommodations. "For one thing, there's only one bed."

"That's easy. Signora Baraca's son owns a furniture shop in town. Every piece is handcrafted. We've been meaning to get those empty rooms furnished and never got around to it. I'll give her a call and you guys can go down and pick something."

Marni rubbed her forehead. "Nella, you should be the one decorating your house. Not me."

Nella laughed. Marni could almost see her waving her hand dismissively. "Why not? It's literally what you do for a living."

True, Marni was an interior decorator. But she usually did commercial work with plenty of input from whomever she was working for.

"I think you know me well enough to pick out pieces I'll like," Nella pressed.

Still. "I don't think Gio will agree, Nella." What if Gio needed time to himself? To deal with whatever he was trying to deal with. She had an urge to ask Nella more about the accident and Gio's scars but decided against it. Her friend would have told her before now if Marni was meant to know.

"Well, then that would be *his* problem, wouldn't it?" Nella answered. "And he'd have to be the one to find another place. He'll come around," she added after a pause. "He's not that stubborn."

"If you say so," Marni answered, not quite convinced. She'd seen Gio act plenty stubborn over the years.

"I do say so. Trust me. And, Marni?"

"Yes?"

"Please have my brother call me as soon as he gets in. I'd really like to talk to him." Was it her imagination, or did Nella sound slightly amused?

She was pondering that question several moments later when a loud sound jarred her in her seat. She took a deep breath. It was just the front door. Just Gio returning.

Honestly, she had to stop being so jumpy. She was

in Capri now. Not back home in Massachusetts where there was someone constantly hovering over her shoulder, ready to hurl an insult or some type of accusation. Someone she'd thought she'd loved once.

When she'd been naive and too trusting. Never again.

"Marni?" Gio called from the doorway.

"In the kitchen."

When Gio entered the room, he brought with him the scent of fresh pastries. He held out a white cardboard box tied with a thin string. "I thought you might want some breakfast."

"Oh. Wow. Thanks."

Without another word, he set the box in front of her. Huh. The gesture was so unexpected, Marni wasn't sure what else to say. She couldn't recall the last time someone had brought her breakfast. Or brought her anything, for no reason other than that she might enjoy it.

Ander would have never treated her to pastries. He considered such indulgences out of the question. Well, she didn't need to give his opinion another thought anymore. He would no longer be monitoring her calorie intake or anything else that concerned her. Never again.

She untied the string and lifted the cover to reveal an array of mouthwatering pastries that looked as delicious as they smelled. Croissants, bagels, a baguette, fruit-topped Danish with rich glaze. There had to be thousands of calories in this box.

But she didn't need to focus on that these days. Not unless she chose to do so. Ander didn't have the right to comment on her looks anymore or check whether she'd logged a calorie deficit or gain for the day.

"Where did you get these?" she asked, just for something to say and to pull herself out of the unwelcome thoughts.

"There's a stand on the beach. You should check it out. They have desserts in the evenings."

Marni sighed. Baked goods on the beach. Exactly the kind of thing she'd been looking forward to when coming here. Could Nella be right? Could she and Gio just stay here? Together but apart? It would solve everything. Neither one would have to worry about finding another place. The only thing they'd need to do was find a bed and some furniture.

The villa was indeed a good size.

But would Gio see it that way? He was clearly here to get away from something, much like herself. What if the last thing he wanted was his little sister's pesky best friend underfoot?

Only one way to find out.

"So, your sister called," she told him. "You just missed her."

"Oh? About time."

Marni nodded. "She wants you to call her back. As soon as possible."

Gio shook his head, reached for a glass from the cabinet and poured himself water from the sink. "She's always so bossy," he complained, but his voice held no sting. Still. He wasn't in a rush to do as Nella had asked.

"I hope you don't mind, but I answered your phone when I saw on the screen that it was her calling."

He shrugged. "I guess that's okay. As long as she's the only one you answer my phone for."

That was weird. Why would she answer it otherwise? But it was apparently important for him to set that boundary. Marni tipped three fingers to her forehead in a mock salute. "Aye, aye."

His privacy was clearly important to him, not surprisingly. Which probably didn't bode well for him agreeing to share the villa with her.

"Bet she was surprised to hear that we're both here."

"She certainly was."

"What did she have to say about it?"

Marni pursed her lips and pointed to his phone on the counter behind him. "I think you'd better call her now. Hear it all for yourself."

Well, that sounded pretty ominous. What had Nella and Marni discussed exactly? Though he'd been delaying returning Nella's call out of pure sibling pettiness—wanting him to get back to her ASAP when she'd taken her sweet time to return his call. As if.

But now his curiosity was piqued. Reaching behind him for his phone, he called up his sister's contact and dialed. When he looked up, Marni was no longer at the counter. The woman could move like a feline, as befitting his nickname for her. He hadn't even heard her leave.

His sister answered on the third ring. With a string of curse words followed by some very specific thoughts about his intelligence and stubbornness.

"Good morning to you too, sis."

"Don't give me that," she snapped back. "What the devil are you doing in Capri? Of all places."

"Sorry. I thought you said I could use this place whenever I wanted."

Nella sighed loudly into the phone. "You know that's not what I mean. Of course any home I have is open to you at any time."

"Huh. You could have fooled me the way you answered my call."

Another Italian curse reached his ear. "Stop playing games, Gio. This isn't the time." Silence followed. A pause during which Nella's aggravation with him had been replaced by sisterly concern. "How are you, by the way?"

Gio was torn between irritation and affection. He was beginning to resent that question. It was all he'd heard for the past several weeks. From Mama, his sister, everyone who knew all the details about what had happened.

"I'm fine."

"Gio, you're not fine. You're supposed to be in Chicago seeing that orthopedic specialist and beginning rehab. Why in the world did you cancel?"

"I canceled because I'm feeling better." Not quite the truth, just a small fib. Gio pinched the bridge of his nose. Who was he kidding? It was a whopper of a lie and he deserved to be hit by a lightning bolt where he stood.

"I'm fine, Nella," he repeated. She may be his sister, but this was really none of her concern. "I just need another place to stay. Do you have any ideas? A neighbor who's away for the season? A hotel you'd recommend? I guess I could go to Naples, stay there..."

Nella sighed with clear resignation. "You don't need to go to Naples. You and Marni can both stay."

"There's only one bed."

"*Nessun problema.* I've already called the furniture store in town, told them to expect you."

Gio supposed that made sense. If Marni was okay with this arrangement, he could make it work.

Nella continued, "Having said that, dear brother, there's just one more thing."

With Nella there always was. "What's that?"

"Marni happens to be my oldest and dearest friend. She's like a sister to me."

"I know all that."

"So I trust you'll know not to toy with her."

Toy with her? She really wasn't going *there*, was she? "Nella, what in the world are you getting at?"

"Let's not pretend you don't have a reputation as a ladies' man, Gio. Marni's too important."

"You've made your point, Nella."

"Please remember it."

Gio said goodbye and ended the call, trying not to feel offended. Did Nella really think she had to warn him off Marni? Of course he'd be mindful not to cross any boundaries with her. He'd known her too long, considered her part of their family.

Given his current situation, Gio was in no position to pursue anything romantic with anyone. Let alone the dear friend who Mama and his sister loved. He'd have the two of them to answer to when things went bad, as they inevitably would. He wasn't built for long-term relationships, especially not now. And Marni deserved more than a meaningless fling.

No, the bigger issue when it came to Marni, if they were going to stay here together for the next several days, was how long he could avoid questions about what was wrong with him.

"Nella thinks we should both stay put here," Gio announced as he walked out onto the patio several minutes later.

Marni looked up from the Italy travel site she'd been perusing on her tablet. Not that she'd been able to pay attention to the colorful pictures of the many tourist attractions. She was much too preoccupied with the way Gio and Nella's phone call might have gone.

"She says the villa is spacious enough for the both of us," he continued. "And that all we need is to furnish one of the rooms."

Huh. Well, he wasn't laughing or grimacing, for that matter. It sounded like he was actually considering it.

"And what do you think?"

He pulled out the lounge chair next to her and plopped down. "It's your decision, *gattina*. I'm the one who came here unannounced."

"True. Which was very inconvenient of you by the way."

"As Nella made sure to let me know."

"But this happens to be your sister's house. And you have an open invitation to be here, unannounced or not."

Not to mention, he was clearly dealing with trauma horrible enough to have scarred his body and give him violent nightmares. A trauma he didn't seem in any kind of hurry to talk about.

"All right, *gattina*. I guess we've established that we both have a right to be here, then."

"I agree."

"Then I say we go furniture shopping," he declared, then grunted out a laugh. "Now, there's a line I never thought I'd say to a woman. And certainly not to my sister's best friend."

Marni bit down on the disappointment that washed through her at his words. His sister's friend. Little *gattina*. Gio had quite the reputation as a ladies' man. He had since he'd barely been a teenager. But he'd never see her as anything more than an extension of his sibling. A little playful kitten. Why that bothered her at this precise moment, she couldn't decide.

One theory that made sense was that her previous relationship had completely destroyed her self-esteem and confidence. So much so that she was now looking for validation from a man she should never view as anything more than a friend. And friends could be roommates. Especially if it was only a temporary arrangement.

Shutting her tablet, she rose out of her chair. "I'm ready when you are."

An hour later, Marni followed Gio out the door. But he surprised her when instead of heading toward the road, he turned toward the beach.

"Where are we going?" she asked his back, following him anyway.

"To town, remember?"

"But the road is behind us."

He turned to give her a curious glance. "But the ocean is in front of us. As is the boat."

"Boat?"

He finally turned to face her. "That's right. You know, it's a mode of transportation that's particularly useful on the water. Has these large white things called sails. And a motor."

Marni gave him a useless shove on his upper arm. He barely moved in response. "Ha ha. I know what a boat is. I just didn't realize we had one at our disposal."

"We do. And it's just as easy to sail up the coast as to try to get a taxi or catch the bus. You don't mind the water, do you, Marni?"

"I'm on an island, aren't I?"

He chuckled then turned back to the stone steps leading toward the water and continued down. Marni silently followed. They walked the beach about a quarter mile until they reached a small wooden pathway leading to the ocean. Half a dozen boats floated anchored at the end. Of course, Gio headed straight for the sleekest, newest-looking one.

"So I lied about the sails," he told her as he helped her aboard. "It's a motorboat."

The amount that Marni knew about boats could fit into a thimble. She could count on one hand all the times she'd been on one. Including the dinner cruise she'd taken with Ander last summer where he'd complained the entire time about the quality of the food and speed of service. Also, about her outfit. She remembered he'd chastised her about showing too much leg with that particular one. If she'd worn a tea-length gown, he would have found something else to complain about.

But that was nothing unusual.

Marni shook away the thoughts and allowed Gio to help her onboard. He walked over to a built-in bin and lifted the cover, removing two life jackets. He handed the smaller one to her. "Do you know how to put one of these on?"

Well, she wasn't that clueless about sailing. "Yes. But is it absolutely necess—"

He didn't even let her finish the sentence. "Yes. We don't even lift anchor unless you have it on nice and tight. Otherwise, you can just turn around and get off right now."

Marni swallowed. Everything about Gio's demeanor had just changed. As soon as she'd begun to ask the question, his eyes flashed dark and the muscles around his mouth tightened.

She hardly recognized this side of him. The Gio she

knew would have made light of her resistance, made some kind of quip about not diving in to rescue her if she were to end up in the water. Gio's expression now held no mirth whatsoever.

"Harsh," she muttered, yanking the preserver out of his hands. Without another word, she put it on then clipped the holster clasps shut. Gio studied her the entire time, as if not fully trusting her to do it properly. She glared at him, lifting her arms. "Do you care to inspect it?"

The corner of his mouth lifted ever so slightly as his eyes traveled down her body.

"As tempting as that is, I've been warned against such inappropriate behavior." With that he turned to stride toward the dashboard, throwing his own life jacket on in the process.

Marni felt hot color flush her cheeks. A tingling awareness skittered over her skin.

He'd been warned? What in heaven's name did that mean?

CHAPTER THREE

GIO TURNED THE steering wheel and began to guide the boat toward the town marina. A bright orange sun hung in a crystal blue sky, and the waves shimmered like liquid gems as they moved along the surface of the water.

If someone had told him a week ago that he'd be spending the day furniture shopping with Marni Payton, he would have told said person to check their mental state. Yet, as ridiculous as it was, he was about to go pick out bedding and floor rugs with little gattina, the same girl who'd followed him around like a pest with his sister for a good chunk of his years growing up.

But she looked very different than that little girl right now. In fact, there was nothing girlish about her. The lanky teen she'd once been had grown into a strikingly attractive young woman. He'd tried hard not to notice those changes over the years. It was harder to do so now in such proximity.

Maybe this living-together thing wasn't such a great idea, after all.

He studied her from the corner of his eye while she sat stern side, her gaze studying the distant horizon. Long, chestnut brown hair secured in a tight ponytail. So tight it seemed to be pulling at the skin around her face. A collared sleeveless shirt atop pressed capri pants. Sensible leather flat-heeled shoes adorned her feet. She looked like she could be going into the office for a day full of meetings.

Did the woman even know she was on vacation?

He would have to make sure she realized it at some point. Tell her to relax, loosen up a bit.

Not that it was any of his business. He had enough to deal with on his own plate.

Still, he couldn't help but wonder what had brought her out here. Alone. And she certainly didn't seem to be in vacation mode just yet. Rather than getting away, Marni looked to be running away from something.

His thoughts led him to remember the last time he'd seen her before this trip. She'd been thin to the point of looking gaunt, dark circles had framed her eyes, her lips continually thinned in a worried line. When he'd asked his sister if Marni was okay, Nella had alluded to a bad relationship. In fact, the look on his sister's face had turned downright murderous when she'd answered his question.

What kind of demons was Marni running from? Were they as bad as his?

Suddenly, he felt like a jerk for the way he'd reacted when she'd scoffed about putting on the life jacket. He could have been gentler. But he wasn't going to risk her well-being in any way. He of all people knew how a split-second moment of carelessness could result in a monumental catastrophe with a lifetime of dire consequences.

Not on his watch. Not this time.

A chuckle rose out of him when he recalled how she'd reacted, challenging him to inspect the life jacket. How tempted he'd been to do just that. To run his fingers down her throat with the pretense of checking the clasps' tightness. To tug her tight ponytail out from beneath the vest, then run his hands through the thick, curly waves.

Whoa. Gio gave his head a shake.

"What is it?" Marni asked.

"Huh?"

She smiled at him. "You were just laughing at something," she said. "Can I get in on the joke?"

He certainly couldn't tell her where his mind had really been.

You see, Marni, I was thinking about the way your skin might feel under my fingertips, how the strands of your hair might flow over my hands, the way you smell of lemon and rose and some combination of spice I can't quite name.

No, definitely wouldn't go over well. Gio scrambled for a response. But it was hard to think with the way Marni was smiling at him as the sunlight danced along her eyes and glimmered in her hair.

What was wrong with him?

No matter. He just had to stop. Best way would be reverting to his go-to behavior when it came to Marni. Teasing her like an older cousin might.

"If you must know," he began, "I was thinking how you look like you're about to go to a board meeting as opposed to spending a carefree day on a Mediterranean island in one of the most gorgeous countries on earth."

Her mouth fell open. "What's that supposed to mean?"

He shrugged, and turned his gaze back to the water. "Start with your shoes for example."

She lifted one elegant leg and looked at her foot. "What's wrong with my shoes?"

"I think Nonno Santino owned a pair just like that, but in taupe."

She dropped her chin to her chest, glaring at him. Okay, maybe he was being a bit over-the-top. In truth, his *nonno* had worn nothing but tennis shoes.

"I'll have you know, these are quite comfortable," Marni protested.

"Is that why you shook sand out of them twice already?"

"I didn't know we'd be walking along the beach, now did I?" Her voice rose just enough to convey annoyance and irritation while remaining steady. "You could have mentioned we'd be taking a boat into town before we'd left the villa."

He nodded. "I could have. And you could have dressed less like a librarian about to begin a full shift."

Marni crossed her arms in front of her chest. "Yeah? What about the way you're dressed?" She gestured toward him with a fling of her hand.

Gio looked down at his wrinkled T-shirt, hip-hugging sports shorts and loose leather sandals. "What about it?"

"We're about to enter one of the most elegant shopping centers in Europe and you're wearing what could best be described as 'frat boy who caught the wrong flight heading to spring break.'"

Gio couldn't help it, he threw his head back and laughed at her put-down. "Touché, little gattina. Touché."

Good for her, she was giving it right back.

She'd felt safe returning Gio's barbs. Marni knew his insults weren't really meant to wound her. A world of difference existed between the way Ander's constant criticisms were delivered and Gio's good-natured joking. She was surprised she even remembered how to verbally defend herself. Leave it to Gio Santino to remind her.

Forget that she'd been totally disingenuous when teasing Gio about his appearance.

The truth was, he somehow managed to look handsome and polished despite his beyond casual attire. No one in their right mind would ever confuse Gio for an out-of-place college student. No, even dressed in a T-shirt and sandals, he looked every bit the successful tycoon and CEO of a global corporation that he was. Now, as they disembarked from the boat and made their way down the sidewalk path along the street of shops, it was clear she wasn't the only woman nearby who appreciated Gio's looks.

Tall, dark, with an angular jaw and toned, muscular body. His hair just long enough to reach his shoulders in dark waves...

Just stop.

This was not the time or place to be admiring Gio's looks or sex appeal. Heavens! Why had she even thought that last part?

Yanking her thoughts from such dangerous territory, Marni focused instead on her surroundings. Glamorous designer boutiques, mouthwatering bakery window displays, the tangy scent of citrus in the air as they passed a limoncello store. They were on a mission with a goal right now, but she made a mental note to come back into town soon and visit every one of these delightful places. Such a shame that she'd be doing so alone. The only reason Gio was here with her now was to pick out the bed one of them would be sleeping in. He'd have no incentive to play tour guide or tourist and return here with her afterward. Hadn't they agreed that the only way the cohabitation would work was to do their best to stay out of each other's way?

If that thought had her feeling downbeat and lonely,

then it was no one's fault but her own. Gio wasn't her guardian. He didn't owe her anything, including his time.

Deep in thought, she nearly walked into Gio's solid back before realizing he'd stopped in front of the revolving glass door of a shop.

"This is it," he announced, then pulled the door open for her.

It was like walking into her own version of heaven. Beautiful works of art in the form of handcrafted wood furniture greeted them inside. It was hard to decide which item to study first: the beautiful bookshelf with the mahogany trim? Or the three-drawer bureau with the intricate carvings. Or maybe the standing mirror with the cherrywood base.

She was startled by a pair of snapping fingers right in her line of vision.

"Earth to Marni. You in there, Ms. Payton?"

She blinked to focus on Gio's face just inches from hers, expecting to find impatient annoyance in his impression. Instead, she found him smiling widely at her.

"Sorry, I was just admiring all the craftsmanship."

He dropped his hand, the grin still framing his lips. "I'll say. I've never seen such pleasure flood a woman's face so quickly. Not from just walking into a store, anyway." He winked at her mischievously.

Marni's mouth went dry at the innuendo. Before she could recover enough to formulate an answer, Gio had turned on his heel and walked farther into the store.

If she didn't know any better, she would think Gio Santino might be flirting with her. Which was preposterous. In all their years of knowing one another, not once had Gio even hinted at any kind of attraction toward her, while she'd harbored a crush on and off for as long as she could remember. It didn't mean anything. Gio couldn't help himself. It was simply his nature to be charming and flirtatious. She just happened to be the only one in his vicinity at the moment. Giving her head a shake, she forced her focus back on the matter at hand: the furniture. They were here to pick something out of this gallery of masterpieces. Something told her she was going to be absolutely torn when it came to settling on just one item.

Despite her professionally trained eye, she felt like the kid in a candy store who wanted to grab everything and run home with her stash. She took her time making her way to where Gio stood, delicately trailing her fingers along the finished lines of the pieces in her path. When she reached his side, he pointed to a bed frame to his left. "What about that one?" he asked.

"What about it?"

He turned to squint at her. "Should we get that one?" he asked, as if his question should have been obvious.

Marni could only shake her head and laugh. He was approaching this outing as if they were replacing the milk carton in the fridge. Poor soul, he had no idea that they'd be in here for at least an hour, more likely much longer than that while she put a room together that would feel both cozy and pleasing to the eye of whoever inhabited it.

She shook her head at him. "Gio. You don't just come into a place like this and point."

His eyes narrowed on her face. "Why ever not? How else would we pick something?"

"We don't just pick something."

More narrowing of the eyes. "We don't?"

"No. We think about what we want the room to feel like for the inhabitant."

He crossed his arms in front of his chest. "Huh. I'd say

it should feel like there's a sturdy piece of furniture in there to be able to sleep on after the day is over."

Of course, he would simplify it that way. "Okay. But beyond that, what do we want to feel when we enter that room? Warmth? Comfort? A sense of solitude?"

Gio rubbed his chin. "I'd say all of the above."

Marni threw her hands in the air. This was hopeless. She turned to walk further toward the back of the store. Gio followed close on her heels. After several moments of browsing, she could practically feel the impatience resonating off Gio's body.

"Fine," she heard him say behind her. "What about this one?"

He had to be kidding. He was pointing to a small child's bed designed to look like a pirate ship. "You can't be serious. You wouldn't even fit in that."

"When did we decide that I'd be the one to have to take the new room?"

Huh. He had a point. She hadn't actually considered that.

"Look," Gio continued. "At this point, I'd settle for a cot and a throw pillow. We've been in here for how many hours already?"

Marni made a show of lifting her wrist and staring at her watch. "We've been in here fifteen minutes."

Gio rubbed his forehead. "Huh. I was exaggerating but it feels longer than just a few minutes."

Marni sighed. As much as she wanted to linger in here, Gio had clearly reached the end of his patience. "Fine. I think your pirate ship just might have given me an idea."

Gio smiled wide, clearly pleased with himself. "Oh, yeah? How so?"

She gave him the "follow me" sign with her finger.

"Here, I'll show you." The bed frame she led him to had tall posts above the headboard, and then she pointed out a round-framed mirror that could easily be accented to look like a porthole window. Rather than bedside tables for the lamps, she picked out two wooden coffers that, with the right studding, could be made to look like treasure chests.

"What do you think?" she asked Gio, after they'd gotten a chance to look at all the pieces.

"Huh. It will be like the bottom of an old-fashioned ship."

She smiled at him. "Maybe even like a pirate ship."

Gio tilted his head, examining her. "I like it, gattina. Well done!"

Marni felt a fluttering in her chest at his approval. It made no sense. She'd simply done what she was trained to do. So how utterly silly of her to feel so giddy at having pleased him.

Unlike the sparse compliments her ex threw her way from time to time, Gio's appreciation of her talent sounded genuine.

She'd almost forgotten what that felt like.

Gio signed the paperwork for the sale of the pieces Marni had picked out and led her out of the store twenty minutes later. For all the complaining he'd done in there, he had to begrudgingly admit that he'd actually enjoyed himself. Observing the way Marni's mind worked out a theme and put together a design had been more entertaining than he would have guessed. Watching her work had exposed him to a side of her he hadn't witnessed or even thought about before. She was smart, talented and had a clear enthusiasm for her chosen field.

Envy blossomed in his chest. He was a man of wealth

and vast resources, but despite all his professional success, he couldn't recall the last time he'd felt accomplished and fulfilled.

Most times, he simply felt empty. Directionless.

Maybe that was why he took so many risks with his life, both physically and financially. Simply to *feel* something on any scale. It was that recklessness that had led him to fast cars and racing. Look how that had turned up. He'd damaged his body and hurt an innocent bystander to boot.

"Where to now?" Marni asked, pulling him out of the black hole of his thoughts.

In perfect timing, his stomach answered with a short growl. Marni's chuckle in response had him laughing as well. "How about we grab a bite?"

She pointed to his midsection. "I don't dare argue after that."

Within minutes they were seated at an outside table of Pescare Delfino seafood restaurant. Later afternoon had turned the sky a bluish gray. Two servers in black bow ties and buttoned vests appeared at their table before they'd so much as pulled in their chairs. One lit a large round candle in the centerpiece while the other poured limoncello in two small shot glasses.

Gio ordered a bottle of his favorite Pinot Grigio then held up his glass of limoncello once both waiters had left. "A toast."

Marni lifted her drink and clinked it to his. "What are we toasting to?" she asked.

"We are now officially roommates. For one."

They both took a sip of the refreshing liqueur, though Marni's could be described as more of a drop. Probably smart. The limoncello in Italy could be potent.

"What else?" Marni asked.

"To your stellar skills as an interior decorator. I'm sure you'll reach the highest pinnacles of success with your talent."

Something flashed behind her eyes, a darkness that shadowed the light that had been behind them since they'd first entered the furniture store.

"Um…thanks," she murmured, setting her glass down without another drink. She looked off into the distance.

Was it something he said? Gio had only meant to pay her a compliment.

Gio went the feigned ignorance route. "Do you not like the limoncello?" he asked, knowing full well that disappointment in her drink wasn't what had dimmed the brightness in her eyes from just moments before.

She immediately shook her head. "No. It's delicious. I guess I'm just hungry."

Sure. That wasn't the issue either. Talking about her professional success had completely soured her mood. Did her career have anything to do with why she was here in Capri for the next several days? Maybe a job she'd done had gone wrong and her ego had taken a hit.

Well, he wasn't one to push. Marni clearly didn't want to talk about her job. That was fine since he definitely didn't want to talk about his accident.

And if he ignored the pain and fought hard enough to continue hiding the limp, he wouldn't have to.

Marni searched for a change of topic. She wasn't in the mood to discuss the train wreck that was her current professional situation. If Ander Stolis had his way, she'd be persona non grata in all the circles that mattered as far as the interior design profession was concerned. And he'd make sure that would be the case for the foreseeable future.

Served her right for falling for the lead architect of the firm she'd worked for. At first, Marni had thought their budding relationship was so romantic. An office romance. Exciting and slightly taboo. Just like in all those rom-coms. Little had she known, she'd be living more of a drama-tragedy.

"Do you know what you're having?" Gio asked across the table, breaking into her thoughts.

"A good heap of regret with a side of crow," she answered, then immediately clasped a hand to her mouth. What in the world was wrong with her? She hadn't meant to say the words out loud. The limoncello couldn't be that strong, for heaven's sake. She'd barely had one sip!

Gio reached out his arm across the table and covered her free hand with his.

"Hey, is everything all right with you?"

He asked so gently, with such care and interest, that Marni felt a lump of emotion form in her throat. She forced a smile on her lips. "I'm fine. Really."

He looked less than convinced and gave her wrist a small squeeze. His palm and fingers felt strong and warm over her hand. The eyes looking into hers held a wealth of concern. "You know you can tell me, gattina. If you want to."

Marni closed her eyes and blew out a deep breath. Gio didn't need to hear how stupid and blind she'd been. How she'd ignored all the warning signs as well as the good advice of her friends and family. The way she'd been certain she knew better than all the people who were only trying to protect her.

But it was so tempting to get some of it off her chest for once. "I made some bad decisions over this past year," she finally managed to answer. "Countless errors of judgment that caught up to me. The gist of it is that I trusted the wrong man."

Gio merely nodded, no judgment clouded his eyes, no subtle admonishment. That made it a bit easier for her to continue.

"I took longer than I should have to break things off with him. When I did, he used his considerable influence and high-profile contacts to smear my name and professional reputation."

She didn't miss the clench of Gio's fists on the table. "I see."

Swallowing, she continued. "He's a highly respected architect with several clients who are members of the media. I know it wouldn't be above him to sully my name in the professional magazines and websites. That's the last thing I need at this point in my career."

"That's why you're here."

She nodded. "That's right. Not only to get away from it all until people lose interest. But also to try and regroup. Figure out how to climb out from under the mountain of mistakes and all their consequences."

Gio swore. "I'm sorry, Marni. If it makes you feel any better, you don't have the corner on bad decisions." He gestured to his chest with his thumb. "Your new roomie here has made a few doozies himself."

Profound hurt resonated in his voice. Gio clearly had his own mountain to climb. Perhaps he would understand her predicament better than most.

Marni turned her hand over under his, reflexively intertwining her fingers with his so that they were holding hands atop the table. She didn't let go until the server arrived to take their order.

CHAPTER FOUR

A SURGE OF protectiveness so strong rushed through Gio that he had to will himself to clamp it down. Marni was gripping his hand as if starved for strength and comfort.

What a lousy stroke of luck for her. He hardly had either of those for himself. He should let go of her, pull his arm back by his side. Find a way to lighten this conversation that had suddenly grown so heavy and deep.

He wanted badly to ask more about the man who'd caused her such deep hurt. But it was her prerogative to share as much or as little as she was ready to. Still, the curiosity didn't settle well in his gut. It was no use trying to tell himself it was none of his business. This was Marni. She'd practically grown up with the Santinos as part of the family. She was the only child of a single mother, and Gio knew how much she'd endured to simply survive her younger years. They'd met her when her mom worked briefly for Santino Foods decades ago.

Despite Marni's disadvantages, she'd grown up to be a successful, confident woman with a list of accomplishments. He didn't know the details but someone had come along and ruined all that for her.

If he ever found out who it was and what exactly he'd done to her...

The waiter arrived with his scratch pad to take their order. They both pulled their hands away at the same moment; a rather awkward moment tempered only by the presence of their server.

When their salads arrived a few minutes later, that awkwardness still hung in the air. Finally, Marni was the one who broke the silence.

"You mentioned your own mistakes," she began, poking at the vegetables on her plate rather than eating any of them. "Do those mistakes have anything to do with your sleepless nights?"

Gio swallowed the plum tomato he'd been chewing, though not tasting. His mind juggled a confusion of thoughts. He didn't know how to talk about the accident and, so far, he hadn't wanted to with anyone. It was bad enough having to go through the details with every doctor and nurse who'd had to evaluate him in the days since. And he couldn't even quite remember all the details.

Where would he even begin to try and tell Marni? The reckless decision to race the car in the first place? How lucky he was that his passenger hadn't been killed? That the man may never walk again thanks to Gio?

Or maybe he could begin with how he might never have full use of his leg, no matter how many long hours of rehab he was made to endure. The dull ache in his thigh muscle mocked his train of thought. Marni picked up on his hesitation.

"You don't have to tell me," she said. "But know that you can," she added. "Same goes for you, because I'm little gattina, remember? Your sister's old friend."

Gio forced a smile he didn't feel. The trouble was, he was starting to view Marni as less and less of his little sister's old friend with each passing moment.

Such a dangerous development. Because the way he *was* beginning to view her spelled nothing but trouble for them both.

On the boat ride back to the villa, the early evening sky had turned navy, full of twinkling bright stars. The day had gone by in the blink of an eye. As tired as she was, Marni didn't quite want it to end. The hours she'd spent in town with Gio had been the most relaxed she'd been since her "walk of shame" through the office hallway. A shudder racked her body at the memory.

"You cold?" Gio asked, mistaking her shiver for physical discomfort.

He took her silence as a positive answer. Lifting open a center console, he removed a thick, zippered hoodie bearing the logo of the Los Angeles Angels across its back. He draped it over her shoulders, giving them a squeeze for good measure. Though it should have felt bulky and uncomfortable over the life jacket, Marni found herself snuggling into the soft fabric. It smelled of him: spicy, woodsy and oh so masculine. She buried her face in the collar, inhaling as she did so.

Suddenly horrified that Gio might have witnessed the small action, she yanked the fabric off her face. A glance in his direction told her he hadn't seen. He was focused on guiding the boat back to their destination. Marni breathed a sigh of relief. That was much too close. She'd be beyond embarrassed if Gio had any hint of her reemerging girlish crush.

It couldn't happen. Her emotions were already strung tight. She had no business crushing on a man so far beyond her reach. Sure, he was easy to talk to and they had a history of being friends. She felt lighter after having confided in him as much as she had about her fiasco of a relationship.

But their differences were plenty. Gio was several years older, and had been linked to women like starlets and models and heiresses. She knew better than to pine for someone like him. She'd just turned twenty-six last month for Pete's sake. She was too old for a schoolgirl crush. How had she not grown out of it already? Then there were the close familial ties. She wouldn't be able to bear it if there was tension between her and the Santino clan for any reason whatsoever.

No, better to just ignore her feelings and hope they went away.

It was just her mind trying to distract her. It had to be. Her brain was trying to stall figuring out all the things she had to deal with as soon as she got back to reality. Like how she might begin to restore her professional reputation. Whether she wanted to remain in Boston or relocate so she could put the past year behind her and move forward with her life.

Then there was the dream of starting her own design business. If she had the wherewithal or the resources or even the motivation to attempt such an undertaking. Another failure might completely undo her.

She was so deep in her thoughts, she hadn't even realized Gio had docked the boat and dropped anchor.

"You're not falling asleep on me, are you?" he asked.

"Guess that dinner was more filling than I thought, not to mention the strong cocktail. I do feel pretty lethargic."

"Then you're in luck," he told her while he finished securing the boat. "Because I happen to make a mean cappuccino. Not too strong, with plenty of frothy milk. It'll perk you right up without keeping you up all night."

Maybe it was wishful thinking, but it sounded as if Gio didn't quite want the night to end either.

"Sounds great." She decided to broach the subject they still hadn't gotten around to solving until the new furniture arrived. "I think you should sleep in the room tonight," she began as they made their way up the stone steps. "I'll be perfectly fine on the couch cushions."

Gio immediately shook his head. "Absolutely not. The bed is all yours."

She wasn't the least bit surprised that he'd immediately refused the offer. "It's only fair," she tried to argue. "I had it last night."

Gio didn't answer until they reached the top of the cliffside. He took her by the shoulders and turned her to him. "Marni. I'm not even sleeping for any stretch of time. Wasting the bed on me doesn't make sense."

Marni knew any further argument would be useless. With a sigh of resignation, she followed him down the path that led to Nella's villa. When they got to the house, Gio fired up the espresso machine while she indulged in a hot shower. He had a steaming mug waiting for her when she emerged a little while later.

"Want to enjoy these outside by the pool?"

That sounded like a delightful idea. Nella's outdoor lounge chairs were so plush and comfortable. And the night was warm with a soft, gentle breeze. Marni couldn't think of a single reason to turn down his offer.

"Lead the way," she answered, taking her cappuccino in hand.

Marni winced when they reached the patio and she eyed her tablet still sitting on the cushion. She'd forgotten her device out here when they'd left earlier. "Darn it."

"What's the matter?"

"I meant to charge that. Hopefully there's enough battery left."

"For what?" Gio asked, dropping onto one of the other chaise lounges.

She ducked shyly. "Don't laugh. But there's a Bollywood show I'm addicted to. I downloaded the latest episode and was looking forward to watching it later tonight."

"A bolly what now?"

She had to laugh at his confusion. "Bollywood. Filmed in India. The script is full of drama and intrigue with lots of song and dance thrown in for good measure."

"How do you understand it?"

She shrugged. "Captions, of course. It's like reading and enjoying an engrossing movie at the same time. You should try it."

Gio gave her a skeptical look. "I don't know. It doesn't really sound like my genre of entertainment."

Marni flipped the lid of her tablet and turned on the device. To her surprise and delight, she had a good amount of battery life left.

Pulling a chaise lounge next to him, she called up the show. "Here. Just try a few minutes. You might be surprised."

He tilted his head. "Sure. Why not. What else have I got to do?" he asked then scooched his chair closer while she touched the play icon. "Just don't tell my sister, or anyone else for that matter, that you talked me into watching a foreign film with captions."

Marni pressed her fingers to her mouth. "My lips are sealed. Our secret."

Gio shifted in the lounge chair and kicked out his legs to give them a good stretch. On instinct, he braced himself for the sharp pain that was sure to shoot down his thigh at any second. But the ache stayed dull and low. That was different. Usually, no matter how gentle the stretch, it always resulted in knifelike pain for several seconds.

In surprise, he blinked one eye open. Huh. The sun was out. But how could that be? The last thing he remembered, he and Marni were watching something on her tablet. A show it would normally never occur to him to watch. It had been close to midnight when the last thing he remembered—a funny dance number—had come on.

Which meant he must have fallen asleep right here. Outside on the lounge chair. More surprisingly, he'd apparently stayed asleep until sunrise…for several hours. A rarity that hadn't happened since the accident.

So that was a bit of stunning news that would take some processing.

It was when he tried to rise that he noticed an unfamiliar weight snuggled against his side. That could only mean one thing. Forcing both eyes open, Gio bit down on a groan at the sight that greeted him. He hadn't been the only one to fall asleep out here. Marni was snuggled against his length, her eyes closed shut in slumber.

Don't you dare react. Don't so much as move.

Not yet. He had no idea what he might say to Marni if she were to wake up right now. He was having trouble putting it all together himself. Besides, what would be the harm in letting her get some more rest? Something told him Marni had had her own share of restless nights recently.

He thought back to the dinner they'd shared the night before, the strain in her voice when she'd talked about her hurtful relationship, the way her lips had grown tight, her eyes clouded over with sadness. She'd trusted the wrong man. Hardly the first woman to do so. At least she hadn't made the kind of mistake that had almost cost someone else their life.

Sweet gattina, how hard are you punishing yourself anyway?

A seagull soared overhead, suddenly dropping to land on the patio by their feet. The noise was enough to have Marni stirring in his arms. Maybe he was being cowardly, but Gio immediately shut his eyes and feigned sleep. Why not spare them both some awkward embarrassment if it could be helped?

He sensed the moment she must have opened her eyes and discovered their positions. He felt her whole body go tense, a small gasp sounded beneath his ear. It took all his will not to open his eyes out of sheer curiosity. It might be worth it to see the expression on her face.

Gio felt her move softly out of his arms and scramble off the chair. The seagull squawked above and he almost reflexively opened his eyes in response. But somehow managed to continue the pretense until he heard the screen door leading to the house open before it softly shut closed again.

He gave her a good twenty minutes before finally following her inside. Marni stood at the counter of the kitchen, brewing tea. She'd changed into a pair of loose gray sweats and a tunic-length shirt that fell low off one shoulder to reveal a small triangle of smooth skin. His nerve endings tingled as he recalled how that skin had felt in his arms moments ago.

How the woman managed to look so sexy in sweats and a loose T-shirt, with her hair a tangled mess, Gio couldn't explain. Her eyes grew wide when she saw him.

"Morning," Gio said before she could speak. "Can

you believe I fell asleep outside?" He shook his head as if amused with himself. "I must have been so tired."

Marni nodded. "Actually, I—"

He pretended not to hear her as he made a show of stretching his arms overhead while executing a perfectly believable loud yawn. Maybe one day they would laugh about the way they'd fallen asleep in each other's arms. He just didn't have it in him to do it today. Not after the way he'd reacted to having her body so close to his. Something told him Marni wouldn't be up for such a conversation either. "Hard to believe, but it's the best night's sleep I've had in forever."

"Huh."

He dropped his arms. "Guess I'll go take a shower."

She blinked several times in rapid succession but didn't say anything. Bingo. He'd been right. Marni was just as content to ignore the fact that they'd fallen asleep in each other's arms as he was. What was the point in dwelling on it? It wasn't as if anything physical had happened between them, after all. No boundaries had been breached whatsoever. And thank God for that. He had enough to deal with right now without crossing any lines with his kid sister's best friend. Nella's warning echoed in his head. *If you do anything to hurt her or make her uncomfortable...*

He pointed to the kettle, which started steaming. "Can you spare some of that for me when I get back?"

Marni nodded. "Of course, I'll have a mug waiting for you."

"Thanks."

See, all casual. Nothing amiss. Just two old friends who happened to be sharing the same living space for a few days. Then they would both go their separate ways and this would just be one more memory of Marni Payton that he'd add to all the other ones.

No one had to know that the shower he'd be taking would be a cold one.

Gio stood under the steaming hot spray, relishing the soothing flow of water over his skin. After a punishing blast of it at ice cold to get his libido under control, he'd turned the nozzle completely the opposite way to the hottest setting.

Not that the cooler water had helped at all. His mind kept going back to that one exposed shoulder. The way the tunic shirt had draped her curves in all the right places.

The way she'd felt in his arms when he'd awakened to find her nuzzled against his side.

Gio swore and pushed the wayward thoughts away, then squeezed more of the soap onto his hand. He usually massaged his sore leg every morning in the shower, the one piece of medical advice he'd taken so far. But the bruised and tattered muscles still felt remarkably less sore.

Had he taken a pain pill and forgotten? No. He hadn't been that out of it. Besides, he did his best to avoid the pills unless he was in absolute agony. The more likely scenario was that he'd done less thrashing about with his legs because he'd subconsciously known that he'd disturb Marni. Or maybe one good night of sleep at last had done both his spirit and body a world of good. Somehow, falling asleep next to Marni while watching a fun, mindless show had given him that rare gift.

Gio sighed and braced his hands against the tile wall. Too bad it couldn't happen again.

Spending time with her was good for him, there was no denying. But there was no way he was going to take advantage of her for his own selfish needs.

The truth was, on his best day, he wouldn't have been worthy of Marni Payton. And these days he was far from his best. Not since the race that had changed him forever.

Before he could suppress them, an onslaught of visions flooded his brain. Losing control of the wheel, veering off at too high a speed toward the other car. The flash of light as the flames burst forth.

He knew he was lucky to be alive. But he felt a mere partial version of the man he used to be. Why would he subject any woman to what his future had waiting for him? Countless days in therapy. A permanent limp. The certain frustration and resulting poor temperament all that was sure to bring out in him.

No. Marni deserved better than that. She deserved better than *him*.

Why was he even traveling down this road of thought? He and Marni as any kind of item were out of the question. He had enough to figure out about his own life without the complication of a romantic relationship. Let alone with someone who meant as much to his family as Marni did.

Nella had warned him about not pursuing this very thing.

That was it. The shower was doing nothing to relax him at this point. Rather than soothing him in any way, now the steam felt oppressively hot and the stall felt suffocating. He pushed aside the glass door and grabbed the thick Turkish towel he'd hung up before his shower.

His phone sounded an alert in the other room. One he'd assigned to his assistant.

Might want to check your email, boss.

Gio did as her message said then cursed out loud. A reporter for New England magazine was asking questions about the accident again after all this time. The last thing Juno needed as he tried to recover was any kind of media attention. The man deserved his privacy as he healed. Gio had to find a way to shut this down as soon as possible.

He was about to text a reply when another message appeared on his screen. This one from his sister.

How are you today?

Honestly, she had to stop asking him that. He wasn't even going to bother to respond to the question. He asked one of his own instead.

Do you know when the new furniture might arrive?

The floating bubbles appeared on the screen once more.

No update yet.

Gio pinched the bridge of his nose and sighed. Nella was still typing.

But I just got word that there's a villa available to buy. If you're still interested in getting your own place in Capri.

CHAPTER FIVE

WELL, IF SHE'D harbored any illusions that Gio was in any way affected by her, she'd been proven sorely mistaken.

He hadn't even noticed her presence next to him last night. She might as well have been a teddy bear he'd been cuddling.

Whereas she couldn't stop thinking about the feeling of being in his arms, the warmth of his body surrounding hers. The scent of him filling her senses when she'd awakened with her head on his chest.

Now she couldn't seem to stop thinking about him upstairs in the shower. Surrounded by steam, water and soapy suds flowing down his hardened muscles.

Marni groaned out loud. This couldn't be happening. She couldn't be reviving her childhood crush, it was completely one-sided. It had to be. Gio may have seemed to be flirting with her sometimes, but that was just his nature, it was how he reacted with any woman in his vicinity.

How could she be lusting after a man who hadn't even realized he'd fallen asleep with her against his side?

Her breath hitched in her throat when she heard him shut the door upstairs and make his way down the stairs. If she was going to squelch this crush, she would have to start with not becoming breathless when she so much as heard the man. He entered the kitchen a moment later, looking fresh and clean, his hair damp. He smelled of pine and mint and his own distinctive masculine scent.

She greeted him with what she hoped was a convincingly friendly smile. "Just in time. Your tea was about to get cold."

"Would have come down sooner, but I was delayed."

"Oh?"

"Nella messaged. Says hello. She tried to call you but I guess you haven't set up your phone yet."

She'd meant to. But she'd been much too distracted last night and this morning. By him.

"I'll make sure to get ahold of her later."

"Sounds good." He took a sip of his tea. "So, how'd you sleep?"

Was it her imagination, or was there a slight smirk to his lips when he asked the question? As if he was teasing her about something.

Maybe Marni was wrong to assume that he wasn't aware of their sleeping positions last night. She felt a slight heat creep up to her cheeks. Well, she certainly wasn't going to bring it up. She'd be horrified if she was wrong.

Besides, Gio was always teasing her in one way or another.

Better to just change the subject. "Too bad we're all out of those yummy pastries from yesterday." It wasn't as if she was lying, she wouldn't exactly turn down a croissant right now.

He shrugged. "We can always go get some more."

"Too wicked, isn't it? To have rich, sugary pastries two days in a row?"

Gio threw his head back and laughed. He winked at her when his gaze met hers again. "Darling, you and I have very different ideas about what we would define as *wicked*."

See, there it was. She was right. He only enjoyed teasing her. It was just his personality.

"Weren't you and Nella having junk food–laden movie nights not that long ago? I seem to recall walking into the viewing room at the house to find the two of you surrounded by snacks and candy. You didn't seem to think rich and sugary were wicked back then. What's changed?"

She ducked her head. He was too observant by far. "It's a rather recent habit. One I'm trying my best to unlearn."

Gio set his mug down. His eyes roamed over her face, full of concern. She shouldn't have given him such a loaded answer. Maybe one day she'd tell him about how Ander had even tried to control her eating habits. But she didn't have it in her right now.

Before he could ask anything more, she jumped off her stool and flashed him another wide smile. "You're right. I am on vacation and can have all the pastries I desire. Finish your tea and let's go get some."

Gio opened his mouth, clearly about to press her, but must have decided against it. He took a long swallow of his drink then offered her his arm. "Let's go."

He led her past the pool and patio area to the stone steps leading to the beach.

"What a gorgeous morning," Marni remarked. It was the truth. Crystal blue water crashed gently against golden sparkling sand in soft waves. A bright, round sun sat majestically above a cloudless horizon. As far as small talk went, it was a handy topic.

What she really wanted to do was ask him about the obvious limp he was trying so desperately to hide. And if it had anything to do with his nightmares and tortured sleep. He must have forgotten how well she knew him after all these years. The Gio she remembered from before this trip was characterized by a flurry of activity. He'd always been a man who moved quickly, never one to sit still or stroll leisurely, no matter the circumstances. That version of Gio would have challenged her to a race down the beach.

How could he think she wouldn't notice the difference?

So maybe he'd overdone it with the amount of pastries he'd ordered. Two of everything the stand offered might have been a bit much.

Silently, he handed Marni another biscotti after she'd finished the sugared almond croissant. She sat on a big boulder, her legs dangling inches off the ground while he leaned his back against it. Gio tried hard to focus on his breakfast but it was hard not to stare at Marni. Her hair had come loose, that all too enticing shoulder remained exposed and there was a smidge of powdered sugar above her lip. It took all the will he had not to reach over and rub it off with his thumb. Or maybe with his mouth.

Instead, he silently handed her a napkin from inside the box. She dabbed at her lips and the smidge disappeared. Thank God for lessened temptation.

A seagull flew overhead, past sandy beach and over the water. Marni shielded her eyes, watching its flight. She sighed deeply. "I know I keep talking about what a beautiful morning it is, but it really is picture-perfect. Like something out of a painting."

"I can't recall a single day it's rained in the week since I got here."

"You were right, Capri is paradise."

"It really is. I'm actually thinking of getting my own

place here." He hadn't even realized he'd meant to share that with her.

She snapped her head in his direction. "How exciting, Gio! I think you should do it."

He bit down on the last of his biscotti, licked the crumbs off his thumb. "Nella mentioned a villa that's up for sale right now. Maybe we can look at it together."

Her mouth formed a small O in surprise. "I'd really like that. Just say when."

He couldn't quite place why, but somehow the moment had grown heavy. Something pivotal had just happened. Though he wouldn't be able to articulate why. Other than the understanding there was something rather intimate about viewing houses together. Something personal.

Gio gave his head a shake. He was being ridiculous. Two friends checking out a villa one of them might buy was purely platonic. Why in the world was he overanalyzing everything all of a sudden when it came to Marni?

"That was delicious," she finally declared after several more moments of chewing, steering the conversation back to lighter fare. "But I think I need to work off some of this sugar high."

Bouncing off the boulder, he watched as she removed her sandals and rolled up her capri pants to above her knees. Then she skipped, actually skipped, toward the water. A chuckle rose out of his chest at the image.

"You coming?" she asked with barely a backward glance.

He couldn't think of a single reason not to.

Kicking off his own sandals, he followed her into the crashing waves. She playfully kicked a splash of water in his direction when he reached her side, just enough to wet the bottom trim of his sports shorts.

"Why, Miss Payton," Gio began in a mock-serious tone. "How utterly childish of you."

Her response was a hearty laugh while she did it once more, getting him wetter this time.

He didn't mind. It was a dry, warm and sunny day. The water felt refreshing on his skin. He tried to think of the last time he'd been on the beach, simply frolicking in the water. Not a single instance came to mind. Not even from his childhood. In his before life, he'd have dived into the waves and began a series of laps, pushing himself harder and harder with each one.

What exactly had he been pushing for all those times?

"I wish I'd brought a swimsuit," Marni said, though she seemed to be getting rather wet enough despite being fully clothed.

"We can always come back."

She nodded with enthusiasm. "Yes! Let's do that. But I don't want to leave just yet."

Neither did he. In fact, he could stand out here and watch her frolicking in the water for hours. The thought both annoyed and amused him. What would he be doing right now if Marni had never arrived at the villa? No doubt, he'd be sitting at Nella's patio table poring over a spreadsheet or making phone calls. He certainly wouldn't be kicking around on the beach after having gorged on pastries.

When he looked up again, Marni had rolled her pants up higher, clear up to the tops of her thighs. She was several feet deeper in the water, much farther away than where he stood near the sand. A particular large wave appeared out of nowhere at that very moment.

Marni seemed to lose her footing as it crashed into her legs. Gio's vision blurred. There was no way he could reach her if she toppled over and got dragged under the water. Was Marni a proficient swimmer? How did he not know?

His heart hammered in his chest as he leaped to try and reach her before she could fall. With his bruised leg and weakened arm, he might not be able to pull her out if she went under and got in trouble. He'd barely made it to her side when he realized that not only had she remained upright, she was bent over laughing, her shoulders shaking with mirth.

Relief surged through him but it was quickly replaced by fury. What if she *had* fallen, what if the wave had taken her under and she'd been caught in the current.

"Did you see that?" she asked him, with amusement dancing in her eyes.

"Yeah. I saw how reckless and foolish you just were." Gio spit out the words, both unable and unwilling to temper his tone. She could have gotten seriously hurt. Or worse. And he would have been nearly helpless to do anything about it.

Her brows furrowed together, confusion clouding her eyes. "What?"

"You could have fallen in the water, Marni. I don't know how strong the current is." He thrust a hand through his hair. "I can't even remember if you're a good swimmer."

A slight breeze blew over Marni's skin as she exited the water. Goose bumps rose along her arms and legs but she couldn't tell if it was from the cold or the sheer terror she'd just witnessed on Gio's face. He was a step behind her when she turned to face him.

"Gio. What just happened? What got into you?" She tucked a wet curl of hair behind her ear. "All those vacations to Cape Cod I took with your family. Those three times I tagged along to the Bahamas with you all. How can you not remember if I can swim?"

Gio huffed out a breath of air and closed his eyes. "I just got nervous in the moment, all right? I thought you might get hurt and I wasn't sure if I'd be able to—" He looked away, never finishing the sentence.

She reached for him then, placing her hand on his forearm. He honestly had been frightened for her. Not that she could surmise why for the life of her. "You had to know I wasn't in any real danger."

Only he clearly hadn't known. "I just—" He broke off again, at an obvious loss for words. Marni found herself torn between genuine curiosity about what was going on with him and the need to be sensitive to his boundaries. If he didn't want to share with her what was causing all these changes in him, who was she to push?

"Look, never mind," he said, turning away. "Let's just forget it happened, okay?"

Right. Like she had any hope of being able to do that.

"I think we should head back now," he announced, then didn't so much as spare another glance in her direction when he walked away.

Marni clenched her hands tight at her sides. She had no reason to feel guilty about how the morning had suddenly gone so sour. She hadn't done anything wrong. She refused to accept the burden of responsibility when it wasn't hers to bear. She'd made a vow to rid herself of the habit when she'd left Ander for good. He'd blamed her for anything and everything that had gone wrong in his life or career. No more.

Whatever Gio had plaguing him at this juncture in his life—and she felt for him, she really did because he was obviously dealing with something major and life-changing—she just didn't have it in her to play the fall guy. Not anymore.

They walked the rest of the way in silence, only broken when Gio handed their remaining pastries to a young mother visiting the beach with her two toddlers. The children hopped up and down with glee when they dug into the box.

A pang of longing shot through her chest as she watched the scene. The mom looked harried and tired, but happy to be with her children. She didn't know if she'd ever have that. Not with the mess her last relationship had turned out to be. She mentally scoffed. What was it with her and her faulty judgment when it came to men? Look at her inconvenient crush on current company. It was wrong enough on the surface, given their past history. But especially now considering whatever was going on with Gio that had him acting so uncharacteristically.

When they reached the house, she didn't bother to let him know that she'd be heading to the shower to clean up and dry off. It would probably be better if they spent the day apart. Obviously, it had been a mistake to deviate from the original plan on day one: stay out of each other's way. Well, she knew better now. Another vow she'd made was to stop making the same mistakes over and over.

Marni took her time in the shower. The stall smelled of him, his aftershave, his soap. The woodsy scent of the shampoo he used. How many times had she imagined running her fingers through the mass of dark curls that fell over his forehead. How often had she resisted the temptation to lean closer to him and inhale deeply of the minty scent of that aftershave?

She was heading down a dubious path here. Maybe it

was just as well that they'd had that little falling-out at the beach. It served as a stark reminder that she needed to keep herself in check when it came to Gio Santino.

Still, she couldn't help the temptation to reach for her new phone when she returned to the bedroom and noticed it was finally fully charged. She knew Nella's number by heart.

If her friend had wanted her to know what was really going on with her brother, wouldn't she have told her by now? Although Marni had to admit Nella might have been hesitant to burden her with her family problems given all that Marni had been dealing with the past few months. Maybe that's why Nella hadn't said anything about Gio.

Marni reached for the phone and dialed the first three numbers before she hesitated. Rubbing a hand down her face, she tossed it onto the mattress and plopped down on the edge. No, she couldn't do it. She refused to call her best friend to ask her to dish about her older brother. How middle school cringe of her to even consider it.

Besides, didn't it also say quite a bit that he didn't trust her enough to tell her himself?

An hour later, try as she might, she couldn't stand to stay in the room any longer. This was silly. They could stay out of each other's way but they would still need to be civil over the next few days. Besides, she was thirsty. Marni would simply acknowledge him if she did run into him downstairs, explain that she hadn't meant any upset, get her drink and go about her day. But when she reached the first floor, Gio was sitting on the armchair facing the stairs, as if he was waiting for her.

He spoke before she could tell him any of the things she'd decided on upstairs. "Nella tells me you're a good listener."

* * *

Gio motioned with one hand to the love seat opposite where he sat. Marni forgot all about her thirst as she made her way into the sitting room and took a seat. They must have jinxed the weather the way they'd spoken about it earlier, because now the sky had grown dark and cloudy, throwing shadows on the walls. It fit the current mood perfectly.

Gio blew out a breath before speaking. "I scared you that first day you arrived. And I know I just scared you again earlier this morning," he began.

"You were concerned," Marni offered. "I under—"

Gio held up a hand to stop her before she could continue. "Please, just let me get through this. Before I have a chance to change my mind."

Marni nodded in agreement, remaining silent. Looked like she might finally be getting some answers, far be it from her to hamper that.

"You know I'm active in the various charities that Santino Foods sponsors."

"Yes, I know." As soon as he'd graduated college and joined the family company, Gio had taken on the responsibility of running the many charitable functions the family global company supported. But what did that have to do with anything that was happening with him now?

"There's an annual event called the Mangola Rally. It's a race across eastern Europe ending in a small town in Turkey. Santino Foods was asked to sponsor a racer. We would donate money and draw attention to benefit a good cause, in this case, a refugee crisis organization." He stopped to rub a hand across his eyes.

Marni waited for him to continue, not daring to interrupt.

Gio went on, "Rather than sponsor someone, I decided

I would participate myself. I'd gotten into racing cars a couple years back. Had even come in first in a few amateur motorsport events. Felt pretty confident behind the wheel. It was for a good cause. Plus, it sounded like fun. So I convinced the organizers I was qualified."

"You always were one to take risks," she offered, not surprised in the least that he'd opted to participate himself.

Gio flinched at her words. Marni wanted to suck them back in somehow.

"Well, it was one risk too many it turns out."

Oh, no.

"About the halfway mark, somewhere in the roughly terrained vicinity of the Austrian border, I lost control of the car."

Gio squeezed his eyes shut as he continued. "I don't even know what happened. I must have hit a boulder, or some other obstruction. The car was going much too fast because I had to be the one who came in first, as usual. I couldn't regain control of the car no matter what I tried."

Gio's hands were clenched tight against his thighs. A muscle worked along his jaw. She hated that he was reliving this, especially considering it was for her sake.

He sucked in a breath and continued. "I must have hit my head at some point, I blacked out. When I came to, the car was upside down."

She could guess the rest. "Oh, Gio. I'm so very sorry." Try as she might, there was nothing else she could think of to say.

"One of the other drivers came upon us eventually and called for help."

Us? Had she heard him correctly?

"You weren't alone in the car?"

Gio went pale and a shadow crossed his eyes. "That's the worst part. I had a codriver in the car with me to navigate the route. A family man with small children."

Marni's blood grew cold. "Is he…?" She couldn't bring herself to finish the sentence. Lucky for her, she didn't have to.

Gio shook his head. "He survived. Thank God." He sucked in a gulp of air. "But there's a question as to whether he'll ever walk again. And that's on me."

The enormity of what he'd just told her registered in her mind. It explained so much, no wonder Gio was in such a state. The nightmares, the restlessness, the tortured look behind his eyes when he thought she wasn't looking. No wonder he'd come here and secluded himself from everything and everyone he loved.

Not only had he suffered a catastrophic accident that could very well have killed him, he blamed himself for destroying someone's life.

A shudder racked through her core. He could have been killed. She felt shaken and unsettled at the realization. He'd been a constant in her life for so long, the thought of not having him in it made her want to weep. She'd been so clueless as to what he'd been dealing with. "I had no idea."

He nodded. "For Juno's privacy while he tries to recover, I did my best to keep it out of the papers and gossip sites. Only close family knew all the details. Luckily, the media lost interest except for a few initial reports. Until very recently, that is."

"Until recently?"

He nodded. "Unfortunately. And I need to figure out a way to make sure the details continue to stay out of the news cycle."

She tried hard to fight it—none of this was about her, after all—but a small, selfish part of her homed in on one undeniable truth: he hadn't thought to include her in that small circle of people he'd entrusted with the full story.

Gio couldn't bring himself to look at Marni's face as she took in all that he was telling her for fear of what he might find on her expression. At best, she'd look pitying and he couldn't handle that. At worst, she'd be horrified at what his carelessness had led to.

He cleared his throat to explain some more. "So you see, that's why I panicked when I thought you might fall in the water and hurt yourself. I might not have been able to help you if you got in trouble. My left leg is shattered, I broke several bones, some of which are still healing, I wouldn't have been able to move too well."

Her chin lifted. "I wouldn't need saving. But I understand."

Good to know. He didn't need to tell her then that the agony of watching her get hurt while he was helpless to help would have broken what was left of his soul once and for all.

He finally lifted his gaze to meet hers. There was nothing behind her eyes but concern.

"Is there nothing they can do?" she asked. "About your friend?"

"I have him set up in a specialty hospital in his native Switzerland. They're doing all they can, cutting-edge treatments. I pray every day that they find a way to heal him."

She nodded solemnly. "And what about your leg?"

He didn't want to get into this now, wasn't in the mood for any lectures. But in for a penny and all that. "I've undergone three different surgeries. The next step is rehab, which was recommended I do in Chicago with a world-renowned team of professionals who specialize in injuries like mine. I'll need more surgery after that."

"When do you start?"

He shrugged, bracing himself for the inevitable fallout when he told her. "I haven't made the appointment yet."

To his surprise, Marni merely nodded. No words of consternation followed, no warning that he was being dumb or stubborn. Could it be that she actually understood why he might be putting off the inevitable? Might she be the only person in his life who understood that he was capable of deciding for himself when and how quickly he'd be able to heal?

For the first time in several months, Gio felt a lightness come over him. The anguish coiled in his gut since the accident loosened. As difficult as it had been to get the words out, he felt as if a heavy anvil was lifted off his chest. He hated when his sister was right. Talking to Marni had in fact lessened some of the burden. He'd seen no judgment on her face, no accusation whatsoever.

Gio felt lighter but also thoroughly worn and spent. The conversation had brought all the dark memories up front and center when he'd been trying so hard to keep them at bay.

As if to match his mood, the afternoon had grown considerably darker since Marni first came down the stairs. The bright sunny morning they'd spent on the beach seemed so long ago. Hard to believe it had only been a few hours since they'd returned. The sun wasn't shining now, no seagulls could be heard outside. A bolt of lightning suddenly flashed outside the window followed by a loud blast of thunder.

"What were you saying earlier about the lack of rainy days?" Marni asked, walking to the screen to slide it shut. She closed it just in time. Fat, heavy raindrops began falling from the sky before she'd had a chance to latch the knob.

"Guess we were due."

She lifted a shoulder. "Darkness and rain have to appear some time."

Despite the seriousness of the moment, Gio had to bite his tongue to keep from laughing. Had she really just made such a blatantly obvious metaphor?

Marni must have come to the same realization, the corner of her mouth lifted ever so slightly.

"Too much?" she asked, the smile lingering on her lips.

"I'll say."

She bowed her head in mock shame. "As reparation, I offer to throw together some lunch for us," she stated, then glanced out the window. "Since it doesn't look like we'll be going out to eat this afternoon."

"Accepted."

"I'll cut up that baguette we picked up yesterday, throw it on a board with some cold cuts and that delicious mozzarella you have in the fridge. Do you mind grabbing a bottle of wine from Nella's rack downstairs? I'll replace it the next time we go out."

"Sure. Maybe for entertainment we can watch another episode of that Bollywood series." Huh, he had no idea he would suggest such a thing. Or that he'd actually thought about watching that show ever again.

Her eyebrows lifted toward her hairline. Yeah, well, he was pretty surprised at the suggestion himself.

"Sure, my tablet's in my room. I'll go get it before I pull the food together."

He wasn't sure how she'd managed it, but somehow he'd gone from suffering the crushing weight of memories of the accident, to looking forward to a relaxing afternoon watching a show while listening to the rain. And it was all Marni's doing.

He couldn't resist teasing her yet again. "But please try not to fall asleep again. You have a tendency to snore."

She turned on her heel to glare at him. "What? How would you possibly know that?" He watched her eyes widen as the realization dawned on her.

"Why you sneak," she threw out, her hands on her hips, though there was no bite in her tone.

"Why whatever do you mean?"

She pointed a finger in his direction. "That night, on the lounge chairs. You knew the whole time. Pretending you were clueless."

He crossed his arms over his chest. "Miss Payton, I have no idea what you are talking about."

"Right. Sure, you don't."

He laughed in response. "Go get your tablet. I'm dying to know what happens after the last dance battle."

CHAPTER SIX

THE NEXT MORNING Marni awoke to a noise she barely registered. Sunlight poured through the half-open blind on her window. She hadn't gotten much rest. It felt as if she'd just fallen asleep moments ago. How was it possible that it was morning already? She'd been plagued by disturbing dreams involving fiery crashes and being trapped in a car after it flipped. If simply hearing about Gio's accident had invaded her dreams, she couldn't imagine how nightmarish his nights must be.

Vaguely, she recalled a late-night disagreement about who would get the bed. The new furniture had yet to arrive, delayed by the freak storm yesterday. Both had insisted the other get the bed and room. She'd won by losing. Or maybe she'd lost by winning. Hard to tell. Gio wouldn't budge, insisted on sleeping on the couch.

Her heart ached for him and all he was dealing with. Maybe she'd been too quick to try and lighten the mood yesterday after he'd told her everything, but she would have given anything to help ease the pain so evident in his face.

There was the noise again. She finally recognized it as knocking. With a groan, she sat up. Why in the world was Gio knocking on her door first thing in the morning?

"Come in."

The door creaked open about a foot and Gio poked his head in. "You decent?"

"I said come in, didn't I?"

He shrugged, stepping into the room. "Didn't want to assume, sweetheart."

The endearment shot through to her center. It was way too early to be hearing sweet nothings from Gio Santino. She hadn't even had any caffeine yet.

"Sorry to wake you," he said. "But I waited and you didn't come down. And we only have a small window."

She blinked at him. "Gio. What in the world are you talking about?"

"The management agency called early this morning. About the villa that's available to buy. They said a rep can be there to let us in until about noon. If you'd rather go back to sleep, I understand."

Noon? Marni glanced at the bedside clock for the first time. It was approaching ten thirty! She couldn't recall the last time she'd slept so late.

"Of course, I'll be down in a fast minute."

Gio's shoulders seemed to drop three inches and he grinned. "Great. I'll see you in a bit."

He appeared relieved that she didn't turn him down. And he'd waited for her instead of just heading to the villa by himself. Did he value her opinion that much? Or maybe he just wanted her company. Either way, she couldn't help the sense of pleasure that pulsed through her.

In her line of work, she visited houses all the time. So why was she practically feeling giddy about visiting this one with Gio Santino?

He was waiting on the patio for her. "It's just up the coast, past town," he informed her.

So another boat ride, then. The sky was clear and blue once again. As if yesterday's storm had never happened.

When they boarded, Gio once again handed her the life jacket. She took it without question this time. Another piece that made more sense now. Gio's adamant insistence that she wear it the first time they'd sailed up the coast the other day.

Now she studied his profile as he steered the boat. Without warning, he turned his head in her direction. Great. She'd been caught staring. *Gawking* might actually be a better word for it.

"What?" he asked, his smile warm and friendly.

No way she could tell him the truth about what she'd been really thinking. "I was just curious about manning a boat. Do I refer to you as captain while we're on it?"

He gave her a mock salute. "I like the thought of you referring to me as your captain."

So he was back to the teasing, flirtatious version of himself Marni was so familiar with. After what she'd leaned yesterday, she would take it. Not that their situations even compared, but it seemed the past year had been life changing for them both.

"Come here," Gio said, motioning her over to his side. "Give it a try if you're so curious."

She stood without hesitation. "You mean I can be the captain for a bit?"

"Let's not get ahead of ourselves."

Marni stood in front of him and gingerly took the wheel. The unexpected vibration threw her off for the first second. He left one hand on it as he helped her to steer. "Steady, we're just gonna keep going straight for a bit."

Marni could feel the strength of the water through her

fingertips as she guided the boat over it. The cliffside rose majestically out of the ocean to their left, giving her the feeling of being yards below civilization. Which she supposed would be an accurate description. Sailing the ocean in Capri felt nothing like driving on land.

She hadn't even noticed until that moment that Gio had removed his hand off the wheel.

"You're a natural," he said into her ear.

That enticing scent of mint and sandalwood drifted to her nose. Even through the life jackets, she could feel the warmth of his body against hers. Her breath caught in her throat. Between the headiness of sailing the boat and the effect of Gio's proximity, her senses were in overdrive.

Finally, Gio reached for the wheel. "I should probably take it from here. We're almost at the shoreline."

Marni reluctantly let go and stepped away. As soon as she got her life sorted and figured out her next career move, she might have to see about sailing lessons back in the States.

Not that anything would compare to what she'd just experienced. For one thing, no lesson was going to feel the same as having Gio guide her.

It wouldn't even come close.

Gio had been looking forward to touring the villa more than he could explain. That had everything to do with Marni. In fact, if she wasn't here in Capri with him, he probably would have sent a representative and asked for pics. After they docked, he guided Marni up the stone steps to the property where a realty agent who introduced herself as Angela let them in.

She led them to the main sitting area first. "I think

this would be an ideal vacation home for a couple such as yourselves," she said, her smile wide.

Marni's hand flew to her chest as she began to correct the other woman. "Oh! We're not—"

Gio interrupted her protest in Italian, quickly changing the subject. A germ of an idea forming in his mind. He and Marni certainly made a convincing picture of a couple touring a home they might share. Cupping Marni's elbow, he motioned for the agent to lead them through the area.

After a quick tour around the rest of the house, Angela allowed them some time to observe the villa alone.

"Well, what do you think?" he asked.

They were standing in what would be his sitting room if he made the purchase. It was spacious with high ceilings and a shiny polished hardwood floor.

"I think you're lucky to be able to afford this. This place is gorgeous."

He would have to agree. Gio never forgot that he'd been born under a lucky star. He was the first son of a prosperous family, who'd managed to grow his own personal wealth. He'd often wondered if he deserved his good fortune. Especially over the past few months.

Marni continued, walking the length of the wall. "I mean, it's roomy and allows in a lot of light. I can think of all sorts of ways to decorate." She turned on her heel to face him, biting her lip. "That wasn't meant as any kind of plea that you hire me. I hope you know that. I'm just making observations. I hope you understand." She seemed genuinely concerned that her innocent statement might have landed wrong. Gio wanted to strangle the person who had done this to her. At times such as this one, she seemed horrified that she'd made some kind of mistake.

"I understand completely." She might not have meant it as a plea, but he would certainly consider it an offer. Of course he would. Who else would he get to help him furnish this place if he bought it?

A look of relief flushed over her features and she continued walking, trailing her fingers along the wall. When she got to the corner of the room, she tilted her head, studied the wall. "There appears to be a gap here, in the wallpaper. Though why anyone would wallpaper these days is beyond me."

She glanced toward the door, as if on the lookout.

"Something wrong?" Gio asked.

"I just want to see what's under this paper, there's some kind of pattern. Let me know if you see the agent approach. I don't want her to think I'm trying to tear the paper off."

Gio had to laugh. Somehow their visit to see an available property had turned into some kind of covert operation. Everything he did with Marni seemed to take on a special or unusual turn. Life was going to seem so flat and boring after they parted ways.

"I've got you covered," he assured her, his eyes trained to the door.

He heard the scrape of her fingernail. "Oh, my God," she said breathlessly a few seconds later.

"What is it?" Gio gave up on guard duty and strode to her side. She was picking at a spot on the wallpaper that had partially come off.

"If I'm not mistaken, there's a genuine mosaic under all this paper. Probably handcrafted."

Gio had no idea what that might mean. Was it a good thing?

"When did you say this place was built?" Marni asked.

He hadn't, it hadn't come up before now. "I think the details online said late nineteenth century."

She tapped the paper back in place and stepped away, her eyes alight with enthusiasm. "You could have a real work of art under all this. I can't imagine for the life of me why anyone would cover it up with plain beige wallpaper."

He wished there was a way to bottle up her excitement. He couldn't remember the last time he'd been so affected by a discovery. Let alone a wall. Maybe that was why he kept looking for ways to take risks. Just to be able to feel things the way someone like Marni did.

He recalled the way she'd reacted when he'd let her steer the boat. Such a mundane task as far as he was concerned. But Marni had been practically buzzing.

"I would kill to see what the entire thing might look like under that paper," Marni added.

He could only think of one way that would be possible.

"I wonder what other delightful discoveries a place like this might hold," she said, palming the wall with a faraway look on her face.

Gio figured she just might find out.

Angela's words echoed through his head...*a couple such as yourselves.*

Gio pushed the thought away. For now.

Twenty minutes later he and Marni were sitting outside on the vast patio by a sparkling blue infinity pool. The realty agent had locked up the house and left, asking them to shut the locked gate once they left.

The pool area felt like a mini paradise, complete with marble statues of cherubs and a plot of colorful flowers in each corner. Marni took her shoes off and sat at the edge of the pool, soaking her feet up to her ankles. The image looked right to his eyes, as if she belonged here.

As far as property went, it wouldn't be a bad purchase. He'd wanted a place in Capri for a while now, ever since his sister and husband had inherited their estate. He could picture himself lounging out here by the pool. Could picture having his morning espresso while seated at the bay window overlooking the cliffside. Funny thing was, in none of those pictures was he alone. The woman splashing her feet in the pool was central in every single one.

What that might mean for his psyche, he didn't even want to analyze. So much in his life was in turmoil right now. Marni was at a daunting crossroads herself. He had no business envisioning her in any part of a future he was so uncertain about.

Marni reached in the pool and cupped a handful of water then splashed his legs with a playful giggle.

One thing he was certain of, regardless of what the future held, Gio planned to be the next owner of this villa.

Marni sighed and took another look back at the villa they'd just toured. The place really was rather remarkable. What she would give to use her skills to decorate a place like that. Who was she kidding? Even if Gio did buy the place and hire her to decorate it—and those were pretty big ifs—she'd have to do it virtually from thousands of miles away in the States. She couldn't stay here in Capri long term. She had to get back and see about putting her life back in order.

Still, a girl could dream.

"Are you in any rush to get back to Nella's?" Gio asked from the bow without looking away from the horizon.

"Not particularly," she answered. "Why?"

"There's something I want to show you. If you're up for it."

His wide smile of enthusiasm was enough for her. "Sure."

Gio turned the boat in the other direction and ramped up the speed. Within half an hour they approached a cavernous opening on the cliffside. A slew of motorboats, small yachts and rowboats surrounded it in the water.

"Let's hope the wait won't be too long," Gio said, then picked up his cell to make a phone call. She couldn't make out any of the Italian.

"What exactly are we waiting for?" she asked.

"You'll see," he answered with a mischievous gleam in his eyes. "Have some patience."

Moments later, Gio got a phone call and maneuvered their boat around the other craft. One of the men in the rowboats close to the cavern opening was waving them over. Gio navigated to his side then turned off the motor.

"Let's go," he told Marni, offering her a hand then helping her onto the rowboat before jumping on himself.

"This is Mario," he introduced, "he'll be our tour guide and rowboat driver."

Tour guide?

Marni cleared her throat. "Wait. Are you telling me we're about to sail into that massive cave in the cliff wall?"

"That's right. This is the Grotta D'Abruzzo. Wait till you see what it's like inside."

Excitement mixed with fear churned in her chest. She'd never been great at closed-in places. Exploring a water cave wasn't exactly what she'd had in mind when she agreed earlier to this outing. But Marlo was grinning and gesturing for them to be seated.

Marni swallowed her trepidation and sat down on one

of the rungs. Then jolted in surprise when Gio took the
one behind hers. Not so much because he'd sat behind
her, but because of the closeness of their bodies in the
small space. Her bottom was nestled against his inner
thighs, his chest close against her back.

Suddenly, her trepidation about entering the cave was
completely overtaken by the fire that shot through her
system at the close contact.

Heat crawled over her skin, her nerve endings afire
with the intimacy of their positions. Surely, Gio had to
feel it too. She was practically sitting on his lap, for God's
sake. His legs spread out, tight against her hips.

She froze when he leaned in to murmur in her ear,
"Comfortable?" Marni didn't imagine the mischief in his
tone. His breath felt hot against her cheek, tickled her earlobe. How in the world was she supposed to answer that?

Marni closed her eyes, willed herself to focus on her
breathing.

Gio leaned into her shoulder once more. "Breathtaking, isn't it?"

Oh, she was breathless all right. But no doubt he was
referring to whatever was in the cavern. Marni opened
her eyes and blinked when she focused on the view before her.

Was she seeing things? The cave was alight with a
bright neon blue. The water below them glowed, the rock
walls glittered indigo. It was as if they'd entered a mono-
chrome painting that somehow lit up from the inside.

"Oh, my," was all she could muster in response.

"Quite a sight, huh?" Gio asked, his chin bopping
against her bare shoulder.

"I've never seen anything like it. What is this place?"

"They say it used to be the private swimming hole of Emperor Tiberius of the Roman Empire." From the corner of her eye, she saw him point upward. "His castle was built above us."

"How is it lit up in blue fluorescence?"

She felt him shrug behind her. "I'm not sure about the exact physics." He asked Marlo a question in Italian. The other man replied with several accompanying hand gestures.

Gio translated when he was done. Something about holes in the cave wall and capturing the sunlight through the openings. But God, it was so hard to concentrate between his closeness, the feel of his breath against her skin and the spellbinding sight before her.

"Imagine having this as your private swimming pool," Gio said after several minutes spent simply admiring the view.

Marni could imagine it all too easily. Had the king come down here for a late-night skinny-dip with his queen? Had they stolen private moments in the water, surrounded by this heavenly light, simply enjoying the pleasure of each other's company? As well as other much more intimate pleasures?

The vignette morphed into more personal images in her mind's eye. Only now it wasn't the Roman king and queen she was picturing. Oh, God, it was her and Gio. What would it feel like to frolic in this water, in the dark, while held in his arms? To have his lips on hers in such a secluded and private setting? Heat rushed to her cheeks. She silently said a small prayer of thanks that Gio couldn't see her face.

No! For all that's holy. No, no, no!

Gio spoke again softly over her shoulder. "I see the sight has left you breathless," he said. "You're practically gasping for air."

If he only knew the truth.

His leg was angrily throbbing. Bolts of pain shot through his thigh down to his knee. It was almost bad enough that he could ignore the more constant ache in his side and rib cage. Almost.

He'd overdone it today.

A voice in his head wholeheartedly agreed. It listed the litany of things he'd done when he should have known better. Climbing stone steps, both at this villa and the one he would be buying. All that walking as he and Marni toured the property. Jumping into a rowboat.

That last one was probably the nail in the proverbial coffin. A perfect comparison since he felt like the pain might actually kill him if it didn't subside significantly.

"You're hurting, aren't you?"

He hadn't even seen Marni come out to the patio.

"What makes you say that?" he said in as light a voice as he could manage. It wasn't easy.

She lifted an eyebrow. "Oh, just the way your face is scrunched up as if you're pushing a heavy boulder up a steep cliff. Or maybe how you keep rubbing the spot above your knee. All sorts of clues I'm sharp enough to pick up on."

That was the problem. She was too sharp by half.

"It's nothing, Marni," he said with a forced chuckle. "Nothing a night's rest won't help. I'll be much better in the morning."

"But you haven't been getting any kind of good rest, have you?"

Well, she had a point there. He should have come up with a better way to assuage her.

"I'll be fine," he repeated, for lack of anything else to say.

"We did too much today. I wondered what you were thinking, jumping onto that boat."

Yeah, the thing was, he hadn't been thinking at all. Just anticipating the joy he might bring to Marni by taking her to the grotto. He was certainly paying for it now.

She walked over and sat down on the lounge chair next to him. "I just wish the new furniture would get here already."

"Hopefully soon. Though things tend to move slower in Europe. Especially this time of year, during vacation season."

Marni's spine straightened and she lifted her chin, as if she was prepping for a fight. "Listen, Santino. If you think for one minute I'm going to take the bed tonight while you try to sleep on the couch or this lounge chair or on a bunch of cushions, you better think again."

Gio rubbed a hand down his face. How often were they going to go through this? Although, this time, he was actually tempted given the thousands of small knives stabbing his leg muscles at the moment.

"I will not argue about this. It's settled."

"Marni—"

"No!" Her tone was sharp enough that he was somewhat surprised. "I said it's settled. In fact, if you don't take the bed, then I won't either. We'll both be uncomfortable while there's a perfectly good bed upstairs sitting empty."

He tried to argue, but found he just didn't have it in him. The pain medication he'd been given left him groggy and disoriented, a sensation he'd hated. And Marni was right, the thought of trying to endure this pain while lying horizontal on anything other than a mattress would no doubt result in a night of absolute agony.

"All right," he said, blowing out a resigned sigh.

"Don't you—" She stopped. "Wait. Did you just agree?"

He nodded. *"Sì. Hai vinto."*

Her eyes roamed over his face. "Huh. I win, huh? That tells me how much you must be hurting."

"Because I actually agreed with you?"

Marni shook her head. "No. That you reverted to speaking Italian."

"Okay. I admit. My leg doesn't feel real great right now. But I don't see why you have to sleep down here."

Marni practically rolled her eyes. "I knew that was too easy. I thought you just said you agreed that you should take the bed."

"I did. But I think you should too."

Her eyes grew wide and her brows lifted clear to her hairline. Her shocked expression made him chuckle out loud. "Marni, it's a very large bed. And I'm hardly in any position to—"

She held her hand up to stop him. "I see what you're getting at. And you're right. We've both had an enjoyable yet tiring and long day. There's nothing wrong with two old friends getting a good night's sleep on the same mattress. Not much different than all those slumber parties Nella and I had at your house."

Gio's ego took a bit of a hit with that one. But she was right. For the most part. "Can we do each other's hair and paint our nails? Write in our journals?"

She nodded. "Sure, we could do all that. Or we could watch another episode of *Lotus Dreams*."

"That works too."

"Sounds like a decent plan to me. I'll go cue it up on the tablet."

"Can't wait." He was aiming for a sarcastic tone but realized he actually was looking forward to the night they'd just planned. Something about watching a mindless television show with Marni by his side was more appealing to him these days than a night out on the town. Or a night scuba diving or parasailing or dirt biking... or any of the countless, rather extreme ways he'd been entertaining himself throughout most of his adulthood.

"Before I do that, I'll go get you some ice for that leg."

There wasn't enough ice in the kitchen, maybe in all of Capri, that would do any good given the condition he was in right now. He was about to tell her not to bother, but she'd already left to go get it for him.

CHAPTER SEVEN

MAYBE THIS WASN'T such a great idea. Gio sighed as quietly as possible so as not to disturb Marni. He desperately wanted to toss and turn but didn't want to risk waking her. One of them should be able to get some shut-eye. They'd just retired half an hour ago. It was sure to be a long night.

"It's okay…"

He heard Marni's soft voice in the dark.

"I know you're not asleep."

"Are you?" The ridiculous question garnered a low laugh out of her.

"Guess," she answered.

Gio chuckled and turned to her. He'd been so concerned about moving toward her in his sleep that he was practically on the edge of the mattress. There was a good three feet of distance between them. "I'm sorry, for keeping you up."

She released a breath, turned over onto her back. "You're not the reason I haven't drifted off. I have a lot to think about and I can't seem to shut my mind off."

Boy, could he relate. It was better for both of them to just do their best to fall asleep. So he surprised himself when he opened his mouth to ask the next question. "What was it about him?"

Gio sensed her discomfort at the question. Finally, she turned her head to face him. "I don't exactly know why. I can only say that he was very charming at first. Until he wasn't."

"Tell me."

She was silent for so long, he figured she had no intention of sharing. Finally, she sighed and began to speak. "I told you about leaving my job, you remember?"

He remembered every bit of their conversations. Something that tended to happen when he truly enjoyed someone's company. "I do.

"All because you broke things off with your former..." He hesitated. He couldn't seem to use the word *lover* when it came to Marni's past relationship. Referring to her as someone else's lover felt wrong on his tongue.

"With your ex?" he finished.

"You do remember. Only I didn't just work with him. I worked *for* him."

"He had the nerve to fire you for breaking up with him?"

"More or less an accurate assumption."

A bolt of rage shot through his chest for a man he'd never laid eyes on. The damage he'd done to Marni was unforgivable.

"What would make it more accurate?"

"He was one of the head architects at the firm I worked for. Interoffice relationships weren't explicitly forbidden but everyone knew they were frowned upon by the higher-ups."

"I see."

"I got lots of disapproving glances and a few outright glares by the other partners."

Gio shook his head. It took two to be in a relationship. "That's pretty unfair."

"Then there was all the snickering and gossip from the other decorators. I could just guess what they were saying behind my back every time I was assigned a job."

He could also guess.

"That I slept my way to getting the assignment," she confirmed.

Again, wholly unfair. But it was the way of the world, wasn't it? Unfortunately, women were the ones who were often the target of bitterness in scenarios such as the one Marni was in. Kudos to her for having the good sense to remove herself from such a toxic situation.

Only, she hadn't walked away unscathed, without any battle wounds.

"What happened?" Gio prompted. He had the feeling it would do her good to get some of this off her chest. And maybe it was selfish of him, but he had to acknowledge it did him a bit of good as well to focus on someone else's woes for a while. If that was indeed self-serving, at least it was a win-win.

"I knew I had to end the relationship. Between the way it was affecting my work environment and the way Ander...treated me. It was all too destructive to my well-being."

"How so?"

"He tried to control what I wore, how I dressed. What I ate, how much I ate. And nothing I did was ever enough to please him."

"Do I have to take a trip back to Mass?" he asked, completely serious and more than willing to do just that. "To pay this guy a visit?"

Marni puffed out a breath of air. "He's not worth it. Believe me. I would much rather just forget he existed."

That was fine with him.

Marni continued, "Only, that's proving hard to do since I was fired on his behalf."

"On his behalf?"

He felt her head bop up and down in a nod. "Ander wasn't happy about the breakup. He didn't try to hide it. In fact, he made sure the tension was thick and heavy every time we had to be in the same room together."

"Not exactly conducive to a work setting."

"Nope. He didn't care, he knew he could get away with it."

"And you were the one who ended up paying for it." Job or no job, Gio believed wholeheartedly that she was better off far away from that sorry excuse for a man.

"That's right," Marni said. "Out of nowhere, I was told they needed to do some cost cutting and could do with one less decorator. Never mind that I had seniority over two of the other decorators who got to stay."

Gio swore in Italian.

Marni repeated the epithet with a thick American accent, earning a guffaw out of him.

"I reached out to colleagues for other opportunities right away. But got a lot of cold-shouldered responses. I guess the gossip was too much for me to overcome. I am persona non grata right now in the Boston interior design scene."

"I'm really sorry, Marni," he said, his heart breaking for her.

"So now, thanks to Nella, I have two weeks to try and put it all behind me."

"If I know my sister, she insisted."

"You would be right," Marni said with a laugh. "But she only has my best interest at heart. And she's smart—what better way to regroup than to do it in paradise?"

He had to agree on that score. It was why he was here in Capri too, after all.

Marni had been through so much. Was still dealing with the vengeful manipulations of a jilted lover. The same nagging thought in his head since they'd toured the villa for sale resurfaced once again. It was hairbrained and ridiculous and nonsensical.

But maybe, just maybe, it might be a way to address both their dilemmas.

Who would have thought she'd be grateful for a bout of insomnia? Marni glanced at the digital clock behind Gio on the bedside table. They'd been simply lying there in bed, just talking, for over an hour. She'd had no idea just how badly she'd needed to purge herself of all that had happened in the past few months. Gio was a good listener. He offered no judgment, didn't pretend to know any of the answers. He simply listened quietly. Turned out, that was exactly what she needed right now.

Nella had been there for her, of course. As always, she was only a call away and checked on her often. But she had her own life to live, now as a newlywed no less, and Marni hadn't wanted to burden her. As for her mom, well, her mom was just too tired these days to care.

"What do you think you'll do?" he asked her now. "When you get back after the two weeks?"

That was the question, wasn't it? She had no plans other than to keep reaching out to people she knew in the field, sending out her CV and hoping for the best.

Except for those times when that one other option

floated through her brain. But that was mere fantasy. How she would attempt to pull it off, she had no idea. Didn't even know where to start.

So she surprised herself when she answered Gio's question the way she did. "Well, during more wishful moments, I fantasize about branching out on my own. If I can figure out how."

"Like opening up your own place?"

"Yeah. But it's a big *if*."

"Marni, I think that's a great idea."

She rubbed her forehead. "I don't know. It would be a lot. I'd have to figure out how to finance it. I'm barely scraping by as it is."

"There are ways to find investors for this kind of thing. Plus, you can start small."

Valid points. Her credit history was pretty good. A small business loan from the bank wasn't out of the question. But what if she failed? Again.

Then she'd be jobless and further in debt. Her school loans were enough to keep her finances in the red for years still.

"Let's pretend you have all the logistics figured out," Gio suggested. "What would you call the business?"

Marni's gut tightened at the question. She was nervous even pretending about having her own place, something she'd wanted so badly for so long. "Nothing fancy," she answered. "Probably Marni's Interior Design. Something along those lines."

"Where do you think you'd set up shop?"

Now that she'd voiced her pretend business name out loud, her stomach muscles loosened just a little. What was the harm in just pretending? "If I had to pick right now, I might say Somerville. Or Medford. Those towns are really growing fast right now. But not enough that I'd be priced out of leasing a place."

Huh. She hadn't even realized the thought had occurred to her.

"What kind of sign would you have above your door?"

"See, that's where I might get fancy. It would have to be big and colorful. With my name displayed cleaRLY in huge, artistic lettering."

The image flashed clearly in her mind as she spoke the words as if a physical sign hung before her at this very moment in the dark. So real, she thought she might be able to reach out her hand and touch it.

"What might your slogan be?" Gio asked.

She surprised herself by coming up with something right then and there. "Comfort, quality and personal attention guaranteed."

"I think that's perfect."

She kind of liked it too. "One of the things about working in such a large firm was not really knowing the clients enough to gage for certain exactly what they would find homey," she explained. "I never knew if I was creating a home interior that went with their innermost personality."

"With your own place, you can personally ensure that happens."

She slapped her palm on the mattress. "Exactly!"

Marni closed her eyes, now fully immersed in the make-believe world she'd just created—sitting at a big mahogany desk, speaking to a client, taking notes about how best to furnish their home. She couldn't guess how much time had gone by when she snapped her eyes open at a grunt from Gio. The moon cast just enough light in the room that she could see him gripping his thigh as well as clenching his lips. In fact, his whole body had gone rigid and tight. He was in pain still.

Marni cupped a hand to her mouth as a realization hit her. "I'm so sorry, Gio."

"What in the world are you apologizing for?"

"Here I am practically wailing about my misfortune then waxing poetic about my dreams. All the while you're lying there literally in pain. I'm being so selfish."

He chuckled. "You're hardly wailing. And you most definitely aren't selfish. Far from it. If anything, you've managed to take my mind off the pain for a bit."

If he really meant that, Marni was beyond grateful that she might have been able to provide even a small iota of comfort, albeit small, especially considering all he'd just done for her. For the first time since leaving the firm, she felt a glimmer of hope for her future. Maybe she'd never be able to start her own place, but the dream was enough to keep her afloat during the tough times.

"Thank you for that. And thanks for indulging in my fantasy design firm creation."

Though she'd be darned if it didn't seem just a bit more real now.

Gio reached over and tapped a playful finger to her nose. "You're welcome, gattina. Anytime."

She couldn't have heard him correctly.

Marni sat up on her blanket-size beach towel and shielded the sun from her eyes. Gio's shadow loomed large on the golden sand beside her. She'd spent the morning lounging by the water. Now he was here handing her a sweaty glass of lemonade.

And also apparently to make a suggestion that seemed too far-fetched to be real. "I'm sorry, I could have sworn you said that we should pretend to be a couple for the next several days."

He crouched down to one knee next to her, so close his scent mingled with the salty sea air. His forearm brushed her shoulder, raising goose bumps despite the heat of the day.

Focus.

"I must have heard wrong," she said now with a soft chuckle.

"Hear me out," he began. "I think a little pretense might be beneficial for both of us."

Marni studied his face, no signs of joking or humor in any of his features. He really was serious. "What kind of pretense?"

"We pretend we're here together intentionally. That we're dating."

Marni shifted in her position. "That settles it, no more of that Bollywood show for you. What you're suggesting sounds like a plot right out of its storylines."

"But it makes sense, gattina. We're seen doing the tourist thing together. Everyone assumes we're a couple. There's no speculation about either of us."

"Speculation?"

Gio sighed and sat down all the way next to her. "It must be a slow news week. Because there's a journalist for a regional publication who's been calling to find out more about the accident. My guess is that others will follow. For Juno's sake, I need to make sure to shut it down before it starts."

"So you want to pretend you're simply vacationing, but why the farce about us being together?" Marni had to swallow after uttering the last few words.

"This way, we avert any interest in digging up the past

and give them something new and shiny to focus on. They'll drool at the human interest angle. A local CEO who narrowly avoided death and has now found love. One who's seen how tenuous and fragile life can be and wants to settle down and give up his playboy lifestyle."

"Huh."

"And you show the world that your previous relationship is well in your past."

His suggestion was still preposterous, but Marni was beginning to see the logic behind the plan. He didn't need to explain how it would be beneficial for her to have the world believing they were an item. It would certainly quiet down the rumors Ander was spreading about her. She would look like a woman who'd truly moved on. "You want it to look like you're simply on some kind of romantic vacation."

He tapped her nose playfully. "Right. What do you say? Do you want to think about it before you make your decision?"

Marni shook her head. "I guess it's worth a try. I mean, we have nothing to lose by giving it a shot."

Gio's grin in response had her insides quivering. "That's my gattina," he said. "All we need to do is just make sure to be seen around town, like we're on holiday together. Visiting attractions, playing tourist. It would settle down all the gossip about the both of us. No one really knows the true circumstances of why we're here except for Nella and Alex."

"How do we explain all this to them?"

He shrugged again. "If they even get wind of it, we'll just tell them the truth. That it's not real."

It's not real. Gio was merely suggesting they playact, put on a show for the rest of the world. So why was her mind flooded with images of the two of them together enjoying the sights and attractions of one of the most romantic places on earth?

Her mind knew it wouldn't be real. But her heart was already wishing it could have been.

Maybe Marni had been right. Maybe this idea was completely insane, a story straight out of the plot of a soap opera. Either way, Gio figured they had nothing to lose by giving it a try. A few leaks to some gossip sites, a few photos floating in the social media sphere, a well-placed comment here or there. That should be more than enough to still the wagging tongues on both his and Marni's behalf.

This dinner cruise along the Capri coast aboard a yacht was a good first stop. Judging by Marni's expression, she was enjoying herself to boot, which was icing on the cake. Wait until they arrived at their destination. She was sure to be stunned.

Speaking of being stunned, Marni's black wraparound dress draped over her curves and brought out her tanned skin. She'd done her hair up in a simple style that somehow made her look both elegant and casual. The woman sure did clean up well.

He'd instructed the captain to specifically have them go by the *faraglioni* rocks on their way to Il Faro, the famous lighthouse on the southern coast. This way, Marni could experience their majestic beauty as well as the lighthouse itself and its views. Just because they were on this outing for practical reasons didn't mean they couldn't make the most out of it. He could show her the beauty that was the Amalfi coast while they were at it.

Her jaw dropped when they approached the sight. "Oh, my," she whispered breathlessly.

He could hardly blame her wonder. The *faraglioni* rocks in Capri were one of the most captivating landscapes in the world. Towering out of the deep sea, waves crashing at their base with a beautiful view of verdant land in the distance.

"It's breathtaking," Marni added, not taking her eyes off the scene before them.

When the waiter appeared at their table to take their order, Gio fished his phone out of his pocket and handed it to the man. "Would you mind?"

Draping his arm around Marni, he pulled her closer to his side, the majesty of the rocks setting the scene behind them. "Smile for the photo, *cara*," he told her.

Taking his phone back, he glanced at the image on the screen. "Picture-perfect," he said to Marni. "This should work just fine."

Picture-perfect. Marni took a deep breath and tried to still the racing of her pulse. That's all this was, just a picture she and Gio were trying to project onto the world. One based on a complete falsehood. So why had her heart quickened when Gio put his arm around her and pulled her close? For his part, Gio seemed single-mindedly focused on their true objective—playing up their false relationship.

Well, she could do the same. She'd force herself to not be distracted by the scent of his aftershave or the way his silver-gray suit brought out the dark specks in his eyes and highlighted the darker streaks in his wavy hair.

No. She'd ignore all that and focus on the now. In the

meantime, she'd enjoy this once-in-a-lifetime early evening dinner cruise aboard a luxury yacht.

The food arrived in short order, helping in her efforts at distraction. Fresh lemon dill sea bass and homemade pasta with a side of grilled vegetables. A few months ago she would have pushed the pasta aside, making sure to only eat the lean fish and veggies. All to maintain her calorie goal in case Ander asked.

What a relief not to have to worry about such things now. Marni's mouth watered. She wasn't sure what her expression must have held but when she looked up Gio was staring at her with concern.

"Is that not to your liking? We can ask for something else?"

"No, it's absolutely perfect," she answered, sticking her fork in the pasta first. "I can't wait for dessert."

Several minutes later, the boat gradually slowed as they approached a redbrick building. Atop it sat a tall lighthouse. They came to a stop just as a waiter appeared with a tray that held two silver goblets half-full of golden liquid. "For the viewing," he said in a charming Italian accent.

Marni took one of the offered drinks and sniffed. They nutty aroma of almonds and spice tickled her nose. "What exactly are we viewing?" she asked Gio after the server walked away.

But he simply winked at her then said, "You'll see."

"Why can't you just tell me?"

"Because there's no way to describe it, gattina."

Marni realized just how true that statement was once they'd disembarked and walked up a stone pathway toward the lighthouse.

"La Punta Carena," Gio announced. "The best place

in the world to watch the sun setting over the Mediterranean."

Marni slowly sipped her drink and watched the horizon as the sun began to lower in the sky. Gio's words had not been an exaggeration. The horizon was a striking hue of red and orange, the water beneath it sparkling like jewelry. It was like watching a live-action view of a masterpiece painting.

Pretense or not, this was one of the most breathtaking scenes she'd ever witnessed. One she'd never forget.

Sighing deeply, Marni leaned back against Gio's chest and simply enjoyed the view, surrounded by his scent and heat.

CHAPTER EIGHT

"I THINK WE'VE floated enough photos out there for this plan to work," Gio announced the next morning. She'd come out to the patio to admire the now familiar view of the ocean in the horizon past the infinity pool. She was going to miss this ritual when she had to return to Boston in a few days. "Combined with the leak that we were seen touring an available villa together, I think we've got a solid foundation for our fake relationship."

Why did she cringe inside every time she heard those last two words?

Gio continued, "But just in case, I've got one more outing planned for us this afternoon."

Marni lowered her sunglasses to study him. "Another outing, huh?"

Gio nodded, his smile growing. If she didn't know any better, she might think he was actually enjoying all this activity. Still, she'd been growing more and more concerned about whether he was overtaxing himself. He'd insisted on walking along the pathway at the base of the lighthouse yesterday so that Marni got the full experience. But she was loath to say anything to him. Gio seemed to take any hint at his vulnerability as some kind of affront.

She could only hope whatever he had planned for today wouldn't involve too much physical effort. For his sake.

"What kind of activity?"

"The Gardens of Augustus. No trip to Capri would be complete without a visit there." He plopped himself down on the lounge chair next to her. "And it will give us another chance to be seen out and about together. The gardens are usually full of visitors this time of year. It's a beautiful day so today will be no different."

Gio was proven right about the crowd size when they arrived by private car two hours later to the winding pathway that led up to the world-renowned botanical garden.

Marni made sure to walk as slowly as she could so that Gio wouldn't overwork his sore leg, taking several breaks along the way. The breaks weren't all that contrived, like the ones yesterday, these views were equally stunning, taking her breath away.

The park's layout consisted of different sections, each made to look like a terrace full of botanicals overlooking the coastline and ocean beyond. Grand statues dotted the landscape, as if a museum of sculptures had its pieces scattered throughout a magnificent garden. Marni had never seen anything like it. She was having trouble deciding exactly which visual feast she should focus her eyes on.

"What do you think?" Gio asked as they stood in a terrace full of colorful dahlias and luscious green leaves. Marble statues flanked them on either side, a cherub to the right and a maiden carrying a load of fruit on the left.

"I think I might have died and am right at this moment walking through Eden," she answered, the awe in her voice clear to her own ears.

A commotion sounded from the pathway a few feet behind them. Excited voices, male and female alike, speaking in what sounded like German.

Marni turned to watch as a bridal procession made their way past the terrace. Half a dozen tuxedoed young men walking alongside elegantly styled women in sapphire blue gowns. Trailing behind them was a bride clad in layers of white silk and delicate lace walking alongside her groom. The couple seemed totally engrossed in one another, oblivious to anything around them, including their own bridal party.

The scene could have been a picture straight out of a bridal magazine. What an absolutely idyllic venue for a wedding. How lucky these two people were, to have found love and were now able to celebrate it with a union bonded in paradise. A bubble of envy formed in her chest, mixed with longing. How could she ever hope to do the same given her disastrous romantic history?

She released a long sigh, which came out sounding much louder than she would have anticipated. Sure enough, when she turned her head, Gio leveled a curious look her way. Maybe it was irrational, but she found herself getting defensive.

"What?" she asked, her tone on the side of aggressive. "Is it so odd to appreciate young love?"

"Is that what you were doing, gattina? Appreciating?" He tilted his head, a slight smile to his lips. He was teasing her!

"Do you mean to tell me that you've never entertained the idea of your own wedding? Where it might be? Not even once?" She found herself asking, against her better judgment.

His smile grew smirk-like. "Oh, sure, we talk about it every time me and the boys get together. Then us guys draw hearts all over our notebooks and sign the names of our crushes on our palms."

"That's ridiculous."

Gio turned with a chuckle to face the view of the Marina Piccola in front of them, crossing his arms in front of his chest. "Fine. To answer your question, no I never gave much thought to my wedding. Or marriage in particular. There was never an occasion to."

So there'd never been a woman who'd inspired thoughts of marriage. Heaven help her, Marni felt a twinge of relief at that notion. Which made absolutely no sense whatsoever.

But she was deflated by the next words out of Gio's mouth. "Now I can't even entertain the thought. Not for a long while," he said solemnly, his gaze narrowing on the horizon.

"Why is that?" she asked. Again, probably another dumb question she didn't really want to hear the answer to.

He shrugged, his jawline tensing. "How could I even think of that? The state I'm in, on top of all my regular responsibilities, how could I even consider tying myself to another person?"

A lump formed in Marni's throat. She had no business feeling so dejected by his words. She was only his pretend girlfriend.

How silly of her to take any of it personally.

For the third time during the span of a week, Gio opened his eyes to the brightness of sunshine rather than watching the onset of dawn. He'd been able to fall and stay asleep. Despite the pain.

Marni. He had her to thank. Again.

As his focus continued to clear, he realized exactly

why he'd slept so comfortably. She was nestled against him and he was holding her in his arms. Sometime during the night, Marni had shifted to his side of the bed. He must have instinctively wrapped his arms around her.

This is wrong. This shouldn't be happening.

His subconscious was simply blurring the lines, had lost sight of what was real and what was pretend. A whisper-soft voice in his head tried to tell him all this but he gave it no need. He made no effort to move or push her away. It didn't help that Marni had been asking him about matrimony and romantic marriage proposals just yesterday.

But...it felt right, lying next to her this way. The scent of her brought to mind roses and fresh berries. The warmth of her body spread over his skin, right through to his soul. The sunrays shining through the window behind her cast her in a halo of light. Several tendrils of her hair fell around her face. She was utterly enchanting. His fingers itched to reach for her, to gently caress those untamed curls. His gaze fell to her lips: full and rose red, puckered slightly in her slumber.

Not for the first time, he wondered what she would taste like if he kissed her. Sweet as honey, no doubt. With a touch of those berries he always smelled whenever she was near.

He sensed more than saw it when she opened her eyes. They widened in surprise before heat darkened their depths. She made no effort to move out of his grasp. And he wasn't even remotely inclined to push her away.

They were a hair's breadth apart. Her eyes roamed over his face and he nearly groaned out loud when they landed on his lips. Did she want him to kiss her, maybe even as much as he craved doing so?

The voice grew louder, more adamant. Repeating the warnings he was trying so hard to ignore.

"Gio?" She spoke softly, her voice low and thick. The sound of his name on her lips had something shifting in his middle. He gave himself permission to gently trail his fingers around the frame of her face, to tuck back a couple of those wayward locks behind her ear.

"Good morning, sweetheart."

Her response was to shift even closer, then tilt her face up toward his. Heaven help him, he wouldn't even have to move his head to take her mouth with his, to finally succumb to the longings he'd been pushing away for so long. A low hungry groan sounded in his ears and he realized it was coming from him. Just one kiss.

Stop. This. Now.

This time, the voice was too loud and too harsh to ignore. Because he could no longer deny how wrong going down this path would be for them both.

With all the will he could summon, Gio moved back away from her, then sat up. Her look of confusion had him cursing inside, made him yearn to return to her. To take those lips with his own the way he so badly wanted to.

But then what?

The possible answers to that question were much too dangerous to explore. What if they didn't stop with one kiss. A very real possibility given his body's reaction and the way Marni had been looking at him just now.

Summoning the last vestiges of his control, Gio turned to sit on the edge of the bed with his back to her. "I should get up. There are some emails I need to check on."

Not exactly a lie. For one thing, he wanted to check for any updates on Juno's recovery progress. For another, he was going to follow up on when that blasted bed might finally arrive.

The sound of her rustling behind him told him Marni was getting up as well. He waited without breath in case she said something, tried to stop him.

She remained silent.

He should have been relieved. Instead he felt a heavy brick of disappointment settle in his chest.

He took his time to get showered and dressed but then there was no longer any reason to delay the inevitable. He would have to face Marni sooner or later. Damn him for not having the sense to turn her down about sharing the bed last night. He would have preferred an uncomfortable and pain-inducing night on the sofa. Too late now.

When he made it downstairs, Marni was curled up on the love seat, still wearing her nightclothes, her hair up in that too tight ponytail again. What he wouldn't have given to set it loose and run his fingers through the strands the way he had moments ago.

"Good morning," he said by way of greeting, then cringed. He'd already said that to her upstairs.

She didn't quite meet his gaze when she responded in kind. Gio swallowed a curse. This was exactly what he'd wanted to avoid. This awkwardness between them. She wasn't even meeting his eyes. So different from before. They'd been so comfortable with each other last night, their conversation so easy.

Now the air was thick with the tension of all that was and had to remain unspoken.

Or he could just go sit next to her, take her in his arms and tell her honestly how badly he wanted to kiss her. Then he would oblige if she said she wanted the same.

No. That was the last thing he should do, as tempting as it was.

"I'm about to brew some coffee. Can I get you some?" he offered.

She shook her head.

"How about some breakfast?"

"No, thank you."

Gio went about the business of getting himself caffeinated and fed. Looked like things were going to remain awkward between them, for now, anyway.

Because he couldn't think of a darn thing to say to make it any better.

Were they just going to ignore what had almost happened between them?

It seemed so, Marni figured as she watched Gio go about his morning as if nothing had changed. He brewed his espresso, offered to make her one or brew some water for her tea, then moved to the patio with his phone to check on those all-so-important emails that he'd used as an excuse to rush out of the bedroom this morning.

While she was still shaking with desire inside. While she was still imagining what it might feel like to have his stubble rub against her cheek. While she longed to be in his arms once more.

When she'd woken up briefly to find herself wrapped tight in Gio's embrace, she'd stayed where she was wrapped in the cocoon of his warmth. He'd seemed in no rush to let her go.

Now Gio was behaving as if none of it had even happened.

Well, he had the right of it, didn't he? He was actually

thinking straight as opposed to the way she was letting her emotions run rampant. It had to be their surroundings.

This was Gio. Nella's brother. She'd practically grown up with him. They'd always had an easy camaraderie, even during all those times she and Nella were being pesky little tagalongs. Surely, they could get back to that dynamic.

Marni scrunched her face and blew out a breath.

Who was she kidding? As if. Even now, she itched to run her hands over his chest, touch her tongue to his lips, ask him to wrap his arms around her the way he had last night.

All this pretending they'd been doing was blurring her reality, bringing to the surface all the attraction she'd tried so hard to curb.

So going back to the way they'd been before this trip was wishful thinking. Still, things between them couldn't remain as tense as they were. She still had eight days here before her return flight. She would need every one of those days to figure out what she intended to return to.

Marni had to forget about the almost kiss like Gio apparently had.

So when Gio finally left the patio to announce he wanted to take a walk along the beach, she didn't hesitate. "I'd like to come with you if you don't mind the company."

He quirked an eyebrow at her in surprise. "You sure? My leg's stiffening up just sitting out there. I might be kind of slow."

"A slow and leisurely stroll. Sounds perfect. Let me just throw some shorts and a T-shirt on."

He tilted his head. "Take your time."

He was waiting for her by the pool when she came back down dressed less than five minutes later.

He hadn't been kidding about being slow. It took him much longer to get down the stone steps this morning. Maybe they should have just stayed put or floated around in the pool rather than tax his already strained leg any more.

She was about to ask him when he spoke before she could. "Feels better already, just being out here by the water in the sunshine."

Why did she get the feeling he wasn't telling the entire truth?

Marni decided not to press, the whole point of walking with him was to overcome the awkwardness between them after the almost-kiss.

"It's beautiful," she agreed. "I wore my swimsuit underneath...the water looks pretty inviting."

So there was that bit of small talk out of the way, then. Now what?

"Have you thought any more about your pretend design business?" Gio asked as they made their way along the water.

Marni waved her hand in dismissal. "Oh, that was just a bit of fun on my part, answering your questions like that. None of it is real." *Like a lot of other things that may have happened last night*, she added silently.

"But it could be," Gio countered. "I thought we established that."

Marni stared out at the horizon. She knew Gio meant well, but dwelling on a pipe dream wasn't going to do her any good right now. She had to get practical and figure out a manageable path forward.

"Maybe," she finally answered. "But I think for now I'll stick with plan A or B. My own shop is probably more like plan Z in the overall scheme of things."

"Huh."

Was it her imagination, or did that one tiny sound hold just a hint of judgment? She felt a prickle of irritation.

Truce, she reminded herself.

"If I understood correctly last night, your plan A seems to be to keep looking for another job like the one you had." And lost. "That's right."

"So what does plan B involve, then?"

She shrugged. "I thought maybe I'd travel to New York City to try my hand there. It's a much bigger market. With more opportunities."

"Is that what you want? To live in New York?"

Why was he asking her all these questions? This was supposed to be a stress-free stroll together to reestablish their friendship. She hadn't realized her very motivations would be poked and analyzed.

"New York is a thrilling place to live," she said non-committally. "The Big Apple and all that."

"Yeah, but it's not your home."

She had to veer this conversation in another direction, away from herself. It was only fair to discuss Gio for a while. Besides, hadn't she shared enough about herself last night?

"What about you?" she asked.

"How do you mean? I'm still CEO at Santino Foods."

"I know that. But you have to admit the life you're going back to won't be the same one you left."

That was one thing they had in common.

Gio wasn't sure why but his pulse had quickened at Marni's words. The truth was, he hadn't really planned for much past this trip. For the first time in his life, he found himself focusing only on the short term. He just wanted to monitor Juno's recovery and continue pursuing his goals for Santino Foods. The company had a highly efficient and competent staff of employees. But with the loss of his father a decade ago and Nella having no interest in the business, the brunt of the responsibility fell on his shoulders. His mother did what she could to help, but with her advanced age she could only do so much. So many people depended on him for their livelihoods. He had a board of directors he had to answer to. Which just made his careless risk-taking that much worse.

Well, he'd learned his lesson.

"The only change I can be certain of is not participating in any more road races for the foreseeable future," he answered, squinting in the bright sunlight.

"I'm glad to hear it," Marni answered. "Nella will be too."

Gio didn't miss that she'd just put herself in the same context as his sister. That had to be intentional. If she thought that was going to make him forget his desire for her, they were way past that stage. He would just have to make the best of the new dynamic and try to ignore the inconvenient feelings he'd developed.

Easier said than done. He had to try. For both their sakes.

"What made you do it?" Marni asked the question completely out of the blue. "I mean, I know you've always been a bit of a daredevil. But why a charity race across rough terrain through several countries?"

He shrugged. "The organization it was meant to support was struggling to find participants that might draw the kind of attention and publicity they needed for the race to be successful."

Having the Santino name attached to the race had done

a lot toward that end, but it wasn't enough. Not until he'd actually been announced as one of the drivers did they see big dollar amount donations.

"Ah, I get it," Marni said. "You knew that if the CEO of an international conglomerate was an actual participant, the publicity alone would bring in more money."

She'd always been clever.

He nodded. "That's right. And there were all those friends and colleagues who wanted to pay for the privilege of taunting me if I didn't win."

Marni laughed. "I'm sure in a very good-natured way."

Despite the seriousness of the conversation, the sound of her laughter lightened some of the heaviness in his chest. See, there was no reason to let any sort of awkwardness continue between them. They could continue as villa mates until she had to leave. He had to admit, he was going to really miss her company when she left in a few days. He probably wouldn't stay much longer after that himself.

The bright yellow tank top she wore cinched at the waist and brought out the golden specks of her irises. Her denim shorts showed off her shapely thighs. Thank God she wasn't wearing those plain leather flats today. The sandals she had on were much more enticing, showing off the bright pink polish on her toes.

When had he ever noticed a woman's toenail polish before? Not a single time he could recall. Maybe he wasn't completely over his concussion, after all.

He focused on the waves splashing near his feet to get his mind to behave. "For the most part," he said.

"So you had the most noble of intentions."

"I guess you could say that." He certainly had in the beginning. The race seemed like a fun way to support a good cause. But it all went so terribly wrong. Now there was a young man laid up in a hospital while he was in pain every night.

She paused and touched his forearm. Gio braced himself, certain he wasn't going to like what was about to follow. "Gio, if you don't mind my asking, what do the doctors have to say?" She swallowed, clearly nervous about asking the question.

He was right, he really didn't want to go down this path of questioning. He shrugged. "The normal doctorly stuff."

"What does that mean? And you don't have to tell me if you don't want to."

Her bright hazel eyes clouded with concern. How could he not give her something?

He shrugged. "Like I told you. There's at least two more surgeries they say I need. But the muscles need to heal first. In the meantime, they prescribe constant and regular physical therapy appointments. Which I'm sure will continue for the foreseeable future."

Marni's hand lingered on his arm. For a crazy second, he wanted to take it in his, lift it up to his lips and plant a gentle kiss on her palm. And wasn't this a fine time to be thinking of doing something so silly and inappropriate for the moment?

"I meant, what are they saying about when you should start the therapy. So that you can move forward with the surgeries."

He was supposed to start them a week ago but had canceled every single scheduled appointment. "When I get around to it. I'm not in any rush."

No need to tell her that decision ran completely against all the medical advice he'd been given. Or that the last surgeon had bluntly and unwaveringly told him that Gio was certain to make his condition worse by delaying the treatment.

But it was as if Marni could read his mind. Her lips thinned into a tight line, and her eyebrows drew together over those piercing hazel eyes. There was no mistaking the disappointment that washed over her features. Along with a solid dose of worry. It was the worry that annoyed him most. "You've been putting it off, haven't you? The therapy and the surgeries."

Like he'd thought earlier, the lady had always been very clever.

"There's no need to look at me like that," Gio said and resumed walking but at a much faster pace—which had to hurt his leg. And for what? Marni wondered. It wasn't as if he was going to get away from her on this beach.

She began to follow fast on his heels and caught up to him in a second. "Like what? How do you think I'm looking at you?"

"Forget it, Marni. Let's just turn around and go back."

A bit late for that. She slammed her hands on her hips. "No. I'd like an answer," she demanded, not even sure why she was pushing him this way. The conversation was getting way too heated. So much for that truce she'd been after. "So tell me."

"I don't know," he bit out. "Why are you badgering me? As if I've tried to drown your pet squirrel in that ocean or something." He thrust his thumb in the direction of the water.

In spite of her frustration with him at what she'd just learned, Marni's mouth quivered with the onset of a laugh. She squashed it. "Why in the world would I keep a pet squirrel?"

He turned to her then, rammed a hand through the hair at his crown. "Didn't you at some point or other have a small furry rodent? I remember Nella having to pet sit."

"That was a guinea pig, Gio. Completely different animal than a squirrel."

How in the world had they gotten so off topic anyway?

He crossed his arms in front of his chest. "Never mind. I suppose you're going to tell me, like everyone else that I'm being stubborn and stupid for not trying to get better as fast as I can."

"No, I wasn't going to say any of that. And I'm not going to ask you why either, for that matter."

Both eyebrows lifted and his jaw tightened. "You're not?"

She shook her head. "I think I can guess. Plus, I'm sure you wouldn't answer me anyway."

He narrowed his eyes on her. "You're right, I wouldn't answer. As for the first part, don't be so sure. You don't know me as well as you think you do."

Ouch. Marni sucked in a breath at the taunt. If he'd meant to be cutting and harsh, he'd hit the mark perfectly. Any trace of amusement flowed out of her. In her head, she knew he was just lashing out because he'd been forced to admit something he didn't want to share with her. But her heart did a little flip at the cruelty.

"Right," she said. "I suppose you're also going to tell me it's none of my business."

He reached for her shoulders, took them in a gentle but firm grip. "Don't put words in my mouth, Marni."

Her mouth went dry at the contact. This was so not the time to notice the fullness of his lips, the way his dark hair curled messily over his forehead, blowing about his face in the breeze. His dark brown eyes blazed with emotion. And something else. Something that had her blood zinging in her veins. Her heart began to pound in her chest.

She somehow got her mouth to work. "So you're saying you are my business, then?"

"I've known you a long time." His answer wasn't really an answer at all.

Suddenly, her own tenuous grasp on her emotions snapped like a dry twig. Marni knew she should step away, out of his grasp. Instead, she did the opposite. She moved forward until they were toe to toe, her face a mere inch from his. Marni knew she was playing with fire, but couldn't seem to help herself.

Once again, her mouth was within a hair's breadth from Gio's. But unlike this morning, there was nothing gentle about the way he was looking at her.

He looked like he could devour her on the spot.

That dangerous, wayward thought had her breath catching in her lungs. Gio noticed, because his lips formed a knowing smile. "What's the matter? Something wrong, gattina?"

Oh, God. Never before had the nickname sounded quite so sexy to her ears. She would never hear it the same way again after this moment.

Yes! she wanted to cry out. All sorts of things were wrong. Like how badly she wanted his lips on hers even though she was beyond angry at him for the way he was risking his health by delaying getting medical treatment. Or how much she wanted to thrust her fingers in his hair and bring his mouth down to hers. How disappointed she'd been that he'd left the bed this morning instead of just kissing her then.

She couldn't even be sure which one of them moved

first. Maybe they both did. But suddenly, what she'd been fantasizing and dreaming about was somehow happening. Gio's lips found hers in a crushing, shattering kiss. His hands moved from her shoulders to wrap around her waist and pull her closer. Her hair was suddenly free from its binding with Gio's fingers threading her loose strands before pressing his mouth into hers harder.

She couldn't get close enough, wanted to feel the length of him even tighter up against her body. Good thing they were out in the open on a beach where anyone could walk by. Or Marni would have been unable to keep herself from tearing his shirt off to run her hands down his chest, over his washboard stomach. Then lower.

This was why he'd been smart not to kiss her in the bedroom earlier. She had no doubt she wouldn't have been able to stop herself from going further, as far as he would let her.

Marni leaned into him now, savoring the taste of him. His warmth seared her skin. Heat and longing curled in her belly and moved lower, and every nerve ending tingled with electricity. The world around her ceased to exist. Nothing mattered but Gio Santino and the way he was kissing her.

She never wanted it to stop.

CHAPTER NINE

HOW COULD HE have lost control like that? Gio bit down on the curse that formed on his lips when he finally let Marni go. Which took way too long.

And he'd gone way too far.

He'd been naive to think they could simply gloss over what had happened between them this morning. Walking away from the bed this morning, rather than facing reality then and there, had only led to a slow simmering of tension between them that had just blown up in spectacular fashion. He had to figure out a way to put out the fire.

He dared to meet Marni's gaze now. His breath caught in his throat at the sight of her. Her hair fell in a mess around her face and shoulders, her lips were swollen. Her cheeks flushed berry red. God help him, she looked ready and waiting for him to do it again.

She looked like some sort of modern goddess, standing on the golden sand. The bright sun highlighted the streaks of golden bronze in her hair. The sparkling blue water of the ocean served as a background as if she were the center of some classic painting. Everything about her called to him, made him want her more.

How totally inconvenient.

It took several moments to get his mouth to work. "Marni, look, I'm so—"

She held a hand up to stop him before he could finish, her eyes ablaze. "Don't you dare finish that sentence, Gio Santino. Don't you dare apologize to me right now."

Gio rubbed his palm down his face. "What do you want me to say?"

She didn't answer, simply glared at him some more. Several beats passed by in silence, the air between them heavy. Gio clenched his fists at his sides to keep from reaching for her again, wiping that angry glare from her face with another deep satisfying kiss.

No! Enough already.

Kissing her again was the last thing he should be thinking about. Instead, he should be trying to figure out how they were going to get past this. Not just for this week but for the rest of their lives. Marni was practically family. They couldn't spend the rest of their days uncomfortable around each other just because he hadn't been able to control himself the brief period of time they'd been alone together.

Marni turned on her heel. "I think I'm done walking now."

Gio watched her retreating back as she made her way toward the house. He debated following her but the tension in her shoulders and the rigid set of her spine told him she wouldn't welcome his presence right now. Just as well, it was probably best for them both to be alone for a while.

Maybe for a long while at that.

Within minutes of docking the boat and arriving in town, Gio's phone vibrated in his pocket and he recognized his sister's ringtone. He pinched the bridge of his nose, not really up for a conversation with anyone right now let alone his chatty sibling. But guilt had him pulling out the device and answering just before it went to voice mail.

Her face appeared on the screen. "Hey, big bro."

Gio did his best to summon a smile and leaned back against the brick wall of a seafood store. Why did she have to place a video call now of all times? "Hey yourself."

Nella's eyes traveled behind him. "You're not at the house?"

"I'm in town for a couple of errands."

"Is Marni with you? She didn't answer when I called her just now. I wanted to speak to you both actually."

Again, she'd called her friend first. Not that he was offended in any way. It just confirmed what he already knew about their relationship. Nella and Marni didn't share any blood, but in every other sense they were true sisters.

Which only proved just how wrong it was to kiss her this morning. His sibling's soul sister should be completely off-limits, no matter how much he was attracted to her.

"Nope. I'm by myself."

Nella rested her chin on her hand. "Why didn't you bring her with you? Marni loves to shop."

He wasn't about to get into any of that. But Nella could be relentless about getting answers when she was curious about something. And she was like a bloodhound if she thought she detected a lie.

Gio really regretted answering the phone. He'd have to give her something. "I just had to come into town for a couple things. Just decided to do it by myself," he answered, hoping it was enough to placate her while still being vague.

No such luck. She straightened in her chair, obviously not buying it. "Well, it was rude of you not to invite her."

Rude. Ha! As if that was the worst of it.

"She wouldn't have wanted to come." Mistake. It was the wrong thing to say.

Nella's head lifted with concern, the casual smile fading from her lips. "Is she feeling okay? She's going through a lot, right now."

Those words only upped his guilt level several notches. Marni was going through a lot. And instead of being a supportive friend Marni could lean on, he was toying with her emotions.

"She's fine, Nella," he quickly assured.

Nella leaned closer to her laptop. Even through the screen it was as if she could see clear to his soul.

"What is it? What aren't you telling me?" she demanded to know.

"Nothing. I mean, you're right. I should have asked her to come."

Nella's eyes narrowed on him, all too knowing. "Giovanni Santino. I swear if you've done anything to upset her."

"Listen, Nella. I have to go. My order's up." So what if he was fibbing. He hadn't actually ordered anything from anywhere. He just had to find a way off this call.

"Fine. But I'm not happy with you right now, big bro. I'll call you later this evening. Both of you," she added in an ominous tone.

Gio ended the call and slipped the phone back into his pocket. Then he made a beeline for the furniture store. Whatever he had to do, that bed needed to be at the villa before tonight. He would hire the delivery van and find a driver if he had to.

Heck, if necessary, he would haul the bed back to the villa himself.

* * *

What do you want me to say?

How could he have asked her that? How could he not know?

Marni pounded the dough harder on the counter, trying to vent some of her frustration. Usually, the vigorous kneading and pounding calmed her nerves. Today it wasn't working so great toward that end.

The gall of that man. First to act like she had no business asking about his recovery. Then to kiss her so passionately that she'd actually felt her knees buckle.

And then the audacity of him to try and actually apologize for it.

Where was he, anyway? It had been hours since their little fiasco on the beach.

She'd already made the new bed—it had arrived a couple of hours after she'd gotten back to the villa following their eventful walk. Then she'd spent some time tidying and dusting. She'd even had a chance to watch another episode of her Bollywood show, which hadn't been nearly as enjoyable now that she was used to having company. Another mark against Gio Santino. He'd ruined her favorite pastime.

Now she was almost done with her kneading and he still wasn't back. She pounded the dough once more for good measure.

"Please tell me you're not picturing my face on that as you smack it that hard."

Startled, Marni whirled around to find Gio standing behind her in the doorway. She hadn't even heard him come in.

"Didn't mean to startle you," he added, walking farther into the kitchen.

Her irritation warred with the urge to run into his arms, and she silently berated herself. She could be such an idiot when it came to this man.

"What are you doing, anyway?"

"Making bread."

"I could have picked some up for you in town. You should have called and asked."

So that's where he'd been all this time. Marni pushed aside the dough and turned to face him, leaning her back against the counter. "And you could have called and told me where you were."

The corner of his mouth lifted. "Why? Were you worried about me?"

Of course she'd been worried. The man had a bad leg and other internal injuries he was just barely recovering from. But she wasn't about to take the bait.

"Of course not," she lied. "Just pointing out the polite thing to do when you're sharing a house with someone."

Gio visibly cringed. "You're the second person today to accuse me of being impolite. Which reminds me, Nella called earlier. Wants to talk to both of us later this evening."

Marni's eyebrows rose. "Is everything okay?"

He lifted his hand in reassurance. "She sounded fine. Just wanted to tell us both something. I was going to ask her more but our conversation got a little waylaid."

Huh. Curious.

What did he mean about a waylaid conversation with his sister? And what would Nella want to tell them both at the same time? So many questions and so few answers. Somehow, her life seemed so much more complicated during this trip when it was supposed to be a way for her to try and find some clarity about her future.

"The bed arrived," she told him, changing the topic. "I've already made it up with some fresh sheets I found in the linen closet."

Gio's response to that bit of news was surprisingly low-key. He merely nodded, then plucked a grape out of the fruit bowl and tossed it in his mouth. "Thanks. What else did you do today?"

So more small talk, then. So be it. She'd play along. For now. "I tidied, started this bread. And watched another episode of *Lotus Dream*."

Gio stopped chewing and swallowed, then tilted his head. "You…you watched an episode without me?" Marni almost felt a twinge of guilt at the dejection in his tone. Almost.

She shrugged. "Guess you'll have to catch up at some point."

"Guess so."

What do you want me to say?

His question from earlier echoed in her mind. So many words he might have come up with rather than asking it. Like, maybe he could have told her that he was just as confused as she was but not sorry about whatever it was happening between them. Or maybe tell her that he cared for her and always would, that they would figure things out together. He could have even told her that he'd enjoyed their kiss as much as she had, but needed time to process.

But Gio hadn't said any of those things. And he probably never would.

What did it matter at this point? In a few short days, she would be on her way back to the States. She'd maybe see Gio four or five times a year when Nella invited her to various family functions. It would be as if this time spent together in Capri never happened.

Her eyes began to sting so she made a dramatic show of working the dough again, not that it needed it. In fact, if she pounded it any more at this point, the bread was sure to be a rubbery, chewy mess.

"Can I have some of that bread when it's done?" Gio asked, a charming, wide smile over his lips. "I'll trade you for some fresh fish I bought in town that I'm grilling for dinner."

She lifted her chin, not quite ready to accept any kind of olive branch. "I'll think about it."

Marni swam the length of the pool then lingered in the deep end just allowing herself to float. She let the warm water wash over her skin and soothe her tense muscles.

Why hadn't she done this before? A serene early evening swim to settle some of her frazzled nerves was exactly the ticket. The salty scent of the sea and the steady sound of the crashing waves in the distance added to the tranquility she'd so desperately needed.

With a relaxed sigh, she immersed herself fully in the water then held her breath for as long as she could. As if she could shut off the rest of the world, if only for the briefest of moments.

Finally popping up for air, she opened her eyes and gasped: Gio crouched by the edge of the pool. Honestly, he had to stop startling her like that. So much for relaxing, her pulse was rocketing again.

"You were under there quite awhile," he remarked. "I was about to jump in to get you."

Unbidden images flashed in her mind of the two of

them frolicking in the pool together. Skin to skin. With complete privacy, unlike at the beach earlier.

She blinked the vision away. Her pulse now a rapid staccato.

"I was about to get dinner started," Gio informed her.

"That's fine. The bread should be done baking. I'll go get it." She swam over to the edge where Gio stood waiting for her. He'd grabbed her towel and was holding it out to her.

When she climbed out, Gio had the towel spread wide in his hands, waiting for her to step in it. Marni swallowed. Nothing to read in the gesture. The man was simply helping her dry off. She walked up to him and turned around, allowing him to drape the thick terry cloth over her shoulders. His hands lingered just long enough. She could feel the warmth of his palms through the fabric, the strength of his grasp. It took all her will not to move back closer against his chest and nestle herself against his length.

Instead, she savored the feel of his fingers on her shoulders. But it was over all too soon. He moved away and the chill of his loss immediately settled over her skin.

"I'll go get the coal grill fired up," he said behind her. "Take your time drying off."

She would need time. Not to dry off, but to quell the yearning in her core that must be written on her face. She could only do so much to hide her feelings for this man. It was exhausting her to try.

"Back in a few," she threw over her shoulder, before walking to the screen door and into the house.

When she returned a few minutes later dressed with her hair in a topknot, Gio was spooning the fish onto two plates. He'd poured them each a glass of wine. A sharp knife of sadness pierced through her heart at what might have been as she took in the sight. In a different life, they might have been a real couple about to enjoy a quiet evening enjoying each other's company, followed by a not so quiet night.

There she went again. Thinking in ways she had no business doing.

Taking a second to compose herself, Marni walked to the table and set the basket of bread in the center, next to the salad and antipasti.

"Fresh and hot," she announced with a casualness she didn't feel. She could only hope it wasn't the texture of gum given the way she'd punished the dough.

Gio pulled her chair out for her, then took the seat across the table. The fish was good, really good. Gio had kept it simple with just a couple of spices and a generous splash of lemon on each filet.

Why did the man have to be so good at everything he did? It was hard to stay angry at someone who'd made this great of a meal for you.

She was about to grudgingly compliment his cooking when he reached for the loaf and broke off the end piece then handed it to her wordlessly. The Santinos always gave Marni the end piece, it was the part she liked most.

When he went to bite his own slice, his eyes widened and his eyebrows furrowed. He chewed once. Then again. Then he stilled.

Marni took a bite and it confirmed her fears. The bread was chewy and dense. "Okay, so it's not my best work."

"I'll say. Not even a whole stick of butter would salvage this."

And he wasn't going to pull any punches.

"I'm sorry, Gio," she said, surprising herself as well

as him given the way he set his fork down and focused on her face.

"Marni, you don't have to apologize for messing up bread. We have plenty else for dinner."

Marni put her fork down as well. "I guess that's not what I'm really apologizing for." Now that the words were out, she realized they needed to be said.

"Then what?" he asked gently.

"I think you know. I shouldn't have pushed you earlier today. You clearly don't want to talk about what you're doing to recover." *Or not doing*, she added silently. "It wasn't my place to pressure you about it."

Gio pushed his plate away. Great, now she could feel guilty that she'd ruined their appetites.

"Marni. You have to realize how important you are to us. To me, my sister, my mother. And my father before we lost him."

She swallowed. "I'd like to think I am. As important as the Santinos have always been to me."

"You remember how strict our parents were growing up. They were hard on both Nella and me."

She nodded. "I remember."

"You were the only one who stuck around, put up with how rigid my parents' rules were. Nella would have no friends if it weren't for you."

The same could be said about her. Her mom was always at work and her dad had long ago left them. The Santinos were more family to her than anyone else.

Gio continued, his eyes imploring her to understand. "So you have to see why I can't break my sister's heart by having a meaningless fling with her best friend."

Ouch. He might as well have thrown the porcelain

plate at her. Well, she'd be damned if she was going to let him see just how much he'd cut her with those words.

She plastered a forced smile on her face. "Of course. You're right, Gio. I completely agree."

Gio wanted to suck his words back in as soon as they left his mouth. He hadn't meant to sound quite so heartless. Just direct and unwavering. Damn. Why did he keep tripping up over himself when it came to Marni? He couldn't seem to stop messing things up with her.

She rose from the table before he could find a way to smooth over the edges of the words he'd used. "I'll take your plate if you're done," she offered, without so much as a glance at him.

Of course he was done. As if he could continue eating now. His delivery may have been shoddy, but surely she had to see the logic of what he'd been trying to say. Gio had nothing really to offer a woman right now, especially not one like Marni. For one thing, he was a wreck physically with nothing to look forward to but months, maybe years, of treatment and surgeries ahead of him. Some days he could hardly manage to walk without cringing in pain. He had no idea how he would juggle all that while manning the helm at Santino Foods.

Marni didn't wait for his answer about his plate. She took her own, grabbed the bread basket and walked into the house.

With a curse, Gio collected the remaining dishware off the table and joined her at the sink. They silently went about washing each piece as he scrambled his brain to think of something to say.

The sound of her phone ringing came from the other room. "That must be Nella," Marni said, shutting off the water and toweling her hands dry. She motioned for him to follow. "You said she wanted to talk to both of us."

For the first time in his life, Gio found himself grateful for a call from his chatty sister. Anything to distract from the tension between him and Marni right now.

He peered over her shoulder as she accepted the video call. Nella's smiling face greeted them on the screen. Her husband, Alex, joined in the frame an instant later.

"Hello, you two," Nella said with a finger wave.

"Hi, Nella," Marni answered and a genuine smile lit up her face, her first one of the day that he could recall.

"Are you both sitting down?" she asked. "I think you need to sit down for this."

Marni cast a curious glance in Gio's direction. He shrugged in response. Damned if he had any clue or insight.

His sister's wide smile suggested that there was no need for alarm. But what exactly was she about to say that was so earth-shattering?

"Go sit," Nella insisted when they still hadn't moved.

Once they obliged, his sister actually squealed before speaking. "So, Alex and I have some big news to share with the two of you," she began.

To his surprise, Marni squealed just then too. "Oh, my God! Nella, really?" she asked.

Really what? What was all this about? Marni sounded as if she'd figured it out already. For the life of him he couldn't figure out how. Nella hadn't even said anything yet.

"Really, Marn," Nella said with a delighted laugh.

"That's wonderful!" Marni clasped a hand to her cheek.

"You and my brother are about to become godparents."

Godparents? But that would mean…

His sister confirmed before he could finish the thought. "I'm pregnant!"

Gio felt his jaw drop. His little sister. His *baby* sister was going to have a baby herself.

"Congratulations you two!" Marni exclaimed. "I'm so happy for you both."

Gio could only manage a nod and a feeble "Me too."

No one else seemed to notice just how dumbfounded he was. "We're only telling immediate family right now," Nella said, glancing up at her husband for confirmation. He gave it to her with a quick peck on her forehead.

His sister's eyes found his on the screen. "Well, what do you think, big bro?"

What he thought was that he was going to need some time to let the news sink in. Somehow, he found a better response for Nella's sake.

"I think you should be prepared for me to spoil this kid rotten. Right before I hand him back to you and take off."

Nella wagged a finger at him. "Or her. We don't know yet, Uncle Gio."

Uncle Gio. His new title. The phrase added another jolt to his already shocked system.

After several more minutes of happy chatter, Nella finally said her goodbyes and Marni exited the call, tossing her phone on the couch. Then she threw her arms around his neck and embraced him in a tight hug. Gio's arms reflexively went around her waist.

"I'm going to be an uncle," he said against her cheek, testing the words out himself, hardly able to believe they were coming out of his mouth.

Marni pulled back to beam him a dazzling smile. "And a godparent. Like me."

That's right. That was the other large piece in all this. He and Marni had yet one more major tie to each other. Nella's pregnancy was not about him of course, but he couldn't help but think it was yet another sign from the universe.

He couldn't play fast and loose with the woman he'd be sharing godparent duty with for the rest of his life.

CHAPTER TEN

MARNI STARED UP at the ceiling in her borrowed bedroom, still abuzz with the news. She was genuinely over the moon for her friend. Nella Santino deserved every bit of happiness. She was the purest, most genuine person Marni had ever met.

She and Alex were perfect for each other. Nella adored her new husband and the feeling was definitely mutual.

Nella's announcement certainly put things in perspective. Her friend had a fulfilling life with a doting, loving husband and she was about to be a mother. Whereas Marni's current relationship was completely made up for the sake of some media clicks. Speaking of which, she reached for her phone and scanned all the relevant websites. No photos of her and Gio, not yet, anyway. Clearly, their selfies weren't having much of an impact.

Marni sighed and turned over to her side, her thoughts returning to her friend's big news. What must it be like to have found the love of your life? To be starting a family with him? Nella was lucky enough to have found her soul mate, and that couple in the Gardens of Augustus had looked so in love as well.

These days, Marni doubted such good fortune would ever be in the cards for her. Just look at her past romantic history. Albeit short, it included a man who'd mistreated her then ruined her career prospects. On the heels of that disaster, she'd somehow managed to fall in love with a man completely out of her reach.

Whoa.

Where had that come from?

Marni bolted upright. She had inadvertently wandered into dangerous territory. Gio Santino had been her crush for years, she rationalized. Her attraction to him was simply at the forefront of her mind now because of their proximity and the romantic setting. She couldn't go believing she'd somehow really fallen in love with the man.

Or maybe you've always been in love with him.

Marni rubbed her eyes, squeezing them shut under her fingers. She needed some air. Despite the late hour, she threw on a thin sweater and made her way downstairs.

The light on the patio was already on when she reached the first floor. Gio was out there, sitting by the pool. She debated turning right around, heading back to the room, but too late, his head snapped up and he gave her a small wave.

With a resigned sigh, Marni went over to the screen door and stepped outside. Silver moonlight bathed the patio and beach in the distance. Bright stars dotted the dark sky like diamonds on dark velvet. If she had to paint a picture of the perfect setting for a romantic interlude, this was exactly what she might put to canvas. Complete with the man of her fantasies sitting front and center.

"My insomnia must be catching," Gio told her once she reached his side.

"I'm too excited for Nella to sleep." That was close enough to the truth. "What about you," she asked, "Don't tell me the new bed isn't comfortable."

He shook his head. "It's perfect. Definitely beats the lounge chair."

"So why are you out here on said chair instead of upstairs in the comfortable bed?"

"Thought I could use the air."

"Hmm."

"You didn't seem all that surprised, about Nella expecting."

Marni shrugged. "I saw how in love she and Alex are with each other. I know family has always been a big part of your sister's life. I guess I just saw it coming sooner or later."

"Well, it was much sooner than I would have expected. Not that I'd given it much thought."

Marni wasn't surprised. Men could be so unaware sometimes. Even about those closest to them. "You'll get used to the idea."

Gio scoffed. "It's still sinking in. Though there might be an advantage for me here with this new development."

"Yeah? How so?"

"Maybe Mama will go easier on the pestering for me to settle down and start a family."

The thought of Gio with a wife, sharing children with some to-be-determined woman, had Marni's stomach clenching in knots. She could just picture him with a doe-eyed, dark-haired beauty as they held hands with their little ones. Maybe she'd be one of the models or actresses he'd been linked to in the past, not that it was any of her business. Marni pushed the image aside.

She was not in love with him! All the pretending was warping her perception of reality.

"She must be over the moon," she said. Signora Santino might have been strict and demanding, but she'd always been one to show deep affection. Marni couldn't think of anyone more fitting for the Italian grandmother role. Straight out of central casting.

Gio shifted his chair to turn and face her. "Listen, Marni. I think this is a good time to get some things straight. I don't want things to be strained between us."

Uh-oh. Marni was afraid to guess where this was leading.

"Especially now," Gio continued. "We're going to be godparents together. Nella's going to need us both to be there for her. And her child is going to need us for the rest of his or her life."

Nothing to argue with there.

"Let's do what we need to, to put whatever started this rift between us in the trash bin. Forget it ever happened."

He meant their kiss. He wanted to pretend he'd never kissed her. Would it be so easy for him to do as he was suggesting? To just wipe from his mind that he'd been shaking with need while he'd held her in his arms with his lips on hers?

What a fool she was. That one kiss had changed everything for her. She went to bed thinking about it at night and woke up with it on her mind the next morning.

"I think that would be for the best," she answered, even as her heart ached in her chest.

He stood suddenly. "Stay put, I'll be right back."

"Where are you going?"

"Since neither of us can sleep, I say we do some celebrating. I thought I saw some nice champagne in the cellar when I first got here. If you're up for it. I know it's rather late."

She was indeed up for it, Marni decided. After all, it wasn't like she was going to get to sleep anytime soon.

"Sure," she answered. "Why not? Let's toast to Nella's news."

He flashed her a dazzling smile. "And we can toast to our newfound understanding too."

Two days later Gio entered the house with a fresh box of pastries, rather pleased with himself. He'd gotten to the bakery stand early enough to get all of Marni's favorites. More importantly, since their little chat on the patio the other night, things between them felt pretty much back to normal. It helped that they had a common interest and desire to talk all the ways they planned on spoiling his niece or nephew.

Well, things were mostly normal, if he didn't count all those times he caught himself noticing the fullness of Marni's lips after she applied her favorite lip balm. Or how her hair became curlier from seaside humidity after she spent time on the beach. Or how her skin was growing more golden with each passing day, leading him to wonder about what tan lines she might have underneath her clothes.

Six days. She'd be leaving in six days. He only needed to hold it together for that long. The thought should have been a comforting one. But the idea of being here at this villa without her didn't exactly hold the appeal it should have. There'd be no one to share pastries with, to grill fish for. To spend sleepless nights with on the patio sipping on champagne or iced tea.

Gio was about to set the box down and transfer the goodies onto a serving plate when a loud thud sounded from upstairs. The sound was followed by a harsh feminine cry. Marni. Something was wrong. Gio tossed the box onto the counter then ran for the stairs and jogged up them to her room, ignoring the bolt of pain that shot through his muscles at the effort.

He found her door open and Marni sitting on the bed. Her hands were clenched at her sides, her cheeks red with a look of horror on her face.

"What's wrong?"

She swallowed, tears welling up in her eyes, and pointed to the floor. Gio followed her finger to where her tablet lay screen down on the carpet.

"That rat!" Marni cried, her voice full of anguish. For a split second, Gio thought maybe she was speaking literally. Had a rodent gotten in the house? But Marni didn't look scared, she looked angry. And panicked.

So a figurative rat then.

Gio bent down and reached for the device. The page Marni must have been reading was still up on the screen. He scanned it just enough to see what Marni was so worked up about. She had every right. In fact, his own blood pressure had skyrocketed as he read the words.

"Why the son of a—"

Marni stood and began pacing the room. "He's making up all sorts of lies about me."

Gio scanned more of the article. It was a piece in a trade mag. Ander Stolis was the featured subject. "Your ex is quite a piece of work."

Marni slammed a fist on the bureau, enough to make her toiletries jump. "He says he was particularly stressed working on his latest designs because of a young colleague who was obsessed with him. That she practically stalked him after he broke things off with her." She laughed bitterly. "What complete bull." She pointed to her chest. "Everyone knows who he means. Me!"

"Marni, you can send out a statement." He held the

tablet up. "Email this editor. Tell him this is all a load of crock. You can set the record straight."

"How?" she demanded, her eyes blazing with fury and shiny wet with unshed tears. "It's his word against mine. And he has much more clout in that world than I do."

Gio clenched his fists tight. If the lowlife were standing in front of him right now, Gio had all sorts of ideas about what he might do. All of it too good for the likes of such a liar.

He knew for a fact none of the claims quoted in the piece were even remotely true. How in the world would Marni be pleading with Ander to get back together? For one, she'd been with *him* almost constantly since she'd arrived on the island.

"He says I sent him countless emails and messages and called repeatedly, begging him to take me back. All conveniently erased I might add. Because he wanted to erase all reminders of me as it was too upsetting and interfering with his work."

"People will have to see how suspect that is."

"Some might. Plenty of others won't. Ander has all the advantage here. I'll have no hope of finding another design position. Most definitely not in Boston. And probably not even in New York now. Not after all these accusations. He makes me sound downright unstable. Who would take a risk on hiring someone like that?"

"This is complete character assassination. He can't get away with it."

Her response to that was to throw her head back and release a guttural groan full of frustration and misery. "So much for our playacting. It's being completely ignored. No one seems to care."

Gio reached for her, pulled her against him, began

rubbing her upper arms. "I guess we'll just have to be more convincing. Our initial attempts at getting our pictures out there clearly haven't been impactful enough. We need to do more."

She leaned back to meet his eyes. The tightness around her mouth loosened ever so slightly. "What does that mean?"

He shrugged. "Clearly, we need to be more high profile about our romance."

Marni wasn't sure she liked the sound of this. What exactly did Gio mean by higher profile? "I'm not really following, Gio."

"Think about it. This Arfin, or whatever his name is—"

"Ander," she corrected, though she could think of plenty other choice words to call the man.

Gio waved his hand dismissively. "Whatever. He's claiming you're still hung up on him. That you've made his life miserable because you can't stand that he's dumped you. We need to be more convincing. And more visible."

"I'm listening," she prompted.

"No more staged photos and appearances in the hope that we might get noticed."

"And we do what instead exactly?" she asked, her eyes still shiny with anger.

"We go to places and events that are sure to be covered. A place where there's sure to be VIPs."

She nodded. "Celebrities and famous people."

"Exactly. Capri is practically a celebrity magnet. And where there's celebrities…" He motioned for her to complete the sentence.

"There's paparazzi."

"Bingo. Then it's just a matter of my social media people sending anonymous notes to various magazines and sites. With the photos to round out the story."

Marni could only nod, trying to fully process all that he was saying.

Gio continued, "Far from a jilted ex who can't let go, you'll be shown as a happy, fulfilled woman who's moved on and found real love. And I'll be able to further redirect any media attention about me to my newfound relationship, as opposed to my near fatal accident. Love conquers all, as they say."

Good thing Marni wasn't drinking or eating anything at the moment. The way Gio kept saying "love" while referring to the two of them would have no doubt made her choke.

"Plus, there's an event we can attend. One with guaranteed cameras present."

"What kind of event?" she asked, focusing on the bare logistics of this plan of his.

"It so happens Santino Foods has an event in Naples in a couple of days."

"I'm listening."

"Every year, we host a charity gala to raise money and awareness for displaced children of wars and global conflict."

"I remember hearing and reading about it. Santino does a lot for worthy causes." Like the one that had led him to personally race in a rally.

He nodded. "Like most years, it's being held at the exclusive Grande Napolitano Hotel and Resort. Black tie, formal, live entertainment. There's always plenty of press there."

"You never mentioned a gala."

He shrugged. "I wasn't planning on going but I'll tell them I've changed my mind."

"You weren't going to go to your own annual event? You're the CEO."

He sighed wearily, rubbed a hand down his affected leg. "People understood why when I sent my regrets. I have plenty of high-level managers and PR people who don't need me there."

Marni let that knowledge sink in. Something fluttered in her chest. Gio had no intention of going to a major company event. He was too bruised and battered to be there. But he was going now. For her.

"I don't know what to say," she told him. The day so far had been a roller coaster of emotion. Waking up to that awful article and all those terrible lies about her had felt like a wrecking ball to her midsection. Now she felt touched and grateful at all that Gio was willing to do to help her make it all go away. "Except to tell you thank you…for being willing to do all this."

He nodded once. "I'm doing it for my sake too. And for Juno's."

Maybe, Marni thought. But she wasn't naive. Gio could have probably found a much easier way to garner some publicity than a sham relationship. No, the pretending was mostly for her benefit.

She looked up to find his hand waving in front of her face. "Marni? Where did you just drift off to?"

"I was just thinking whether we can pull this off."

He cast a smile her way that had her insides quivering. "Of course we can. I know just where to start tomorrow night."

"Where?"

"There's a nightclub in town. Owned and run by a

trained musician. Every weekend night he plays live music with a full band. At least one or two international celebrities are bound to show up."

"Which means cameras and picture taking."

He winked at her. "You got it. We can go tomorrow night. Make it a night on the town."

"Gio, I don't know. For one thing, are you up for it? You were in so much pain after the grotto."

His eyes narrowed on her, and a dark shadow passed over his face. "Don't worry about me, gattina. I can handle it."

Great. She'd offended him. She was about to tell him that acknowledging his injury was nothing to be insulted by. Did Gio honestly think himself lesser because of his injuries? Before she could get a word in, he thrust the tablet toward her until she took it.

"The only question is what will you decide to do," he told her, his voice challenging. "Are you going to push back and defend yourself? Or are you going to let him continue to get away with taunting you?"

With that, he turned away and left the room, shutting the door firmly behind him. Marni heard a slew of Italian words and curses as he descended the stairs.

Marni flopped backward onto the bed and swiped the slanderous article off the screen. Then she deleted the entire app for good measure.

No. She certainly wasn't going to let Ander Stolis get away with repeatedly smearing her name.

She *would* push back. She *would* defend herself.

Her friend was positively glowing. Even through her computer monitor Marni could see plainly how radiant and happy Nella appeared.

"You look great, Nella. Pregnancy definitely agrees with you."

Nella flashed her a wide smile. "Thanks, Marn. It may appear so, this time of day anyhow."

Concern flushed through Marni's core. "What do you mean? Are you not feeling well?"

Nella placed her palm above her rib cage. "The morning sickness is kind of kicking my behind. Takes me a good two hours to get past the queasiness and get out of bed."

Oh, no. Nella had always been a morning person. Being hampered the first part of her day had to be difficult for someone like her.

"I could use some of your vanilla pancakes. Been craving those," Nella told her.

"As soon as I'm back, I'm going to make them for you every morning."

"Thanks." Nella wagged a finger at her. "But don't even think about coming back early on account of me. You promised me you'd take it easy for the full two weeks."

If Nella only knew. This vacation had been less "take it easy" and more "what curve ball is next?"

"Don't you dare renege," Nella added.

"I won't. Promise."

"Good. Besides, Alex is trying his hand at those pancakes and he's getting better every day."

The twist of Nella's lips indicated that Alex might still have a way to go. How sweet of him to try for his wife. A wave of sadness rose in her chest. She couldn't recall any time a man she'd been involved with had tried to make her breakfast.

Though Gio made sure to keep the breakfast pastries in full supply. Hardly the same thing. Still...

"So, what's new?" Nella wanted to know, pulling her out of her thoughts. "You just calling to check on me and the bambino?"

Primarily. "Of course."

"And?"

"I just wanted to tell you that if you see anything on-line, about Gio and me, that it's not real. We're just trying to put on a show. I'll explain more later. You have enough going on right now."

Nella tilted her head. "Okay..."

She had to laugh at her expression.

"What else?" Nella asked.

Her friend could always read her so well. Marni wasn't surprised she'd picked up on the fact that there were more than a couple reasons for this call.

"Actually, there is one more thing," Marni began. "I also had a question."

"Shoot."

"I was wondering where you went in town to get your hair done. And where you'd shop if you needed a new dress."

CHAPTER ELEVEN

SOON AFTER HANGING up with Nella, Marni walked the mile and a half down the beach to the water taxi station her friend had informed her about. Gio was deep in emails on his laptop, so she'd simply left him a note.

She did some mentally calculations taking into account her bank balance, upcoming expenses and the exchange rate. Depending on how much the beauty salon was going to charge, she would no doubt have to skimp on the dress. One thing was certain, there was no way Marni could afford the upscale boutique Nella had suggested. She'd have to make do and find something relatively inexpensive.

A text popped up on her phone screen while she waited for the taxi boat. It was as if Nella was reading her mind.

Tell Gio to charge the salon and dress to a company expense account. You're attending a corporate function so it checks.

Marni smiled with appreciation but there was no way she was going to take the Santinos up on that. She wouldn't type that to Nella, however. Or she'd end up having to ditch the other woman's calls all day. She sent the heart emoji instead.

The floating dots appeared immediately on the screen.

You're not going to do it, are you?

Of course she wasn't. This time Marni sent a smiley face.

When she reached town twenty minutes later, the salon was only a brief walk away.

Using the translation app on her phone, along with the rudimentary Italian she'd learned spending so much time with the Santinos, Marni explained what she was after.

The stylist, a stunning brunette with bright red lips and dark wavy hair, gave her a dubious look.

"Sei sicuro?" the other woman asked.

Marni nodded. *"Sì."* Yes, she was sure.

She'd given this a lot of thought. No matter what happened with this little facade of theirs, Marni planned to go into it as a different person. She would start with her looks. She couldn't remember the last time she'd altered her appearance. Marni was due.

The woman who'd allowed Ander to control and belittle her, with hardly a word in her defense, was gone for good. Never to return. She was different now.

Marni was going to make sure to look the part.

Something on her face must have convinced the stylist, because she grinned and got to work. Marni spent the better part of the afternoon in the chair. When she was finally done three and a half hours later—transforming yourself was a long process—she nearly squealed in delight at the results.

The stylist was a genius. She'd taken what Marni had

said and expanded on it. The result was a stunning and modern hairstyle that brought out the shape of her face. If she did say so herself. Despite her measly bank account, she gave the woman a generous tip. The stylist had earned every penny.

Let's see Gio make fun of her ponytail now... She stopped herself mid thought. No. These changes were for her and her alone. Gio's reaction was sure to be just a bonus.

So why did her heart pound with nervous anticipation at the thought of what he might say about her new hair?

Marni would find out soon enough. Right now, she had to move on to the next phase of her trip into town. The dress.

Even looking at the window display of the boutique Nella had recommended was enough to confirm what she already knew. Her credit card might not have been declined, but it would take Marni a good long time to pay it off.

It didn't help that everyone around here was impeccably dressed in the latest styles. Her simple beige wraparound dress fell far short. Particularly compared to the young lady Marni eyed sitting alone sipping a coffee at the café next door to the shop.

Marni shoved away her shyness and walked over to the woman. What did she have to lose?

"Scusa," she began, approaching the woman's table. "Er... *Dove posso trovare."* She indicated the woman's outfit with her hand.

With a warm, friendly smile, the woman gestured for Marni's phone. When she handed it back, a name and address had been typed on the screen.

"Un piccolo negozio. Poco costoso," the woman said, pointing across the piazza to a side street.

Marni wanted to hug the other woman with appreciation. *A small store. Not too expensive.* Exactly what she was looking for.

The next time she saw herself in the mirror of a small dressing room, Marni had to pinch herself to confirm it was really her in the glass.

The new her.

Gio heard the door shut from the first-floor study and finished off his email then hit Send. Finally. Marni had been gone most of the day. With nothing but a note informing him she'd gone into town.

Why hadn't she asked him to take her?

They could have had lunch together. Done some sightseeing. Plus, they needed to talk about their exact plans for this evening. Shouldn't they discuss how they wanted to act? The image they wanted to project to the world?

Gio knew tonight would be all for show. But he wanted it to go smoothly. For Marni's sake.

Right. As if that was the only reason. It had been so long since he'd been out with a woman, and he'd never had to do so while in pain before. What if Marni had been right to ask about his readiness. What was he going to do if the pain became too much? It wasn't as if he could find a bag of ice or elevate his foot as he fought the waves of agony. Could he keep the pain at bay for a few hours given the stakes?

Well, before the night was over, he'd find out one way or another.

By the time he rose and went out to the sitting room,

she had already dashed upstairs. A moment later, he heard her voice echoing from above. She must have called Nella.

Great. Marni had been gone all day and now she was holed up in her room talking to his sister, a conversation that could very well take over an hour. Those two always spent forever talking to each other once they got started. And now that Nella was pregnant, there was a litany of baby topics they could chat about.

Gio swore and went back to his laptop. His mood had been sour all day, now it was downright acidic. He couldn't even explain why.

He didn't need to spend every day with Marni. They'd be together all evening, after all.

It wasn't as if he'd missed her while she was gone.

Gio adjusted his tie and glanced at his watch, a ritual he must have completed at least a half dozen times in the last hour. He and Marni would have to leave in a few minutes if they wanted to make any kind of noticeable entrance.

He debated icing his leg yet again but decided against it. It was on the brink of frostbite as it was.

Instead, he loosened the knot of his tie for the umpteenth time. He was out of practice as far as wearing one. The last time he'd gone out in a suit was before the accident. He'd been a completely different person then. His highest priority had been the next growth opportunity for Santino Foods and his main concern the latest sales figures and profit margins.

He still paid attention to those things, of course. Gio still made sure to monitor the industry, kept up with the distributors and read up on all the newest, trendiest Italian restaurants in major cities across the world. But numbers on a spreadsheet seemed much less life-and-death now. He supposed his turnabout was hardly surprising, given that he'd survived an actual literal life-and-death scenario.

What was taking Marni so long? He'd heard the shower shut off a good forty-five minutes ago. Was she stalling? Losing her nerve to go through with this?

After about ten more minutes of waiting, Gio made the decision to go check on her ETA. The turn of her doorknob sounded just as he reached the first step and he sighed in relief. He hadn't realized until that moment how nervous he'd been that she'd changed her mind about tonight. Which made no sense whatsoever. It wasn't as if he was looking forward to being gawked at on his first night out since the accident.

And then Marni descended the stairs and he lost all ability to think at all.

"I'm ready to go," she announced but he could hardly hear over the pounding in his ears.

Marni was…different. Her hair was cut and set in a completely different style with subtle bronze highlights throughout. It fell around her face in soft willowy strands, the ends reaching just above her shoulders. The waves were no more, replaced by a straightened thick mane that glittered where the light hit it.

He cleared his throat, finally managed to summon some words. "You, uh, got your hair cut."

Her hand reached up and she ran a finger through the fringe of her bangs, also new. "A good four inches. What do you think?"

What he thought was how much he wanted to be the one running his hands through those tresses. Of course, he wasn't about to actually say that. Trouble was, he couldn't come up with anything *to* say.

Marni's eyes widened with what looked like alarm. "You don't like it? Is it too drastic a change?"

Oh, no. He couldn't have her go thinking he didn't like it. He did. He liked it very, very much.

Then there was the dress. Gio ran his gaze down the length of her. Whisper-thin straps sat over golden tanned shoulders. The navy silky number draped over her curves in all the right ways, the skirt coming to a stop right above her knees. Her legs were bare but, heaven help him, did they have some kind of glittery powder on them? He didn't even know that was a thing. Strappy dark blue high heels adorned her feet. The pink polish was gone, replaced by a scarlet red that reminded him of the finest Toscana Rossa.

"Gio," she asked, "what do you think?" She gestured toward her midsection. "Will this do for tonight?"

Somehow, he kept himself from yelling outright that Yes! it would more than do. The only problem with it was how much he wanted to slip the dress off her and then proceed to muss up her stylish hair in all manner of ways.

Marni pointed to her head. "Is it the hair? Or the dress?"

That had him dumbstruck. It was the whole package. Where had all this come from? Where had this Marni come from? Gone was the familiar, conservatively dressed prim and proper gattina he'd grown up with. In her place stood a strikingly stunning woman who could easily fit walking down a runway or featured in a magazine fashion spread.

Marni had always been pretty. But now she was absolutely beautiful.

He had to stop gawking somehow and find something to say.

When he met Marni's gaze again she was staring at him, her lips tight with apprehension.

"Should I change?" she asked. "Or wash out my hair to bring the curls back?" She searched his face. "Both? Should I change all of it?"

The question had him snapping out of his stupor. "Don't even think about it, Marni," he finally managed. His voice sounded thick and strained to his own ears. "Don't you dare change a thing."

She felt like a princess on her way to the royal ball. Her companion certainly fit the image of the handsome prince. Of course, she'd seen Gio dressed up in the past. Prom night came to mind, and various formal functions she'd attended as a guest of the Santino family. But never before had she been the one on his arm.

The thought made her light-headed. She stole a glance at him now as they made their way into the club. In a dark navy suit Marni was certain was custom-tailored, Gio looked polished and devilishly handsome. A light gray shirt topped with a silk tie rounded out the image. He looked every bit the successful, coveted bachelor that he was. How unexpected that she was the woman he'd be spending the evening with.

Steady there, girl. This is all just for show, don't forget.

Still, she couldn't help but think of the way Gio had stared at her as she made her way down the stairs, and the memory sent feminine pleasure surging through her chest. He'd truly appreciated her new look. No doubt, her ex would have found a way to put down her makeover. Or even mock her for trying something different with her appearance.

Marni gave her head a shake. No more thoughts about Ander tonight. He wasn't worth it.

The band wasn't onstage yet but already the place was packed. Not one empty table. She wondered how Gio had snagged the last one.

The place was decorated to look like an ancient roman castle. A large mural painting of the Parthenon covered one wall.

Marni scanned the others in attendance: definitely an A-list crowd. Subconsciously, she fingered the costume jewelry earring on her earlobe. The other women in here were decked out in high-karat diamonds and other precious stones.

Who did she think she was fooling?

The better question was whether she was only fooling herself thinking she could fit into a place like this, with her bargain dress and faux leather shoes.

Gio must have sensed her self-doubt, maybe her expression had given him a clue. "You look beautiful, Marni. Absolutely beautiful," he said. A darkness settled over his eyes that left her insides quivering. His compliment served as a boost to her wavering confidence, and Marni suspected that was exactly what Gio had intended.

"Thanks, Santino. You clean up pretty nice yourself."

"Good thing. Because I haven't worn a suit in ages and I feel like I'm wrapped like an Egyptian mummy." Gio stuck his finger in his collar and made a choking sound.

He was trying to get a laugh out of her, must have sensed how nervous she was. Marni reached for his other hand on the table. "Thank you, Gio. For doing all this." She meant it. He was uncomfortable and achy, out on the town when he should be home resting his bruised and battered body. For her.

Gio's hand clenched under hers. "You can thank me by trying to relax and have a good time. Just because we're here on a mission doesn't mean we can't enjoy it."

"I'll try." She knew she should pull her hand away right then but let it linger, skin against skin. Finally, she pulled her arm back to her side when their server arrived.

Marni understood enough of the language to know that Gio ordered the night's special cocktail for them both and a bottle of champagne to share, along with an antipasto tray. Within moments of getting their food and drinks, the band appeared onstage and took their seats.

Soon the sound of traditional Neapolitan music filled the air. Before the end of the first song, several couples had already moved onto the dance floor.

Gio leaned over to speak in her ear. "Do you recognize the young lady in the leopard print dress?" he asked her.

Marni zoned in on the subject of his question. A petite blonde in impossibly high stilettos. She definitely looked familiar. It dawned on her why in a few seconds. "She's the latest addition to the cast of those superhero movies."

Gio nodded. "That's right. I'm certain at least a dozen people are snapping pictures of her right now. Pictures that will find themselves onto various gossip sites by morning."

Marni scanned the crowd. He certainly wasn't wrong. Several cell phones were held in the young actress's general direction.

"So if we want to be in any of those pictures, and hence on the websites, we should go up there now."

Marni swiveled her head and blinked at him. Was he suggesting that they actually join her on the dance floor? What about his hurt leg?

Before she could figure out how to ask without offending him again, Gio had stood up and was holding his hand out to her.

"Dance with me, gattina."

Marni's heart jumped in her chest. Silly as it might have been, it had never occurred to her that they'd be dancing together at some point tonight. Gio remained standing with his hand extended. He tilted his head questioningly when she still didn't rise out of her seat.

She swallowed, shoved her doubts away and stood, taking his hand. Gio's shoulders dropped with relief. He led her onto the dance floor. And then she was in his arms, her cheek against his shoulder, his arms around her waist.

The song was a soulful melody. She may not have understood all the lyrics but she knew the tempo of a love song when she heard it. Reflexively, she nestled closer against Gio's frame, allowed herself a deep inhalation of his aftershave.

Gio rubbed his cheek against the top of her head. Being in his arms again felt like being home. She hadn't even realized how badly she'd wanted to be there.

The song ended but Gio didn't let her go. Instead, he lifted her chin with his finger, then placed the gentlest of kisses on her lips. Marni's heart stopped, a jolt of electricity shot through her core. She wanted to ask him to do it again. But for longer this time, so that she could once again savor the taste of him. The way she had on the beach that day.

A small flash of light shone in the corner of her eye.

"There it is," Gio said with a satisfied tone and it hit her then: someone had snapped a photo. That was the whole reason he'd been kissing her in the first place. Shame and embarrassment had heat rushing to her face.

When would she learn? It served her right. A reminder of why they were here. How could she have forgotten for even a moment that all of this was meant for the photos?

None of it was real.

He was in no mood.

Nella had picked the wrong time to tease him. He wasn't even going to bother replying to her text. She may be pregnant, but she was still the pesky little sister who knew exactly how to get under his skin.

Saw the pictures from last night online. You and Marni make quite a striking couple.

That part wasn't so bad. It was the kissy face emojis, at least a dozen of them, that she'd stuck on at the end that rankled his nerves. Nella knew why he and Marni had been out last night. She'd even called yesterday to tell him he was a sweetie and a *tesoro* for helping Marni to thwart her ex's toxic campaign against her.

What Nella didn't know, nor Marni for that matter, was just how real it had all felt in the moment. On the dance floor, he'd simply meant to pose for a picture when he'd planted that kiss on Marni's lips. Just another way to continue the facade. But something had shifted in his center when he'd had his lips on hers. Their momentary loss of control on the beach had been full of emotion, with tensions running high for them both.

In contrast, the kiss last night had felt tender, delicate. Yet all the more powerful somehow. It had shaken him to the core the way he'd wanted to take her mouth again. Right there on the dance floor. He hadn't even cared that they were in a crowded nightclub, surrounded by strangers. And he no longer cared about getting some silly photo to send to a magazine.

She appeared in the doorway a moment later. Gio did a double take when he saw her, still not quite used to her new look. Short hair suited her. He hoped she kept it that length.

What was wrong with him?

The way Marni wore her hair was none of his business. And he had no business wallowing about a chaste little kiss they'd shared in the middle of a dance floor.

"Anything yet?" She pointed to his phone.

Gio shook his head. "Yes and no. It's just hitting the mainstream sites now. It'll take a couple more days before people figure out who you are and it gets to the trade mags."

She pushed her bangs off her forehead and blew out a frustrated breath. "It stinks that we have to do this. I wish there was some other way."

Did she mean having to go out with him? He thought she'd had fun last night. Enjoyed his company.

Last night was the most fun he'd had since the accident. Maybe even before it. Despite the way his leg and torso had screamed all night at the punishment of dancing.

He ignored the lump of disappointment that seemed to have formed in his gut. "We'll just have to get through the launch party tonight. Hopefully it will generate more publicity and attention."

She blew out a breath. "I really hope so. Then we can be done with this farce once and for all."

Gio flinched where he stood, hoping Marni didn't notice.

CHAPTER TWELVE

MARNI RAN THE brush through her hair one last time and adjusted the scarf around her neck. Last night had been magical. Until she'd realized that like most magic, it was all smoke and mirrors. All the joy and thrill she'd experienced burst like a needle-pricked balloon in that moment. Then she'd just wanted it to be over.

At least she was more mentally prepared this time. She wouldn't allow herself to get carried away like a schoolgirl if Gio kissed her again. Or fake-kissed her, that was.

When she made it downstairs, Gio was dressed and waiting. He offered her a rather weak smile that didn't quite seem genuine.

"Ready to go?" he asked. Unlike last night, he didn't offer her his arm this time.

"As I'll ever be. The sooner we get there, the sooner we get this over with."

He gave her a curt nod and led her out the door.

Hard to believe but he looked even more dashingly handsome than he had at the club. Tonight he wore a tux that matched the black of his hair. He'd used some kind of gel to keep it in place, whereas yesterday it fell in waves over his forehead. If the man ever got tired of this business tycoon thing, he definitely had a future as a men's cologne model.

She, for one, would be ready to buy anything Gio Santino was selling.

A speedboat with a uniformed skipper awaited them when they reached the beach. Gio helped her onboard and led her to a comfortable seating area below deck with a circular table larger than the one she had in her apartment. A tray of fresh fruit and a variety of cheeses sat in the center, along with an airing bottle of wine and two stem glasses.

Gio poured them each a glass but she only took a sip, guzzling from the frosty water bottle instead. Best to try and keep her wits about her for as long as she could manage.

"I've never been to Naples before," she said by way of conversation. Gio was being oddly quiet. She wished he would tell her more about what to expect. The last Santino function she'd been to was a corporate Christmas party when she was seventeen in the North End, Boston's equivalent of Little Italy. This one tonight would actually be in Italy.

The motor roared to life and soon they were making their way across the ocean, the craft accelerating gradually until they reached a speed that had the scenery outside the windows zipping by.

For the second time in two nights, Marni wondered if she was going to be underdressed. Maybe she should have saved last night's dress for this evening instead, it was just a tad fancier. But last night, she'd been concerned about impressing Gio. Such a wasted effort on her part.

She checked her reflection in a side panel mirror. And thought she heard Gio snort.

Her eyes snapped on his face to find him looking at her with pursed lips and darkened eyes. "Something wrong?"

"You seem overly concerned again about your appearance. I told you yesterday you looked beautiful. How many compliments are you fishing for?"

Marni felt her jaw drop and her chest stung with a sudden flash of anger. "What?"

Gio rubbed his jaw. "Never mind. Forget I said anything. You look great, okay? Stop worrying about it."

Well, he'd seen to that. Now all she'd be worried about was why he was being so surly and offensive. Clearly, he didn't want to be here on this boat on his way to a function he'd had no intention of attending if it hadn't been for her. None of that was her fault, damn it.

"May I remind you that all this was your idea?"

His eyes bore into hers and he shook his head. "No, you don't need to remind me. And I'm sorry it's so taxing for you to go through with it."

Marni sucked in a breath. Where was all this coming from? "I never said that."

"You didn't exactly have to spell it out."

The chime of an incoming text interrupted her reply. From Nella.

Too bad it can't be real.

She'd attached a well-known meme of a disappointed cartoon character. Marni squinted at her screen. What exactly was that supposed to mean? Damned if she could guess. Honestly, the Santino siblings were insistent on testing her nerves tonight.

She was about to text her back to ask for some clarity

when Gio spoke. "We're here." He then stood, adjusting his gold cuff links.

Marni was surprised to look out the window and see the spectacular sight of Naples. Bright lights reflected off the water and lit up the clear night sky. She might have been looking at colorful fireworks somehow suspended in the air. The scene took her breath away. She imagined this was what Mount Olympus might look like.

Marni couldn't help but gawk at the sight as Gio led her off the boat and into a waiting limousine.

Less than ten minutes later, they arrived at the circular driveway of a sprawling resort. Marni could have sworn she'd seen this exact hotel in a spy movie not too long ago. Definitely worth an internet search to confirm as soon as she got a chance.

They walked down the brightly lit hallway toward the open double doors of a ballroom. The party appeared to be in full swing already.

Gio guided her through the entry with his hand at the small of her back. Marni forced herself not to react to his touch.

Even now, when she was furious with his behavior and at a complete loss to guess what might have caused it, she felt a current of electricity travel from the palm of his hand, clear through her skin and up the length of her spine.

The room seemed to still as they entered, the noise level decreased several decibels. Many heads turned in their direction at once. Marni supposed it made sense, the CEO had just arrived, after all. But there was something else she sensed in the air, a wave of curiosity.

She heard Gio utter a curse in Italian under his breath.

On instinct, she reached for his hand and gripped it tight behind her back. He squeezed back.

"Let's get a drink."

"All right." Sounded good to her; she was beginning to regret turning down the wine on the boat. Being the subject of such widespread scrutiny was not a comfortable feeling, nor one she was used to.

"I'm afraid we're going to have to mingle," Gio told her after he'd ordered them a couple of cocktails.

Sure. She could do that. All she had to do was smile and nod, right? Gio was the main attraction here, not her.

He looked less than pleased about it.

But he didn't falter. No less than half a dozen people approached him as they waited for their drinks. A couple simply wanted to say hello. The rest had urgent grievances and important matters and weren't going to waste this opportunity to bend the boss's ear.

Gio listened patiently, offered solutions or provided follow-up guidance. He really knew his stuff and was good at what he did.

Not that she'd ever doubted it.

Still, it was something else to see him in action. No wonder the company had grown several-fold under his guidance. Santino Foods was lucky to have him.

It was after they'd gotten their drinks and were headed toward their reserved table that the world shifted. Marni felt a splash of ice-cold liquid over her arm and middle. A heavy weight pushed against her side, followed by a hard thud by her feet. Marni's heart stopped as she processed what was happening: Gio had lost his balance. In horror, she looked down to find him braced on one knee gripping the base of a nearby table to keep from, going all the way down. His face a tight mask of agony.

"Oh, my God! Gio! Are you okay?" She dropped down next to him, reached for his arms. "Here, let me help you up."

The look he gave her had her breath catching in her throat. Red-hot anger burned behind his eyes. His voice was low and thick when he spoke. There was no mistaking the fury behind his words as he bit them out through tightly gritted teeth. "Marni. Don't."

Never in his worst nightmares had Gio imagined the scenario he found himself in. A room full of his colleagues and his employees, all present to see his horror. Then there was Marni. She'd had a front-row seat to it all.

His leg had actually given out, refused to support him. It had happened in a split second, without any kind of warning.

Check that. He had been warned, hadn't he? Warned by all the doctors, nurses and specialists.

He couldn't even bring himself to look around and see who might have observed his literal downfall. Clenching his teeth against the pain and embarrassment, he put as much weight as he could on his good leg, then used the thick base of the table to rise to a standing position.

Marni rose immediately as well and the look of worry on her face had competing forces warring in his chest. He was both touched by her concern and shamed that she'd witnessed such a stunning moment of weakness.

"Gio?"

He clenched his fists at his sides, here came that question again. *Are you all right?*

Marni didn't voice the words out loud, just continued scanning his face, her eyes imploring. He had to give her something. He thought about lying, telling her he'd tripped over some nonexistent object that was now miraculously gone or over a leg of a table. But what was the use? For one, she'd see right through the lie.

"I think I just put too much pressure on my bad leg. It'll be fine in a few moments."

Marni opened her mouth before closing it again, clearly at a loss for words.

He gestured to her middle. "Sorry about the drink. Your dress is all wet." Luckily, he'd ordered a vodka tonic for himself, at least she wouldn't have to walk around with a large stain on her dress. Just a large wet spot.

She blinked. "It will dry."

Gio finally dared to look about the room. No one seemed to be paying them any attention. If anyone had witnessed what had just happened, they had the good sense not to stare.

Still, he had to get out of this room. He didn't think he could handle even one person approaching him. "Excuse me for a few moments," he told Marni. "I'd like to get some air."

He turned away before she could respond.

Marni watched Gio's retreating back and debated what to do. Should she follow him? What if he fell again? She gave her head a small shake. No, he needed time alone and appeared steady enough on his feet as he navigated the crowded ballroom.

She would give him a minute. If she knew Gio, he was stinging with an imagined hit to his pride, which was ridiculous. He couldn't help what had just happened. He'd overdone it, pushed himself too far and ignored the fact that he wasn't one hundred percent. It had all taken a toll at the worst time.

But Gio Santino had never been one to show any weakness. And to think, Nella had said a couple days ago that he wasn't so stubborn. Ha! If she only knew just how stubborn her brother was acting these days.

A twinge of guilt fluttered in her chest. A lot of what he'd done had been on her behalf. Marni wanted to kick herself. She should have never agreed to this silly plan, should have just taken her lumps from Ander's conniving and not involved anyone else in her problems.

Along with an apology, she was going to tell Gio all that as soon as he returned.

Marni pulled her phone out of her clutch purse and mindlessly scrolled through various sites to kill the time until he returned, not paying any kind of real attention to what she read. Several moments passed and she continued scrolling.

Gio still hadn't come back. She dialed his number but he didn't pick up. No shocker there. Marni couldn't decide whether to be annoyed or more worried.

Finally, when she couldn't take any more anxious wondering, she went to look for him. Gio wasn't in the lobby nor was he outside by the main entrance. She ran back through the lobby area and down the opposite corridor to the back of the hotel facing the beach.

Lit fire torches dotted the sand beyond a wide stone patio furnished with cushioned wicker furniture. All of the chairs and sofas sat empty.

Marni strained her eyes down the length of the beach.

Countless people were walking along the water or enjoying an evening swim. It could take her hours to find Gio if he was down there. He'd had quite a head start.

A deep, masculine voice sounded behind her. "Looking for me?"

Marni clasped her hand to her chest, her heart racing. It was anybody's guess whether that was caused by Gio unexpectedly materializing from behind her or because of the figure he posed. Framed in shadows, he looked almost ethereal.

She sucked in a breath and forced her mouth to work. "Gio. There you are. You startled me."

He stepped out of the darkness into the pool of light cast from a nearby lantern. "My apologies."

She knew better than to ask him if he was all right. That had never worked out quite so well in the past.

"I'm guessing you don't want to go back into the party just yet."

He thrust his hands in his pockets, tilting backward on his heels. "You would be correct."

Good. Because neither did she. Marni stepped to the wicker seat closest to her and dropped into it, then tucked her feet under her. The fresh air felt good on her skin, the ballroom had grown much too stuffy.

Gio didn't make any kind of move to sit himself, he merely lifted an eyebrow. She couldn't help but notice that most of his weight was solidly on his good leg. Saints give her patience with this man. He thought he'd appear weak by sitting down.

Oh, Gio. You don't have to prove anything to me.

"So when are you making the call?" she asked, feeling a little disconcerted with the height difference now that she'd taken a seat and he'd remained standing.

"Call?"

"The hospital in Chicago. To schedule those appointments finally. First thing tomorrow morning, I hope."

His head tilted. "I told you a few days ago. I'm in no rush."

He couldn't be serious. But there was no sign of joking on his face. "But that was before—"

He cut her off. "I'll call when I'm ready."

Marni covered her face with her palms, hardly able to believe what she was hearing. "Gio, you need to get started on those therapy sessions. And then you need to go through the surgeries. You can't put it off any longer."

"Is that your expert opinion?"

Marni's temper flared. How could he take this so lightly? It made absolutely no sense.

"Please explain to me why you plan to put this off any longer than you already have. Especially after what just happened."

A muscle jumped along his jaw. "Nothing happened, Marni. I lost my footing. It happens to everyone."

Maybe so, but it didn't often happen while simply walking on a flat surface. "Are you trying to convince yourself of that or trying to convince me?"

He shrugged. "I don't have to convince you of anything."

Marni pushed past the hurtful barb, one meant to imply that this was none of her business. She'd deal with the wound it caused to her soul later. Right now, she really wanted to learn why Gio was doing something so harmful and dangerous to himself.

She took a deep calming breath. "I'm just trying to understand. Don't tell me you don't believe the doctors can be of help? Gio, you have to trust in the professionals who have spent their lives helping heal others."

He scoffed at that. "Of course I have faith in doctors and professionals. I'm in regular contact with Juno's medical team. I'm making sure that he gets the best care and that he's being seen by the best specialists this side of the world."

It dawned on her then. Suddenly, all the puzzle pieces fell into place and everything made sense. She'd been so wrong in all her assumptions. Gio wasn't only putting off his recovery because he was too proud to admit he was wounded. He was delaying to punish himself. For the accident he'd caused which had tragically altered the life of a young father with a family who needed him. It was a vicious circle—he refused to get the treatment he needed because of his guilt, which only grew his frustration at his injuries. He was going around and around and couldn't even see it.

"Gio, it was an accident." She emphasized the last word. "You didn't intend harm. You have to see that."

His eyes hardened on her face. "Marni, let this go."

She couldn't. For his sake. "What if I don't want to?"

His jaw visibly tightened. "It's not up to you."

She knew he was simply lashing out, but his coldness still broke her heart.

"Good night, Marni," he said in a flat voice. "The limo and speedboat are waiting to take you back to the villa whenever you're ready."

Marni's mouth went dry. He was really doing this. He was really pushing her away because he'd rather keep punishing himself than move on with his life and his future. A future that might have included *her*.

"I've decided to stay here in Naples for the time being," he added with finality.

Gio didn't even wait for a response before walking away without so much as a glance back.

Sitting in the *piazetta* sipping coffee wasn't doing much to settle her emotions. But Marni had had to get away from the villa. She'd been going stir-crazy wandering around the grounds all morning, waiting for word from Gio. The throngs of people bustling about the square and those enjoying the cafés and shops should have made for a worthy distraction of people watching. But Marni hardly noticed her surroundings.

The biscotti she'd ordered with her cappuccino was one of the freshest and most flavorful she'd ever tasted. But she might as well have been nibbling on cardboard.

Not a peep from him since their disastrous argument last night. Not so much as a text or a phone call, despite several attempts to reach him. His silence had Marni torn between anger and worry. What if his leg had gotten worse? What if he was holed up in a hotel room right now, lying on the mattress in agony and pain?

A shudder of anxiety racked through her at the image in her head. Still, even that drastic scenario, heaven forbid it be real, wouldn't have prevented him from sending her a quick text.

No, he was ignoring her because he wanted to. Because he clearly thought Marni had overstepped when she'd insisted he get the medical care he needed.

Gio thought she had no right to weigh in on his decisions. Her opinion or thought held no import for him. And here she'd gone and foolishly fallen further in love with the man. There was no denying that now. If she couldn't admit it before, she damn well had to face reality now.

She'd always loved him, since they were preteens. Now she was head over heels.

A hiccup of anguish tore from her chest and her eyes stung behind her sunglasses. She reached for her phone once more, but she wasn't holding her breath. It pinged just as she glanced at the screen. Heart pounding, Marni unlocked the message only to have her hope plummet. It wasn't Gio but his sister.

Your plan was a success! You and Gio are all over the sites.

Marni tossed the phone back on the table as if it had burned her palm. The plan. What an insignificance. Little did Nella know she could care less now about the blasted plan. Even less about what the world thought about her. She'd take her chances to get her career back on track. If that meant leaving home and moving to New York then so be it.

Right now, regaining her professional career was pretty much all she had in her life. But she'd do it on her own terms. Without a pretend boyfriend.

One challenge at a time. For right now, she had to focus on herself and the best way to move forward toward her future.

She'd done it again—carelessly trusted her heart to the wrong man. Unlike Ander, this particular man would be impossible to get over.

Gio was the one who'd made her feel like a princess. The one who'd encouraged her to dream of more for her future and told her he had faith that she could accomplish it. He was the only man who'd sent shivers down her spine when he so much as touched her.

No matter what the future held for her, Gio Santino would forever claim her heart. All the more tragic given the family connection.

They were to be co-godparents for heaven's sake! How in the world would she even navigate that? How would she hide her true feelings and keep from shattering inside every time they were in the same room together?

With trembling fingers, she reached for her cup and took a tentative sip. Well, she was done waiting. There was no sense staying in Capri any longer either. Her goal to come here and take two weeks to recharge and regroup had completely backfired. She had nothing to show for herself but a broken heart. Looked like her days in paradise were over. Gio had clearly moved on.

Somehow, some way, so would she.

He sensed it as soon as he let himself in the front door. Gio didn't need to walk through the villa to know that she was gone. He should have answered her calls. But he couldn't bring himself to do it, couldn't for the life of him figure out what he might say. Now that he was ready to find her, it was much too late.

He knew that made him all kinds of a coward.

He'd spent hours wandering the city last night until his leg had screamed at him to stop. When he finally returned to the hotel, Gio hadn't been able to fall asleep, hadn't even bothered to crawl into bed. Just simply sat on the sofa in his hotel room, staring into the dark until the sun rose. And it had nothing to do with the regular insomnia that had plagued him since the accident.

When his eyes had finally drifted shut sometime late in the afternoon, his mind played reels of images in his head: Marni pouncing into his bedroom that first day she'd arrived; the marvel on her face as they'd sailed over blue water in the grotto; how her eyes had widened in the Gardens of Augustus… The way her lips had tasted on his.

With a curse, he strode to the patio and dropped down on the lounge chair only to have more memories of her flood his mind. He even replayed the moment in the garden when the wedding procession had walked by. Only, the bride in his mind was Marni. And he was her groom. He had to push the vision away. Because it was complete fantasy.

Maybe it was just as well she was gone. She was better off without him. He wasn't anywhere near the man he used to be.

Marni deserved better than the man he was now. Broken both inside and outside. Unable to tell the woman he loved how he really felt. Too broken for the likes of someone like her. Hopefully, one day she would see the truth of that and forgive him for his cowardness.

Heaven knew, he didn't deserve such grace from her. Just like he didn't deserve *her*.

CHAPTER THIRTEEN

Four months later

MARNI READ THE email once more, then rubbed her eyes to make sure she wasn't imagining the message. Was it really possible that they were about to be hired by their first client?

"Huh," she said out loud, scanning her laptop screen once more.

"What is it?" Nikita Murtag asked from her desk across the small office. Nikita was Marni's new business partner of approximately three weeks now. A former colleague at Marni's old firm, the other woman had contacted her the day Marni left Capri. Niki told her how low morale had turned at her old place of business. How most of the female employees knew Ander to be a predatory liar and didn't want to be next in his crosshairs. So Niki had quit. Somehow, within days after Niki's call, the two women were cosigning a business loan and painting the walls of their new shop in Boston's South End.

The signage even worked out, just as Marni had envisioned in her fantasy that night. Her mind reflexively pushed the memory aside before it could fully form. Any thoughts of the time she'd spent with Gio Santino were too painful and raw to entertain. Her heart couldn't take it.

What mattered now was that Mar-Ni Designs was officially open for business. And if this email wasn't some king of spam or junk, they might even have their first client.

"Come look at this," she told Niki, then turned the laptop toward her when the other woman reached her desk. Niki read the message over her shoulder then let out a whoop.

"We have a job!"

It certainly seemed so. "It's odd, isn't it, though?" Marni questioned. "We've barely been open more than a few days."

"Word of mouth is a powerful force, Marni. Don't discount it."

"They sent the email through the new website."

"Looks like they're asking for you specifically." Niki gave her shoulder a squeeze. "You must have impressed somebody through the years. Go ahead and confirm."

Within minutes of her replying, another message popped up.

"You're not going to believe this," she told Niki. "Whoever this potential client is, it says they're in a hurry and want a meeting this afternoon if possible."

"Are you going to say yes?" Niki asked.

Marni shrugged one shoulder. She couldn't think of one reason to turn down a potential opportunity. "Why not?" she answered. "It's not like I have anything else to work on just yet."

Three hours later, Marni made her way to the most exclusive restaurant in Boston's Seaport District, the requested meeting place, with her portfolio tucked under her arm. The dining room was relatively empty given the early afternoon so she was surprised when the maître d' led her to a private room on the top floor.

Whomever this potential client was, looked like he carried a lot of clout in the city. Marni took a seat at the large mahogany dining table, nervous anticipation humming through her veins.

A shadow fell over the table from behind her seat. A familiar scent carried in the air.

It couldn't be. Marni squeezed her eyes shut, afraid to turn around.

"*Ciao, gattina.*"

That voice. *His* voice.

Her mind had to be playing tricks on her, trying to conjure a false reality she wanted so badly to be true. Gio Santino wasn't really here, standing behind her.

Only one way to find out.

Sucking in a shaky breath, she made herself get up and turn around.

Even as her eyes fell on him, she couldn't quite believe what she was seeing. Gio stood in the doorway, his shoulder leaning against the doorframe. He flashed her a devilishly handsome smile that made her heart skip a beat.

"Gio?"

"*Sì, bellisima.* It's me."

Marni felt as if her mouth had filled with sawdust and her tongue felt too heavy to move. Somehow she managed to form a single word. "Why?"

Gio squeezed his eyes shut, tilted his head up toward the ceiling. "You have every reason to be upset, *cara.*"

That got her mouth working. "Of course I do! You—you just left me. Without a goodbye. Not a word!"

He paused before returning his gaze to her face. "I

know. For the life of me, I couldn't come up with a thing to say to you. Please know that I will spend the rest of my life trying to make up for that."

A sudden war was being waged in her soul. Every cell in her body wanted to tell him he was forgiven, that she was overjoyed to see him. But a calmer, saner part reminded her how hard she'd worked these past few months to focus solely on her own growth and fulfillment.

Whatever his intentions were for being here, she had to set him straight on at least that one thing. "You can't just walk back into my life, Gio. It's not that simple. I've done a lot since we last saw each other."

He took a step closer, his eyes dark and compelling beneath those black lashes.

Focus.

"I know. From all outward appearances, it seems your new business is exactly what you'd envisioned. You should be so proud of yourself."

Her chin lifted. "I am. And I don't have room or time to waste if my feelings are one-sided."

Gio moved closer to her once more. Something nagged at the back of her mind when he took several more steps. It took a beat, but she finally figured out what her brain was trying to tell her. "Your limp," she began. "It seems to be better."

He gave her a thin smile. "It should. After the countless hours of therapy and all the grueling muscle building exercises."

Marni sucked in a breath. "You went to Chicago."

He nodded.

"You were right to push me that night. And I was so wrong to push you away. I'm so sorry, *mi gattina.* Please forgive me for being such a *stolto.*"

She couldn't help herself, didn't even realize what she'd intended until she was across the room and in his arms. He wrapped himself around her, nuzzled his chin against the top of her head.

"You're really here," she said against his chest, savoring the feel of him, inhaling deeply of that scent she'd missed so much.

"I had to come. To find the woman I love."

The woman he loved? If this was indeed a dream, Marni didn't want to ever come back to reality. Gio Santino had traveled across the country to be with her, to tell her he loved her.

But there were so many things as yet unsettled. She couldn't celebrate until she had the answers she'd been asking for that night in Naples. Marni made herself pull away. "What about your treatments?" If she was remembering correctly, he still had surgeries to complete after the therapy was over. "Don't you have to go back to Chicago for the surgeries?"

He tilted her chin. "Chicago is so far, *mi amore*."

She was about to argue when he pressed a finger to her lips. "I'm already seeing a specialist. Right here in Boston. I refuse to be so far from you again. I intend to stay right here and do all I can to work on becoming the man you deserve."

Marni thought her heart might burst in her chest. Then she couldn't think at all as his lips found hers.

When he pulled away all too soon, he took her by the hand to the table. "Now, let's get down to business, shall we?"

Marni blinked at him in confusion. "What business?"

He chuckled. "You're here about an assignment, aren't you?"

Marni didn't miss the mischief behind his eyes. What was he getting at?

"I thought that was just a ruse to get me here." As if she'd turn him down if he'd just asked her. He couldn't have really thought so.

He shook his head. "No ruse. There's a property that needs a professional decorator. As a fan of your previous work, I believe you'd be perfect for the job."

Marni tilted her head, whatever game he was playing, she'd play along. "What property?"

"Here, let me show you." He reached for a leather binder sitting in the center of the table, pulled it toward her and lifted the cover.

Marni knew immediately what she was looking at. "This is the villa in Capri. The one that was for sale." He must have bought it.

She looked more carefully at the photos and paperwork. "There's a mistake here," she said, pointing at one of the documents. "This has my name listed as the owner."

Gio flashed her a wide smile. "No mistake. The villa is yours."

Before Marni could so much as absorb that bit of information, he continued, "Consider it a wedding present for my new wife. That's if she'll have it." He took her hand in his over the table. "And if she'll have me. What do you say?"

Marni thought her heart might burst in her chest with joy. It had nothing to do with any villa. And everything to do with the man she'd loved for as long as she could remember.

"Sì, mi amore," she answered, wrapping her arms around his neck. "I say yes!"

EPILOGUE

UNLIKE THE LAST time they were here at the Gardens of Augustus, the sky was dark and overcast. In fact, it appeared as if it might rain any second. But none of that hampered the joy flooding through her heart and soul.

Let it rain, Marni thought. An all-out thunderstorm would not be enough to dampen the celebration of her wedding day by so much as even a fraction.

As she approached the man who would soon be her husband, Marni fought the urge to pinch herself to prove all of this was real. Gio stood beneath a circular archway of flowers, the view of the ocean behind him. He looked so devastatingly handsome, his eyes shining with so much love that Marni thought her heart might burst in her chest. His sister stood next to him, beaming. Cradled in her arms was Marni's infant goddaughter, surely the cutest flower girl to have ever been in a wedding. The grand view of the Faraglioni rocks framed them.

Marni's eyes stung with happy tears. She was surrounded by love and affection and everyone who'd ever mattered in her life. The Santinos had always been her family. Now it was simply official.

Her tears refused to be contained as she reached Gio's side and they began their vows. Marni felt like she was living a true fairy tale, right down to marrying her own prince.

Afterward, through a blur of happy emotion as they began posing for their wedding photos, Gio gently took her elbow. He leaned in to whisper in her ear after the photographer snapped several pictures. "I've been thinking, *cara*. Something has occurred to me and I can't seem to get it out of my head."

Marni couldn't help but giggle at the clearly exaggerated mock seriousness in his voice. "What thought might that be, dear husband?" She had to suppress a cry of glee at the last word as it left her lips.

"I was thinking how much little Alexandra would appreciate a cousin to play with. Wouldn't you agree?"

Marni gave him a useless shove on his upper arm. "Gio!"

The photographer was trying to direct them in another pose but it was so hard to process the man's direction. She was utterly, wholeheartedly focused on her new husband.

Gio continued, "As responsible godparents, it behooves us to give our little niece all that she may desire."

"Anything you say, my love."

His expression turned suddenly serious. The photographer had apparently given up at this point and stepped to the side to wait patiently before continuing.

"Of course, the timing is entirely up to you," Gio told her. "I know you're quite busy with your growing clientele back in Boston."

"I am quite busy," she said, just to tease him.

He tapped her playfully on the nose, then dropped a soft kiss on her lips. "That's fine. Just gives me something to look forward to."

Marni cupped his face in her hands and rose on her

toes to give him a deeper, longer kiss. She felt breathless and heady when they finally pulled away.

"Me too, my love," she whispered against his lips. "I'm looking forward to all of it. All that we have in front of us."

* * * * *

FAKE ENGAGEMENT WITH THE BILLIONAIRE

ALLY BLAKE

MILLS & BOON

To my rubber band friends—
Cassandra, Rowena and Sangeeta.

For your foundational friendship,
the lockdown Zoom drinks and, of course, Binga.

I'm so grateful that, despite time and distance,
we keep tugging one another back. xxx

CHAPTER ONE

PETRA GILPIN HAD made a huge mistake.

Since she was knee-high to a butterfly Petra's intuition had been her navigation system, bewildering her highly successful Type A parents, and delighting her older brother Finn.

It had sent her meandering down garden paths in search of soft pink feathers and sparkly pink stones to add to her collections. It had sent her to art school, where she'd discovered her skills were more in the appreciation than the doing. And it was entirely to blame for her losing her heart to the first boy who'd found a pink feather on the ground one day and saved it for her.

Petra's instinct was not infallible by any means. It had got her lost more times than she could count. But only in the best ways.

Now, sitting in the swanky Gilded Cage nightclub, the deeply luxurious purple velvet couch making the backs of her knees itch, that same intuition buzzed at her like crazy.

Petra glanced at her bag—the tip of her flamingo phone case in particular.

Read it, her intuition whispered, referring to the email that had lured her back home to Melbourne for the first time in over a decade. *Read it one more time. There's got to be a loophole, a way out—*

"This place is insane!" said Deena—one of the few friends from her weekly boarding school days she'd actually kept in touch with—climbing through the actual cage curving around their private booth, huge bottle of bubbly in hand. "Did you see the disco ball over the dance floor? It's bigger than my office. And I made partner last year. Having fun?"

Petra twinkled a smile her way. And wondered at what point she could call it a night.

Deena refilled their glasses generously, before lifting hers in the air. "What shall we toast to?"

Petra always raised a glass to the same thing—her big brother Finn. But Deena hadn't met him, which would be a little weird.

"You choose," Petra said.

"Your welcome home?"

Petra felt her nose twitch.

Deena laughed. "Okay, not that. How about beauty, love, art and...hot men with roping arm veins?"

Petra perked up and clinked glasses and said, "To favourite things!"

As the excellent bubbles dived deliciously down her throat, Petra pondered if *huge mistake* might be pushing it. For Deena was good value. And the club's design elements were exquisitely brassy and bold. It was just that Petra was more a behind-the-scenes, get-it-done-then-head-home-for-a-glass-of-red kind of girl.

A burst of joyful noise saw Deena on her knees on the couch, leaning through the bars, making friends with the hen's night party in the private cage next door.

Petra took her chance, grabbing her phone.

DARLING!

That was how the email in question began. Because that was her mother's way of showing she felt fondness towards her daughter, even though she'd spent Petra's entire childhood acting as if Petra had simply wandered in from the garden one day, and Josephine had decided raising her as their own was the civilised thing to do.

And all in caps because her mother had read that it expressed urgency, and deemed every message she ever sent out into the world to be of great import.

Petra nibbled at her thumbnail as she read on.

YOU MIGHT REMEMBER THAT YOUR FATHER AND I ARE ON THE BOARD OF THE GALLERY OF MELBOURNE.

THE GOM HAS FOUND ITSELF IN A BIT OF A FIX AND IN NEED OF SOMEONE WITH YOUR UNCOMMONLY SPECIFIC SKILL SET, AS WELL AS A NAME THAT WILL INSPIRE TRUST IN THOSE BEST ABLE TO DONATE THE FUNDS THAT IT NOW RATHER DESPERATELY REQUIRES IN ORDER TO KEEP ITS DOORS OPEN.

I MUST INSIST ON YOUR DISCRETION ON THIS POINT. AFTER SOME YEARS OF MISMANAGEMENT THE SITUATION IS DIRE. WE'VE THUS FAR HELD OFF THE WHIFF OF SCANDAL AND WISH FOR IT TO REMAIN THAT WAY.

YOUR FATHER AND I REMEMBER HOW MUCH YOU ENJOYED YOUR TIME SPENT IN THE GALLERY AS A CHILD, AND HOPE THIS MIGHT ENCOURAGE YOU TO DO WHAT MUST BE DONE.

ARE YOU UP FOR THE CHALLENGE?

Petra's response—lots of *wows* and exclamation marks and Some of the best memories of my childhood, followed by a final Challenge accepted! were all typed in a shocked flurry, as if it was the best news ever.

Yes, art was her field, but not the business side—more the enchantment that came with stumbling on a work that made a person *feel* something. An affinity that had led to her procuring private collections for princes and pop stars, curating modern art collections for famous galleries, and breaking records hosting auctions of digital art.

All of which she'd put on hold so that she might help her parents save the august, old Gallery of Melbourne.

The sounds of the club whumped back to her, and Petra lifted her glass to find it empty.

"Phone down!" said Deena, literally yanking it out of Petra's hand and tossing it up the other end of the couch. "No work. Or cat memes. Or whatever your kink is these days. And no photos. What happens at the Gilded Cage stays at the Gilded Cage."

Petra held out her glass and Deena happily refilled it. "What exactly do you imagine happening tonight?"

Deena reared back, hand to her throat. "I am happily married! It's my mission to see *you* hooked up."

Petra flinched. "You're meant to be giving me a rundown on who the movers and shakers are in Melbourne these days. Hooking up was not on the agenda." Or bubbly, for that matter, but there she was, glass in hand.

"It can be!" said Deena. "Unless you have a man back in London?"

Petra shook her head rather more vehemently than was probably necessary. It wasn't as if she didn't *date*, it was just another *normal person* thing that didn't come naturally to her.

She *had* thought herself on the way to falling in love a couple of years back, with a soft-spoken junior taxidermist at the American Museum of Natural History. It had taken her longer than it ought to realise that rather than being a strong silent type—her catnip—he was pathologically shy. And what she'd liked *most* about him was that he didn't make her feel as if she had to *work* to impress him.

Had she imagined she'd still feel the sting of her parents' lack of insight into who she was at thirty? Heck, no. Then again, she *had* imagined she'd be married to her favourite football player and living in some beautiful, gloriously eclectic hideaway in the Dandenong mountains by now.

"Humour me," Deena begged, then poked her head through

the bars of their cage as she looked down on the dance floor. "Nope. Not him. Wait a minute... *Ding! Ding! Ding!* I do believe we've found a winner! And—holy mother of Thor—he might just be the most beautiful man who ever lived."

"Big call," said Petra, snuggling deeper into the couch as she sipped on her bubbly.

"Big's the word," said Deena. "This guy is huge. Rugged. Beastly. Smells like summer rain."

Petra laughed, the sound now bubbly too. She spun, fluffing her long dusky pink tulle skirt behind her so she could hop up onto her knees and see what the fuss was about. Only for the lights bouncing off the glassy mosaic ceiling to do funny things to her balance, making her wonder exactly how many times Deena had refilled her glass.

"How can you possibly tell what he smells like from here?" Petra asked.

"It's a skill. Hang on, I've lost him. How could I lose him? Dark curls, the build of a giant, brown leather jacket... There!" Deena called, finger pointing madly.

Petra followed the line of the finger. And before she could mouth the words, *Which one?* a voice inside her head said: *That one.*

The seething Saturday night crowd seemed to pause and take a breath, clearing a path to where a hulking, dark-haired man leant his heft against the circular neon bar in the centre of the room. Even from that distance Petra could sense the slow roll of a meaty shoulder before the guy lifted a glass to his mouth, the dark hair curling wildly and overlong over the collar of his beaten-up brown leather jacket.

It was enough for Petra to plonk her backside back into the seat, the tulle crinkling as it settled around her.

It couldn't be *him*, could it?

He was *always* travelling, from country to country, city to city, even village to village, spreading Big Think Corp fairy dust—aka tech, or insight, or provisions—on whoever needed it. It had been years since they'd been in the same time zone, much less the same city.

And yet…

If her intuition had been humming before, now it filled her head with a delirious high-pitched scream.

"Hey," Deena cried, "why are you not down there, shoving people out of the way to get to him? I would if I wasn't, you know, happily married."

"Too brooding for my taste," Petra lied as she downed the remains of her bubbly in one mighty gulp. But, rather than loosening her up, it tightened her insides like the squeeze of a rubber band.

Deena settled her chin against her hand and sighed. "Yeah, you're probably right. All that testosterone must be a lot to handle. A guy who knows how to rock cycling gear, and brings you coffee in bed every morning, that's the ticket. That's *my* man and I'm…"

"Happily married." Petra shot Deena a smile.

Deena smiled back. "Now, I have to take a quick trip to the ladies' room. Then I might find someone to dance with me. Platonically. Wanna come with?"

Petra saw the bottom of yet another empty glass. "I might grab some water."

Deena patted her on the knee before climbing over her legs and out of the cage. "See you in a bit, then."

"Here goes," Petra said, ducking under the arch of their twirling gilt cocoon, strappy high heels carefully navigating the small steps down to the dance floor below. The music felt as if it was rising from the floor, through her knees and into her spine.

Once she reached the other side she ducked into a spare slot at the busy bar, then lifted onto her toes and glanced along the bar. Finding no familiar faces at all, she slumped back to her heels in disappointment.

Then stared dreamily at the pink lights dappling her skin,

reflected off a thousand tiny mirrors embedded in the roof above, wishing she could bottle it somehow.

"What can I get you?"

Petra looked up to find a bartender smiling her way. The word *water* danced on her tongue before it was somehow replaced with, "Tequila. Slammer."

The bartender clocked her fob, their private booth coming with its own eye-watering bar tab.

The moment the bartender put the ingredients in front of her she dabbed salt on her wrist, licked it off with a quick determined swipe of her tongue and downed the clear spirit in one go.

Wincing as she bit down on the sliver of lemon, she reached up into her hair, fluffed the roots till her auburn waves settled around her face like a cage of their own. And she let the tequila do what the bubbly had not, sear her fluctuating intuition away.

"Good evening," a male voice said beside her, the cloying scent of cologne following.

"Nope," said Petra, not even turning.

"Let me buy you a—"

"Nope," she said again. Eyes now closed, she smiled as she felt the space beside her cool as the interloper moved away.

But it was short-lived, as soon a wall of heat filled the gap. A deeper male voice said, "Of all the gin joints in all the world."

Only this time the rusty tone made her skin prickle, her breath catch and her instincts rise within her like a hurricane.

Eyes fluttering open, Petra braced herself and turned. But there was no amount of bracing to combat the rush of heat swooping her insides as she came face to face with the man in the battered leather jacket.

"Sawyer," she said on a heady exhalation of breath.

Sawyer Mahoney. Her late brother Finn's best friend. The one who'd gifted her a pink feather all those years ago. The most beautiful man who had ever lived.

The last time she'd seen him in the flesh had been a year or so after Finn died. At her eighteenth birthday party. Where they'd made one of those romcom movie pacts, promising to marry if neither was hitched by her thirtieth birthday. Not that that was why she hadn't seen him since. She didn't think.

Sawyer looked just the same, only different, if that made any sense. His lashes were still impossibly long, though creases now branched from the edges of his clear blue eyes, while sparks of grey glinted within the curls and the thick stubble covering his hard jaw.

It suited him. Boy, did it suit him.

As she stood there, cataloguing every part of him, his mouth cocked at the corner, his expression questioning.

And finally the very fact of him there, *right there*, overwhelmed her completely and Petra threw herself into his arms.

"Whoa," he said, his voice muffled by her hair.

Then, after the merest hesitation, his arms closed around her too. Strong arms, thick, like tree branches. Tightening. As if he too was more than merely glad to see her.

They'd kept in touch over the years. Long, zingy text chains, funny social media comments—his to her, as he never posted a thing—memes shared. Though it had taken Petra a couple of years to realise Sawyer was trying to fill the gap Finn had left somehow.

Not that he'd ever admitted as much.

Not that that was what she'd *ever* wanted from him.

This, she thought, *this was what coming home was meant to feel like.*

Like a pool of warm lamplight. Like curling your feet beneath you on the couch.

Which was why she held on tight, even when she found herself noticing the press of his thighs against hers. The dig of his jeans button at her hip. The scent of him filling her nostrils. No cologne. Just him. Earthy and warm and delicious.

When she began to imagine the grip of his fingers around

her waist shifting, pulling her closer still, she knew it was time to let go. Her ability to see magic where others did not might be her greatest asset when it came to her work, but when it came to Sawyer Mahoney it had always been a one-sided affair.

After indulging in a final deep breath, Petra lifted her head out of the cocoon of his chest and pulled herself completely from the circle of his arms.

"It's so good to see you!" she said, thumping him on the chest with a fist, reminding herself that they were old chums.

Had been since she was fourteen, and he sixteen, and Finn had brought him home from footy practice looking like a Labrador puppy, all muddy limbs and knotted hair, and eyes so clear she'd had to blink to make sure he was real.

Only her fist bounced. He was harder than he used to be. Time had hewn him into solid rock. And if her knees gave way, just a little, she covered it well.

"What are you doing here?" She glanced pointedly at the huge mirror ball over the dance floor, the hot pink bar stools, the confetti painted into the bar.

Sawyer's half-smile kicked higher again. She imagined the deep, sensual bracket bracing the edge of his lips, now hidden beneath a beard, as he said, "Right back at ya, kid."

The bubbles in her blood went *pop-pop-pop*.

Kid. He hadn't called her that since she was, well, a kid. She'd always be Finn's little sister in his eyes, and it was better to remember that than, you know, lust.

"Oh, I'm fancy now," Petra said, hands out, rocking back and forth to show off her pink tulle dress. "Gave up the overalls and bare feet for grown-up clothes a while back now."

His gaze didn't shift, but she felt him take her in. And move closer as the crowd pressed in around them. The music seemed to lift a notch. Faster, deeper, vibrating in Petra's chest now, her belly. Lower.

Before she did something really silly, like sigh, or grab his sleeve and roll it up to see if he still had those amazing veins,

Petra leapt in with, "Aren't you meant to be in Guatemala? Or Istanbul? Or Flub...istan...ovia?"

"Flubistanovia?"

She waved a hand. "I don't keep tabs."

She did, of course. It wasn't that hard.

Just after her eighteenth birthday party he'd run off to become an Australian Football League star—which had been his, and her brother's, dream. After a career-ending injury, he'd been in rehab for months and had used his spare time to fight for better rehab funding for vulnerable kids. Which had won him the Young Australian of the Year award.

To say he was beloved by the press—and therefore easy to cyber-stalk—would be an understatement.

And that was all before he'd co-created Big Think. A *multibillion-dollar future-proof powerhouse focused on world health, innovation and invention, and Third World equity*. Yes, she'd memorised the mission statement on their website by heart.

No wonder he was one of the most written-about men in the country.

As if he could hear her thoughts, he turned a little to face the bar, keeping the crowd at his back. Petra gazed about but couldn't see anyone paying them any attention. Probably because he looked so scruffy, so rough.

"Are you in town long?" she asked, mirroring his pose.

"A bit. A few weeks at least. You?"

"Same," she said, bumping her arm against his, as if needing to make sure he was really there.

"What are the odds?" he said, his voice low.

Something flickered behind the blue, something warm, molten, too quick to catch. And the rubber band feeling was back, tugging her towards him. But, despite the tequila-induced warmth moving through her, she held her ground.

"You here on your own?" she asked.

His mouth quirked. "I was meant to be meeting Ronan."

"Ronan's *here*?" Petra had known Ronan Gerard, one of his Big Think co-owners, longer than she'd known Sawyer, and could picture him in a place like this even less than she could Sawyer.

Sawyer lifted his drink and downed the last sip. "Not, as it turns out. I believe he thought it a great joke to have me come here, straight from the airport, under the guise of an important meeting."

"Ah," said Petra, chuckling.

Like the Gilpins, the Gerards enjoyed the rarefied world of trust funds and private schooling and summers in Europe. Ronan had fought against it, in his own way, whereas Finn had leaned in, enjoying the trappings. Petra had simply *never* fitted in. Ever.

While Sawyer, having come from more humble beginnings, with far more responsibility loaded onto his shoulders from a young age, stood up, fought the good fight and did what had to be done.

"Finding new and interesting ways to amuse himself is a mental health necessity where Ronan's concerned."

Sawyer nodded. Then ran a hand up the back of his neck. Was that dust he'd dislodged, now floating about his head?

She reached and brushed some from his shoulder. "How did they even let you on the plane, looking like this?"

"We have our own jet."

Of course. "Well, you're a grub. Wherever you've come from, you brought it with you."

Spying a few stray flecks, she swiped a finger down the bridge of his nose, her thumb grazing the line of his cheek. She felt him still. Her gaze flicked back to his in time to see a shadow pass over his eyes.

Swallowing, she let her hand drop. And when she caught the bartender's eye she motioned for another drink.

"You never mentioned you were coming home," Sawyer said.

Petra explained her mother's email, the job offer that came

with it, her hope that Deena could help her make some local connections.

In fact... She looked at Sawyer. *He* was a connection. He and Ronan could fulfil her budget with their spare change. Then she could head off into the sunset, having proven to her parents that she was, in fact, pretty fabulous and worthy of their regard.

"You okay there?" Sawyer asked, his gaze dropping to her mouth.

No doubt because she was nibbling on her bottom lip as if it was made of chocolate. "Yep! Fine. Great."

His eyes narrowed, and she felt the shift in him. He stood taller, rolled his shoulders, made himself even bigger somehow. Protection mode engaged. "If you need my help—"

She held up a hand, close enough to his face his eyes crossed slightly. Close enough to feel his breath against her palm. She moved it back. A smidge. "I've got this."

When his eyes found hers they were glinting. "What if I want to help the art?"

Her resolve faltered under the warmth of his tone. "And how would you propose to do that?"

"Say, if the gift shop is selling a poster of a kitten with a funny saying written over it, you could put one aside for me."

"Not dogs playing poker?"

He thought about it then shrugged. "Nah. Kittens all the way."

"Fine," she joked. "That'll be a hundred grand."

"Mercenary." Sawyer flashed a grin.

Petra couldn't help but grin right on back.

For Sawyer was in town. For a bit. As was she.

Yes, her contract with the old Gallery of Melbourne might come with complications, but for the first time since she'd read her mother's email daring her, *ARE YOU UP FOR THE CHALLENGE?* Petra felt a thrill of anticipation rush through her.

"Here you go," the bartender said, placing her tequila on

the bar. He gave Sawyer a second glance, as if trying to place him, before shaking his head.

"Want one?" she asked, lifting her drink. "Or are you going to make me drink alone?"

A muscle flickered under his eye. Then he nodded his acquiescence to the bartender.

A minute later a second tequila shot was lined up beside hers.

Petra flashed her fob. "On me," she explained to Sawyer.

"There's no need. I—"

"I'm paying. Told you I'm a fancy grown-up now."

Sawyer let that sink in before lifting his glass. "What should we drink to? Good health? Good weather?"

"To Finn," she said, closing her eyes and sending out a small happy thought to her brother, as she always did.

She opened her eyes in time to see myriad emotions flashing across Sawyer's eyes—shock, sorrow, and a flicker of something that looked a hell of a lot like guilt.

"Sorry," she said, not quite sure what she was apologising for. "We can toast something else?"

Sawyer pulled everything back inside himself, locked it down, breathed out and shook his head. "No, it's fine. It's a good choice."

It was, right? For Finn was there between them in every conversation they had. When it came down to it, everything they were, everything they were *not*, all came down to Finn.

"You *absolutely* sure?" she asked.

"Petra," he warned. Her name, in that voice, was enough to stop her arguing further.

"Okay then," she said. Then, with gusto enough for both of them, she added, "To Finn."

A muscle ticked in Sawyer's jaw before he nodded, downed the drink in one go and said, "Another?"

Petra knew water was probably a really good idea. But so was flossing, and she didn't do that nearly as much as she ought to. Doing what she was *supposed* to do had never been her thing. That was where her instincts came in. And in that moment they were feeling pretty buzzed.

"Bring it on," she said.

"May as well leave the bottle," Sawyer said, raising his glass to the bartender.

Petra shot Sawyer a look. "Like that, is it?"

"It's been a hard few months," he said.

"Hard?" she said, leaning her chin on her hand and batting her lashes his way.

"Long."

Petra grinned as the words floated between them in a bubble of double meanings, while Sawyer slowly shook his head, trying to hide his smile.

The bartender lined up their drinks, then accepted the sneaky hundred Sawyer passed across the bar.

"Ready?" Petra asked, watching him as she licked the knuckle of her thumb.

"Not even close," he said, shaking his head before licking his knuckle too.

Petra poured salt on the slicks of damp. Took the lemon slice he offered. Then tapped her glass against his.

"To Finn," he said, his voice like sandpaper, as if it was the first time he'd said Finn's name in years.

"To Finn," she echoed back. Strong and sure. Then finished her shot before Sawyer had even lifted his to his lips.

Huge mistake? she thought as she sucked on the lemon slice and looked right into Sawyer's beautiful blue eyes, joy now flooding into all the places her earlier concern had resided.

And that was the final thought she remembered having for some time.

CHAPTER TWO

MONDAY MORNING, dressed in her favourite dark caramel jumpsuit, an autumnal-toned floral jacket and her lucky high-heeled aubergine boots—lucky because she'd been wearing them when a certain crooner had called her *personally* to beg she deck out his Aspen chalet—Petra dropped off her dry-cleaning on her way to her first day at her new job.

Only to find herself stuck, as the woman behind the counter was impressed by what she called the "uber-rummy scent" of one of Petra's dresses.

"Not a rum drinker," Petra assured her.

The woman raised an eyebrow. "Daiquiri, mojito, piña colada, Mai Tai, Dark and Stormy?"

Petra's mouth popped open, ready to assure her otherwise, till she saw the dusky pink tulle and realised it was the dress she'd worn on Saturday night. Meaning she couldn't be sure.

She *thought* she remembered Deena dancing on someone's shoulders. And had there been *karaoke*? There were remnants of a deep and meaningful conversation with someone from the hen night crowd regarding whether it was wrong for a mother of three kids to see a film just because it starred Timothée Chalamet.

What she remembered most vividly, though, was Sawyer. Hugging him so hard she could feel his imprint along her entire body, dusting his nose with a swipe of her finger, curling her hand through his arm and leaning into his meaty shoulder.

But the rest? Not so much.

So Petra merely smiled, asked when her dry-cleaning might be ready, then with big dark sunglasses in place to ward off the last lingering vestiges of Saturday night ickiness she went in search of a hearty breakfast.

Belly full, hot coffee warming her hands, only then did she switch off the Do Not Disturb function on her watch. Her wrist buzzed immediately.

For a second her heart leapt, imagining it might be *him*.

Sawyer had messaged her the day before.

Morning. Hope your head's okay.

She'd assured him it was not, returned a laughing emoji and that was that.

Maybe this time he was calling to ask when they could catch up again. Since they were both in town. At the same time. For a bit.

But no.

Petra found her phone in her bag and read the full message.

DARLING!

Her mother again, with the caps lock on.

ASSUMING YOU'RE ON YOUR WAY TO WORK? FIRST DAY... GOOD IMPRESSION... A REMINDER THAT DISCRETION IS PARAMOUNT. THE GALLERY'S REPUTATION DEPENDS ON IT!

Petra considered using caps lock back, then reminded herself that passive aggression was not her favourite thing. So she typed:

On my way! Ready and raring! Can't wait!

Then, feeling as if she were about to get a sugar toothache, she tossed her phone back in her bag.

This trip had better improve things between them, or they were doomed to play out the Ingenuous Daughter/Disappointed Parent dynamic for ever. And, well, they were now all one another had.

One last quick check of her phone in case she'd missed any important messages—aka any from Sawyer—then Petra grabbed her coffee and made her way down the hill towards the gallery.

Where she planned to magically figure out how to beg for money, from people who didn't know her, in as timely a manner as possible, while not scandalising anyone, or thinking of Sawyer Mahoney much at all.

Around an hour before opening time Petra showed her ID to the lovely old security guard. Before heading up to the admin floor she made a quick trek to the heart of the gallery—the *Then and Now* exhibition, an impressive array of classic Australian art, including a familiar-looking Sidney Nolan painting.

"On loan from the collection of the Gilpin family," she read off the plaque on the wall. It brought with it an unexpected wave of nostalgia.

Petra's big brother Finn had been the golden child. And fully deserved too, for he'd been handsome, smart, funny, athletic and a dauntless extrovert. Exactly the kind of child that well-to-do go-getters like Josiah and Josephine would expect.

Petra, on the other hand, had been dreamy and quiet and odd. The one thing they'd seen eye to eye on was art.

And once they'd realised they couldn't convince Finn to give a jot about painting, Petra had become their go-to companion at any gallery event, given tacit permission to wander freely through the basement collections, and the restoration floor, while her parents did whatever they did to help keep the place running.

The clearing of a throat from a security guard somewhere nearby had Petra shaking off the bittersweets, lifting her chin and making a beeline for the lifts leading to the administrative floor.

Her relief when the lift doors opened was immediate. Behind the scenes, in the messy hustle, was where she belonged.

Petra meandered around big peeling pylons decorated with layers of posters stuck over one another, wrapped in fake ivy and fairy lights, under an amazing domed skylight letting in the weak Melbourne sunshine.

She noted the *many* empty desks, the piles of merchandising material yet to be stored, or tossed. And thought it looked as if they were still moving in. Or in the process of moving out.

In the far corner, according to the information her mother had sent, was HER OFFICE. Petra had been told it would be READY TO USE, so had imagined a utilitarian desk, a chair, a phone. An elegant jail cell.

Imagine her surprise at finding a wall of fantastically rugged exposed brick covered in framed pictures of all the special collections she'd attended as a child. Add a funky cream leather office chair, big blond wood desk, pink blanket thrown over the back of the comfy-looking caramel-coloured sofa and a kidney-shaped coffee table boasting a vase of fresh pink peonies.

Her mother's attempt at making it Petra-friendly? Her intuition hiccupped in surprise.

When her watch buzzed she looked at it through a single squinted eye, in case she was attacked by capital letters, only to find a message from Sawyer.

You've got this.

Grinning, she grabbed her phone and typed back.

Heck, yeah, I do!

"Ms Gilpin!"

Petra looked up to find a petite brunette in oversized glasses standing at her office door. "Hi?"

The young woman swept into the room, leant over the desk and held out a hand. "Firstly, I have to tell you I am such a huge fan. I've watched the video tour of that rapper's ranch a zillion times. The collection you curated is the reason I tacked a fine arts minor onto my business degree."

"Wow. Thank you," said Petra, honestly taken aback. Being a curator meant she was the one behind the art that went into the homes of the kind of people who had fans.

"I'm Mimi, by the way. Your assistant. At least I'd like to be considered for the role."

Petra crossed her legs and sat back. "Do I not already have an assistant?"

Mimi grimaced. "As far as the whispers around here go, you're on your own."

Petra felt a moment of surprise, before she coughed out a laugh. Beautiful office space, but no help. That sounded about right. "May I ask how you survived the redundancies?"

Mimi said, "I'd only been here for three days when it all went down."

"Three *days*?"

Mimi grimaced. "I know, right? My dream job and *whoomph*. Up in smoke before I'd even figured out how to use the coffee machine."

Petra tapped her fingers on her desk. "Figured it out yet?"

Mimi grinned. "Test me."

"Big. Strong. Whisper of milk."

"Coming right up."

Mimi bolted from the room, though she took a moment first to tap something into the computer on the desk just outside Petra's office. "Check your email!" she shouted before hustling off, presumably to make coffee.

Petra pulled her laptop from her bag, turned it on, trailed a finger over the mousepad, to find a message from the desk of Mimi Lashay, Interim Assistant to Petra Gilpin.

Mimi with the Business Degree and Fine Arts Minor had put together a thorough portfolio of the gallery's legacy benefactors, including those who'd lapsed, and made a list of Melbourne's untapped up-and-comers, entitled *Legacy*, *Lapsed* and *Opportunities Missed*.

And Petra wondered which gods she had to thank for Mimi Lashay.

She opened the file and went straight to the latter section. The unexpected was much more her bag than the establishment.

Right up at the top—alongside corresponding accolades, awards, titles and articles, including one entitled *Top Ten Sexiest Single Billionaire Bachelors Under Forty* and an estimate of individual net worth boasting a staggering number of zeroes—were three names she recognised in an instant.

Ronan Gerard, Ted Fincher and Sawyer Mahoney. The cofounders of Big Think Corp.

Petra burst into laughter.

One thing she remembered, for sure, about Saturday night was deciding *not* to ask Sawyer for a donation. The lines of their friendship were blurry enough without giving him explicit permission to go all knight in shining armour.

Though she did take a minute to read Mimi's report before moving on—Mimi had put so much effort into it after all—and quickly found herself flabbergasted at how deep, how wide, their interests ran. Including, hilariously, full ownership of the Gilded Cage, which explained Ronan's choice of location.

With their resources and investments, Big Think could accede and become their own nation.

"Big. Strong. Whisper of milk!"

Petra's hand lifted off her keyboard as if caught watching

porn, only to find Mimi carefully placing the hot coffee on her desk, her eyes on the Big Think page.

"You should totally start there," Mimi said, nodding giddily.

"You think?" Petra said noncommittedly.

"Have you *seen* those guys?" Mimi pulled out her phone and fiddled with the thing, then turned to show Petra a photo of Ted, Ronan and Sawyer in tuxedos at some benefit or another. "They're like a real-life *GQ* spread."

"Mmm…" Petra mmmmed.

"So, the dark frowny one," said Mimi, pointing at Ronan. "His family are off-the-charts wealthy. If we could convince him to flick us his fun money allowance, we'd be golden."

Fun money allowance? Petra hid her laughter behind her coffee as she imagined making that call.

"And the redhead, the big guy in the glasses." Mimi pointed at the picture of Ted Fincher, who Petra had never met. "He's like this amazing science brain. The projects he has in the works, the patents, the tests—game-changing!"

And there was Sawyer: grinning, clean-shaven, so beautiful it hurt to look at him. "What about the last one?" Petra asked, going for nonchalant.

"That's Sawyer Mahoney. He used to be this superstar AFL player. When I was five I had a jersey with his number on the back. My mum claims I cried for a week when he broke his leg. He never played again."

Petra understood Mimi's young crush all too well. "Great job. Honestly."

Mimi grinned and said, "I'll be at my desk if you need me."

Leaving Petra to swing back and forth on her office chair. And think.

Old money, venerable benefactors, dusty family names—that was how the art world had flourished for a long time. That was her parents in a nutshell.

Whereas Petra was most in demand with musicians, movie

execs, crypto success stories, influencers, mumpreneurs. If she could find a way to tap into *that* audience, they might not be dead in the water.

Movement outside her office. More staff were arriving. If Mimi was right, they didn't belong to her. But their jobs still depended on whether or not she could fix the gallery's problems.

Considering the place had not changed a bit since she'd last been there—the same tired displays, same stale heritage wall colours, same scent of antediluvian dust on the back of the tongue—she feared its problems ran deeper than mere funding.

Meaning she needed to get cracking.

Only she couldn't get Sawyer Mahoney out of her head.

She grabbed her phone, pressed call, lent back in her very nice chair and propped her feet up on her very nice desk.

"Mahoney," he answered.

"Sawyer, hi." A hand on her belly to settle the instant swoop, then, "It's Petra."

"Hey," he said, and she felt the deepening of his voice like a fingertip tracing her spine. A few seconds beat past, then the call sounded different. As if he'd pressed the phone closer to his ear. Or closed a door. "Everything okay?"

"Brilliant!" she said, her voice overbright. "You?"

"I'm fine. But I didn't absorb a bottle of tequila on Saturday night."

"Half a bottle," she shot back. For he'd had the other half. Hadn't he? Like an echo, or an echo of an echo, she heard a Kylie song in her head.

It disappeared as Sawyer said, "If you're worried about the picture, Ronan's Doberman of an assistant, Hadley, is on it."

"What picture?"

Silence.

"Sawyer! You can't say something like that then leave me hanging!"

"There's a picture circulating. From the other night."

"Of me?" Petra asked, the words *whiff of scandal* kicking about inside her head.

"Of us."

The Kylie song was back, stronger this time, and Petra's instincts flickered like a pilot light on a cold night. Not quite awake, but stirring. As if there *was* something about Saturday night that she knew she ought to remember. Or was best left forgotten.

"What were we doing?" she asked, now madly typing her name and Sawyer's into the search bar on her laptop, but nothing came up. Nothing new anyway. Only old youth football images from when Finn and Sawyer played together.

"Nothing," Sawyer said. "Just talking."

"Right. Of course." As if they'd ever do anything else! "Is that a concern?"

"Not for me. You, on the other hand, mentioned quite a few times that *what happens at the Gilded Cage stays at the Gilded Cage.* So I was concerned *you* might be concerned."

"Ahh!" Deena's maxim must have made an impact after all. Though... "My mother did make a bit of a big deal about not wanting even a *whiff of scandal* surrounding my appointment. Due to some old behind-the-scenes stuff. So maybe that was on my mind?"

"Right," he said, his voice dropping into protector mode. "Do you want me to continue with the cease and desist?"

"No! That sounds extreme."

She'd been in plenty of press photos over the years. In the background, unnamed, untagged, mere ambience, like the décor she'd curated. "So long as they caught my good side."

A beat. Then, "Which is your good side?"

"Isn't it obvious?"

Another beat, that stretched into several. As if Sawyer knew it was a trap. Which it totally was.

Then, "Sorry, Petra, can you excuse me for a sec?"

"Sure."

The phone muffled as if Sawyer had put his hand over the microphone and she heard his deep voice as he spoke to someone.

Petra tapped her finger against her mouth, popped the call onto speaker, then checked her social media notifications. Bingo! She'd been tagged in a story.

She opened it to find a glaringly bright, colourful image of a bunch of young women in pink veils, the hen night group from the Gilded Cage. And in the background, nibbling on a thumbnail and frowning at her phone was *@petrart*.

How on earth had they found her handle? *Deena*. At the edge of the photo, holding up a glass of bubbly and grinning for all she was worth.

Petra tapped through the rest of the stories. Lots of dancing and toasting. Photos of disco balls and clinking glasses.

A 'who has the longest arm' selfie with a bunch of faces crammed into the shot.

Petra held a finger to the screen, so that the image paused.

For in the background, paying them no heed, she and Sawyer faced one another at the bar. No tag this time, pure coincidence.

Her hand hovered near his chest, her hair tumbled wildly down her back as her face was tipped up to his, the tulle of her skirt lifted as her knee was cocked his way. She could feel the warm crush of the crowd and a heady looseness in her body. Could feel her happiness in that moment with a kind of dizzying assurance.

Then, just before she lifted her finger, she noted his knee was cocked too. In fact, it was touching hers—

"You there?" Sawyer asked.

"Yep!" she squeaked, swiping the story off her screen.

"Was there a reason you called?"

Apart from needing to hear his voice, she could put him

out of her head and get on with her day? "I have a question about the other night."

A pause, then, "All right."

"Did we drink rum?"

A beat, then a bark of laughter, as if he'd been holding his breath. As if he'd been expecting her to ask something else.

"No," he said, before she could imagine what that something might be. Then, "There was tequila. And champagne. Though what you got up to with Deena, and those rowdy hen night girls, before I finally poured you into a taxi, I can't be sure."

Oh. So he'd stuck around, dusty and jet-lagged as he'd been, waiting till she was done for the night. Which ought to have made her growl, considering the whole little sister thing, but instead it made her feel...safe. Made her feel valued.

"Let's have lunch," she said.

"Lunch."

"It's a meal some people enjoy in the middle of the day. I'm thinking I order a salad, steal chips from your plate and make jokes about how much you need a haircut."

Sawyer laughed, a rough-edged hum that did things to her insides that were wholly unfair.

"How's the Elysium sound? Around one."

"Sure," she said, jotting down a note to find out where the heck the Elysium was.

"See you then." He hung up.

And Petra let out a lusty sigh.

A knock at her door, then, "Ms Gilpin?"

Mimi sure knew how to interrupt a daydream. Which, to be fair, happened a lot in the land of Petra. Meaning, this might already be the most perfect relationship she'd ever had.

"What's up?" Petra asked.

"Need another coffee?"

"No. Thank you. But do you want to drag a chair in here and we can work on the Opportunities Missed list together?"

Mini nodded. Ran out of the room. Grabbed her chair, dragged it in and sat. Tablet and stylus at the ready. "So, we ditch the legacy list?"

A small part of her wanted to say yes. To prove, in a big way, that she and her kind, her ways, had merit. But this place was bigger than her.

"Art isn't about gilt frames," Petra said. "It's not about provenance or exclusivity. It's about exploration and empathy, connection and revelation. It bravely leaves itself wide open to interpretation and judgement, from and for everyone. So we won't leave any avenue unexplored when it comes to ensuring its survival."

Mimi said, "Find more donors."

And Petra knew she'd found her assistant. "One more thing."

"Yes, Ms Gilpin?"

"Call me Petra."

They spent the next hour coming up with lists of influencers and young artists and designers and creatives.

When Mimi went back to her desk, Petra grabbed her phone, found the earlier tag, saved the picture of her and Sawyer to her camera roll, before tossing her phone into her bag with only a mild case of self-disgust.

Sawyer flipped his phone, with its beat-up case, back and forth between his hands, a smile tugging at his mouth, a frown pulling at his forehead.

Petra Gilpin, blithely befuddling him for half a lifetime.

He'd been thinking of her all morning, hoping she was settling in okay. On Saturday night, he'd been given a detailed rundown as to the many reasons why she wished she'd not taken on the job.

Then Hadley—Ronan's executive assistant—had sent him the photo, something she liked to do when any of the three of them were photographed in any way that had not been sanctioned by her.

Yes, the photo was innocuous. And, so far, isolated. But Ted had put himself squarely in the firing line a number of months earlier, having taken up with the journalist writing a feature story on him. Ted *did* end up marrying Adelaid, and having a daughter – reaching peak of wholesomeness Hadley was still twitchy.

Sawyer was not interested in Hadley's twitches. His sole interest was to make sure Petra was okay.

Liar, growled a voice in the back of his head.

He growled back.

Fine, so he was also still working his way through all that had gone down at the club. Not that anything had *gone down*. Not really. But he had been…unnerved.

Could have been the surprise at seeing her.

Could also have been the shock of realising just how much time had passed. Last time they'd been together she'd been a dreamy, soft-spoken eighteen-year-old. Saturday night's Petra had been all wild waves and a kind of magnetic self-awareness.

It didn't help that the club had been so packed they'd had to stand danger close all night long. That she'd kept lifting onto her toes to speak into his ear, her breath brushing over his neck again and again and again. As for her story about Russell—

Sawyer shut his eyes tight. Nope. He was not going to think about Russell. Ever again.

Now, it seemed—considering the rum query—that *she* didn't remember all that had gone down. Not that anything *had* gone down. Not really.

But maybe it was best it stayed that way. They could put a line under Saturday night and move on.

Using the murmur of voices on the other side of the hallway wall as a lifeline, Sawyer ducked through the doorway of the near-mythical Big Think Founders' Room they'd allotted for themselves when designing the fancy-schmancy new Big Think Tower. Anyone outside the group would be dismayed to find it looked—and sometimes smelled—a heck of a lot like the university lounge in which they'd first become friends.

Sawyer opened the door to find Hadley standing darkly in the doorway. He swore, all but tripping backwards over himself to avoid smacking into her.

Ted looked up from his spot on the dilapidated old blue lounger that used to belong to his dad, then back at the research paper he'd been annotating.

Ronan barely spared him a glance from what looked like a throne at the head of the table. "Finally ready to join us, Mahoney?"

Sawyer rubbed discreetly at his leg. Specifically, the scar tissue beneath which pins held his leg together. Then he narrowed his eyes at Hadley, before giving her a dramatically wide berth.

"A lot to get through," Ronan drawled. "Considering how long it's been since we were all in the same room."

Knowing that was a dig at him for taking an extra few weeks at the end of his last trip. But the chance to work one-on-one with actual communities, actual people, rather than committees, or governments, or bureaucrats he was assigned to, had been too rewarding to pass up.

Though, as per usual, having taken a rare chance to do something for himself, he was now paying for it.

"Begin away," Sawyer allowed magnanimously. Straddling a chair, he grabbed a handball from the bowl that lived permanently on the table for his use.

"Hadley?" Ronan demanded.

Hadley glared at Ronan for a moment before turning to Sawyer. "Any idea how long you'll be in town this time?"

Sawyer thought of his mum's phone calls, her growing concerns for his youngest sister, Daisy. The weight of familial responsibility that had finally tugged him home.

Then he thought of Petra. Her insistence they have lunch.

"For a bit," he said.

"Excellent," said Hadley. "The Big Think Ball is coming up in a few months, so this is prime schmooze time. We don't need any antics that will pull focus. Ted has been forced to pull your weight, Mahoney, so you're going to make up for it."

"Suits me," said Ted, offering a thumbs-up.

Sawyer rubbed his leg again.

Not that it hurt. More a phantom echo. One that seemed to appear any time he was forced to smile and wave and stick to the neat and tidy Big Think origin story.

Of course he was grateful to have broken his leg playing footy. Otherwise he'd never have learnt about the disparity in rehab between the haves and have-nots, which had sent him back to university to study Social Work and International Relations. Which was how he'd met doctorate student Ted Fincher and MBA candidate Ronan Gerard.

Not that he had any intention of sharing the other moments in his life that had brought him to that point.

"Why do they call you the brawn of Big Think? Is that a reference to your football days?"

"My dad died when I was eight, making me the man of the house, so doing what has to be done is the only way I know how to be."

"And what motivated you to be such a fierce competitor? If you'd played with a little less vigour, might you have saved your sporting career?"

"I broke my leg playing footy; my best friend broke his neck. I was lucky, while Finn, at nineteen, had barely begun to grow into his own possibilities. Since that day I've felt it my duty to achieve enough for the both of us."

Not that he believed either of those happenstances were his

fault. But his literal job, on the team, was to be the hard man, protecting Finn's flights on the wing. How could he not help wondering: what if he'd been there that day, rather than off on a representative footy camp? Would it have happened at all?

Sawyer grabbed another ball, juggled them with one hand.

"Can you commit to all of this?" Hadley asked, holding up her tablet.

Sawyer looked up, realised she was talking to him.

"Have you been paying attention at all?" Hadley asked.

"Some." He grinned, the kind that distracted. "I'm assuming you each gave a speech, in thanks, as to how much I achieved in Big Think's name these past months. Then apologised for being so slow at doing your bit and giving more world-saving projects to go out there and hawk."

Ted grinned, Ronan muttered under his breath, and Hadley snorted. Then death-stared him for daring to make her succumb to such indignity.

"You assumed wrong," Hadley said.

"Ah. Then, till then I'm yours to wield as you see fit. Except—" said Sawyer.

"Here we go," Ronan grumbled.

"Except lunchtime today. I'm busy."

"Doing what?" Hadley asked, frowning at her tablet.

"Having lunch." Sawyer tossed a ball and caught it behind his back. "With Petra."

At that Ronan's gaze finally lifted. "Petra *Gilpin*?" For Ronan and Petra had known one another as kids, running in the same Brighton rich kid circle.

Hadley said, "I'm assuming this is the same Petra Gilpin with whom you were photographed in a nightclub looking like a caveman who'd slept in a cement factory. Said photo you want taken down under threat of death and dismemberment."

"About that," said Sawyer, clicking his fingers at Hadley. "Turns out it's not a problem after all."

Hadley rolled her eyes before tapping at her tablet, likely sending a directive to whichever shadowy figure or family member of hers took care of such things.

Ronan tapped his fingers on the desk. "Petra is doing well for herself these days. Her parents are old money. And none of them are Big Think benefactors. Romance her at lunch. See if she or her parents might come on board."

Sawyer tossed the ball again, but he missed completely. The thing bounced off the table, then off at an angle, just missing Ted, before landing in a pot plant in the corner.

He had zero intention of *romancing* Petra. Protecting her, the way her brother would have, had he still been around; that was his purview where she was concerned.

Hadley swept her stylus over her tablet and Sawyer's battered old phone buzzed on the table. "Your calendar is now updated."

He hopped out of the chair when his leg began to hurt for real, and moved to a spare couch along the back wall. Twisting to lie back, his feet on the opposite armrest, he continued to toss the ball.

Till the familiarity of the banter, the mind-boggling ideas thrown about, the determination in that room to actually make a difference, settled over him like a warm blanket.

For it was a rare room in which he could justly share the weight of responsibility and didn't feel the burning duty to shoulder all. Only because the people in that room wouldn't have allowed him in otherwise.

CHAPTER THREE

"I'D FORGOTTEN HOW wild Melbourne traffic can be. And I lived near the Arc de Triomphe for two years," said Petra, as she dropped her big soft bag onto the table and flumped dramatically into the chair across from Sawyer.

Sawyer said nothing, for he was still coming out of the fog that had descended over him at the sight of her sweeping into the restaurant, all long and loose and so comfortable in her own skin she shone with it.

"How's your first day so far?" he asked.

"Strange," she said, "but not terrible. How about you? Ronan as painful as ever?"

"More so with every passing year."

"Ha." She gave him another quick smile, before looking around the hotel restaurant. No doubt clocking the stark white walls, the neon art, the chunky composition which was as natural to her as breathing.

"What do you think?" he asked.

"It's…sunny."

He laughed, for she sounded as if she was making polite noises regarding his hovel under a park bridge. It was refreshing to find that although Petra had taken herself out of Melbourne, you couldn't quite take the Gilpin out of her. Not that she'd want to hear that.

Then she was flicking through her phone, before sliding it across the table. "I found the photo's origin, by the way—the one from the other night. One of the hen night girls put it on her Instagram."

Sawyer looked, jaw clenching. For it wasn't, in fact, the same picture at all.

The one Hadley had sent him had been much closer, taken over Petra's shoulder. A deliberate shot taken of him, looking, as Hadley had pointed out, more caveman than billionaire philanthropist.

This one, while incidental, was far more provocative. The way they curled towards one another, her hand pressed against his chest, their knees touching. Anyone seeing this image would be forgiven for thinking they were moments from—

Nothing. Nothing had happened. So it wasn't even worth considering.

Sawyer handed back the phone. "If it concerns you, I can still do something about it. We have ways and means."

"Like what?"

"The blushing bride?" He mimed a finger slicing across his throat.

Petra barked out a laugh, her mouth wide, her eyes sparking devilishly. And while it felt so familiar, so her, it hit him just how much she'd changed, her gentle sweetness having morphed into effortless cool.

"Not necessary," she said, before looking to her phone for a moment, her tongue darting out to wet her lower lip, before she put it away.

"Now, I have a bone to pick with you." She waggled a finger at him. "Why didn't you tell me you own the Gilded Cage?"

Sawyer sat back in his seat, glad to have moved on. "I did."

"When?"

"Saturday night. Some time between 'Copacabana' and 'Raspberry Beret'."

She blinked at him, clearly trying to remember the moment. But, as he'd expected, her memory was patchy.

"And you own *this* place too," she said accusingly. "I looked it up."

"Big Think does, yes."

Petra pointed a thumb over her shoulder. "Is that why there's a photographer in the bushes outside?"

The hairs rose on the back of Sawyer's neck and his feet flattened against the floor. "Did he bother you? Is he still out there, do you think?"

"What? No!" She held up both hands in surrender. "I mean, he kind of looked like a tourist in his khakis and matching puffer jacket, so he was probably just taking a photo of the hotel and I got in the way."

Maybe. But maybe not. People taking photos of him was one thing, anyone making Petra feel uncomfortable was quite another.

"Drink?" Petra asked, changing the subject and catching the attention of a passing waiter.

She asked for a particular brand of iced tea, it was pink. It made Sawyer smile. So he ordered the same.

After the waiter left, her smile turned down at the corners. "What? Is there something on my face?"

Caught staring, Sawyer leant in, stared harder. "Just reconciling the Petra sitting before me with Petra at fourteen. You and your pink feathers, and stones, and sea glass and whatnot. You had bowls of the stuff all over the house."

She flicked her napkin and laid it across her lap, then lifted narrowed eyes his way. "I like what I like."

"That much was clear."

"To you, maybe," she said.

"It was," he reiterated, aware that her parents had favoured her brother. "Though fourteen-year-old Petra was a girl of compelling contradictions. Off with the fairies one minute and screaming at footy umpires if they did me wrong the next."

Petra's eyes widened, as if surprised he'd noticed. It had

been hard not to, for she'd been the third musketeer, always around. When not yelling at umpires, she'd been so unruffled—by Finn's boisterousness, or her parents' vexation. Coming from his crazy house, with his loud sisters and despairing mother, her sweet unflappability had been a balm.

"Then you turned fifteen," he said, "and began sighing moodily over paintings by... Who was it? Caravaggio?"

At that, Petra leant her chin on her hand and batted her lashes. "All those men with their big muscles and sweaty limbs. Their faces, twisted in pleasure."

"Pain," Sawyer said, his throat a little tight. "I think you'll find their faces were twisted in pain."

"Same-same," she said, before she turned and smiled at the waiter who'd brought their drinks.

Allowing Sawyer to breathe out. Hard. And shift on his seat.

Petra ordered her salad, and for Sawyer steak and chips.

"Charge it to room 1201," he said, before the waiter nodded and left.

"What? You're actually staying *here*?" said Petra. "In a *hotel*?"

"I believe we just established that it's a very nice hotel."

"I'm sure, but—"

"Twenty-four-hour room service. A dozen cabanas by the pool. Award-winning design. And the beds are like sleeping on a cloud."

"I'll take your word for it."

An innocent response, and yet something flashed between them. A spark. Some acknowledgement that time and distance had both of them seeing one another with fresh eyes.

Then she levelled him with a look that was pure Petra. "Unlike me, *you* actually live in Melbourne. And I know you can afford it, Mr Big Shot. If you didn't fork out for houses for your entire family the moment you could, I'll eat my boots. And these are my lucky boots. So, what gives?"

"I travel more than I don't, so I don't see the point."

"Where's all your stuff?"

"What stuff?"

She coughed and spluttered, as if unable to compute the thought of living out of a suitcase permanently. "Your stuff! Your things, your treasures, your memories. Your art!"

"I think we established my eye for art is less than exemplary."

"Rubbish. If you know when something feels beautiful to you, then you understand art."

Another moment of eye-contact, another spark.

Sawyer squinted towards the bar. "An unused house is surplus to requirements. Nothing but a big dust-collector. A blight on the environment."

"Mmm," she said, unable to curb her smile as she sipped at her pink drink through a striped paper straw.

"So where are *you* staying?" he asked. "With Josiah and Josephine?"

Petra choked on her drink. "Apartment in the city," she eventually managed. "A six month lease."

"I bet it's nice."

Her mouth twitched, a delicate arc flashing at one corner. "It's getting there. Two bedrooms. Two bathrooms. Too big really, for one person. In fact—"

She stopped and came to a conclusion he ought to have seen coming.

"Stay with me!" she said.

"We're a little old to play sleepover, don't you think?"

"Seriously, the apartment is huge. It's fully furnished. I have a cleaner. Groceries delivered every three days. I'll be working a lot, so you'd barely see me."

"You say that as if it's a selling point." Yeah, even he heard the note of dissent in his voice with that one.

And again that spark seemed to flash between them. Like a crackle of lightning forming in mid-air.

"We *never* see one another anyway, Sawyer. The fact that we are both here now, it feels like serendipity. Don't you think?"

He did think. He just wasn't sure that was what he should be thinking.

"You *just* said I'd never see you," he said, prevaricating.

"Ignore what I said. I'm riffing here."

Sawyer laughed. Only a Gilpin would consider a real estate deal riffing.

"No pool cabanas, but the showers are phenomenal. Both rainforest and wall-mounted heads. With several settings. Not that I've tried them all out," she said, before he had the chance to go there. Then, with a very grown-up grin, followed up with, "Only because I haven't had the time."

And, just like that, Russell popped into his mind.

Dammit. He'd tried really hard to forget there was a Russell. Without even the slightest measure of success. Another reason why staying with her would *not* be a good idea.

She plucked her oversized bag from the table and pulled out a set of keys, slipped one free and slid it across to him. "I'll text you the address and let Security know I'll have a guest."

"Petra," he warned, overwhelmingly sure that he needed to simply say no.

"Come on!" she said. "You can be my guard-dog. Any robbers scouting the street would take one look at you, with your battered jacket and all your tats, and this new bad boy beard you have going on, and they'd move on fast."

Sawyer's back teeth ground. Did she know she'd just pulled out the single reason why he'd agree to such a scenario? The knowledge he'd be right there if anything happened.

"I'll think about it," he growled.

"Brilliant. Now, is it warm in here or is it just me?" she said, sliding her floral jacket free and laying it over the back of her chair.

No, Sawyer thought, it wasn't just her. The spark had found kindling, the temperature only rising as Petra lifted her hair from her neck before twirling it over one shoulder.

Sawyer deliberately racked focus, only to find she was wearing the thin gold necklace Finn had given her one Christmas.

He knew as he'd helped pick it out…

"Rose gold."

"What now?" Finn asked as they stood outside the jewellery store.

"She'd like the rose gold."

Heat crept up Sawyer's neck as Finn looked at him as if he were speaking another language.

"It's kind of pink. Look."

He gave Finn a shove and pointed in the direction of three necklaces draped over a puffy velvet pillow—one normal gold, one silver and one rose gold.

"Oh, yeah! You're right."

Finn put him in a headlock before they shuffled inside.

"Where would I be without you?"

Sawyer blinked, his chest tight, uncomfortably so, as he looked up to find two girls in their late teens linking elbows and staring at him.

"It's not him!" said one. "He doesn't have a beard. And he's not that old."

"You're Sawyer Mahoney, right?" said the other.

Sawyer thought about telling them no. With the beard, a random accent, he could probably fake his way out of it. Then he remembered Hadley and her rabid insistence they play extra nice till the Big Think Ball.

He said, "So, I've been told."

"Told you! Can we, like, have a selfie?" said one.

"Her mum *loves* you," said the other.

Petra snorted from the other side of the table.

One of the girls was already leaning in towards him and holding her phone at arm's length up high in the air. "She'll totally scream when she hears we met you."

A few click-click-clicks and they were done.

One of the girls jerked back when she noticed belatedly that Sawyer had company. To Petra she said, "Are you somebody?"

Petra waved her hands madly and said, "Not even slightly."

"Okay. Well, thanks!" And with that the girls bounced off, giggling and checking their phones.

Petra squinted at him. "Is *that* normal for you?"

"It comes in waves. And usually only when I'm home."

She leant her chin on her hand, no batting lashes this time. "So when you're *not* here you have anonymity. That must be a relief. Unless you *love* the fawning fans. The sighing girls. The adoring mums."

"It's a hardship, but I cope."

"Mmm. So if we keep hanging out, what *are* the chances of getting through drinks or dinner without someone taking your photo?"

"Slim to fair."

"Meaning I might end up in more photos that give Hadley hives."

"Chances are."

She looked at him for a long while then, her mouth twisting side to side. "So long as you don't rob a bank, or trip an old lady, or say 'art sucks' while with me, then I can't see any problem with the world knowing we are friends."

Not his best friend's little sister, and her big brother's best friend. Friends of their own accord. Surely he could handle that too.

Then she looked at him as if it was her turn to reconcile Sawyer at sixteen with the man before her now.

He'd been knackered by then, working two jobs, playing

footy any chance he had, when not looking after his mum and sisters.

But he'd also been *sixteen*, and fuelled by hot air and ambition. Determined to be scouted by an AFL team. Family folklore telling tales of how his dad had nearly made it to the big leagues, but not quite. While also quietly hoping that life might give him an out. A chance to carve out his own niche.

He didn't realise he was rubbing his leg till his knuckles cracked with the effort.

"How do you cope?" Petra asked.

"With?"

"Attention. Photographers. Fans. People telling you how amazing you are all the time. The pressure. The *judgement*."

Sawyer ran a hand up the back of his neck, to find he really could do with a haircut. "I engage, but don't encourage. I smile, take the photo and thank them, as if it was my idea. I never deny any accusation, no matter how wacky, as my denial will become the story. You want to control your own narrative as much as you can. Do all that and it's over sooner rather than later."

"You could just tell them to eff off."

Sawyer laughed. "I could. If not for the very real fear Hadley would have my guts for garters."

Petra grinned. "You're a saint. Are you even real?"

"Pinch me," he said, holding out an arm, "and I'll let you know."

She didn't pinch him. Or even deign to glance down. Neither did he, caught as he was by the slight hook at the corner of her mouth. The humour in her eyes.

When they'd done nothing but look into one another's eyes for a few seconds, she broke into a grin. Then a bout of breathy laughter. Patently glad to be with him.

He wanted to tell her how good it was to see her again. How much he'd missed her lightness, her smile, her ease. Missed the way she'd never wanted anything from him bar his company. A quality he'd not realised was so rare, how precious, till now.

Then their food arrived, the steak steaming, the salad gleaming. And the moment was gone.

Later that evening, after sending a zillion expressions of interest packages to their A-list of possible new donors, Petra turned the key in her apartment door. Slowly, quietly.

Then poked her head around the door and listened.

"Hello?"

No response. Meaning no Sawyer. Her heart sank.

She swung open the door, threw her keys, bag and tote containing the pack of pink fairy lights and the triptych of happy face paintings she'd picked up in a small shop on the way back to the apartment on the hall table. Then unzipped her aubergine boots, dragged them off one by one and let them fall where they may.

Twirling her hair into a messy bun and rubbing her neck, tight from spending so many hours behind an actual desk, she chose a playlist on her phone and cast it to a portable speaker, the music playing throughout the vast space taking the edge off the quiet.

Then, pulling a bottle of red from the fridge, she poured herself a glass and a half, pressed it to her cheek and stared into the fridge.

What had she been thinking? Asking Sawyer to stay with her. Expecting him to say yes!

Catching up some more would be fantastic. And just being in the same room as the man, for as long as she could have him, would fill her fantasy bank for a good long while.

But she wasn't back *for* him.

She was there to save a crumbling institution she now she feared was being mismanaged on multiple levels, all while proving to her parents that trusting her had been a good decision.

The last thing she needed was a distraction. And Sawyer was as big a distraction as she was likely to find.

Shutting the fridge door, the apartment grew dark, the only light coming through the gauzy curtains covering the balcony doors.

Petra padded towards the view, opened the sliding door and stepped outside, a rush of cool evening air pressing against her, the lights of Melbourne twinkling back—

"Hey."

Petra cried out, sloshing her wine over the rim and spinning to find Sawyer splayed out in one of the outdoor chairs.

Jacket gone, he wore jeans and T-shirt, tattoos poking out under the edge of the sleeve and over his shoulders. One bare foot up on the table, hand gripping some battered paperback with the cover falling off. She could not have painted a hotter picture if she'd tried.

"Hi," she said, her voice breathless, her heart stammering in her chest.

"You okay?" he asked.

His instant protectiveness was enough to take the edge off, turning her attraction to the guy down from a strong eleven to a ten point five.

"Yep! Just didn't realise you were here."

He leaned forward, dropping both feet to the floor, taking up even more of the small space. "I mean your neck."

She was rubbing at it still, her fingers pressing deep. "I'm fine. Not used to sitting for so long."

"I give a mean massage," he offered.

Oh, she bet he did. But crushing on him from a distance she could do. Had done, for ever. Massages, mean or otherwise, were a definite no-go zone.

Maybe she'd try out that fancy showerhead after all. On her neck. Yep, just her neck.

She let her hand drop and said, "So what did you do with the rest of your day?"

A quick frown, then a longer smile. "Visited home."

"How's your mum?"

"Good. Great, actually. Besotted with her grandkids. Though she thinks I need to take a break. Slow down."

Petra snorted. "You'd go off your tree if you didn't keep yourself busy."

A smile hooked at the corner of his mouth. "True."

Petra basked in the fact she knew him better than his own mother.

Sawyer kept smiling at her, while looking all warm and comfortable and delicious. And big and hot and tattooed. And—

"Nice nails," she blurted, in need of a subject change.

He knew it too, by the flicker of his mouth. But he let it go, wriggling his purple, glittery, messy toes as he said, "When I popped in to see Mum my sisters turned up within minutes. And everyone stayed for dinner."

Sawyer's family were a rowdy bunch. Rambunctious, noisy and really close. And they leaned on him like crazy. Had done after his dad died when he was really young. A little too much, from what she'd gathered, but she was hardly the expert when it came to healthy family dynamics.

"And how's Daisy?" Petra's favourite, bar Sawyer, of course.

"Not sure," he said, brow furrowing. "She wasn't there. She's proving to be hard to get a hold of."

"Right." From memory, Daisy had always been the black sheep of the Mahoney clan—creative, rebellious. "I remember her being a lot like me. She adores *you*. Keep trying, she'll relent."

Sawyer shot her a look, and it took her a moment to realise

that the way she'd worded things she'd made it sound as if she adored him too. Which she did. She just had no intention of telling him so.

Petra turned away, leant against the balcony and said, "Pity she wasn't there, though. She'd have done a better job on that pedicure than your other sisters."

Sawyer laughed, the sound deep and rough and chaotic to her senses. "My five-year-old niece painted the left," he explained. "Four-year-old nephew painted the right."

"Sure sure," she said, glancing over her shoulder in time to catch a quick grin. The kind that came with canines, and a glint in those clear blue eyes.

"Did you find your room?" she asked, looking back into the apartment. "Mine's the one closest to the kitchen."

"I figured it out."

Which was when Petra remembered—having left the apartment that morning not expecting company, she'd not thought to tidy up. Had she put her undies in the dirty clothes basket or were they draped over the end of her bed? Bed, for sure. Having grown up in a house that looked like something from a magazine she liked a little noise in her home, a little lived-in mess. And—

Oh, no. What about *Russell*? Awake crazy early, filled with nerves and the last vestiges of tequila, she'd brought him out that morning. Had she put him away? Too late now!

As for Sawyer's room—she'd have to avert her eyes any time she passed. The last thing she needed was to discover what kind of underwear *he* wore. Or to see his toothbrush leaning nonchalantly, intimately, in a glass on his sink.

Sawyer lifted an eyebrow slowly and she realised she was staring.

"So, you've eaten?" she asked, her voice peppy.

"I've eaten."

"Me too. Wine?"

"I'm good."

"Okay. Well, I'm going to—"

She was going to say *have a shower*, but thought better of it. She didn't need to imagine him imagining which shower-head setting she might use. Not that he would. Argh!

"I'm going to string up some lights I bought today, then head to my room to get some work done. Then sleep."

"'Night, Petra," Sawyer said.

"'Night, Sawyer," she said, then hotfooted it inside.

Reminding herself that as hot and delicious as he'd looked on her balcony, she had to be sensible here.

Sawyer had been the one constant through her life. Her biggest support. Her parents might never have understood her choices, but she had *someone* on her side. She couldn't mess with that. Couldn't lose that. For she wasn't sure who she'd be without it.

After finding places for the lights and the paintings, Petra downed her wine in one go, rinsed the glass and turned it upside down by the sink, before she hotfooted it into her room. Where she planned to stay till the next morning.

Some plans simply weren't meant to be.

"How is it that I heard from Deena Singh's aunt that you spent the night with Sawyer Mahoney?" Josephine Gilpin said by way of hello.

It took Petra a couple of seconds to make the connection.

Petra said, "I wasn't aware you knew Deena's aunt."

"It's late," her mother said on a sigh. "Humour me. Is it true?"

Petra rubbed her forehead. "Sawyer and I didn't *spend the night*...we bumped into one another a couple of nights ago. When I was out with Deena."

Letting her mother know he was asleep didn't feel necessary. Besides, her parents had always liked Sawyer. How could they not when he'd been so close to their son?

But there was a strange tightness in her mother's voice. Was it still about *Finn*? The same way Sawyer had baulked when she'd brought Finn up, her mother never talked about him. Ever. There was a pandemic of silence in the people around her. And it was not healthy.

Petra sat on the edge of her bed, curling her feet into the rug. "You know what? Finn's birthday is coming up soon. Maybe we can all—"

"Shoo. Shoo," her mother said. Then, "Honestly, those old man bike riders in their shiny Lycra. It's obscene. I've told your father that if he even thinks of taking it up, he can think again."

So much for that, then.

"Where are you?"

"In the car. On my way to the hospital." Where she'd been the head of Thoracic Surgery for the past fifteen years. "I'm on the Bluetooth. One of your father's old article clerks had to set it up for me."

Petra heard the words that had been left unsaid: *Because Finn's not here to do it.* Finn the tech whiz, as opposed to Petra, who'd spent her tech-learning years mooning over moody paintings by long-dead Dutchmen.

She ran a hand over her forehead. "So, quick update on the gallery. I have a great assistant named Mimi. We have a plan in place to lure fresh money—"

"We trust you have it all in hand."

Petra blinked. They did? Well, of course they did, or they'd not have asked for her help. It was just they'd never said anything of the sort. Out loud. To her.

Meaning maybe she should try one more time. "So, Finn's birthday—"

"I'm nearing the hospital. Must go."

Then Petra found herself on the end of a dead call as her mother hung up.

Wide awake now, Petra poked her head out of the bedroom door, waited till she was sure Sawyer wasn't around, then snuck into the lounge.

She switched on the fairy lights she'd bought that afternoon, smiled at the way the pink lights dappled her skin, a kitsch twist on the fantastical lighting in the Gilded Cage, and knew she'd use it in a show one day.

Lying back on the couch, TV on mute in the background so as not to wake Sawyer, she read an article on her phone about a new local art prize, making notes on how the gallery might opt in.

Not imagining Sawyer in the spare room. Stretched out on the king-sized bed, wearing flannel PJs, or T-shirt and boxers—or nothing at all—tattooed arms akimbo, one knee cocked, the sheet draped just so—

"Hey," Sawyer's deep voice said from just behind her.

Petra screamed, arms flailing, the image she'd been building in her head exploding into glitter.

"You have to stop doing that!" she cried, cricking her neck to find him standing behind the couch. The blue light of the TV playing over his face, the T-shirt he'd worn earlier and his jeans, the top button unsnapped as if he'd only just pulled them on.

"Doing what?" Sawyer asked, his voice low, rusty, in the cool quiet of the night. Leaning to curl his hands over the back of the couch, right near her shoulder.

"Just...being there."

A raise of the eyebrows. "What happened to *'Stay with me, Sawyer...fight off the robbers for me, Sawyer'*?"

Petra coughed out a dumbfounded laugh, glad the darkness could hide the heat shooting up her neck. "For a big guy you have delicate footsteps, just saying."

"I have really good arches." He pushed away and padded slowly around the couch. "Back in the day, when my teammates were starting to suffer from collapsing arches, mine were perfect. Our team podiatrist used that exact word."

"Was she young? And female?"

Sawyer grinned, his teeth a flash of white in the low light. Petra rolled her eyes.

"Thought you'd gone to bed," said Sawyer.

"Couldn't sleep. You?"

"Jetlag still playing havoc. I think."

In the quiet that followed, Petra considered heading back to her room. Tossing and turning till eventually she fell asleep. But she'd convinced him to stay with her, to spend time with her, so why not make the most of it?

"Sit," she said, pointing to the matching single-seater.

Sawyer either misread her instruction or ignored it and he moved to *her* couch, lifted her feet, sat and plonked her feet on his lap.

Her instincts buzzed, a little pre-warning warning. She told them to shush. She had this.

"What you watching?" he asked.

She somehow tore her gaze away from his big warm hands resting on her bare ankles to glance at the screen. "I wasn't watching; not really." Then, *"Camille Claudel."*

They watched in silence for a minute, his thumb moving on her ankle, tracing the bone, before he asked, "What's it about?"

Art. French. Restrained desire and impossible attraction. She'd been obsessed with it in her teens. No two guesses as to why she'd felt a sudden nostalgic need to watch.

"Rodin," she said. "And his relationship with sculptor Claudel."

The only sounds in the room were their steady breaths, the occasional squeak of the couch and the hum of the fridge in the kitchen behind them.

Petra grabbed the remote and turned up the volume, and quickly found herself caught up in the language, the angst, the tension, the longing looks the leads shared on the screen.

"If you'd asked teenage me what I wanted to do with my life, I'd have said art school. But really, *that* was my dream."

"To sculpt?" Sawyer asked.

"To inspire."

Sawyer's hand stopped moving. She braved a look his way to find his eyes glued to the screen, his jaw tight. The night air felt thick around her.

Yeah, it was time to go to bed.

She made to move, to gather her feet towards her. Only Sawyer's thumb pressed into the arch of her foot. Finding the exact spot her favourite boots hurt by the end of a long day.

"This okay?" Sawyer asked, his gaze sweeping back to her, the usual clear blue all dark and smoky. "That same podiatrist taught me a trick or two."

"I bet she did."

Sawyer laughed softly, but did not, Petra noticed, deny the insinuation. Or stop massaging her foot. All intense, painful pleasure. The kind that hurt but you let it happen in the hopes it would soon feel so, so good.

His voice was low as he said, "My fourteen-year-old dream was to wake up and find one of my sisters had turned into a brother. Not quite so lofty as yours."

And Petra laughed, grateful to have been given a reprieve. "I loved having a big brother. Not sure Finn would have said the same about having me as a sister some of the time."

At that Sawyer stilled. And it felt as if all the air had been sucked from the room.

It had been such a long time since Finn's accident. Petra still felt the loss of him, for sure, but she'd chosen to take that empty space and fill it with all the best memories.

She'd long since wondered if Sawyer had filled this empty space by looking out for her.

She opened her mouth to address it somehow. To talk about Finn in a way that didn't make him flinch.

But then he pressed harder again, running his thumb along the pad of her foot. And every thought fled her head as she focused on the magic of his touch.

The movie played on. Sawyer's strong hands moved from her foot, to her ankle, then up her calf. And Petra let it happen.

Till Sawyer shifted, his body rolling against the couch, as if relieving some discomfort.

When she realised she'd braced her spare foot against his thigh, in the effort at keeping herself still, her eyes flickered open to find Rodin undressing Camille, her dress falling off one shoulder, his mouth tracing kisses along her collarbone.

She didn't have to glance at Sawyer to know he was watching it too. She could feel it in the sweep of his hands, moving in time with the vision on the TV.

It was so freaking sensual Petra could barely stand it.

And when he let her go, his hands reaching for her other foot, it was too much. She jerked away from the touch. The fact that she was so turned on her whole body hummed.

"You sure?" he asked. "You might walk funny if I don't even you up."

Yes, it was dark, and yes, it was night, but there was no mistaking the heat in his eyes. The way his nostrils flared as he dragged in a breath. And while she might dream that she was the one making it happen, she was well aware of the allure of nineties French cinema.

Slowly, lest he try to stop her, lest she let him, Petra dragged her feet over the crest of his hard thigh and onto her end of the couch.

"I'm sure. So tired," she said, feigning a yawn as she heaved herself to standing, her limbs a little shaky. "Shall I turn off the TV?"

Sawyer sank deeper into the couch, hitching his jeans in a way that had Petra's mouth watering. "I'm invested now. Got to see how it ends."

She considered telling him Claudel was later committed after exhibiting signs of paranoia—aka accusing Rodin of stealing her work—but instead went with, "It's French. If you like a happy ending, keep your expectations low."

His grin felt real. Like a gift. Then he held out his fingers to give them a stretch as if he too could still feel her skin beneath their touch. And it was enough to send Petra scooting back to her bedroom.

Where she fell face first onto her bed, her body thrumming as if she were wearing the wrong skin.

She glanced at her bedside drawer, where Russell was tucked up alseep, and whimpered at the knowledge that he was far too noisy to bring him out to play.

CHAPTER FOUR

THE NEXT MORNING Petra waited till she was in the lift before pulling on her ankle boots. She'd not dared risk the *chock-chock-chock* of her heels, or the loud *burr* of the espresso machine, in case she woke Sawyer.

As far as she could tell, he wasn't up yet. While the couch where she'd left him, all long and warm and gorgeous, had been tidied, as if the night before had never happened.

But what had happened? A movie night between mates with a quick platonic foot rub thrown in. Nothing at all!

Petra waved to the security guard behind the front desk, slid her big sunglasses onto her face and headed out into early morning grey.

To find a guy pointing his phone her way.

She shot him a quick smile, innate politeness kicking in, before she made to go down the hill, only he moved to step in her way. Which was when she noted the khakis and matching puffer jacket. It was the same guy from outside Sawyer's hotel. Meaning this was actually happening.

Instinct had her holding up her hand in front of her face. Instinct *then* had her dropping it when she realised it only made her look like some poor man's Greta Garbo.

"You and Sawyer Mahoney?" he said, looking at her through the viewfinder. "You guys shacked up? What's your name?"

She'd had a little media experience, but the questions had been directed to the artists, had not been about *her*.

This was very different. She could feel his judgement. Feel his antagonism. As if this stranger had taken one look at her and decided she was lacking.

"Who do you think you are?" the guy asked, or maybe he'd just asked her name again.

Either way, her vision began to blur, her ears hummed, the way they had when she was a kid and her parents had paraded her before their friends and colleagues. Their gazes hard as they waited to see how she might fail them yet again.

The urge to spin back into the apartment building was a strong one. But she wasn't a kid any more. She wasn't failing anyone either. And she had to get to work.

Enough blood rushed back to her feet that she was able to remember some of Sawyer's instructions:

"Engage, but don't encourage...take the photo...control your own narrative..."

What was the narrative? They were friends who watched sultry French cinema together?

"Do all that and it's over sooner rather than later. Bring it to a close quickly."

That she could do—hopefully.

"Sorry!" she said in a sing-song voice, giving the guy a big smile and a friendly wave, even as her heart beat in her throat. Then she kept on walking. "Can't chat. Have to get to work! Have a great day!"

Heart racing, knees wobbling, she made it to the end of the block. Ducking around the corner, she glanced back to find he'd not followed. She pulled out her phone, sent Sawyer a text, letting him know what had happened.

Pretty sure he'd go all caveman if he thought she'd been in any real danger, she added that she was fine, his advice had worked, she'd handled it like a pro. Then wished *him* a great day, as clearly that had become her go-to sign-off.

Seriously. When she'd first agreed to come home she'd

imagined herself sweeping in, magically whipping up a bunch of money, her parents gasping at how capable she truly was, then heading back in time to take up the offer to curate the art for a certain award-winning actress's new villa at Lake Como.

Instead she was tiptoeing out of her apartment so as not to wake her houseguest, and now hiding from paparazzi, or whoever that guy was. And she'd yet to raise a single cent.

She pushed herself away from the wall and headed to the dry-cleaners, where she handed the woman her ticket stub. And checked her watch for her latest notifications, in case Sawyer had replied to her messages.

He had not.

"Sniff it."

Petra looked up to find the dry-cleaner holding up her garment bags, one of which had been zipped open, revealing the dusky pink tulle she'd worn on Saturday night.

Petra duly sniffed. "New detergent?"

The dry-cleaner shook her head and smiled proudly. "It took some doing, but we were able to save the dress *and* remove the heady scent of rum."

Petra opened her mouth to insist, once again, that she did not drink rum, when she heard club music thumping, saw rainbow lights swirling about her head, tasted tequila on the back of her tongue.

And from nowhere a memory from Saturday night unspooled in her mind...

"It's been so long, Sawyer," she said, twirling a hot pink feather she'd gathered up after it had fallen from one of the hen night girl's boa.

"Since?"

"Since I've let down my hair, you know?"

Sawyer watched her hand as she ran it over her hair, checking she had, in fact, let it down.

"It's busy business, being a wanted woman." Petra tipped up onto her toes, her cheek all but brushing against his as she shouted to be heard above the music. *"It doesn't leave much time to swipe right, or date, or...or find myself backed up against a hard surface."*

At that, Sawyer reared back, swallowing hard, his eyes dark.

Too squiffy to care, Petra said, *"Then, and this is the real kicker, any time I do go on a date with some random, it feels like I'm cheating on Russell."*

"Who the hell's Russell?" Sawyer asked. *"I thought you just said you were too busy to...you know."*

Petra wiggled her fingers over her ears, intimating Russell's particular shape. Then stage-whispered, *"Russell's my favourite vibrator."*

Sawyer swore. Rather a lot. Though with his hand rubbing over his beard it was kind of hard to tell.

"You?" Petra asked, realising she'd been talking about herself for quite a while.

"No favourite vibrator," he murmured.

Petra rolled her eyes and poked him in the chest, her finger bouncing off the hard flesh beneath. *"Women,"* she said, placing her hand over his heart, or, to be precise, his left pectoral muscle, which was impressive as hell. *"Flesh and blood. Soft skin and wicked moans."*

Sawyer's chest lifted under her palm and she looked up at him to find his eyes on hers. Those clear blue eyes, now smoky and warm. Then his knee brushed against her. An electric shock shot through her. Enough that she gasped. But she did not move clear. And neither, she noticed, did he.

Some latent self-protection instinct that the tequila could not touch had her pulling her hand back to her side and saying, *"I bet you have no such problems. Groupies galore beating down your door."*

Sawyer breathed out hard, a mix of humour and exasperation now lighting the dark depths of his eyes.

His fingers tapped the space next to the half-empty tequila bottle as he said, "I've rarely spent more than a few nights in the same city, much less country, for months. Slept in tents, atop a Range Rover, in a treehouse just last week. Haven't had an actual shower with soap and hot water and a clean towel in some time. So I've hardly been in a position to..."

He stopped, with smoke still swirling in his eyes, his voice low and intimate, leading Petra to finish his sentence.

"Back a woman up against a hard surface?"

He laughed at that. Or choked. Again, she was finding it tricky to pick up on his signals. Darned tequila.

"Come on, Mahoney," she said, her voice feeling a little thick. "You must know that none of that fancy stuff makes a lick of difference where you are concerned."

"Fancy stuff?" he said, his gaze warming. And had he moved in closer? It sure felt as if he had.

"The Sawyer Mahoney appeal goes beyond showers," she said loftily, her hand flying out sideways as if to emphasise her point.

Which was when it landed smack in the face of a passing drinks waiter.

A tumbler of rum, filled with ice, splashed over her dress—

"Here. Pocket stuff."

Petra blinked to find herself still at the dry-cleaners, several garment bags hooked over her elbow, the dry-cleaner handing her a small Ziplock bag containing what looked like a receipt, a hot pink feather and the pull tab from a soft drink can.

Head spinning, Petra popped the pocket stuff into her handbag, thanked the dry-cleaner and left, certain now that there was a *lot* she did not remember about that night with Sawyer.

Sawyer, who'd not been with anyone in goodness knew how long.

Sawyer, who was now staying in her apartment.

Sawyer, who knew she had a favourite vibrator. Named Russell.

Some random paparazzi wannabe was suddenly the least of her worries.

Giving up on the idea of walking to work, she held out her hand for a taxi, slipped her garment bags onto the back seat and gave the driver the gallery's address.

Feeling ninety-three percent sure that putting it all out of her head and simply pretending everything was hunky-dory was not only the right way to go, but possibly the most Gilpin thing she'd ever done.

Sawyer swung back and forth in the office chair he'd pulled up to Hadley's desk, checking the weather, the footy news, his messages, to see his little sister Daisy still hadn't responded.

Then he found a pencil and flipped it around his fingers. Till Hadley grabbed it from him and threw it across the room.

She said, "Go away."

"Give me something to do," he begged. "To fix. To disentangle. Give me a day trip. Anywhere."

"Not happening. You have things to do here. People to charm. So that we can afford to send you places. Now go away."

"I will," he said. "When the others get in."

"Ted is working from home today as his little one has a sniffle. Ronan took the jet to Perth overnight." She spared him a glare. "Can't you go for a run? Or lift something heavy, over and over again?"

"Did that already."

Awake with the birds, despite the late movie, and subsequent dreams of hands sliding over wet clay, over warm skin, he'd left the apartment stupid early that morning to sweat it out in the Big Think gym. Not that it had helped. Clearly.

His phone buzzed and he whipped it from his pocket. *Petra.*

Just seeing her name gave him an electrical charge. Only this time it came with the memory of her feet on his lap, her skin beneath his touch. Petra, whose eyes had turned dark, cheeks a warm telling pink when he hit the right spot. Petra, who knew how to pick a movie.

Then he read her message.

Hey, so there's a photographer outside the apartment. If you can call a goofy guy with an iPhone a photographer. He took some photos. Asked questions about us. I took your advice and played nice and then he left me alone. I'm fine, just letting you know so you can avoid him. Okay. Have a great day!

And every other thought dried up in a flash.

He'd left before her, left her alone, and this had happened. On his watch.

He typed back:

I'm on my way.

And then pushed back the seat so hard as he stood it smacked against the wall.

Hadley, used to working with the Big Think men, kept on typing. "Problem?"

"It's Petra. She had a photographer take photos of her outside our apartment this morning."

Her tapping came to a halt. "*Our* apartment?"

Petra had typed back.

No need. I'm fine. Just wanted to give you the heads-up.

Hadley said, "I thought you'd taken the Big Think suite at the Elysium."

"I did. Now I'm staying at hers." Sawyer's thumbs hovered over his phone as he figured out…how to convince her she needed him. Yep, that was his thought process. Which was nuts. If she said she was fine, then she was fine.

"Sawyer—"

"Not now, Hadley."

"Yes now! It might seem ridiculous to you, but *I* need to know these things. You go rogue for months, playing hero on your metaphorical white steed, while Ted goes from saving the world to changing nappies, and Ronan is pissing off as many investors as he brings in due to his innate lack of humility. I'm the one holding this place together with my bare hands. So if you plan to add to my workload by taking part in some click-bait romantic entanglement that takes focus off the Big Think Ball—"

Sawyer held out a hand. "Petra is an old friend. We haven't seen one another in years. I'm staying in her spare room so we can catch up. That's all."

All true, and yet he felt his eye twitch.

Hadley raised her eyebrows. "So long as you know what you're doing."

Sawyer did not, as it turned out, know what he was doing. He just knew he had to do something. "I have to go."

"Best news I've had all day!" Hadley called as he left her office.

Adrenaline too high, he took the stairs.

Not because he liked playing hero, as Hadley asserted. But someone had to stand up, do the hard thing, do the right thing, and as usual that someone would be him.

Outside the Big Think skyscraper the sky was a murky grey. No rain, but no sun either, giving the architecture a kind of gloomy elegance. It was Melbourne at its most Melbourne.

Sawyer scanned the area and spied no paps, meaning this guy—whoever he was—wasn't interested in where he worked, only where he slept. Not great.

He turned the collar of his leather jacket up against the cool and set off, hustling past designer shops and stately hotels, past theatres and alleyways and converted churches. Past fences covered in posters for bands stuck up over older posters for bands. And walls covered in graffiti that reminded him of his sister, Daisy.

Needing something to settle his mind, he pulled his battered phone from his pocket and tried calling his youngest sister again, not expecting her to answer. But she did. And his relief was palpable.

"Hey, brother," said Daisy.

"Who is this?" he said.

A beat, then, "You called me, you doofus."

"You Called Me, You Doofus…? Hmm. Not ringing any bells."

Daisy groaned, while Sawyer checked both ways before jogging across the street.

"Where the heck have you been, kiddo?" he relented. "I've been trying to get onto you for days, to let you know that I'm in town so that you might rejoice."

"I've been about. Doing my thing."

Her thing being skateboarding and 'street art' which had led to him having to quietly get her out of trouble more times than their mother would ever know.

"Want to do me a solid and find a moment in between *things* to call Mum? Story around town, she's been lovingly requesting a check-in for a few weeks now."

"Hounding, more like."

Sawyer ran a hand over his mouth, not liking the tone in her voice. His other sisters were uncomplicated, high-spirited creatures prone to creating babies, which was keeping his mother blissfully happy for the first time in his living memory.

Then there was Daisy. Solemn, shy, prone to depression. A lot like their mum used to be. Which was why his mum worried. And called. A guy could only try to save the world for so long before family responsibility wanted its turn.

"You think that's hounding?" he said. "Try this. Tell me where you are. Right now. Do it, do it, do it."

She laughed, as he'd hoped she would. "Yeah, maybe."

He rounded a corner and the spires on the Gallery of Melbourne popped into sight. "How are you? Really?"

A slow exhalation of breath. Then, "I am good. I'm actually starting to make a name for myself with my work, which is really cool. Mum just doesn't understand it."

He opened his mouth to say he didn't much understand it either, but the trundle of trams making a racket as they rocketed past gave him just enough pause to hear the words in his head. Which were embarrassingly similar to what Petra had heard daily as a kid. And he'd seen how divisive that lack of understanding could be.

Josiah and Josephine Gilpin were smart people. Yet they'd never been able to see how impressive their daughter was, and had always been, in her own unique way.

"Sawyer?"

"Yep. I'm here. And I'm chuffed for you, kiddo," he said, stopping to let a dogwalker with ten yappy dogs in a myriad of fancy collars make their way around him. He looked down to find a small pink gem, likely from the collar of one of the dogs. He picked it up and slipped it into his pocket. "Still, if you need me, need anything—"

Daisy sighed gustily. "I know the others live for your knight-in-shining-armour thing, but I don't need all that, okay?"

Sawyer reared back. What was it with the women in his life and their sudden need to psychoanalyse him?

A guy walking the other way glared at him, so he took a step sideways and set off on his mission once more. For it was who he was and they could all just handle it.

"Fine," Sawyer said, not meaning it. He'd turn himself up to annoyingly painful older brother level soon, but the gallery was in sight and he set off at a jog. "I'll be in touch again soon."

"I have no doubt," Daisy said, before hanging up.

When Sawyer barrelled into the gallery, a security guard looked up, and smiled. A few old ladies on a day out checked their bags and umbrellas. A toddler ran past his legs, a beleaguered-looking mother chasing.

It was all so pedestrian, it hit him – was he looking for problems to fix just to keep himself busy?

No. Unlike his family's loss, or Finn's accident, or the people he helped all over the world, Petra's current problem was all because of him.

He found signs pointing the way to admin.

When he found Petra in the back office area, she was sitting behind a desk in a glass-walled office at the far end of the space. Her small form was swamped by her oversized mustard-coloured jumper, beneath the desk dark fitted jeans were rolled at the cuff, over chunky ankle boots, showing off a sliver of pale skin in between.

And the memory of holding those ankles in his hands hit him like a truck. The warmth of her skin, the softness. How good it had felt. How right.

He leaned against the doorjamb and watched her rock side to side on her office chair, tapping a pencil against her teeth while she read something on her phone that was making her smile. Music played via a portable speaker set up on the corner of her messy desk. Surrounded by noise and light and a little mess, so sure of herself, in her element, it was clear she was not in need of someone to ride up and rescue her. Not in need of him.

And that hit harder than a truck ever could.

Then she looked up, saw him and cried, "Sawyer!", nearly dropping her phone, the pencil clattering from her hand, having to reach for it to stop it rolling off the table.

"Petra," he said, easing into the room as if he weren't in the midst of an existential crisis.

"Please tell me you're not here because of what happened," she said, pressing her chair back and standing. "I told you, I'm fine."

He rolled a shoulder. "I can see that. It's just—"

A shadow moved in beside him. It belonged to a pocket-sized brunette with a tablet in hand. Like a mini-Hadley in the making.

"Petra," she said breathlessly, "Murray Landis just emailed. He's in. Everything you asked for is yours."

"Yes!" Petra clapped her hands and bounced up and down, joy radiating from her.

The young woman at Sawyer's side grinned at Petra, then looked at Sawyer and said, "Oh! Sorry, I didn't see you there. It's... Oh, my, it's you!"

"It's me."

"Sawyer," said Petra, "this is Mimi Lashay, my wondrous sidekick in this endeavour. Mimi, Sawyer Mahoney."

Mimi juggled her tablet and held out a hand. "Big fan. Big. Huge. So good to meet you."

Sawyer smiled and shook. "Likewise."

The young woman looked from Sawyer to Petra and back again. Then she left, muttering about wanting to be Petra when she grew up.

Petra hustled Sawyer into the room and shut the door. Pointed at the couch. "Sit."

Sawyer sat, waiting for Petra to sit at the other end. But

after a moment's hesitation she leant her backside against her desk instead. He wondered if she was thinking about the night before too.

"Murray Landis?" he said, knowing a little about the up-and-coming tech guru.

"A new donor. We put out a lot of feelers yesterday, Mimi and I. Throwing spaghetti at the wall hoping something might stick. A few have shown slight interest, Murray the biggest so far. A tech trader looking for some good PR and to invest in his private collection. I offered advice as a sweetener."

"You're not mucking about, are you?"

"Right." Petra smiled, radiating confidence. Which was new. No, not new, just more overt than it had once been. She'd grown into her gravitas. "Which is good news, because while I keep getting these big fun ideas as to how this place could really be turned around, it's not in my purview. The sooner I raise the funds the sooner I can get back to my life."

"I thought you said you had the apartment for six months," he said, a strange tightness in his chest.

She blinked. "I do. Just in case. But my hope *was* to blitz this gig then head back to London as soon as humanly possible."

Emphasis on the *was*. As if that hope had since changed.

"So," she said, looking away, "as you might have gathered, Mimi is a big fan."

"Huge," Sawyer corrected. "Which is nice, but can we talk about the elephant in the room?"

"Elephant?"

"The photographer."

"Oh, right." She nibbled at a thumbnail and he knew he'd made the right decision, coming to her.

"Was he polite? Did he touch you? Threaten you?"

"No! None of that. It all happened so fast." She shrugged. "Do you think it will keep happening?"

He sat forward, resting his elbows on his knees. He didn't want to worry her but also wanted to give her enough so that she could make an informed choice.

"In my footy days I couldn't have coffee without being tagged in a hundred pictures. People were usually pretty nice, unless they went for another team. But even then—"

"You were beloved," she said.

He couldn't help but laugh. "I was lucky. These days, I'm relatively boring as far as the paps are concerned. Out of sight, out of mind."

"Till now."

Sawyer nodded. "In the end it comes down to access. Without pictures there is no story."

"And with them…they can make up any story they like?"

Sawyer held out his hands, face up, in agreement. Then opened his mouth to offer help, but she held up a hand, halting him, while she had some thoughts.

The urge to take over, to fix everything, was not a surprise. The tightness in his chest as he waited to see what she chose to do was.

Petra looked through the glass wall and said, "I reckon I can handle it. It was a surprise, which was why it caught me off-guard. But I'm tougher than I look. Inured to judgement!"

Only because, as a kid, she'd had to be. Which made this kind of thing much harder. For her and for him.

"My one concern," she said. "Just quietly, the last guy who was in my position left under a cloud. I'd hate for any story to mess with what we are trying to do here."

Ready with a ten-point plan, including carrying her off to the nearest tower and locking her up inside, Sawyer heard Hadley's words, and Daisy's, and instead found himself asking, "Tell me what *you* need? Would you like me to move back to the hotel?"

"No!" she said, eyes flashing. "Don't even think about it.

I've missed you, Sawyer. I didn't realise how much till I saw you the other night. I'm not about to let some stranger get in the way of us spending whatever time together we can. Okay?"

The violence of her response yanked at something inside him. Some thread that had been living, latent inside him, just waiting for her to tug. Now tugged, the floodgates opened and all kinds of feelings flew about inside him.

"Screw 'em," she said.

"Screw 'em," he agreed, his voice ragged.

And Sawyer felt, no, he *knew*, that they were in this thing together. Which, for the guy who usually shouldered the load single-handed, was a hell of a thing.

Then she had to go and shift against the desk, all slinky and loose. Her gaze locked on his in a way that made the feelings rushing through him spark and twist.

"At this point," she said, "I think I need to know what happened the other night. If anything happened. Forewarned is forearmed and all that."

"Like?"

"A few things have come back. The rum—a spill down my dress. And…" Eyes half closed, she lifted her hands to the top of her head and waggled her fingers.

Russell, the vibrator.

Hearing her wax lyrical about her favourite vibrator while two sheets to the wind was one thing, but sitting in her office, her standing there looking all warm and lovely and making him feel as if he was sitting by the fire on a cold day, was like heaven and hell all at once.

"That was educational," he drawled.

She lifted her hands to her face, her voice muffled as she said, "That has to be the worst of it, right?"

"You're a happy drunk. Chatty. Friendly. But there was no tabletop dancing, or bra-tossing, or fistfights, if that's your concern."

"It kind of was." Then she let her hands drop, crossing her arms, crossing her ankles. Those damn ankles. And she asked, "And us...? There's no particular reason we are suddenly of interest to the press?"

"Such as?" he asked, his voice rough.

Thinking of how she'd found any chance to touch his arm, or smack him on the chest, or pluck fluff from his hair.

Thinking of how he'd felt as if he could have stayed there, talking to her, for the rest of his life. And how if it had been any other girl he'd have been entirely within his rights to believe they'd both been flirting their hearts out.

But this wasn't any other girl. This was Petra.

Her glance was deadpan. "Do you want me to list possibilities and you nod any time I'm right?"

No, he did not. "We talked, we laughed, we told stories. We reminisced."

"And that's all?"

Sawyer nodded. *Pretty much.*

"Great," she said with a huge sigh of relief.

Sawyer found himself glad she hadn't asked for a blow-by-blow account. For while there had been nothing the press would find interesting, not while they'd been at the main bar, there had been moments he'd be hard pressed to explain. He could barely make sense of them himself, and figured they were best left to fading memory.

"Still, after this morning's fun, I'd like to pick you up and take you home tonight."

She blanked him. "Because the more they see the two of us together, the more likely they are to back off?"

Sawyer's jaw worked. She had him there.

"I'll be fine. I have the Sawyer Mahoney Rules of Engagement in my head. And a neat right hook." She shifted back and forth, fists raised in such a way she'd break her thumb if she made contact at all. "Now, leave. I have to get back to work."

Making it clear, there was no knight in shining armour position for him as far as she was concerned.

And when she lifted her chin, daring him to contradict her, out of nowhere he was reminded of Finn. And it was like a bucket of ice water poured over his head.

If Finn had still been around, watching them circle one another the way they had been, would he have warned him off? Or would he have laughed it off as inevitable?

It was something Sawyer would never know.

He pulled himself to standing. "Is it okay with you if I try to get Daisy over for dinner one night?"

"Of course! Did you get onto her?"

"I did."

"Oh, that's fabulous! I still picture her in pigtails, all ringlets and red bows. How is she?"

"No longer wearing pigtails. And painting Melbourne in graffiti."

Petra burst into laughter, before it came to a sudden stop. "Oh, you mean literally. Wow. Is she any good?"

"At tagging fences near train lines?" He had no clue. "What's the criteria?"

"Does she have a site? Socials?"

He nodded.

"Show me."

"Her eyebrow rings?"

"Her work."

Sawyer found his sister's Instagram page and handed over his phone. Moving to lean his backside against the desk beside her, he watched as she scrolled and scrolled, gaze intent on the screen, her profile a study in delicate architecture.

"How have I not seen this before now?" she asked, turning to face him, their faces danger close. Her eyes now filled with fire and determination. "What does she eat? Any intolerances or predilections?"

"I can cook."

She shook her head. "I know a great place round the corner. I'll order in."

"I. Can. Cook."

She blinked at him, big eyes, tangled lashes, a constellation of pale freckles scattering the bridge of her nose. "How?"

"The usual way. Ingredients, heat."

She swallowed; her pupils dilating. And he *knew* it had nothing to do with talk of food. "I wouldn't know," she said, handing him back his phone.

His thumb brushed hers as he took it back. Deliberately? Hell, yeah.

When he felt her gravity pulling him in, he stood. Then reached into his pocket, found the pink gem, waited for her to hold out her hand and dropped it into her palm. "Found it on my walk here. Thought of you."

"Oh," she said, her face lighting up with delight.

Figuring it best to quit while he was ahead, Sawyer moved to the door and said, "I'll leave you to it then."

Knocking the doorframe in goodbye, he left. If he whistled as he walked back towards the lift, not caring who was watching him, then so be it.

CHAPTER FIVE

"HURRY UP!" Petra called. "I can't believe you take longer to get ready than I do!"

After a few days of successfully avoiding men in khaki and puffer jackets, that Sunday morning Petra sat at the small round dining table, one leg crossed over the other, flicking lint off her leopard print skirt and olive-green polo neck.

"You don't look ready."

Petra looked up to find Sawyer standing near the kitchen, his hair a little damp from his shower, wearing dark jeans that did great things to all the bits they enclosed and a navy Henley, the crease marks from the packaging down his chest.

"Have you been shopping?" she asked, when what she wanted to say was *Phwoar!*

He glanced down and tugged at his shirt till half a pec peeked over the top of the neckline. And she came mighty close to having an aneurysm right there on the spot.

"I have a person who sends me clothes when I need them."

"A *stylist*?" she asked, loving the pink creeping over the top of his beard.

He let his shirt go and narrowed his eyes her way. If he realised she was babbling to cover her lust, then he didn't say so. Except his eyes did glint just a little before he asked, "You okay?"

"Yep!" she said, snapping out of her fog and shooting to her feet.

"Because you look a little flushed."

"Nope. Trick of the light. Now, let's go bother your sister!"

They were on their way to see Daisy. Unable to lock her down to a dinner—*too bourgeoise*—she'd agreed to a catch-up when she'd heard Petra was coming. Which Sawyer had taken in his stride.

The truth was, after days of making very few inroads into scraping up donations, Petra finally had the seed of a plan. A plan that could see the gallery not only get itself out of its current financial straits, but to become a true destination for art enthusiasts, in a city that prided itself on being the cultural hub of Australia.

As fun as Deena was, she fitted into the Gilpins' world, not Petra's. The contacts Deena had would likely look at Petra as if she had two heads. Whereas Daisy? Now *she* might be the key.

Petra grabbed the gift she'd picked up for Daisy on her way out of the door. Sawyer held it open, forcing Petra to pass him nice and close. The scent of his skin, freshly washed, the size of him swamping her made her feel all buoyant. And woozy.

She let out a great big sigh. Then looked up to find him smiling, as if he knew exactly why. And while it ought to have her in a panic, the truth was, the more time they spent together, making new memories, ones that were wholly their own, the more she found herself hoping he'd hurry up and figure it out.

"Oh, shut up," she said, heading to the lift with the sound of his laughter in her ears.

In the lift, and out, Petra walked backwards towards the rear doors, grateful the building manager had given them permission to use the emergency exits any time they left the building. "Cab? Walk? Tram?"

"Wait—" said Sawyer, his expression suddenly grim as he held out a hand, but Petra was through the doors before she saw the crowd gathered in the back alleyway.

Camera flashes snapped and mobile cameras hovered in front of her face.

"What the hell?" she said, rearing back. Hitting smack bang into a wall.

I can handle it, she quickly reminded herself. *I'm tougher than I look. I'm inured to judgement!*

And yet she froze. The same way she had when her parents' colleagues barked questions at her. Questions Finn had answered as if born with them lined up inside his head. While she'd just wanted to hide under a table and trace the wood patterns she found there.

Then the wall at her back moved. It was Sawyer stepping in beside her and taking her by the hand.

"I've got you," he said, his words brushing over her ear as he smiled into the distance. Then, his voice warm, charming, strong and sure, cutting through the throng, he said, "Excuse us, guys. My friend and I are running late."

Questions came at them, too fast, too convoluted for Petra to pick out a single thread. The blood rushing behind to her ears didn't help. Or the fact her feet had gone numb, as if all the blood had left her body. She hated it. Hated that it made her react this way.

Sawyer's voice, her lifeline in the stormy sea, said, "Petra, sweetheart, we need to go." Then he slipped an arm around her waist and used it to herd her forwards.

And she stuck by him, like glue. Her body pressed against his. And before she knew it, they were in a taxi, Sawyer giving her a small push across to the far end of the back seat so he could climb in after her.

She heard him bark an address, and they were off.

Her hearing came back fully after a minute or so, to find Katie Melua singing through the tinny speakers. And she turned to face Sawyer, who was watching her, his whole body tensed, as if readying to strike anyone who dared disagree with her, much less jump out and take her photo.

"Taxi, then?" she asked.

And after a beat Sawyer burst out laughing. Then, as if that had magically broken the bodyguard spell that had come over him, he ran his hands over his face and swore, an impressive array of language choices all focused at the mob.

Energy flowing around him like a summer wild aura, he said, "It's been niggling at me, how this has all gone down. And I think I've figured it out. The guy, the one who took your photo the other day, khakis and puffer jacket? He was there. Only he's not a pap. He's just some guy who was at the bar the other night. He asked for my autograph, but I was heading to the bathroom so made an excuse and brushed him off. I'd to-tally forgotten about it till I saw him just now."

He breathed out hard. "I'd put money on him being a fan, with zero intention of selling any photo he took. Something changed that, clearly. And he made the rookie mistake of also giving up where we were."

"Who needs paparazzi when you have superfans?" she said. "As for the rest of them, are we—as in me—really that in-teresting?"

Sawyer lifted a hand as if writing across the sky. "Hand-some, Beloved, Footy Star Billionaire Philanthropist with a Heart of Gold Tempted into Secret Tryst with Little-Known Society Princess." A small sorry smile lifted his mouth as he said, "The headline writes itself."

Petra groaned. Then leant forwards and let her head fall into her hands.

She was going to have to call her mother, let her know that there might be…something. Not a *whiff of scandal* by any measure, but in her mother's eyes anything that wasn't neat, tidy, proper was disquieting.

Petra herself included.

Adrenaline levels having dropped, the backs of Petra's eyes burned. She bit her lip and forced herself to keep it together.

"Do not ask if I'm okay," she demanded when she heard Sawyer's intake of breath.

"I was about to assure you the *heart of gold* bit would *never* happen."

At that she laughed. Then groaned again.

"Are you okay?"

"Stop! Seriously. You need to stop asking me that! It is doing my head in!" She glanced over to see a muscle twitch beneath his eye.

Other than that, he seemed wholly unfazed by her outburst, as if his reasons trumped hers. "It eases my mind."

"I'm aware. I am. And I get why."

He stilled. Braced. But it was time he faced up to this. Truly. Now seemed a good time, considering the only way he could avoid it was to leap from a moving car.

For he had it in him to run, if she pushed too hard, too fast. He'd done it before. Twice. Just left, with no word, for a long time.

After Finn's funeral. And after her eighteenth birthday party.

A memory flickered—something to do with her eighteenth. But not the party itself, something from the night at the Gilded Cage. A conversation? Reminiscence? Re-enactment? She tried to reach out for it, but it fluttered just out of reach.+

"You feel the need to look out for me, because of Finn," she said.

His jaw clenched.

"It hurts you when I say his name, doesn't it?' she whispered. 'I'm sorry that it feels that way. Especially because I love telling stories about him. It gives me such solace. I won't force you, it's not my place. But I'm here, ready and willing, when you are. Till then, I need you to know that I would tell Finn the exact same thing, if he were still here: I've been looking after myself for a really long time now. And I've done a pretty good job of it. So take it as a given, unless I tell you otherwise, I'm just fine."

He said nothing, and she could only hope it had sunk in.

As for her, she'd not loved having to push through the mob, but she'd hated more the fact that she'd frozen. As if all the work she'd done to know herself, and love herself, even if her parents could not, was for naught.

She was not going to let that happen again.

"Teach me your ways."

"Regards?" he asked, his jaw still tight.

"Connect Four," she shot back. Then gave his leg a nudge. And kept her knee there, near his, annoying him till he looked her way. "If you didn't notice, I just asked you for help. Which should have you on cloud nine. So can you get over yourself for a second, and help me?"

He looked at her then, his clear blue eyes taking her in. Then he glanced at her hand, resting by his thigh.

She wriggled her fingers, warning him she'd squeeze again if he didn't comply. "Teach me how not to freeze up."

He took a deep breath in, let it go, then said, "After my dad died, my mum had it hard—alone, young, four kids to raise. So she leaned on me." Then, "Stop me if I've told you this story."

Petra shook her head. "Go on."

"I'd been a bit of a handful, a class clown. But I had to stop making waves so my sisters could slide through on my wake. I taught myself how to cook. Did assignments on my lap while waiting for my sister to finish her after-school job, or with Daisy at the skate park.

"Then Daisy started to run away, all the time—from shops, from school. My heart would be in my throat the whole time, imagining all the terrible things that might have happened to her. But I'd not let Mum see. Because how much harder would it have been for my mum if she knew how hard it was on me?"

Smile, she thought, *take the photo and thank them. As if it's your idea.*

He made it look so easy. When it wasn't. Not at all.

Oh, Sawyer.

"You became good at pretending," she said.

He nodded. "Looking back," he said, "those years are a total blur. Till—" A quick frown marred his forehead.

"Till?" she encouraged. Knowing in her gut what was coming next, and hoping, *hoping* this time he might be the one to bring it up.

"Till your brother ditched that fancy private school footy team and joined mine."

There, she thought, an overwhelming sense of gratitude coming over her. If that craziness outside the apartment building had led to this, then she'd take it.

"He was quite the light-bringer, that brother of mine," she said.

Sawyer let his head fall back against the seat. "Yeah. He was all right, I guess. But your house—spotless, quiet, food prepped by a cook. Now that was bliss."

Petra shivered. "Your reprieve was my nightmare."

Sawyer laughed, the sound rough. Then he opened his eyes and tipped his head to face her. That face, those eyes, that soul. She let out a sigh before she'd even felt it coming.

His gaze dropped to her mouth, and her instincts began to hum.

"Now it all makes sense," he said, dragging his gaze back to hers. "The shoes you discard at the door, the jacket tossed over the back of the couch, the constant music playing or the balcony door open to let in the noise of the city. You're still rebelling."

She laughed. "A little bit."

He smiled. She smiled. And when his chest rose and fell, she wondered if maybe there was even the slightest possibility that he wasn't completely immune to her too.

Then his hand found hers, curling around her fingers, before he lifted it onto his leg, where he traced the lines on her palm and she literally forgot how to breathe.

"Do you remember the day we met?" she asked, then cleared her throat to dislodge the bur within.

"I remember feeling terrified I'd get footy mud on the clean floor. Till you walked in, sticks in your hair, a pink flower tucked into the knot of your overalls, trailing grass up the hall. It was like spotting a unicorn in the wild. And I knew that I'd never have to pretend for you."

Petra swallowed as the sweetness of his words climbed under her skin, curled up and purred.

Then the taxi stopped suddenly, the tyres screeching for a half second. The driver looked over his shoulder, saying, "Sorry, guys. Learner driver just pulled out in front."

"All good, mate," Sawyer said, instant charm.

Then, with one last swipe of his thumb down her palm, he gave Petra back her hand. She curled it into her lap, her nerves singing, her instincts dancing in circles.

"So what happens now?" Petra asked.

"We visit Daisy."

She'd meant with the photographers. "But—"

"We visit Daisy. You guys chat art. Then we get on with our day. You can't let it sit with you. Or worry you. You can only control what you can control, which is you. Your behaviour, your response. Which for me means acting as if I'm not enraged by a bunch of strangers camped out in the alley behind my unicorn friend's building, taking photos and yelling at her, because that would only give the story legs. And because she wants to learn to handle it herself."

Petra reached out and took his hand, holding it between them.

And they stayed that way for the final couple of blocks' drive down the street to meet his sister.

* * *

"Here will do," Sawyer told the taxi driver, peeling off some cash so they could hop out fast, just in case.

But no one had followed. They were interesting on a slow news day, but they were not royalty. Meaning the day was hers. And she was going to make the most of it.

"This way," said Sawyer, shooting her a smile as he held out a hand.

And she took it, because apparently that was now a thing that they did. Yep, the day was looking up already.

He led her down a tall, dark, narrow alleyway and Petra was instantly transported. For on both sides of the alleyway, every inch of reachable wall space was covered in colour. Some dull, some recent. Some paint. Some chalk. Including a glorious mural of Frida Kahlo—untouched by the graffiti tags covering every other wall.

"Honour among thieves," said Sawyer, who'd stopped beside her, hands in pockets, admiring the artistry.

Then he pointed to a bright white painting of a daisy in the middle of a mural filled with quotes over the top of quotes till it was too hard to pick out where one started and another began.

Petra stood back and took it in, her heart now beating hard in her chest, a feeling she'd not had since coming home, no matter how many triptychs she had leaning against the hallway wall, or light installations she'd installed. To know that her inspiration could spark here was a huge relief. "Wow. This is…"

"A cry for help?" said Sawyer.

"Glorious," Petra chastised, before noting that he was smiling, his eyes filled with wonder as he looked over what was clearly his sister's work.

"I jest. But the first time she was caught," he said, "the owner of the building called the police. Daisy was arrested. Mum rang, panicked. The entire family was up in arms. I, of course, was called on to sort it out."

"How?" Petra asked, spotting a piece of pink chalk and picking it up.

"I bought the building."

Of course he did.

"Best big brother ever," she said, then realised what she'd said. An unexpected flash of sorrow poured through her, in the place she usually saved for nothing but lovely memories. "I mean, not *the* best, but—"

"I know," he said, taking her hand and tucking it into his elbow. "And I am happy to share the title with Finn."

"Petra!"

Petra turned to find Daisy barrelling towards them. Short dark hair dipped in hot pink. Studs in her ears and on her clothes. Black lipstick. The same bright blue eyes as her big brother.

Petra gathered Daisy in for a hug, then pointed to Daisy's work. "I'm blown away. Truly."

"You love it," she said, with a measure of pride that Petra adored.

Sawyer moved in to give his sister a big bear hug, which she took. And again Petra found herself awash with bittersweet feelings.

"I love it too," Sawyer assured his sister.

"Sure you do," said Daisy, pulling back to roll her eyes at her brother.

"Sprung." Petra laughed. "Art is subjective, and that's a good thing. If we all loved the same painting, there would only be one painting. And then where would you be?"

Daisy took that in, and nodded at her wall. "I like that. Can I quote you?"

"I'd be honoured. Also…" Petra reached into her oversized bag and pulled out the sculpture she'd found a couple of days before on one of her lunchtime jaunts. "A present."

"Is this a Tabitha Mendez?" Daisy asked, her voice overawed as she took in the sharp angles and bright colour.

Petra nodded. "I saw it and thought of you."

"I can't. That's way too much."

Petra held up both hands. "My dream in life is to bring art to the person who'll love it the most. Do you love it?"

"I love it."

"Then it's meant to be. Now, I know you're busy—"

Daisy wasn't, but she puffed up at the thought Petra assumed she was.

"So I'll get right to the point. I'm working with the Gallery of Melbourne, and playing with an idea that would bring a whole lot of freshness to the place. I was hoping you could be my conduit. Show me what's new in town. Introduce me to some of your artist friends."

Daisy blinked, still slightly stunned by the gift, which Petra had fully expected she might be. "Sure. But they are hardly Gallery of Melbourne types."

"I get that. But that's what excites me about them. This idea, it's more of an…epic dream, if you will Drinks on me one night, so I can pick your brains?"

"That'll do it," Daisy said with a grin.

Petra glanced to where Sawyer was standing back, a smile on his face, his eyes on her. Eyes filled with warmth. And something else. Some slice of himself Petra knew was all for her.

She could feel the heat of it, a knife-edge, hot and focused, like the run of his thumb down her palm, the brush of his breath over her ear when he'd called her *sweetheart* before ushering her to the taxi.

Then she remembered he'd *just* told her a story about how good he was at pretending. That he'd spent his life fitting himself into whatever mould he needed to be. Perfect son. Protective brother. Football star. Social justice warrior. Billionaire philanthropist. Friend.

Not with her, he'd assured her. He'd not had to pretend back then. But now? With so many more ghosts now heavy on his shoulders?

"Your brother looks hungry," Petra said, pushing her toes into her shoes when his eyes flared with a different kind of hunger.

She turned back to Daisy. "Come with me while I feed him?"

Aware that it was a ruse for her big brother to look after her by proxy, Daisy waited a beat before heading up the alleyway. "Go ahead and hold hands again, if you like. I don't mind."

"What?" said Petra. "That was... It wasn't..."

But Sawyer shot her a grin that had her mouth drying up. Then he had his sister in a headlock as the two Mahoneys strutted up the alleyway.

Leaving Petra with no choice but to follow.

I will not search for my name online. Or Sawyer's name. I will be calm and Zen and focused on the things that I can control.

That evening, after having messaged her mother to let her know that she and Sawyer might be in some photos, doing nothing but leaving her apartment building, and not to worry, she had it under control, Petra set her watch to Do Not Disturb.

Then she sat on the floor of the lounge room, TV playing a home renovation show on low volume, couch at her back, papers and highlighters and sketchpad at the ready. A glass bowl holding the gem, feather and piece of chalk sat before her like a talisman—a reminder that simple things could be the most beautiful. As she collated the zillion ideas she'd had since breakfast with Daisy.

Ears attuned, having lived with him for a few days now, she heard Sawyer's footsteps coming down the hall.

Like a moth to a flame she turned to find he was shirtless, his chest bare, showing off so many tattoos her poor eyes had no chance of absorbing them all.

Then there was the V-shaped muscle working its way from

his abs to his…below ab area, loose pyjama bottoms hanging low off his hips.

And as he scrubbed his hair dry with a towel, the veins roping down his forearms were very much deserving of their own toast. And a statue. And maybe a public holiday.

Then, when he dropped the towel, she saw that he'd shaved.

And it was all she could do not to expire on the spot.

Rough and scruffy, he was a big, beautiful bear of a man. But like this…hair slicked back, hard jaw clean-shaven, that sensual mouth no longer hidden… She felt as if she had fallen into a deep hypnosis.

"Whoa," she said, the word falling from her open mouth before she could catch it.

Finding her in the semi-darkness—for night had fallen while she'd been busy working—his face broke into a grin, lines bracketing his mouth, the flash of a canine or two.

He lifted his hand to his jaw and gave it a rub.

"It's been itching like hell for days," he said. "I kept it in the hope it might give me a little anonymity, but that horse has clearly bolted. Still going?"

It took Petra a moment to figure out what he meant. She turned back to her papers. "I am. But it's good. Really good. And much more up my alley than calling people asking for money. Art is a connector. It's a conversation. It's collusion and community and colour and cool. Making the gallery the home for *that* kind of experience will bring in the money, I know it."

The couch behind her back shifted as Sawyer sat at the other end, bare foot beside her hip. The man half-naked, and damp and warm and smelling so good.

Feeling itchy, and twitchy, she twirled her hair into a bun atop her head. Only for it to fall loose within a minute.

"Can I put on the pre-game instead?" he asked, nodding towards the TV.

"Mm-hmm," she said, not trusting her voice.

He moved closer to reach past her to grab the remote from the coffee table, the heat of his skin washing over her. "I can watch it in silence if it'll disturb you."

"Sound up," she said, "white noise always best."

She gathered her hair and twirled it tighter this time, needing as much air around her as possible. But it wasn't to be.

"Let me help." Sawyer, lifting his foot, scooted in behind her, trapping her between his knees. Then he gathered her hair in his hands.

"What's happening now?" she asked, pulling her head away, spinning on her butt, hands lifted as if she might fight him off.

"I'm helping."

"I thought you meant with work."

"What do I know about art?"

"What do you know about hair?"

"Three sisters," he reminded her, his clear blue eyes sparking, his mouth lifted at one corner, unimpeded by the beard, and *whoa*...

She knew she should say no, but instead found herself turning back to face the TV. Then his hands were in her hair again, lifting it gently from her neck, running through the lengths, gently detangling as he went.

Then he gave her head a gentle shake, her brain rattling against her skull.

"Hey! What was that for?"

"Stop thinking so much. I can practically hear it from here."

Petra doubted it very much. Would he be sitting so close if he knew how aware she was of his thighs? His bare chest? How she was memorising every place he touched her?

Then he leaned past her to grab the remote again and she glanced sideways, catching his beautiful profile, the curls brushing over his ears, the scent of his skin. And it took every bit of self-control not to lean in and drink him in.

He turned up the volume just a smidge more. Went to sit

back and stopped when he saw her notebooks. The sketches she'd made.

"Is this about Daisy?" he asked.

"Mmm hmm."

He turned to face her, close enough she could see a small patch on one cheek where he'd shaved not quite close enough. Could taste his clean skin on the back of her tongue.

His nostrils flared and he looked back at her notes. "Have you told her any of this?"

"Not yet. I'd hate to get her hopes up if I can't pull it off. I need this approved by the gallery management, which will take some Sawyer-level charm."

"What is it, exactly?"

Petra wriggled forward on her backside, glad to have a little breathing space, then found a larger sketch she'd made of the forecourt. "I want to showcase a slew of young artists in some kind of wild, bright, loud, joyous, family-friendly, ticketed special collection out front of the gallery."

He nodded.

"If successful—which it will be, because this is my wheelhouse—it would lead to future pop-ups, a constant rotation, each of which could have their own corporate or community sponsor, which will keep the gallery relevant and making money going forward. And I want Daisy's work to be the centrepiece. Her flowers, her quotes. She's seriously talented. And innovative. And cool. And her work is so joyful people will love it. They'll love her."

He handed back her sketch and said, "You're good."

"I know."

"I mean the sketch. I can see exactly what you mean. You've got talent."

"A little. I am a woman of many skills," she said, then sat back, her shoulders sliding into the gap between Sawyer's thighs. And she motioned to her head.

Laughing, he settled back into place and gathered her hair once more.

Only this time his hands moved to her scalp, sparks racing over her skin like static. Uncomfortable and fantastic, all at once. Till she felt restless. And unsettled. And lit up with want.

She could just make out his reflection in the TV while the commentators talked stats and scores regarding the last time the two teams had met. She watched the flexing of the muscles in his arms, the dark shadows of his tattoos reaching over his meaty shoulders, the way he watched his fingers move through her hair.

His voice was low, quiet as he said, "A big part of why I came home when I did was because Mum was worried Daisy was feeling a little low, which for Daisy can mean a lot low. Then you stepped up and made everything a thousand times better than I ever could."

"Oh, I doubt that."

He shook his head. "Your confidence and lack of fuss; it was a masterclass in caring for someone without overstepping."

Petra wasn't sure she'd ever been given a compliment that meant as much. Coming from Sawyer, her heart fluttered like a bird in a cage.

"She's amazing," Petra said. "Which is why I want to do this. But I'm glad I could help. This is where you say, *Thank you, Petra.*"

Sawyer's gaze dropped to hers in the reflection. His mouth quirked and he said, "Thank you, Petra."

Then his fingers moved over her skull, tracing her temple, then down her neck, dipping below the collar of the oversized shirt she'd thrown on that evening. And there was no hope of stopping the sound of utter pleasure escaping her throat.

Then he carefully separated three chunks of hair at her crown.

Petra's eyes opened wide. "Are you...*braiding* my hair?"

"Best way to keep hair out of your face, yes?"

"How on earth—?"

"The girls all went through a Katniss Everdeen obsession. Now, shush, or I'll have to start all over again."

They sat in silence, the football on the TV, Sawyer's fingers gliding across her scalp with a tenderness she'd not have expected from those big hands of his.

And she let herself imagine what it might be like if this was her actual life. Not a blip, not serendipity, but actually *being* with Sawyer. Talking about each other's work, their stresses, their delights. Not having to find excuses to touch one another.

Only to find that imagining it lasting for ever made her realise they were already living on borrowed time.

Then his fingers reached the bottom of her skull, the soft spot where her baby hairs tickled her neck, and a shiver rolled through her. If he noticed he didn't say anything. Though he did take his time finishing the final strands.

"All done," he said when he tucked the end into itself.

She turned slowly to face him, hands running over his work, the plaits a little bumpy and uneven. Which only made her love it all the more. "I'm seriously impressed."

He half smiled, his eyebrows raised. "This is the part where you say, *Thank you, Sawyer*."

"Thank you, Sawyer."

Gratified, he sat back, his thighs still pressing lightly against her shoulders. And rather than getting back to work, Petra stayed right where she was.

The noise of the crowd on the TV grew as the Magpies, Sawyer's old team, Finn's favourite, ran out.

"Do you miss it?" she asked.

"Sometimes," he said, not having to ask what. "The training was a bitch. But the mate-ship, the clear intent, the finesse of the game itself. Nothing like it."

"I know it was your life's dream, the both of you, to play

professionally, but I do wonder sometimes if Finn would have gone on with it, or if he'd have been swept up into law as our folks intended."

"Mmm…" Sawyer said in a way that made her turn. Her arm hooked up onto his knee. His legs splayed before her, his chest sculpted perfection.

"What does that 'mmm' mean, exactly?"

He ran a hand through his hair, the curls springing up in damp whirls. "It wasn't my dream, in point of fact."

"Excuse me?"

"It was Finn's. And my dad's. A story my mum told me before every footy season, tears in her eyes."

Petra twisted further, accidentally gathering the fabric of his thin pyjama pants till they cupped him in a way that took every fibre of her being not to look.

"Are you telling me," she said, "that you were a first-round draft pick for the most successful football club in the country, and you were doing it for…your best friend, and your dad?"

"Do you hear me complaining?"

His gaze dropped from the TV and landed on her. With no hair to hide behind she felt raw. Exposed. But she couldn't let that stop her. Not when she felt so close to unlocking some part of him she'd not even known was there.

"No!" she said. "Not at all. It's just… What *was* your dream? Your passion? That one thing you always felt you were meant to do?"

"Not everyone has that, Petra. You were born lucky."

Born lucky? Not something she'd ever considered before.

"What about now? Your Big Think work; it's amazing, right?"

He breathed deep, thought hard and said, "When the pre-organised jobs are done and I can wander, talk to the locals, find out what they need and make it happen, that feels pretty good. More buckets to collect spring water? Done. Wood, nails, tools to repair fences to keep out predators? Done."

"That sounds amazing," she said, and meant it. "Can you do *more* of that?"

"It's hard to find those kinds of stretches of spare time. Though…"

"Though what?"

"The one time I did have the time was during the long months of rehab, after busting my leg. Meeting with those kids, the ones whose parents couldn't afford regular sessions, then hustling to find places for them to get access to the level of care the club had afforded me, begging for funds for a brand-new rehab facility in Darwin, that was seriously rewarding. With Big Think the big stuff has to happen first. Ted's innovations. Ronan's greasing of palms and circumnavigating bureaucratic red tape. Only then do I get to do my stuff."

"So you do love it?"

"Mostly."

"Sawyer!"

"Mostly is pretty damn good."

Petra shook her head. This was blowing her mind. To think that, after all Sawyer had achieved, it was all down to what? Duty? Ability? Skill? Rather than impulse and desire and happiness, which were the things that drove every decision she made?

"Name one thing, off the top of your head, that you want. With a kind of urgency you can feel in your gut. Right now!"

He breathed out hard, shifting on the seat, and she couldn't help herself, she glanced down. And she had her answer.

Me, she thought. *He wants me.*

But she couldn't say it. Could barely believe it. Couldn't reconcile her daydreams of for ever with something *actually* happening between them. For it would change their dynamic, messy as it was, for ever.

So she slowly untwisted, let his pyjamas fall back into place and pretended nothing was happening. And said, "What about a hobby, then?"

At that he laughed, the muscles in his chest clenching in ways that had saliva pooling in her mouth.

"A hobby?" he repeated.

"Like…macramé. Or golf. Or…" *What hobbies did other people enjoy?* "Rolling cheese down a hill."

"Cheese rolling?"

"It's a thing. Right?"

"What are your hobbies?" he asked, leaning forward, elbows resting on his knees. Abs crunching, not a lick of spare skin. "Petra?"

Her eyes lifted to his. "Sorry, what?"

"Hobbies," he repeated, his voice low, intimate. "Outside of work? Do you knit? Bowl?" A pause, then, "Date?"

Petra opened her mouth to tell him her work was her hobby, her hobby her work. Who needed to knit, or bowl, or run their hands down a man's chest, or slide their hand up his thigh, or press their lips to his smooth hard cheek when their work was so very satisfying?

"This isn't about me," she said, her voice barely louder than a whisper.

His gaze hooked on hers. Then he reached out to capture a stray curl of hair he'd missed and tucked it behind her ear. "I'm starting to wonder if it is. About you."

And there his hand stayed, his fingers gently cradling her jaw, his thumb running along her cheekbone. His gaze hazy. His jaw tight.

While spot fires lit up all over Petra's body. Pockets of heat and hope and flashes of panic, as Sawyer Mahoney looked at her like…

Like he wanted to kiss her.

Petra swallowed. And Sawyer's gaze dropped to her throat.

To her chest, rising and falling as she sucked in great gusts of air. Then lifted to her mouth.

His thumb moved down her cheek to slide over the corner of her lips. Then along the crease. Tugging at her bottom lip, so gently, but enough that her mouth opened, and stayed that way.

While she didn't move. Didn't even breathe, in case it broke whatever magic spell had come over them both.

Then the siren blared on the TV, the opening bounce of the game, and Sawyer shook his head. Literally. As if clearing away a brain fog.

His hand dropped away.

He dragged his gaze to the TV, his jaw hard, his expression fierce. As if he was having a hell of an argument inside his own head.

Then he pushed himself up on his palms, the veins in his forearms bulging as he shot out of the chair.

"You're not going to watch the game?" she asked. When what she really meant was, *You're just leaving me here, now, filled with this longing?*

"Nah. Put your home reno show back on, if you like. I'm going to take your advice."

"What advice?"

"I'm going to go find some cheese to roll."

Completely flummoxed, Petra waited till he came out of his room again, having pulled on jeans and a jumper, heading towards the front door.

"It might take a while," she called out, "considering we're in the middle of the city!"

She could have sworn he muttered, "Here's hoping," before he called, "Don't wait up," and was out of the door.

Leaving Petra to stare at the TV, then her notes, and wonder what the heck had just happened.

CHAPTER SIX

AFTER A RESTLESS NIGHT, waking up every time she thought she heard the front door open, the urge to check Sawyer's bedroom before she left for work was so strong it hurt.

But in the end he was his own man, who could come and go as he pleased. It had nothing—*nothing* to do with her. Of that, she was eighty...eighty-five percent sure. And he'd said it himself—all she could control was her reaction, her behaviour.

Which was why she called an early morning meeting with the gallery management team, making it clear it was in their best interests they all attend.

Dressed to impress in a forest-green belted silk dress, and her lucky aubergine boots, sparkly clips in her hair, she watched the faces of the gallery management team—most of whom had worked there since she was a kid, and all of whom looked more than a little overwhelmed by the Epic Dream Festival idea she'd just presented to them.

But she *knew* what she was doing. This—bringing art to people who needed it—was her happy place. *Her dream.* Where the years spent wandering, collecting seemingly disparate things, had purpose.

The rest of her life, not so much. Clearly, if a conversation about hobbies and knitting and rolling cheese could send a guy running for his life.

She shook herself back into the meeting. Leant forward and looked each person dead in the eye. "Pulling together this kind of event, from idea to fruition in the blink of an eye, it's my superpower. It *will* bring a whole new cross-generational audience to the gallery. It will create media buzz. It will be joyful, and sustainable, and—"

She was losing them. Glazed and fidgety, she could see them pulling back.

The only card she had left to play was the Gilpin card. Something she'd never done before. But she was hoping her parents could bend her way, just a smidge, then surely she could too.

"You know my parents," she said. "They've been on the board here longer than some of you have been alive. They brought me here, knowing my skill set, knowing my abilities, trusting me to do what had to be done to help the gallery survive—"

A loud knock on the glass wall, hard enough the thing shook, took everyone's attention. It was Mimi, frantically pointing at a mobile phone in her hand.

Petra widened her eyes and mouthed, *I'll call them back*.

Mimi, whose eyes looked about to pop, madly shook her head.

Petra dropped her hands to the table and pushed herself to standing. "Excuse me, folks. It seems we've landed in the midst of a pantomime."

The management team laughed politely, or in relief that she'd no longer be badgering them, and Petra excused herself to meet Mimi in the hall.

"Is the building on fire?" Petra asked.

Mimi turned her phone to face Petra, and then began to scroll.

A series of grainy images slid up the page. A bar. A chandelier. Selfies of smiling, happy, drunken people. At the Gilded Cage. Yes, she'd seen all this.

But then the images moved on to what looked like a private

room. Studded red velvet walls, gold velvet couches, a mini chandelier, drinks and snacks laid out on a small table. All of this seen through a door left slightly ajar.

And inside Sawyer in his battered leather jacket, his jaw covered in stubble. And she in her pink tulle-skirted dress, her hair a little wild, her shoes tossed onto the couch.

The next shot—she was holding Sawyer's hand. Her other hand touching her chest as she grinned at him. Grinned *down* at him.

Since he was *down on one knee.*

And just like that the floodgates opened, and image after image from the night at the Gilded Cage came swarming back to her.

Begging the DJ to play Prince and Kylie and the Bee Gees.
Someone suggesting karaoke.

Sawyer saying, "Leave it to us," then holding her hand as he led her through the crowd to a private room he'd nabbed at the flick of a wrist because he owned the place.

Then a beat, a moment, a window in the night where every-thing went quiet. The air felt cool without the crush of people. And she leant against a couch in a private room, filled with such release and joy at having Sawyer all to herself.

Sawyer. All dusty curls and beautifully smiling eyes.

Sawyer, down on one knee, asking her to—

"There's a video too," said Mimi, snapping Petra back to the present, her voice hushed, reverent.

She clicked on a news article—*a news article!*—*Mystery Mistress Revealed in Exclusive! Heiress to Society Couple Sweeps Billionaire Bachelor Off His Feet! Literally!*

It was so close to the headline Sawyer had joked about, her knees nearly gave out.

And Mimi kept on scrolling. Then, stopping on a video, she clicked.

In the video—taken sneakily, seedily, through the half-open door of the private karaoke room—Sawyer dropped to his knee, held out his hand, while Petra stood barefoot, swaying and smiling so widely she was sure she'd never looked so happy.

"And—?" said Mimi.

"There's an *and*?" Petra asked.

"Your mother keeps calling."

Petra checked her watch, on which she'd set Do Not Disturb during the meeting, to find that, yes, her mother had called. And messaged. As had Deena. A number of media sites had emailed. Even a top wedding dress designer, with the subject line *Symbiotic Opportunity*, which she assumed meant they wanted to offer her a free dress so long as she promoted the heck out of them. Along with a bunch of numbers she didn't recognise.

She stopped only when she found a message from Sawyer. He'd pinned an address. Nothing else. As if he knew that what they had to say to one another had to be said in person.

"Petra?"

She spun to find the gallery manager poking her head around the door.

"Sorry to interrupt, but we do have to get back to the floor before the gallery opens—"

"Right. Of course." Petra gave the tablet to Mimi, who patted her on the arm, her expression saying *You've got this, boss*.

Petra walked back into the conference room to find the others huddled over their phones. As one, they looked up.

The assistant manager, a guy around Petra's age, said, "Is it inappropriate to admit I had such a crush on your fiancé when I was a kid?"

Get in line, Petra thought, laughter gathering at the back of her throat. Then, *My fiancé?*

She opened her mouth to deny all.

Then remembered Sawyer's adage. *"Never deny—no matter how wacky—denial will become the story."*

The last thing the gallery needed was a 'story' taking focus away from the event she was determined to launch.

The term *whiff of scandal* started beating a tattoo inside Petra's head. As if it had been inevitable somehow, from the moment her mother had typed those words. Inevitable that she would disappoint them.

Sawyer warned you this wouldn't magically go away, a voice said, and tut-tutted in the back of her head.

Only she'd been so determined to see him, to do what *she* wanted to do, she might as well have stuck her fingers in her ears and cried, *La-la-la-la-la-la!*

She needed to talk to him. Now.

"I'll let you guys go," Petra said to the room, sounding far calmer than she felt. "Please think over my idea. Any questions, ask. And trust me, I can do this. It will be amazing. And it might just save the gallery."

They all left, smiling and full of beans, where they'd been hesitant and obstructive only minutes earlier.

"I have to go," Petra told Mimi as she hustled to her office.

"No worries. I'll hold the fort." Mimi closed Petra's door and hopped straight on the phone as if nothing had happened.

Petra sent her mother a quick text.

Hey, Mum. Busy now. Talk soon. Don't panic. Everything's fine!

She wondered if she should use all caps to really hit that home.

Then, ignoring all other notifications, she searched her name, and Sawyer's. And there it was—Sawyer dropping to one knee, holding something in his hand. It had been cropped, enhanced like something out of a police procedural TV show.

Petra gasped. Literally. The sound filling her ears. For if

nothing else about that shot made any sense to her, one thing sealed it.

She grabbed her handbag, tipped the contents onto her desk and rifled through the detritus till she found what she was looking for.

The small Ziplock bag the dry-cleaner had handed her.

The *pocket stuff.*

And there, inside, the ring pull from the soft drink can.

The one Sawyer was handing her in the pictures.

Her engagement ring.

Petra's high heels clacked and wobbled as she strode along the dock looking for the address Sawyer had pinned: the berth number for the Big Think yacht at Melbourne Marina.

A yacht, a nightclub, a graffiti installation/building, at least a couple of hotels… No wonder the guy didn't need a house, he had a thousand places to stay. And yet he'd stayed with her. Till he hadn't.

Why? That was one of the many burning questions she'd be asking him. *Why did you stay? And why did you leave last night?* And the big one, *Why on earth did you propose to me? Then why not tell me when you had the chance?*

Petra slowed as the berth number neared, then looked up to find herself facing the kind of boat usually only seen in Netflix series about fake heiresses. She'd figured the billionaire thing was some tricksy PR angle, but in that moment realised it must be true.

Discombobulated, overtired and all mixed up inside, she went to yell his name, with gusto, until she saw the name of the yacht. *Candy.* And all the wild thoughts swirling about inside her head quieted.

Candy had been Sawyer's nickname, back in his football days, so good was he at selling fake hand-balls—aka candy to babies—before wrong-footing the opposition and getting clear. The nickname given to him by Finn.

He struggled to talk about her brother, yes, and the way he tried to take Finn's place could be frustrating, but everything pointed to him still feeling the loss in a big way. Which made it hard for her to stay angry at him. People did dumb things when they were hurting.

A flash of something on the top deck caught her eye.

"Sawyer?" she called.

Then there he was, easing around the stern. Decked out in a T-shirt and shorts, his skin tanned and beautiful, his hair ruffled by the sea breeze. If she didn't feel so hamstrung by the whole situation, she might well have swooned.

"What on earth are you wearing?" he asked, as if he was the one who deserved answers!

Petra looked down at her ridiculous get-up, having forgotten she was in disguise. "I borrowed a coat from one of the security guards, and we found a scarf in some leftover merchandise for a Monet exhibition to cover my hair. Then Mimi organised for a car to pick me up from the storage bay so I could get away unseen. By some miracle, it worked."

He gripped the handrail and shielded his eyes from the sun. Was he...? He was laughing!

"None of this is funny!" she cried.

"You're absolutely right."

"We have things to discuss!"

"Then come on up."

She tipped her sunglasses forward, clocked the distance between the bobbing stern and the dock, imagining how her heels might manage it. "Why don't you come down here?"

Sawyer leaned against the railing and squinted her way, as if he was auditioning for an aftershave commercial.

They'd be so lucky, Petra thought, remembering his hand on her cheek, his eyes clouding, all that smoulder focused her way. Before he'd done a runner and ended up on a million-dollar yacht.

Gaze locked onto hers, Sawyer said, "Because out here, on the water, there is a thousand percent higher chance that we can have a conversation without a telephoto lens bearing down on us. And shoes off," he called. "House rules." Before moving to unhitch the boat from its mooring.

Petra, realising she had about half a minute to either join him or be left behind, unzipped her boots, tucked them over her handbag, then hitched her coat and climbed on board.

Sawyer met her up top with a bright yellow safety vest in hand.

"Do I really need that?"

"Humour me," he said. And the heat in his voice, the dark glint in his eye, had her doing as he asked.

Stripping off coat, scarf, sunglasses and dumping her gear in a big pile, she donned the vest over her silk dress, then found herself a seat in the cockpit.

"Can you even drive this thing?" she asked.

"I'm willing to give it a crack," he said, before the rev of engine filled her ears, the deck beneath her swayed as Sawyer nudged them out of the berth, neatly past the line of boats, out of the marina and out to sea, where he really let it rip.

Petra held on tight to the bench beneath her, lifting her hand only to try to get her wildly flapping hair out of her mouth.

While Sawyer looked as if he'd been born on the sea, the creases around his eyes crinkling as he squinted against the light bouncing off the waves, his curls fluttering back off his face. The cotton of his T-shirt pulling tight around his biceps, the edges of one of his many tattoos poking out the bottom, the veins roping down his forearms making her mouth water.

Sawyer looked over his shoulder, as if he'd heard her thoughts.

She waved him to face the front. To watch where they were going.

For, feeling both terrified and strangely ready for it, they were about to have it out. Taking things to a place their friendship had never been before.

But it was time.

Sawyer pulled back on the rudder, the boat slowing. Then, using lots of fancy radar and autopilot tech, dropped anchor.

After which he leant back against the dash, his feet crossing at the ankles, and looked Petra's way.

The last time she'd been in the same room as him, he'd nearly kissed her. She was *sure* of it. She could still feel the heat of his touch. See the intent in his eyes. Feel the press of her heart against her ribs as it yearned for him.

And now she must look like a crazy person, with clown hair, no shoes and a bright yellow safety vest.

She tugged herself free of the thing, swiped her hair off her face, then said, "I'm assuming, judging by the size of this thing, there's somewhere more civilised we can sit."

Sawyer pointed to a doorway to the right, leading to a set of internal steps.

Petra left her gear upstairs, made her way down. A kitchen took up one end and a large comfortable-looking couch spread bench-style around the outer rim. Smoky blue windows cut out the glare.

"All this," she said, waving an arm around, "is not normal, you do realise that?" Then she plonked onto the couch, the exhaustion of the night before, the importance of the meeting that morning and the shock at finding herself the subject of a viral video finally overwhelming her.

Sawyer leant against the bar, hands gripping the bench. "I'd have come get you—"

"I know," she said, expelling a huff of breath. It must have taken some major self-control for him not to storm the gates and slay the dragon, especially where she was concerned. She appreciated the restraint.

Her gaze swept to his, to find him watching her, his expression wary. Ready for anything. And for the first time since she'd seen the video she wondered how this might all be affecting *him*.

"Are *you* okay?" Petra asked.

He blinked, his lashes bussing his cheeks. "I think you'll find that's my line."

"And yet. Are you?"

"I'll let you know in a minute or two." Because he was waiting on *her*, on her reaction to all that had unfolded that morning. "We know the video came from the puffer jacket guy. We know he contacted a footy journo who declined to pay for the footage. So he found a gossip site that would. We've approached him and found he's all apology and contrition. Sheepish, I believe was the term bandied about. I feel confident we've seen the last of him."

Yes, the video itself was a problem. But she'd put that into a box for later, the implications far too vast for her to imagine. All the space in her head had been taken up with figuring out what the heck had been happening *in* the video in the first place.

She reached into her bag, pulled out the pull tab and flashed it at him as if it were a Watergate tape.

"You kept it," he said, his voice gravelly.

"I didn't *keep* it. The dry-cleaner gave it to me and I forgot to throw it out. For, at the time, I had no idea it had any significance." She curled the strange little artefact back into her hand, as if it was something precious rather than merely evidence. "What were you *thinking*?"

He didn't say.

Which was fine, because Petra wasn't done. "And when I

asked you point-blank if anything happened that night, you looked me in the eye and said we just talked."

He shifted a little.

"I know we were in a private room at the time, so there was an expectation of privacy, but you got down on one knee and—" she stopped, swallowed, unable to believe she was about to say the next words "—proposed to me. Using a pull tab. Why? Were you *that* drunk?"

"I was not."

Now he speaks!

Petra raised an eyebrow. "*It's been a long trip. Hard. Tequila, and leave the bottle...*"

"Is that meant to be me?" he asked, his voice low, ominous.

But she was not to be stopped. "Uncanny, right?"

Sawyer's eyes flashed. "I had a couple of shots. Then I stopped. I wasn't about to put myself in a position where I couldn't look out for you."

Petra breathed deeply, and slowly, her voice roiling into a growl, she said, "It's *not* your job to look out for me, Sawyer! What we are to one another, it goes beyond your friendship with Finn, or...or it doesn't work at all."

Otherwise this was all it would ever be: her crushing on him, he protecting her. Now and for ever. And she simply refused to play that game any more.

"Sawyer, I need you to...to respect that I'm fully capable of making my own choices. Making my own mistakes. Dealing with embarrassment. And cleaning up my own messes. All things that I am well-versed in."

Sawyer ran a hand up the back of his neck, looking discomfited. But then he pressed away from the bar, prowled to the couch and sat by her side. Bent over, elbows resting on his knees, he looked to her and said, "You're thirty."

"I'm thirty?" she said. "What has that got to do with...?

Do you mean the promise we made at my *eighteenth* birthday party?"

"It came up."

"You mean *I* brought it up?"

A single nod.

Her eighteenth birthday party had been a formal affair, populated by her parents' friends and their kids. The only highlight? Sawyer. Showing up unexpectedly, for the first time in several months, having disentangled himself from her grieving family not long after Finn had died.

High from seeing him, she'd jokingly—or not so jokingly—convinced him to make a 'let's get married if neither of us are by the time I'm thirty' pact. Which neither had brought up again in all the years since. Except she had. At the Gilded Cage. Leading to him getting down on one knee.

Sawyer hadn't told her, because to him it didn't register as important.

Because it wasn't real.

Done, cooked, over and out, Petra sank low in the chair, her legs poking out in front of her, her eyes squeezed shut. Only for the taste of lemon, salt and tequila to suddenly hit the back of her tongue.

"Petra," Sawyer said, his voice deep with anguish. And apology. But she was not having it.

"Shh!" she insisted, holding up a finger as she felt a swell of memories break the surface...

"Do you remember my eighteenth birthday party?" she asked as she leaned against the velvet couch in the private karaoke room.

She was waiting for the hen night girls to join them. Till then, the relative quiet was a relief.

Sawyer stood by the door. "I do."

"Do you remember your gift to me?" said Petra, holding eye contact for all she was worth.

Sawyer's nostrils flared.

In case that was a no, she said, *"If neither of us was married by the time I turned thirty, you'd...do the deed."*

Sawyer coughed out a laugh, but there was no humour in it. In fact, it appeared as if he was masking a measure of pain. *"Were you drinking tequila that night too?"*

"Grapefruit Vodka Cruisers. I thought they were the height of sophistication."

"And now?" he asked.

"Haven't touched one since that night." A pause. *"And I turned thirty last summer."*

She tipped forward, flashing her left hand at him, to prove it was devoid of rings. *"I know,"* she said, *"big shock, right? I mean I have a crazy cool career. I'm well-travelled, I have great taste in movies, I'm cute."*

She awaited confirmation.

"Am I not cute?"

"As a button," he said, a muscle twinging in his cheek. *"Instead of karaoke, how about I see you home?"*

No way was she going home when Sawyer Mahoney had just admitted he thought she was cute. Yes, she'd forced it out of him, the same way she'd forced him to promise to marry her. But still.

"I'm flexible," she said, pressing away from the couch to tiptoe around the small room, as if she might do a split leap at any moment, only to forget what she was saying when she noticed the fabulous wallpaper and the cool vintage op shop art. *"I can't cook, but I'm a champion at take-out. And I have stamina. Like super-human stamina. Just ask Russell."*

At that Sawyer looked to the ceiling and seemed to whisper some kind of prayer under his breath.

"You know what?" said Petra, spinning to point a finger

Sawyer's way. His face wavered at the end. Or maybe that was her. "I'm a freaking catch!"

Sawyer, who'd been glancing between the exit and Petra, as if readying to step in and rescue her if required, shot his gaze to hers, his eyes dark, strained and...hot. As if he was using copious amounts of energy to fend off her attributes. In case they hit their target. Which was, of course, him.

Sawyer, who smelled like a summer storm. And apples. And leather. And kindness. Did kindness have a smell? Sawyer, who made her feel all the feely feelings.

No other man had made her feel that way. Not the shy taxidermist. Not the drummer who was obsessed with the pre-Raphaelites. The good men, the loud men, the arty men. She'd tried them all on for size, hoping one might stand out, might see some stray pink found thing and think of her.

"I'm never going to find someone," she said, "and it's all your fault."

"Petra..." he said, his voice wary.

And through her fuzzy gaze she saw him start to think, to put two and two together. Meaning soon he'd figure out that she'd been in love with him for sixteen-odd years.

Her chest tightened. She started to panic.

She blurted, "The promise! What if it's the promise holding me back? Like it's a curse. Or there's some psychological block stopping me from finding my person."

Outside the small room Kylie sang about spinning around. While inside the room Sawyer looked at her as if he believed her. And she found herself counting down to the moment he bolted for the door.

Instead, he dropped to one knee.

Petra's hands flew up in the air. "What are you doing?"

"Breaking the curse," he said.

Then he leapt back up again. Or stood with a wince, considering his old injury. Found a can on the coffee table and twisted off the pull tab. Sank slowly back to one knee and held the "ring" on the palm of his hand.

Petra's senses sharpened, as if she'd sobered up quite a bit.

Then everything seemed to slow, to unfurl, as Sawyer's deep, husky voice said, "Petra Gilpin, will you do me the honour of fulfilling the promise we made all those years ago, when you were young and knew no better, and tipsy on Vodka Cruisers, and say that you will marry me?"

Petra opened her mouth to answer, only to find her mouth was already open and no sound was coming out.

Sawyer went on, "After which you will rightly change your mind, so that the curse of the promise is broken and you can get on with your life. Unhindered. Open to find your person." A quick smile. A heartbreaking smile. Then, "What say you?"

Feeling silly, and more than a little hurt—mostly by herself for letting it get that far, Petra grabbed Sawyer by the hand and hauled him back to stand.

Just as Deena and the hen night girls piled into the room.

Petra fluttered her eyes open to find she was still on the yacht, muted sunlight slanting through the tinted windows.

Sawyer had gone down on one knee to break the curse of a promise he'd made all those years before, so that she could feel free to love someone else.

If she hadn't known what heartbreak felt like before that moment, she knew now.

CHAPTER SEVEN

IN THAT MOMENT Petra felt a clarity she'd not felt since she'd arrived back home, as the entirety of her situation unspooled before her.

Taking on a job she was not fit to do, in the hope of finding some connection with her parents. And throwing herself in Sawyer's path, in the hopes he'd see how important he was to her.

All of which was now out there, in the public domain, for anyone and everyone to pick apart at their leisure.

It was all such a mess that she began to laugh. Till her eyes streamed and her stomach hurt. Till she wondered if she might, in fact, be falling apart.

Sawyer slid along the couch till his thigh bumped hers, his hand landing on the back of her neck gently, warmly, sending goosebumps skittering all over her already fraught body.

No, he didn't get to do that to her unless he meant it. She sat up and shook him off, turning to face him with an accusing finger keeping him at bay.

"You pretend proposed to me because of some silly joke made years ago."

Not a joke.

"In order to break my bad dating curse."

Not a curse.

"But I never actually said yes."

Why hadn't she said yes? Some latent self-protective in- stinct that had beaten the tequila?

For a second she felt fiercely proud, while also terribly be- reft.

"Which matters not a jot, for the whole world *thinks* we're engaged. Which we can't deny, because that will somehow only make it more true."

Sawyer held up a hand and said, "May I speak?"

Petra's glare could have burned holes in his clothes. But then she'd be dealing with glimpses of Sawyer's bare chest, and the last thing she needed to add to the mix was Sawyer- lust. Which, despite being upset with him right now, never seemed to go away.

"Forget about the video," he said. "Forget about that whole night. We were, neither of us, at our most lucid. So I suggest we give ourselves a break, let that go down in flaming his- tory, and figure out what to do from here." A beat then, "How does that sound to you?"

It sounded…like a good place to start. She nodded and said, "Fine. So what's the plan?"

"You tell me."

Right. So this was where her *I'm fully capable of mak- ing my own mistakes* speech came back to bite her. That was quick. But at least he was listening. Trusting her to take the lead. Reminding her that he *was* on her side.

"Where do I even start?" she relented.

"What do you want, Petra? What do you want to get out of this? What do you want to happen?"

"I want," she said, "to be able to do what I'm really damn good at, without anyone looking over my shoulder and judg- ing how I go about it."

He nodded. "So, what can we do to facilitate that?"

"We control the narrative."

A smile shot across his face, and she softened towards him

a little more. Despite how much easier it made things to think that way, Sawyer was not the bad guy here. They were truly mixed up in this thing together.

He sat back, his knee shifting to point her way, his meaty arm resting along the back of the couch. "So, what's our story?"

"It's not what it looks like? Just a drunken misunderstanding?"

"We can go that way. Sure. If you think you can smooth things over with the gallery, I can deal with Hadley. Or?"

"Or," she said, warming to this now, "I could push you overboard. Or smother you with one of these cushions. Then everyone will feel sorry for me and give me everything I want."

A grin. The kind that shot straight to her middle and lit a fire deep down inside. "That's a story all right. Unfortunately for you, my survival instincts are pretty good. I'd fight back. Any other ideas?"

Just one. The most dicey one. The one she was sure—considering past actions—would send him jumping overboard without need of a push.

"We honour the original promise."

Something flickered behind his gaze, as if he'd been expecting it. All of it. All along. And he'd been patiently waiting for her to come to the same conclusion.

"We remain," she set out, just in case he wasn't following along, "for all intents and purposes engaged. Until some cat is born that barks like a dog and we become old news. Then we gently go back to the way things were before."

"Right," he said, with a finality that she felt scoot down her spine.

"*Right* as in you would buy a poster starring the Barking Cat, considering your affinity for such things, or *right* as in... the rest."

His smile was smoother that time. More focused. "All of the above."

"Really?" she asked, her voice kicking high. "You'd do that? For me?"

He cocked his head, as if to say, *Petra, I'd do anything for you. And if you don't know that by now, then you've not been paying attention.*

Feeling it now, how it might work, how it could make all the *whiff of scandal* stuff go away, she turned to face him, her knee bumping his as it swept up onto the couch. "There is a lot *not* to like about the idea. We'd be lying, for one thing. To our families, our friends, our workplaces. I just... I don't think I can do that."

"It doesn't have to be a lie."

Petra's heart forgot itself for a beat, seizing up, before slamming against her ribs. "Meaning...what, exactly?"

He held out his hand. When she stared at it, he wriggled his fingers and said, "Gimme the ring."

She opened her hand to find the pull tab still tucked up safely inside.

Sawyer plucked it from her palm. Then eased himself off the couch and onto the floor, where he landed. On one knee.

"Oh, get up!" Petra said, rearing back, her voice echoing around the small space. "Seriously. It was ill-thought-out the first time and now you're just being ridiculous."

But he remained there, kneeling before her, looking strangely at ease. Sawyer the knight in shining armour, in his element. Then he held up the pull tab, twisting it back and forth so that it caught the light.

And despite the fact that it had been yanked from a random can at a bar, she found herself captured. By the enormity of his offer, the deference with which he'd gone about it, and the talisman itself. This strange, sharp-edged thingamajig that had no meaning to anyone but them. Which made it a thing of beauty in itself.

"Petra Gilpin," he said, his voice sombre, his expression fierce, "will you do me the honour of agreeing to be my fiancée?" Then, "Till the time comes when it's no longer necessary to pretend."

She knew what he meant, but for a blissful few moments her brain took his words a very different way.

Drunk, bolshie and high on lemon pulp, she'd managed to protect herself from a moment such as this. Now, in the cold light of day, she found the wherewithal to say, "I have one provision. You can't do what you did last night."

His gaze flared. And for a moment she wondered if he thought she was referring to the near kiss.

"By that," she explained, "I mean you can't just leave, not without warning. Not without reason. I mean, you can do as you please, because you are your own person, and this will all be pretend. Just… I'd appreciate it if you could give me a heads-up, and some context, so that I don't worry."

And don't consistently feel like it's my fault that you go.

Sawyer breathed out hard through his nose. "Were you truly worried last night?"

"I wasn't, because I'm aware that you can handle yourself. And yet I was."

Because I wasn't entirely sure if you'd come back.

"So long as we're in this I won't go far, not without notice. Fair?"

"Fair."

"So, what'll it be?"

Which was how, the second time Sawyer Mahoney got down on one knee to ask Petra Gilpin to marry him, she let him slide the pull tab onto the tip of her finger, for the thing was not built to go past a knuckle, and she said, "Fine. What the heck."

"What the heck?" Sawyer repeated, clearly bemused.

Petra coughed out a laugh, feeling as if all the tension inside her had been replaced by helium. "Well, what did you expect me to say? *Yes! A thousand times, yes*?"

"That level of enthusiasm wouldn't go amiss." Wincing, Sawyer pressed his hand onto his thigh to find leverage to get himself back up.

"Your leg!" said Petra, reaching to help him up onto the couch, dragging him so that he sat right by her. Her skirt caught under his thigh, her hand hooked around his arm. Their faces danger close.

"Seriously," she said on an exhalation of breath that shifted the hair by his ear. "The one knee thing was not necessary."

"Except now, when anyone asks, we can tell the truth—I fell to one knee and begged you to be mine."

"You didn't have to beg all that hard."

His eyes swept over hers, and she wondered if he saw the truth behind the joke. Saw how being this close to him messed with her completely.

"I mean, come on," she said, doing her best to keep things light. "I'm now officially fake-engaged to one of the *Top Ten Sexiest Single Billionaire Bachelors Under Forty Alive!* Or maybe they didn't have to be alive... I can't remember."

Sawyer laughed, though it sounded far more as if he was in pain.

"Truly, though," she said, using her hand at his elbow to yank him a little closer, the feel of him all up in her space making everything else feel secondary, "I am so grateful to you, Sawyer Mahoney. Grateful that you are good-looking enough that people might *actually* believe I'd want to marry you."

"Is that right?" he said, and something changed in his gaze. As if one second he was Sawyer Mahoney, the next he was *Sawyer Mahoney*. Bringing her right back to the night before, his hand on her face, the *certainty* that he'd wanted to kiss her.

And she wondered—just how far *would* he go for her?

If she wanted to touch him, would he let her? If she moved to kiss him, would he lean in? He shifted on the seat, adjusting himself, and she knew. Knew in that deep, most feminine place that all she had to do was ask.

"What is going on in that head of yours?" he asked, his voice deep.

Petra felt completely hollow now. As if she was made of the most delicate shell. But she managed to say, "Watch many Netflix romances, do you?"

His surprise at the change of subject was clear. "Not a lot of time for Netflix on the road."

"Imagine a princess who's not really a princess, who becomes fake engaged to a carpenter who's actually a prince. For terribly good reasons. Only now they have to decide how far they'll go, in public, to sell the story."

She licked her bottom lip and Sawyer's gaze moved to her mouth. Where it stayed.

His voice was rough as he said, "Still no idea what you're talking about."

"They must agree, the non-princess and the carpenter prince, the boundaries of their fake relationship. Enough to convince the world that the relationship is true, not so much either party feels uncomfortable."

"Define 'so much'," Sawyer said. Then he shifted again, dragging the edge of her swishy silk skirt underneath him more, so that her legs were bare from her chipped pink toenails to halfway up her thigh.

Which he noticed, she noticed, the whites of his eyes turning to smoke.

"Okay," she managed, even as her skin began to flame, her breath now hard to come by. "Do they make goo-goo eyes at one another? Do they hold hands? Do they…?" She took a quick breath. "Do they kiss? If so, is there a time-limit on the kiss? Do they—?"

"Who are we talking about again?" Sawyer asked, his eyes so dark she could barely make out the colour.

"The non-princess," said Petra, her voice cracking. "And the carpenter prince. They have to prove they don't hate one another, remember?"

"Right. But I don't think anyone would ever accuse the two of us of *hating* one another."

An innocuous claim, only the way he said it made it feel as if it was crystal-clear to the whole wide world that they felt something very different from hate.

"So this is about *us* now?" she asked.

His gaze returned to hers, and the little finger of the hand at the end of the arm she still held began to trace circles on her bare thigh. "Petra, it's always been about us."

And Petra nearly expired on the spot.

"So," she said, "what do we do? To convince everyone we're—" She paused when she felt the lift of his chest, so close to hers now they nearly touched.

"Madly in love?" Sawyer finished.

"Well," she said, "I was going to say convince everyone we're hot and heavy behind closed doors, but sure. Let's go with madly in love."

He laughed, the rough sound vibrating through her, his breath rushing over her hair. He was so close now, every time she breathed she caught the scent of him. She wished she could run her fingers over his cheek, his jaw, his lips. Or her lips. Tasting him. As if simply finding out if he was as warm and tough as he looked would fulfil her for the rest of time.

"Do you think," she said, "that we can pull it off?"

The moment felt like a soap bubble—precious and precarious—and she wanted it to go on for ever.

"Yeah," he said, brushing the back of his hand against the

edge of her skirt, before his hand landed on her knee. "I reckon we can."

Petra had never let herself believe there was the remotest chance that he felt for her the way she felt for him. If she had, she'd never have dated, much less tried to muddle her way through a relationship. She'd have been doomed to a life lived alone, without even the chance of reprieve.

But what if he *did* feel the same way she did? All this—the sleepovers, the massages, the hair play, the hot glances, the touching, the near kiss, the proposal, the second proposal... Surely that added up to something? Something bigger than she'd allowed herself to believe?

"On that note," she said, before she lost her nerve, her voice barely above a whisper, "last night, before you felt a sudden need to go water a horse, I got the feeling that... That you wanted to kiss me."

There, bomb dropped. Whatever happened from here, that could not be unsaid. Good. Great! It was about time!

Except Sawyer said nothing.

Petra, already rolling downhill, added, "I want you to know, for the sake of the current conversation, that I'd have been amenable to that. If that were, in fact, the case."

Nothing. Only the dark clouds in his eyes, the stroke of his thumb over her thigh.

"Now's really not the moment to go all stoic on me, Sawyer," she said, her voice croaky. Her need for him to meet her halfway verging on panic. "Tell me I was wrong. Or tell me I was right."

She could see the argument going on behind his eyes. *Years'* worth of convincing himself that she was Finn's little sister warring against the attraction that had pulled them together, till she was a heartbeat away from curling up on his lap.

Then he shook his head slowly back and forth. Only she

knew it wasn't a *No, I feel nothing for you* shake but a *Petra, do you know what you're asking?* shake.

The slow build, the fast burn, the years of yearning. It all pulsed within her. And she knew that if this wasn't going to happen when she was engaged to the guy, then it was never going to happen at all.

"Screw it," Petra said and, grabbing Sawyer by the shirt front with both hands, she dragged him to her and planted a kiss on his mouth.

Direct hit. So unexpected to the both of them, their teeth clashed, just a little.

While Petra winced, Sawyer did not react, not in the optimal way a man might act after finding himself kissed.

He. Did. Not. Kiss. Her. Back.

Seconds slunk by. Two, maybe three. Or maybe a hundred. An interminable amount of time in which Petra regretted every decision that had led her to this moment. A feeling that worsened when her eyes sprang open to find his staring into hers.

Oh, God...oh, God...oh, God.

What had she done?

There was no taking this back! No jetlag or tequila to blame. No amount of pretending in the world that could make this go away. Mortified, devastated, she made to pull back, her breath rushing past her lips and over his on a ragged, aching sigh—

Then Sawyer's eyes slammed closed, his hand dived into the back of her hair and he angled the kiss, slanting his mouth over hers with the most perfect, soft, warm seal that had ever existed on planet Earth.

He wanted this! He wanted her!

Telling herself to stop thinking and just *be*, for this might *never* happen again, Petra let herself let go. Let every feeling she'd ever felt for him rush to the surface, filling her with sweetness, and magic, and joy.

Sawyer's arms slid around her waist, pulling her close, spinning her up and onto his lap. Till they were entwined round one another, clothes twisted, hands lost in touching one another.

And his kisses, those drugging kisses, took her down, down, down—till she could barely see for the fog.

Needing more, needing all of him, she shifted, turned, tucked her knees either side of his hips. Her hands reached for the hem of his shirt, lifting, yanking, till she found skin.

All that hot, hard, smooth, glorious skin. She traced his ribs, his sides, the rough of his tattoos, the whorls of hair on his chest.

And when her hand dived to the waistband of his shorts he rasped, "Hold on," against her hot mouth.

But she didn't want to hold on. She wanted to keep going. Forward. No looking back. Sinking down into his lap, her centre notched to his. His…hard, hot, ready centre, pressing against the seam of his shorts. Pressing against her.

And they pulled apart as one. Their eyes met. Wild and reckless.

His were asking, *Are we really doing this?*

She answered with a roll of her hips, her teeth biting down on her bottom lip to hold in the moan.

Breathing out hard, Sawyer used both hands to press back her hair. Then, holding her face, he pressed a soft kiss to her mouth. To each cheek. To each eyelid.

Then, with her eyes still closed, he kissed his way down her neck, easing the loose neck of her soft dress aside as he grazed his teeth over her collarbone.

Then, with the utmost care, he dragged one shoulder free as he nuzzled his nose over the edge of her lace bra, his teeth grabbing the edge and pulling it down, down. Till she felt the waft of his warm breath over her exposed breast, a moment before his mouth closed over her nipple.

And there he remained for the longest time, tasting, licking, biting, sucking. Learning her breaths, her gasps, what made her roll against him as she chased the pleasure he gave.

He licked his way across to the other side, tugging her shirt so that her arms were now pinned to her sides, before yanking the bra cup aside and sucking her breast into his mouth.

She cried out, no amount of lip-biting could hold her back.

When the pleasure built inside her so thick, so rushed, so wild that she thought she might finish from his kisses alone, she managed to lift her arms enough to cradle his head and drag his mouth back to hers.

Sawyer lifted her from the couch in one easy move, as if she weighed nothing, as if she gave him superhuman strength. Then they were moving through the lounge.

She could sense the boat around them—the tight furniture, the lull of the water, the angled walls. But she trusted Sawyer to navigate it. To protect her.

She hitched herself higher, wrapped her legs around his waist. One hand thrust into her hair as he kissed her as if she was the very air he needed, his other hand held her backside, her skirt and the flimsiest of underwear all that kept him from touching her where she wanted him to touch her most.

Inside a double bedroom, he tossed her to the bed. She landed, she bounced and she laughed, the sound echoing off tinted windows with a view of sky and ocean and nothing else.

Then she realised that she was alone on the bed.

Sawyer was standing at the end, his hair a mess, his T-shirt skew-whiff, the evidence of his desire tenting his shorts in such a way her mouth went dry.

She could see him overthinking, see him second-guessing. Was he really about to pull a Sawyer and do the right thing, putting an end to it all?

"Stay with me," she said, lifting up onto her elbows. Not a request, a demand. "I *want* this." Then, in case he needed it to be as clear as it was possible for it to be, she braved up and added, "I've always wanted this."

She let her knee fall to one side, her dress sliding down her thigh. His gaze dropped, the heat therein enough to scorch her from head to toe.

Then he tugged off his shirt, in that seriously sexy back to front way men used, and she felt so happy, so overjoyed, she lay back on the bed and laughed.

The bed moved as Sawyer climbed into the end, crawling up her body till he rested on his hands over the top of her. His face was so close she could count the three perfect freckles beneath his left eye, the tangle of lashes, the rough scrape of stubble on his beautiful jaw.

And that bare chest, with the wings of the phoenix tattoo that covered his upper back curling over both shoulders. Myriad tattoos, curling and merging over that warm brown skin, some hidden beneath swirls of coarse dark hair. It was all she could do not to growl.

Hooking her foot around his backside, she pulled him to her, eyes fluttering as his centre met hers. Then he moved, so that they could fit together more fully, and so that he didn't crush her with his bulk.

Then he leaned in and brushed his lips over hers. Gently. Sweetly. Tasting her. Taking her lower lip between his and tugging.

She felt drugged. Loose. Limp. Her skin on fire.

When her mouth popped open on a sigh he took advantage, covering her mouth with his, his tongue sweeping inside.

She used her leg around his backside to press herself closer, to rub against him, to give herself some relief. Before his kisses sent her swirling into madness.

Then he moved away, enough that she grabbed for him.

"It's okay," he promised, a smile in his voice, and wonder and heat. "Just evening the score."

With that he peeled her dress down her arms and over her hips, his skin rough, his hands gentle. His gaze fierce as he drank her in.

Then it was hot damp skin on hot damp skin. Hands everywhere. The taste of his skin in her mouth as she dragged her teeth over his shoulder in a way that had him crying out. And pressing himself against her in a way that sent her mind blank with pleasure.

Somehow they were both naked, protected, and when he kissed her then there was no holding back. No thought, just feeling. Touch. Worship. Chasing one another's sighs and gasps.

No boundaries, no questions, just raw feeling and relief.

Till Petra was gone. Lost to sensation. All the feelings she'd ever felt for this man rolling through her like a summer storm.

And when it broke, when *she* broke, it was wild, and vast, and inevitable.

CHAPTER EIGHT

SHEET HALF FALLING off the too-small bed, one arm crooked behind his head, the other hand unconsciously tracing the tattoos covering his left pec, Sawyer lay back and stared at the panelled ceiling of the cabin.

He could almost feel the rocking of the waves if he concentrated hard enough. Though concentration was nearly impossible with the sound of the shower just behind the bathroom door. His mind playing out every move he imagined Petra making as she took that shower.

He pulled himself to sitting and ran both hands over his face. Hard. Trying to pin down some crummy feeling that he could grip onto. Shame? Disappointment? Only he felt none of them. Not a lick.

From the moment he'd seen Petra standing on the jetty looking so damned adorable in that oversized coat, dark sunglasses, scarf around her head, he'd felt as if some inevitable force had finally caught up with him.

The fake engagement, play-acting how that might look and finally, *finally*, kissing her, holding her, tasting her, taking her to his bed, he'd almost seen it unfold before it even happened. As if it had been written in the stars.

But, for all that, he *had* crossed a line. A line he'd been nudging for years.

Every time he'd waved to her in the stands of a youth football game. Or sought her out in the gardens of her family home, offering to carry her collections, when he was meant to be hanging with Finn.

At her eighteenth birthday party, having gone specifically to apologise for not being around after Finn died. Only to see her and feel as if his twenty-year-old heart had been blown wide open.

Then that crazy night at the Gilded Cage.

After years spent keeping himself in check, it had taken one night to screw it all up. As if everything he knew about responsibility and duty had fled his head as soon as she'd hit him with that smile.

He'd been treading water ever since. Not sure if he was coming or going. There was a limit to how long a man could hold out under that pressure. And he'd finally reached his.

It was the only way he could make sense of their conversation the night before. When she'd asked about his dreams. His passions. What one thing he'd do with his life if he was given the chance.

And he'd told her the truth. That he had no dream of his own. Something he'd never really admitted to himself, much less out loud.

But rather than feeling as if his foundation had been pulled out from under him, it had been a relief to say so. A relief to tell her. The truth had set him free.

Leaving room for more truths to rise to the surface. Specifically how lovely she'd looked, sitting on the lounge room floor, her shirt half falling off one shoulder, her dark auburn hair pulled back off her face, leaving her with nowhere to hide. The attraction she felt written in every swallow, every flicker in those big hazel eyes.

He felt punch-drunk simply being with her. And now he'd not only walked over the line, he'd demolished it completely.

A bump came from the bathroom. Followed by an oath. The

shower wasn't big, as he'd discovered when he'd fled there the night before, as his last thread of self-control had begun to fray.

And, crossed line or not, he wanted to join her there. So badly he ached. He rearranged himself over the sheet, his hand staying where it was. Cupping himself. As if he might be able to hypnotise the thing into submission.

His brain wasn't helping, flashing up memories of her pink cheeks, her mouth open, her eyes hooded, back arched, her hair trailing over her bare breasts as she straddled him.

Gritting his teeth, he left *himself* alone, hauled himself to standing and paced.

He'd not join her in the shower. She needed space. Time. To think. To decide how she felt about all that had happened.

She already knew how *he* felt about it. Screwed. In every way imaginable.

Engaged—to Petra. Sleeping with Petra. Imagining ways he could actually make this work, with Petra. After spending a lifetime determined to keep her from harm, the only reason she was in this mess in the first place was because of him.

And all because of an ancient birthday promise...

It was a year or so since Finn's death when Sawyer opened the invitation, splayed out on the busted mattress in his university dorm room, paid for by a football scholarship that was looking precarious after his having asked the Dean for yet another shift in major.

The snick of the envelope, the feel of the card—a soft, buttery pink, the paper like linen over silk—was like something out of another life.

So, having not seen the Gilpins for some months, after having slowly, regretfully, necessarily disentangled himself from their all-consuming grief, he walked up the front steps of their stately Brighton house to the sound of a jazz quartet spilling across the manicured front lawn, the sight of golden lan-

terns lighting the way to the huge back yard. Neither of which seemed at all like choices the messy-haired, slow-blinking, sweet-smiling Petra he knew would have made.

So he wasn't surprised to see dozens of people in their fifties and sixties—no doubt business associates of the elder Gilpins—as well as a hundred-odd rowdy teens, dancing beneath a marquee, leaping into the pool, taking advantage of an impressive champagne fountain.

Then a shaft of moonlight fell on a willowy young woman talking to a group of suits. She wore a pale peach dress that began with a big bow gathered behind her neck and then floated around her to her ankles. Her long, smooth auburn hair was gathered in a braid over one shoulder.

It took him more than a second to realise it was the birthday girl. But his reaction to seeing her again was visceral. He felt it in his gut, behind his ribs, in the sweat of his palms, and deeper.

She took a sip of her drink and looked around. As if searching for something. Or someone.

Till her eyes found him.

Pale hazel eyes made vibrant by the moonlight and clever make-up widened. Her wide mouth fell open. Then, with a squeal, she hitched up her dress and ran across the yard.

"Sawyer! Oh, my God!"

Then she was in his arms, having thrown herself there and holding on tight.

"Thank heavens you're here. I wasn't certain you'd come."

His arms wrapped about her, holding her tight lest her momentum take them both down. "Of course I came."

She nodded into his neck. Her hair tickled his nose. Her skin felt like velvet against the roughness of his cheek. His hands dipped into the very real curves at her waist and her breasts pressed into his chest.

She smelled drinkable. There was no other word for it.

His heart beat a hard, fast, telling tattoo behind his ribs as he slowly led her to the grass, uncurled his arms from around her and shoved his hands in his pockets.

"Nice party," he said.

She pulled a face. "This has nothing to do with me," she said. "Clearly. But when they offered...after the past year, how could I say no?"

Sawyer nodded, the lump in his throat stopping any actual words from coming forth. For the loss of Finn still raged inside him. The unfairness of it all.

"I'll be at the same uni as you soon," she said. "You're looking at a Fine Arts major."

"Good for you," he said, his mind spinning to what it would be like, seeing her around campus.

He imagined her knocking on his dorm room door. Barefoot, hair loose, an eighteen-year-old's smile on her face.

"Ah!" he said. "But we might just be ships passing in the night."

"You're leaving uni?"

He'd not considered it seriously till that moment. "I'm thinking of entering the rookie draft."

His coaches were pushing him. And his teammates. And the state league organisers who couldn't understand why the consistent Best and Fairest wasn't out there. But it felt wrong, because Finn would never get the chance.

Would Petra think so too?

Her mouth popped open, her big eyes grew wide. Then she smacked him on the arm. "Sawyer, that's brilliant!"

"Yeah..." he said, and the idea now hooked in his gut.

His sisters were all doing okay. His mother loved having her first grandchild to help look after. Maybe this was the right time to do something for himself.

"It's been your dream for as long as I've known you," said Petra. "Yours and Finn's. You have to do it. Do it for him."

Her words rocketed around his chest like an out-of-control firework. The weight of responsibility settled back over him like an oft-worn cloak.

She lifted her bottle—some kind of vodka mixer—to her mouth as she looked about at the party, her glossy lips leaving a soft pink smudge on the rim.

"So, which one of those meatheads is your boyfriend?" Sawyer asked, needing to say something. "I'll need to give him a good talking-to."

Her left eyebrow kicked into a point. "I think you're mistaking me for someone else."

So, no boyfriend... Good. "Girlfriend, then?"

She grinned and shook her head. "I'm not their type. Any of them. Not cool enough. Or stylish enough. Nor do I know enough about stocks or stats and markets to keep up with them. But that's just fine, as none of them are my type either."

And something in her gaze, a level of adult knowledge, had him looking away.

Gutless, the voice inside his head spoke up.

He squished it before it could draw another breath. This had nothing to do with a game. Or intent. She and her parents were only just emerging from the worst of their grief. It was important he keep himself removed from that. For his sake, and for hers.

Then there was the fact he'd never let on to Finn about the feelings he had for his little sister. Never gauged whether they'd have his friend's blessing, figuring they had time. For her to grow up and for him to make sure he was worthy of her.

Sawyer reached out as a waiter passed, grabbing another pink bottle for Petra.

Petra deftly popped her empty bottle on the tray of the next waiter and grabbed him a can of beer. His favourite. And he wondered if that was why it was on offer.

Lifting the pull tab with a click and a swish, Petra took a sip from the can, then handed him the rest, her kiss mark right there, where his mouth would go.

He took a quick sip to get it over with. Then, with nervous tension riding high, he bounced the pull tab on his hand—palm, back of hand, palm, back of hand. A habit from his footy days, staying dexterous.

Watching his hand, Petra said, "I do wonder, though. What if I die, never having had a boyfriend?"

"Petra..." he said, unable to tell if it was warning or want grazing the edge of his tone.

"No, truly—what if I don't? It could happen. What if some disease takes out half the men on the planet? Or climate change means we all live in caves and I never get to meet anyone—?"

"If all of that actually happens then I'll help you. Somehow. Okay?"

She nodded, as if that was what she'd been asking of him all along. Then she said, "Now, where's my present?"

"Ah... My presence is the best gift of all."

"Hmm..." she said, eyes narrowed. Then she laughed, as if she'd known it somehow. Known him. That he was a show-up kind of guy rather than a pepper-with-trinkets kind of guy.

Only now he had the feeling that she'd been leading him to this point the whole time.

"How about we come up with something I want that only you can provide?" She tapped a finger to her lips.

And for a second Sawyer thought she was asking him to kiss her. For another second he wondered if he had it in him to refuse.

"I know!" she said. "How about if neither of us are married by the time I turn thirty you marry me?"

It took him a moment to pivot, before he burst out laughing.

Petra did not join him. In fact she reared back as if...as if he'd slapped her.

"Whoa! Wait... You don't mean that."

Realising his reaction had not been what she'd hoped for, he shot out his spare hand, touching her waist, his fingers dipping into the fabric till her warmth seeped through. He moved his hand to her elbow instead.

She glared at him. Said, "I mean it with every fibre of my being."

Then she hiccupped. And his panic eased. A little.

"Why?" he asked.

When what he meant was, Why me?

For he was a mess. He'd missed the draft the year he'd been meant to enter, pulling out after Finn's death. Since then he'd struggled to find any real purpose at uni. And he was still looking after his mum and sisters, who were becoming more work as they grew up rather than less.

"Why not?" she said, reaching out to touch his arm.

"I think it's the pink fizzy drink talking."

"It's not," she said, her voice now a little hoarse. "It's something I think about. A lot."

At that she lifted her chin, as if daring him to make fun. Then she shivered, goosebumps springing up all over her arms. And he realised that he still had his hand on her elbow, while hers was on his arm.

He slid his hand away. Only he took the long way round, his fingers tracing her bare arm, finding her skin so smooth and warm beneath his football-roughened palm. When his hand reached hers it was facing upward, her impossibly pale skin catching the moonlight, showing the vulnerable trace of veins beneath the surface of her wrist.

Then her hand was in his.

His, a voice reiterated inside his head.

He let her go and said, "Sure. If that's what you want for your birthday. If you and I are both single, free and clear, without even a hope of a relationship on the horizon by the time you turn thirty, let's get hitched."

"Yes!" she said, grabbing his hand and yanking him close.

So close he could see the swirl of greens and greys dancing in her eyes. So close he could almost taste her scent on the back of his tongue. That heady, wild, warm, drinkable scent.

"We can travel," she said, "and go on adventures, and eat too much, and seek out amazing little galleries in remote places. Or find some fabulous little place with a view and stay in bed all day long. And it'll be fabulous."

He started bouncing the can's pull tab on his hand again, trying to keep the image of staying in a bed with her all day long from embedding itself in his brain.

Petra caught the silver ring in mid-air and shot him a grin. Then she bounced it on her own palm, saying the letters of the alphabet along with each bounce.

"What are you doing?" he asked.

"Shh..." she said, frowning as the thing missed her hand and fell to the grass.

She picked it up and did the same on the back of her hand. Starting the alphabet under her breath again.

"I'm figuring out the initials of my future husband. Did you never play that game as a kid?"

The pull tab fell. She picked it up and tucked it into her palm.

"And?" he asked.

"Turns out you're off the hook," she said, handing the pull tab back to him. "I'll be marrying some lucky guy with the initials XO. Still, just in case, you're my backup."

He lifted his can, and she clinked it with her bottle. And they smiled at one another over their drinks. As if they both knew, somehow, that if this XO guy came along Sawyer would send him packing.

And in that perfect moment, with zing and spark swirling around them, it felt like a dance. Like no one else needed him.

Not his sisters. Not his teammates. Not even Finn.

Only her.

Sawyer pocketed the pull tab and listened as she told him about her degree, and her plan to eventually move to Paris and steep herself in coffee and paint dust and become a world-famous artist. Or a curator if it turned out she had zero talent.

She rocked from side to side as she spoke, so that her dress swished about her legs, hugging her lithe curves before floating out again.

It brought back another memory. Another time. Of her standing in the doorway of Finn's bedroom, with the boys on the floor doing homework—aka predicting the end-of-year AFL ladder to see if their favourite team, the Collingwood Magpies, might make it—asking if they'd like some snacks.

It was as if someone had shot a hose filled with cold water at the back of Sawyer's neck.

This was Petra. Finn's. Little. Sister. He'd been promising to marry her in some distant dystopian future when what he should have been promising was to fill the hole in her life Finn had left behind.

He decided then and there that he would be her safe harbour. He would not muddy his mission with feelings, or want, or anything that could jeopardise that. For however long she needed it.

Petra wiped a hand over the mirror, clearing a smear of condensation.

Baby curls had sprung up around her face, her eyes dark with smudged mascara. She turned her head to the side and a whole-body shiver rocked through her as she remembered the feel of his mouth on her neck, the murmur of his voice, the slide of his tongue, leaving stubble rash on her neck.

If anyone doubted their story, that'd clinch it!

Laugh-crying—her new go-to mood—she let her head go till her forehead hit the mirror.

How had all that sprung from a conversation about *boundaries*? If she'd known that was all it would take, she'd have brought them up years ago!

Petra lifted her head away from the mirror. "What now?" she asked her reflection.

Did they take the boat back to the marina, walk hand in hand to her work, or his, smile at any photographers who tracked them down? Say, *Surprise! We're engaged!*

Maybe. Maybe not. First, she had to leave the bathroom.

Moving to the door, she pressed her ear against the wood and listened. What was Sawyer thinking out there? Was he still in the bed where she'd left him, splayed out, his big buff body covered in half a sheet? Or was he up and dressed and just going about his business as if all that was totally normal?

For the first time in her life, calling her mother felt like the easier option.

After all the messages her mother had left that morning, it went to voicemail. Of course, it did.

"Hey, Ma, it's Petra." Well, duh. "Just in case Deena's aunt has yet to fill you in, I wanted to tell you myself that Sawyer Mahoney and I are engaged! Woo-hoo!"

Woo-hoo? She squeezed her eyes shut.

"That night we reconnected, well, it turns out there *was* a spark. And always had been. For both of us."

Gosh, she hoped Sawyer couldn't hear any of this through the door.

"I didn't tell you before, because, as you can imagine, people are pretty interested in Sawyer's life and we wanted to keep it private, for just us, as long as we could. And quiet, so as not to overshadow things, such as my super-important work at the gallery. But alas. We could not hold back that tide."

She looked to the ceiling.

"I also didn't want to upset you. Considering his connection to Finn. Because of that, this wasn't an easy thing, for either of us. It took a lot for us both to get to this point. Just so you know."

A deep breath in and out.

"Anyhoo… The secret is out. Yay us. And yay to *no whiff of scandal*! And I won't let it get in the way of my work. So. That's it. Okay, 'bye."

Tossing her phone to the bench before she made it any worse, Petra wrapped the towel tighter around herself, took a deep breath and left the bathroom.

To find Sawyer was sitting on the edge of the bed, naked, the top sheet draped over his hips. The bed in which they'd just spent the last couple of hours. Or weeks. Who could be sure? They'd certainly left no stone unturned.

Sawyer lifted his head, his expression inscrutable as he took in the small towel, the messy bun atop her head, her face scrubbed clean.

She shrugged. *This is me.*

And when he smiled, breathing out hard as he slowly shook his head, as if he'd never found her more lovely, the emotions that swept over her were like nothing she'd ever felt before.

"So," she said. "That happened."

"Mmm… Do you reckon your princess and your carpenter would be proud?"

"Ha! I think they'd be blushing to their little PG cotton socks."

His smile was different. Easier somehow, lit with some new calm she'd never seen in him before.

When he asked, "You okay?" she didn't mind at all.

And this time she thought about her answer.

She'd imagined that being with him might get him out of her system, or take the edge off at least. Only that wasn't the case.

For the Sawyer she'd spent her life adoring was the Sawyer she'd built up in her head—the good, clean-cut, endearing, supportive, beautiful boy of her youth.

The Sawyer sitting before her, rumpled and scarred and tattooed, sparks of silver in his stubble, was complicated, and stubborn, and lonesome, and over-protective, and imperfect. Add to that the knowledge that he was also the most attentive lover imaginable. Generous, open and raw.

And what had once been a river of feeling that flowed through her was now all the oceans of the world.

"I am more than okay," she said.

"Glad to hear it." Then, gripping the sheet in one hand at his hip, he stood, looking like some Roman god. He walked over to her, placed a finger under her chin, turned her head and winced. "I did that?"

"You did that."

She braced herself for an apology. But instead he smiled. No, he grinned. As if glad to have left his mark on her.

Then his gaze dropped, and the smile slipped away. Petra looked down to find her small towel had dropped open, revealing a sliver of skin down her right side. Her right thigh, the curve of her hip, the edge of her breast.

Sawyer's jaw clenched, his eyes glinting. Every muscle seeming to switch on, in the effort not to reach out and whip the thing away.

The last twenty-four hours had been a lot. The push and pull—all of it had come to a head, leading to them falling into bed.

But from here? From here it would be a choice. Whatever happened between them from this moment would redefine the parameters of their friendship for evermore.

It took her half a second's thought to let the towel fall. To move into his arms, press up onto her toes and kiss his jaw. His neck. The edge of his mouth.

It took him a little longer to make the same choice. But she got that. With Sawyer it always had.

He dropped the sheet and pulled her into his arms, kissing her with a ferocity that turned her bones to mush.

"So," she said as he kissed his way down her neck. "Just so we're on the same page, when we go back out into the world, which we will have to do eventually—"

Sawyer cut her off with a growl. And a light kiss on the gravel rash that her had ovaries sighing.

"We are engaged."

"We are," he murmured, his mouth trailing along her shoulder and back to her earlobe.

"And neither of us has a problem being touchy-feely."

"Looks that way," he said, hands sliding down her back to cup her backside as he lifted her and carried her back to the bed where he sat, her knees settling each side of his hips. Where his gaze trailed over her body, his eyes dark and murky, like a man drunk on the view.

"And we are doing *this* now too," she managed to say, even while words and thoughts were becoming hard to find, as his mouth brushed back and forth over her collarbone.

"Seems so."

Then he lifted her and tossed her to the bed. Laughter shot from her lungs as she bounced, her hair splayed behind her head. Then her still damp skin brushed against his as he crawled his way up her body. Mouth brushing her belly, her breasts, before landing on her mouth, staking his claim.

As if he'd not staked it years before.

Then he made his way back down. Licking along her ribs, into her navel and pressing her legs apart, he made himself at home.

"Tell me," he said, his deep voice rumbling against her. "Tell me you want this."

"Yes," she said, pleasure already building inside her. Roiling like a wild thing.

"Tell me."

"I want this," she whispered. "I want you."

With the sense that he'd finally let himself off the leash, Sawyer licked her centre, before dragging her into his mouth.

Petra arced off the bed. Her nerves singing, her muscles aching. Her body still recovering from the past few hours. And yet she held on. Balanced on a knife-edge between too much and more *more*—

"More," she said, hardly recognising her own voice.

And he gave her more. He gave her everything she'd ever wanted.

But not for long.

Not for long.

For soon there was nothing left to want.

CHAPTER NINE

THE NEXT TWENTY-FOUR hours were a whirlwind. Starting with a quick trip to Sawyer's mum's place to tell her the news.

As Sawyer had suggested she might, Mrs Mahoney had given them both a pat on the cheek before showing off some of the grandkids' art on the fridge, her newfound priorities clear.

He'd then messaged Daisy on the way into Big Think. Her response was:

Punching above your weight much?

Then:

For Petra: He's a total pain. Good luck to you.

Hadley had made it clear they were to head into Big Think through the *front* door. "You're not rock stars," she'd apparently said. "Its past time you own this, so that the focus can shift back to where it belongs. On the work."

And she was right.

So, hand in hand, Petra and Sawyer passed another throng of 'reporters' shouting questions. This time they were asking when the big day would be, who'd be best man, and if Petra was knocked up.

Sawyer had talked to Petra the whole time, keeping her

attention on him, his face, his smile, the protective glint in his eye, even while her heart had banged about in her throat.

Once inside the foyer of Big Think Tower, a grand three-storey atrium that took Petra's breath away, Sawyer had put his arm around her shoulders and pulled her close. While she'd taken the hand resting over her shoulder in her hand and held it tight.

Then upstairs, in an office she'd have picked as Sawyer's in an instant—considering the understated colours, the beautiful vintage map on the wall and the grand final medal draped over a bust of Groucho Marx—Hadley had sat them both down for "media training", to "get their stories straight".

While waiting for the hairdresser who was prepping them for their "candid engagement photo" to finish faffing with her fringe, Petra lifted her eyebrows at Sawyer, mouthing, *Does she know?*

Sawyer laughed. "That's just Hadley. Warm and fuzzy to her is like sunlight to a vampire."

"I heard that," said Hadley.

"Don't be mean," Petra said, smacking Sawyer on the arm by way of apology. "Hadley's put this all together for us with half a day's notice. She's a freaking queen."

Hadley had lifted her chin in agreement, while shooting Petra a quick smile. And in that moment Petra knew she'd made herself an ally.

Which had been quickly balanced out by her mother finally responding.

PASS ON OUR CONGRATULATIONS TO SAWYER.

With an unexpected addendum:

AND DO TAKE CARE.

Then that afternoon, while working from the apartment, Mimi called to let her know the gallery management had been in touch to let her know they were fully on board with the Epic Dream Festival.

Mimi was over the moon when she relayed the phone call she'd received. "They said it sounds amazing! They can't wait to see what we come up with! Oh, and they sent congratulatory flowers as well, from the whole team. In fact, there are flowers everywhere in your office. From so many people. I hope you don't get hayfever."

Petra gave Mimi the required *rah-rah-rah*, while quietly noting they'd only found her idea exciting after Big Think had started leaking news of a possible announcement.

It was a relief to know she had a mandate going forward. One she could sink her teeth into. That was the point of the whole endeavour after all. But it was also deeply disquieting.

As Petra, the internationally renowned art curator, the gallery management had been unsure. Her boho clothes, her hand-drawn pitch making them look at her as if she wasn't worth their faith.

As Sawyer Mahoney's *fiancée* she was in like Flynn!

After spending a lifetime carving out her own space in the world, a space she'd had to work her ass off to make her own, once again a label she knew did not rightly belong to her defined her.

But the time she heard Sawyer's key in the apartment door lock she was pacing by the door, nibbling at her thumbnail, ready to vent.

Only the moment he opened the door and saw her there, waiting for him, he dropped his stuff to the floor, swept her up in his arms and had her up against the hallway wall before she could catch her breath.

And later, lying curled up against his side, her body humming with pleasure as she played with his hair, her head resting on his chest so that she could breathe in time with his heart, Petra decided not to bother him about it.

She'd made it pretty clear that she did not want his help. Meaning she had to find her own way through the mental mire.

Which she could do just fine. She'd spent a lifetime doing just that, on her own, after all.

Hopping out of the taxi that dropped her to work the next morning, Petra saw the throng of photographers milling about the gallery entrance.

Determined to start as she meant to go on, and to claw back as much of her identity as she could before it was completely subsumed, Petra had insisted Sawyer head to his job, she to hers.

Armoured in her favourite swishy caramel velvet flares, a bottle-green top with a big soft bow at the neck, with teetering purple heels, she felt as ready as she could possibly feel as she headed towards the front doors.

"Petra!" called the first one, the rest perking up and racing her way.

"Over here!"

A camera flashed right in her eyes.

Sheesh.

"How did *you* land Mr Unlandable?" a reporter asked, a definite stress on the *you*. "Must be a hell of a prenup? What did you pop into his drink to get him to say yes?"

The others laughed. She knew that tone, having heard it in her parents' voices when she was really young. It was pure judgement.

As the way to the gallery seemed to lengthen before her, Petra missed a step, her sharp heel teetering sideways for half a second before she found traction again. She hoped they couldn't see the pulse that had suddenly begun beating madly in her throat.

It hit her then. She was going about this all wrong. She was trying to do it *Sawyer's* way, not her own.

While he was all about protective armour, Petra was the human version of an exposed beating heart, her soft spots always on display for anyone to poke. She'd never faked it till she made it because she liked who she was, and relishing that had brought her more happiness than trying to please others ever had.

Which was why, chin up, shoulders squared, she spun on her heel and faced the throng. Like something out of a cartoon, their shoes squeaked on the concrete as they shot past her before circling back around.

Her heart still beat madly in her throat—because the whole thing was mighty intimidating—but of all the plans she'd made over the past few weeks, this one felt the most right.

"Hi." She waved. And waited till one of them waved back. "I'm Petra Gilpin. Assuming you're all here today because my fiancé..." still sounded weird "...is a public figure. While I'm not. So, I get why that makes you all a little curious. I hope it helps you understand why this—the swarming and the shouting—well, it's a lot!"

A couple of those nearest laughed, and her heart settled the tiniest bit.

"So, here's what I'm going to do," Petra said. "I'm giving you three answers to three questions. And that's it. So make 'em good."

One guy who looked like an old pro came on board fastest. "Where's the billion-dollar bling?"

Sawyer had offered. Petra had flat-out refused. It would be taking things a step too far. Or *another* step too far, at the very least.

"Just not a ring girl," she answered truthfully. She held up her hand and counted off. "That's one."

"Petra! Over here!"

She blinked into the waggling microphones and the wall of phones. For all that this felt better than the alternative, she wasn't sure how anyone got used to it.

"What's in the prenup?" a reporter at the back called.

"There isn't one."

Also true. Which felt better than *not denying*.

"But now you mention it, I feel a particular fondness for the Gilded Cage. Should I ask for that if it all goes pear-shaped?"

A smattering of laughter.

"Who've you signed with for the wedding photo exclusive?"

"I've been engaged for all of five minutes and I can't leave the house without you lot there to say good morning. So, needless to say, any wedding questions will be answered with an *Um...*"

Much laughter at that one.

"The wedding exclusive-why do people do that?" she asked, genuinely interested.

"For the money," someone answered.

"Ah. Well, have you met my fiancé?" Laughter rolled through the group. And Petra felt such relief she was sure she was a foot taller. "Okay, well, that's three. Now, I have to get to work. So..."

She glanced back at the gallery, which looked lovely, all gothic and venerable in the early morning light. One guy lifted his camera and took a photo of the sign. She took that as a win! Petra gave them a wave and tried really hard not to run towards the doors.

She could have kissed Mimi, who met her there, sweeping her inside. While the photographers stopped, like a wave battering a beach, before subsiding back from whence they came.

"Wow," said Mimi, jogging beside her. "That was wild out there. But you were so cool. And I can't believe you're really engaged to Sawyer Mahoney. I mean, I can, because you're amazing, and he's amazing, but hot damn, Petra."

Mimi lifted her hand for a high five, which Petra duly returned.

"You're not secretly married, are you?" Mimi asked out of the side of her mouth as they waited for the lift.

"What? No! Who's saying that?"

"People."

"What people?"

Mimi bit her lip, then said, "People on the internet. Or pregnant?" she whispered. "I know I'm not meant to ask, but just in case you get morning sickness I can be on alert."

After her win outside, Petra deflated. What if none of their efforts brought an end to the wrong kind of attention? What if no Barking Cat was born, and the heat didn't die down? What if everyone figured out it was fake, and the gallery was embroiled in yet another scandal, and her *actual* reputation ended up in tatters?

She had to get the Epic Dream Festival off the ground ASAP. There was no time to lose. Not only because it would make her parents look at her *differently*, but so that she could go back to looking at herself the same way she always had.

If she could sleep with Sawyer Mahoney, several times over, and not wake up to find he'd fled to Peru, then anything was possible.

"Are you ready to co-organise the biggest pop-up art collective this town has ever seen, have it marketed, ticketed and running in the next two weeks?"

Mimi blinked, then sat straighter in her chair. "What do you need me to do?"

Petra rattled off her ideas as they came to her. A stream of consciousness more than an actual plan. There were no wrong ideas—no wrong paths. Allowing the big, the bold, the wild, the wonderful some air made magic happen. And the more she spoke, the more she felt herself coming back into her own skin.

When Mimi left to get started, Petra called, "And lastly, set up lunch with Daisy Mahoney? I'll send you her number. She's stubborn, so do not take no for an answer."

"Consider it done."

Petra met Daisy for lunch. "It's happening."

"Really?"

Daisy bounced on her chair, looking like a kid again, hot pink tips and nose rings aside. "I have so many friends who are super keen. Can I send you their details?"

"Yes! Please! I'll make it my mission to check out each and every one asap. We need all hands on deck. Now and into the future. This is going to change the art scene in this town for ever."

"Wow. When you dream big, you dream big."

Petra breathed out and thought, *Hell, yes, I do.*

A notification buzzed on her wrist. A quick check of her phone found an article forwarded from Deena. The headline: *Art World Virtuoso Petra Gilpin and Big Think Partner Sawyer Mahoney Announce Engagement.*

It reeked of Hadley. Lots of lovely wholesome buzzwords, and Petra's name first, which she appreciated more than she could say.

Only the photo Hadley had gone with was not one of the media-friendly, smiling-into-the-distance shots they'd taken, it was a candid shot snapped when she was leaning into Sawyer, whispering into his ear.

Petra's hand was on Sawyer's knee, to get his attention. He was looking down at her, a small smile on his mouth, his eyes crinkled. They looked close, intimate, comfortable, and as if—

"Could there be any more goo-goo eyes and heart emojis?" said Daisy, half off her chair so she could gawp at Petra's phone.

Petra turned her phone face down on the table, having seen

it too. And feeling more confused than ever as to what was real and what was not.

Daisy sat back. "Gross."

"Harsh!" Petra argued. "What's not to love about your big brother?"

"Plenty."

"Come on. He's a good guy. He'd do anything for you."

"Except stay."

Petra coughed on her drink, having to catch the dribble before it hit her shirt.

Daisy looked stricken. "I didn't mean he won't stay for *you*. I just mean he's away, a lot."

Petra smiled, even while she felt as if Daisy's simple statement had hit a gong inside her. One that wouldn't stop chiming.

Ask her, and Petra would tell you Sawyer had always been there for her. But when she needed him *most*? The man carried the world on his shoulders. But when it came to intimacy, to putting down roots, to *love*, he was as reliable as a bucket with a hole in the bottom.

Which was when all the pieces of the puzzle seemed to slot together in her mind. Big Think wasn't his dream, but it had given him the chance to fall off the edge of the earth any time he needed to do just that.

"His work is important," Petra said. "As is mine. We'll figure it out. Now, lunch?"

It had been a long day at Big Think, starting with much the same treatment for Sawyer on his way into the tower.

"How'd a rogue like you land a lady like that? When's she due? Come on, mate, you'd think a guy in your position could afford to give her a damn ring!"

He found it far easier when such questions were targeted towards him. He did not feel near the same urge to take them by the scruff of the neck. And there had been another layer atop-the sense that he wanted to keep his answers private. As if it wasn't pretend.

He'd breathed easier once inside the lobby of Big Think Tower, a spectacular monument to all that he and the boys had achieved in a mad few years.

The building was Ronan's dream, not his. Much like Big Think itself. But still, an incredible adventure to be a part of, something he'd never taken for granted. Also something he'd been thinking about, a lot, since Petra had made him consider his place there.

He'd taken his time walking through the lobby, noting how the soft sunlight fell through the three storeys of smoky glass windows, over an atrium filled with long leather couches and low tables, around which staff sat, drinking coffee and making plans. And he'd felt a wave of nostalgia come over him. As if he was looking back years from now.

Enough that he'd stopped to chat to everyone, checking what projects they were attached to, giving anyone who asked updates on the progress he'd made on his last trip. And accepting congratulations for his recent engagement.

By the time he'd even made it to the lift the expansive inlaid marble floor had done his leg no favours.

Nor had Petra climbing back into his bed that morning, bringing him a coffee—*"The one thing I can cook"*—before climbing on top and having her way with him. Totally worth it.

Now, back at the apartment, Sawyer searched for the video he was after and rolled out his leg on a foam cylinder, adapting the instructions on the screen to suit.

He could still remember the moment he'd broken his leg. *Catastrophic,* the commentators had called it. They'd put up a screen so that the crowd and cameras couldn't see, and even allowed an ambulance onto the field.

But he'd forgotten that he'd woken in the hospital with the strangest mix of emotions—fear that he might not walk again, and relief that one of the multitude of responsibilities he spent his life juggling had been taken from him. Till he'd felt the same sense of relief in asking Petra to marry him.

Fake or not, it didn't matter. What mattered was that, after butting heads about it for so long, she'd finally asked him for help. And it felt as if some deeply held truth had been unlocked inside him, leaving him free to let it be.

Near the end of the session, the front door rattled before it opened. The sound of Petra's bag hitting the floor, her shoes kicked off her feet, her keys landing somewhere on or near the hall table.

"Hey," he called, his voice strained, a yoga band wrapped around his big toe as he stretched out his hamstring.

Her face popped over the back of the couch. That lovely face. Soft hazel eyes, creamy skin, swishy auburn hair. All rumpled after what must have been a long day for her too.

"So, I saw you decided on an ad hoc press conference?"

She pulled a face. "I know, it just kind of happened. I tried to stick to your advice, but added a twist of my own. Hope that's okay?"

More than okay; she'd been phenomenal. Engaging, a little giddy, and utterly real. "Did it feel okay?"

"It felt…amazing." A nod, then she trailed her hand over the back of the couch as she rounded it, before she fell onto the thing and leaned up onto an elbow. "Now what are you doing?"

"*Pilates with Penny,*" he grunted, motioning to the TV.

"I can see that," she said, her gaze flitting between his bare torso and the twenty-something American telling him to *"stretch, stretch, stretch…"*

He lifted up, his stomach muscles clenching as he found the remote and pressed pause. Liking the way her eyes widened as she stared.

"It's physical therapy," he said, falling back flat to the floor, sweat dripping down his cheek now that he'd stopped moving. "For my leg."

Petra's gaze roamed over his shoulders before moving over his ribs, then to his scars, plural, the result of multiple operations, running down the outside of his left leg, finishing just above his knee.

"Did we," she said, "hurt it…this morning? Or last night when I had you…"

"Backed up against a hard surface?" he finished, harking back to a particularly memorable conversation at the Gilded Cage.

She dropped her head to the couch, hands covering her face.

Sawyer laughed, letting his foot fall to the side so he could breathe. Then he heaved himself to sitting. Leaned an arm along the edge of the couch, his chin on the back of his hand.

Waiting for her to look at him.

Which she did, tipping her head sideways. Close enough he could see the myriad colours in her glorious eyes.

"Physical therapy is part of my life. You can't hurt me. I promise."

Her eyes moved from one of his to the other, wheels turning, before she asked, "When are you thinking about heading off again?"

Her voice was light, as if totally bored by her own question, proof to him it was anything but a throwaway line.

"No plans in place," he said. Which was true.

The fact that he'd spent most of the day thinking, seriously, *about* his next trip, he kept to himself. No point talking it over till he had something concrete to say.

"I'm going to finish stretching," he said, "then have a shower. You're welcome to watch."

Petra waved a hand his way. "Go ahead."

Lying back, he twisted his good knee to the side, stretching out his glute. "I meant watch me in the shower."

She rolled her eyes before hauling herself to sitting. Then nibbled at her bottom lip, still thinking thoughts that put frown lines above her nose.

Sawyer distracted her with, "I'm going to the footy Saturday night. To shake hands with some Big Think big investors. Wanna be my date?"

Something flashed behind her eyes, wiping away her thoughts. Good. "You need a wingman?" she asked.

Dammit, she was incisive. Heading to the football was always a bit of a mind bend. Which, he was sure, it had to be for her too. "Think of it as a chance for us to take our engagement out for a spin."

"Okay, let's do it."

She gave his bare torso one last look, her gaze clouding with lust, before she hopped up and padded away. And it hit him how quickly things had changed. How openly she drank him in, when he used to catch the occasional telling flickers before.

It was hard not to imagine what it might be like living like this, living with her, for real. But that wasn't on the cards. He might be fake fiancé material but the rest was beyond him. He was busted, for one thing. Stretched too thin. And too used to not staying in one place too long.

She deserved better. She deserved the world.

In the shower, Sawyer turned the water scalding hot, letting the room fill with steam. A light knock had him lifting his head out from under the spray.

"Hello?"

Petra's voice came through the door, "I'm coming in."

No question. She opened the door and found her way through the mist. Her hair still a tumbled mess, only now she wore nothing but that same thoughtful expression.

He turned the water to a manageable heat, then opened the shower door and welcomed her inside.

And, without a word said between them, her hands glided

up his chest as he moved back to let the water stream over her sleek skin. Pebbling her nipples. Gathering in pools at her décolletage.

His hands followed the streams, around her waist, over the curve of her bare backside.

She slid her hands over his shoulders, lifted up onto her toes and placed a kiss on his lips. Gentle. Intimate. So much so an ache hit right in the centre of his chest.

"How does your leg feel now?" she asked.

"What leg?" he said, and then he kissed her thoroughly. And made love to her against the shower wall with the dexterity of a man with four perfectly able limbs.

Making every hour he'd had to endure *Pilates with Penny* worth it.

CHAPTER TEN

SAWYER HAD TRAVERSED some of the most spectacular places on earth, but there was still nothing quite like looking out over the Melbourne Cricket Ground, the home of Australian Rules football—the grass a pristine green, the sky cerulean blue, the energy of the football crowd creating an electric storm in the air.

Watching Petra lean over the railing as she tried to count the rows of seats on the level below he did not love as much.

"Finn would have loved this," she said.

"The best seats in the house?" Sawyer reached out and hooked a finger through her belt loop, readying to haul her back if she tipped too far. "Hell, yeah, he would."

Then realised belatedly that they were talking about Finn and none of the usual heaviness settled on his shoulders. He felt more a phantom pain than immediate and raw.

She looked back at him when he added an extra finger. "You all right there?"

"Just can't keep my hands off you," he said.

She stilled. The way she had again and again over the last few days as they'd settled into their new normal. As if waiting for the other shoe to drop. "Shouldn't you be saving that gold for when we have prying ears listening in?"

Sawyer gave her jeans a little tug. "Trying it out on a test audience first seems a smart move."

Petra spun about slowly, taking his hand with her till his

arm was wrapped around her and he had her backed up against the railing. "What else you got?"

He leaned in, calling her bluff. Only for her scent to hit the back of his tongue—so sweet and warm and heady, making him forget what he'd been going to say. So he kissed her instead, sweeping his tongue into her mouth when she gasped.

When they pulled apart her eyes were dark, her cheeks pink. "Aren't we here to project a *wholesome* image?"

"You, Ms Gilpin, are here today to trawl the private room behind me for those with the deepest pockets, so that you can sweet-talk them into sponsoring one of your pop-ups."

She grinned. It was blinding. Literally. He felt his brain go blank for a second. Meaning he wasn't ready for her when she lifted onto her toes and nipped at his bottom lip.

Then she pulled back, ducked under his arm, grabbed his hand in hers and dragged him up the stairs towards the corporate box.

"Mahoney!"

Sawyer looked up to find a bunch of footy fans decked out in black and white on the third level, waving. And filming. Petra looked up, smiled and waved. And they cheered.

Because since her "three questions and three answers" chat out in front of the gallery she'd become quite the hit. According to Hadley, *Have you met my fiancé?* was a trending meme on social media.

Petra looked back at him then, pink-cheeked, eyes filled with laughter. Heart-achingly beautiful. And he found himself wishing, hoping, that none of that had been for an audience. That it had all been for him.

The glass doors leading to the corporate box slid open and Sawyer spotted Hadley and Ronan.

Petra made her way straight to them, leaning in to kiss Hadley's cheek.

"Aren't you a dark horse," said Hadley, eyeing her sideways

as if she was checking to see what other skills she might be hiding.

Petra made a *pffft* sound, brushing it off, before giving Ronan a big bear hug. Which he accepted with a grumble.

"Why are you wearing those colours?" Ronan asked.

Petra flapped her black and white scarf in his face. "Why aren't you? Sawyer *played* for Collingwood—you can't possibly go for anyone else."

Ronan tapped the small navy and red pin he wore on his dark suit lapel. Petra rolled her eyes. "Of course, you go for Melbourne. You are such a cliché."

Sawyer moved to Hadley's side when it became clear the other two were happy to go toe-to-toe. "Checking up on me?"

Hadley brought a glass of wine to her lips. "I'm here to watch the players. I like their short shorts."

"I still have mine, if you'd like to borrow them—?"

"No," said Hadley, shivering from head to toe. "You've done your time, for now. So, I found you a trip. Wanna go to the Northern Territory for a couple of days?"

He opened his mouth to say *Hell, yes*. For he'd been nudging Hadley for the chance since telling Petra about the clinic he'd started up there, in his pre-Big Think days. Only now he had someone else to consider.

"Hey, Petra." He whistled to get her attention. "You okay for me to go to Darwin for a couple of days?"

Hadley coughed on her drink. Then made a whip cracking sound.

Sawyer, ignoring her, waited for Petra to blink. And say, "Oh. Ah...sure. Of course."

"Yep," he said to Hadley, "I can go to Darwin." Then, with a waggle of his eyebrows, he moved to Petra's side as Ronan asked, "How'd you get roped into trying to save the gallery, that old dinosaur?"

"I'm an altruist."

Ronan snorted. "It's on its last legs, from what I hear. Be my conduit, help me buy the gallery building. I'll give it to Ted for more lab space."

"Care to sponsor a pop-up modern art collection instead?" Petra asked. "Give me enough money and I can name a gallery wing after you." She held out a hand as if writing the name across the sky. "The Ronan Gerard Experience."

"That's all we need," Hadley muttered, then lost interest, ambling off to find another drink. Ronan followed.

"So, Darwin," Petra said. "Just a couple of days?"

"Just a couple of days."

"You could check on the rehab clinic!"

His smile came from some deep place inside him, loosening everything in its path. "I certainly could. Now, come with me. I see some Melbourne supporters who look in need of some wallet-lightening."

The Magpies won in a thriller, with a goal after the siren.

Add the several enthusiastic contacts Petra had made, who were keen to talk more about her pop-up collection sponsorship plan, as well as pick her brain about their private art collections, and Petra could not have had a better night.

But it was the Darwin thing that had her feeling as if she were floating an inch off the ground.

Sawyer was going away. Only this time he'd let her know. And she couldn't help but feel as if they had turned some corner in their relationship. As if it might, maybe, truly be leading to something real.

Once home, while Sawyer was getting a drink, Petra checked her messages to find one from her mother.

Squinting with one eye, she read it.

YOUR FATHER SAW THE PHOTO OF THE TWO OF YOU ON-LINE. STILL AS HANDSOME AS THE DEVIL, THAT ONE...

Petra's eyes opened wide as she coughed out a laugh. No passive aggression. No dig. If not for the capital letters, she'd wonder if she was being catfished by someone pretending to be her mother.

She replied:

My father? Or Sawyer?

FUNNY GIRL.

Petra smiled, and popped her phone on the small dining table, spun on her heel and reached for her talisman, her necklace with the engagement pull tab attached, only to find it wasn't there.

"What's wrong?" Sawyer asked as he set a pot on the stove.

"I can't find my necklace. The rose gold one. The one with the... The one Finn gave me."

Sawyer stopped what he was doing, ready to spring into action. And while that side of him had always frustrated her, now she found it endearing.

"Were you wearing it today?" he asked.

"I wear it *always*. I was definitely playing with it, in the game's dying minutes."

Her scarf! She plucked it from the floor pile and gave it a shake. Only for the necklace to fling free and land with a delicate slump.

Sawyer picked it up, the thin chain so small in his big hand. The aluminium pull tab he'd offered up as an engagement ring, twice, a clunky dented silver thing glinting up at him.

She watched him run his thumb over the silver circle, his expression unreadable. Then he bounced it up and down on his hand, the chain dragging lightly behind, before his gaze swept to hers, full of questions. Most likely regarding why she wore a fake engagement doodad so close to her heart.

But Petra was deep inside a memory of her eighteenth birthday party. The pull tab from his beer. Bouncing the thing up and down as she'd played a silly game about who she would one day marry.

Was that *why* he'd chosen it that night at the club? Because it had meaning for them? For him?

She walked to him on shaky legs. Placed her hand over his, trapping the necklace and the "ring", their torrid history, the push and pull of their story, right there, between their palms.

And waited for him to look up.

"That night," she said, feeling brave and terrified all at once, "at my party, when I was bouncing the pull tab on my hand, I was trying to stop at the letter S."

His throat worked, as if fighting against what she was trying to tell him.

"I had such a crush on you back then."

Sawyer's chest rose, his brow tight, as he said, "I knew."

"You *did*?"

"You wore your heart on your sleeve back then. Just right out there. Fearlessly. Everyone else I knew, Finn included, hid behind charm, or politeness, or fear. But you…you were so wholly yourself. You were mesmerising."

"And now?" she asked, feeling breathless. Hollow.

"Can't read you quite so well," he said, his eyes now searching hers. "But the mesmerising thing still stands."

With that, she took the necklace from his hand, lifted it till the pull tab dangled between them. A big shiny sign of how she'd once felt about him. How she felt about him still.

He motioned for her to turn around, lifted her hair off her neck and fixed the clasp. Then he kissed her, the clasp between his lips and her skin, before letting her hair drop back into place.

"When do you leave?" she asked, knowing she'd miss having him near. But so staggered he'd let her know. Not that it negated Daisy's point, that he *couldn't* stay. But it was something. She was *sure* it meant something good.

"Tomorrow morning," he said. "If that suits you."

She nodded. "Then we'd better not waste any more time."

Petra took him by the hand and led him into her bedroom.

Her clothes were messily draped over the end of her bed. A jacket and a bra over the back of a padded chair. And a small cut-crystal bowl with a pink stone, a pink button, pink chalk and a pink feather had pride of place on her chest of drawers.

She gave Sawyer a small shove and he dutifully lay back on her bed, watching as she slowly took off every item of clothing, bar the necklace carrying his ring.

Then, as if he knew that she needed this, that she felt strong and brave, he let her divest him of his clothes too.

Planning to take her sweet time, she worked her way up his body, touching, stroking, caressing, nipping where she saw fit, before she lay along his side, her leg hooked over his, as she traced the massive phoenix tattoo curling over Sawyer's shoulder. "When did you get this one?"

He lifted his chin and watched her finger. "Started it the week I walked on my own for the first time after I broke my leg. Took several sessions. And a few touch-ups."

"Did it hurt?"

"Like a son of a bitch."

Knowing him, she imagined the pain was part of the reason why. "And yet you got more. Tell me about them. I want to know them all."

He lifted a little, pulling at his tight skin to show a mountain scene. "I got this one in a little hole in the wall in Mexico City last year. It was the most gorgeous place I'd seen in some while. I found a hospital full of kids with limb injuries. Burns. All in need of rehab. It felt as if I'd come full circle."

"You light up when you talk about that, you know? The rehab." Lit up and lightened up. "It could be something you turn your focus to, if you ever lose the will to sleep on jungle floors."

She felt his chest rise and fall under her hand. Then under her mouth as she kissed her way over the mountains. Running her tongue along its ragged edges.

She knew she could have talked more about her idea. Her certainty that he'd find real purpose in that kind of work. But Sawyer was not a man to be told. He had to figure it out for himself. So she kissed her way over the ocean waves, the spring flowers, the AFL football, the magpie, the date of the grand final he'd won his first year. This map of the life he'd lived without her.

Only to stop short when she saw the single feather floating over his left pec. It was tiny, delicate, pink, with a watercolour finish. It looked ethereal, magical, the only tattoo that wasn't pure black.

It was her.

His eyes lifted to hers and he knew what she'd found.

The urge to ask him about it, to know how long he'd had it, for him to tell her why, was so strong her throat burned with the need to ask.

But she could feel the rubber band holding him back. The same one he'd used to keep himself in one piece while everyone in his life pulled him in a thousand different directions, knowing he was strong enough not to break.

Petra didn't want to be something he had to navigate. She wanted to be the one he came home to when he was done.

So she kissed him, and held him, and sighed as he did the same to her.

Then he reached towards her bedroom drawer, in search of another condom.

"Wait!" she cried.

"What?"

"Not that drawer."

"What's in that drawer?"

She bit her lip so as not to say.

A smile spread across Sawyer's face as he figured it out. "Now I have to open that drawer."

"Why?"

"I want to meet the competition."

"Russell's not your competition."

"Oh, I know that," he said, shooting her a look that made her blush all over. "I'm his."

Laughing despite herself, she waved a hand to her bedside drawer. Eyes closed, biting her lip as Sawyer slowly opened it with grave ceremony, only stopping when he found the man of the hour.

"Good God," he said, pulling out her big, bold, bright purple vibrator with its cute bunny ears.

Petra's hands flew to her face.

"Oh, *now* you're hiding. You brought him up easily enough that night at the club. Russell this and Russell that. Mind you, he's impressive as hell."

She laughed and wriggled till she had the sheet over her head.

Then she heard the tell-tale buzz. Russell was turned on.

The sheet was tugged gently before Sawyer whipped it away, leaving her bare. Laughing, she held up her hands to push him away.

He waited for her to calm down before lowering the vibrator till it hovered, buzzing just above her belly, "May I?"

His eyes were dark, his jaw tight. That face, that beautiful face, wanted her. And while she now knew that he knew she'd wanted him for ever, she'd take it. Whatever she could have of him.

She nodded. Then, "First, are you sure you know how to wield that thing?"

"I'm an athlete," he said, "I learn quick."

And boy, did he.

A few days later, longer than he'd intended, Sawyer stood beneath the large covered porch area annexe outside Petra's apartment building, collar turned up against the chill and the rain now coming down so hard it was near sideways.

Enough to keep away any press.

Or maybe they'd given up on him and moved completely to team Petra.

There was the chance that their ruse had worked. With no new nightclub vision coming out, just a well-written announcement and Petra's openness, it was possible they were no longer of interest.

It was also possible that the fact that he'd not been around had given Petra a reprieve. Which, if true, needed consideration.

Then again, a barking cat *might* have been born and the press were merely distracted. Better leave things as they were till he found out for sure.

Now, where the heck was Petra?

He was itching to tell her about the rehab centre. The feeling of rightness that had come over him the minute he'd set foot in the place. The ideas that had unspooled.

And to see her, hold her, maybe even wrap her up in his coat and not let her go.

She wasn't at the gallery. He'd called. Their closing hour had long since passed. She wasn't home, in their apartment. Her apartment? *The* apartment. And she wasn't answering her mobile.

In fact, she'd been mighty hard to get onto the whole time he was away, having apparently gone into hyper-focus mode, working crazy long days the way he knew she usually did when she was in the midst of a project she really loved.

Meaning everything must have been going brilliantly in his absence.

Another thing to consider that, it turned out, he wasn't in the mood to consider.

Not until he saw her. Held her. Kissed her. Told her that she was absolutely right and that it turned out he was, in fact, a man with a dream.

Till then he stamped his feet to ward off the cold and tried not to imagine other places she might be. Such as stuck in a lift somewhere. Or lost down a well. How long *had* it been since he'd last heard from her? Eighteen hours? Twenty-four? He checked his battered watch. It was after nine at night. Late home for her.

He found himself remembering the times Daisy used to run away, as a kid. The times his mother would call, her voice slurred, and he'd drive home, imagining the worst, only to find she'd had a glass of Baileys on an empty stomach. Then there'd been the phone call telling him Finn had broken his neck.

He looked to his phone. Who could he call, just to ease his mind?

There was only one.

He called Petra's mother.

"Dr Gilpin," she answered in her clipped tone.

"Josephine, it's Sawyer. Sawyer Mahoney."

A beat, then, "Well. Hello."

Sawyer swore at the sky, wishing he'd not been so rash, but he was there now. "Sorry to call so late, but I was wondering if you've heard from Petra in the last day or so."

"No, not in that time-frame. Why? Has she meandered off somewhere? She used to do that a lot, as a child. If you're really going to marry her, do keep that in mind."

Sawyer's jaw ached from not throwing back, *Of course I'm*

going to marry her. But he didn't want to make things more complicated for Petra with her parents than they already were. "I've been away, and now I'm back and she's not home, and... And I sound like a fool."

Josephine laughed, the sound so like her daughter. "Not at all. I remember what it was like those first years Josiah and I were together. Young love can be quite the rush. Don't worry. She'll find you when she's ready. She always worked on her own timeline that one."

It surprised him to find a note of affection in Josephine's voice, considering what he knew of how they'd interacted when Petra was younger. And Petra's continued lack of faith in her parents' affections.

It surprised him and gave him great relief. To know that he had support in supporting her.

"You're right," he said, his voice a little rough. "I should let you go."

"Not at all, it was lovely to hear from you, Sawyer. It's been a while." Then, "It's *his* birthday soon, you know."

Sawyer nodded. "I know. Petra keeps trying to nudge me to do something with her to celebrate. Has she done the same with you?"

"She has at that, but I fear I've not been as receptive as she might have hoped."

"She'll give you another chance," he said.

"Full of infinite chances, that one," said Josephine.

The memory of Finn – stubborn and restless, compared with Petra and her wide open heart-wavered between them before it fluttered away.

"As for my younger child," said Josephine, as if she'd read Sawyer's mind, "while she might appear as if she's far stronger than us all, her tender side is stronger still. Do remember that."

With that, Josephine Gilpin rang off, leaving Sawyer feeling as if a weight that had been on his shoulders all these years had been lifted.

Pocketing his phone, he looked down the street and—

There. Petra. Walking up the footpath.

Rain was now pelting down, but she didn't even seem to notice. In fact, she tilted her face to the water and soaked it in. Her hair was dark red as it stuck to her cheeks and neck. Her boots splashing through puddles.

Only Petra, he thought, his chest tightening at the sight of her, as if he missed her more now that she was so close. *Only her.*

"Petra! What the hell are you doing out here?" he called when she was close enough to hear him, stepping out into the rain as he waved his arm in the air.

Petra stopped when she heard her name. Grinned when she saw him. Then ran into his arms.

He lifted her, twirling her about on the spot till the rain ran down his face, down the back of his shirt, into his shoes. When she slid down his body she kissed him. Hard.

"You're back!" she said, as if slightly surprised.

"That I am," he said.

"And no press?" she said, glancing around.

"Seems they've grown weary of us."

"Oh, I doubt that. A magazine called me today, asking if I could do three questions and three answers for their online stream."

"Wow, that's... You tell me?"

"I said only so long as it was about my work. They're yet to get back to me." She smiled from ear to ear. "Today was a good day. I wanted it to last as long as possible. So I walked home. And then it started to rain. And here I am!"

"What was so good about today?" he asked.

"The Epic Dream Festival is good to go. We bump in from

tomorrow, and it begins over the weekend. Despite evidence to the contrary, the weather is going to be perfect!"

"It wouldn't dare be otherwise."

"Right? Then Mimi, the wonder that she is, started a whisper campaign. And everyone is talking about it. Including major sponsors, which brought in more artists willing to do pop-ups. Which are now booked for months to come!"

"That's incredible."

"And then I hear my favourite gallery in New York is looking for a guest curator for their autumn season. And Daisy put me onto this fantastic underground German art club that I'm dying to check out. It's as if the universe knew I was missing you and did everything possible to make me feel better."

Sawyer smiled, even while his brain was suffering from an overload of information.

She missed him. She was making plans, far-away plans, for the not-too-distant future. She'd nearly done what she'd come home to do.

He'd gone to the Northern Territory to reconnect with his past. Only, instead, to find himself seeing a future. Not a future spent living for someone else, but one he wanted for himself. One which Petra could be part of.

Only now, seeing how happy she looked at the thought of doing what she'd set out to do, which was to help the gallery get back on its feet, before heading back to her amazing real life, he realised how selfish that would be.

Right as he was ready to put down roots for the first time in his adult life, his reason why was just learning to fly.

"How about you?" she asked, flicking water from her eyes. "Anyone at the rehab centre who remembered you? Was it hot up there? Did you eat crocodile?"

"I'll tell you all about it later. But first..." He lifted her bodily and walked her out of the rain. And there, beneath the bright light of the annexe, he kissed her.

He kissed her as they made their way up in the lift. Kissed her as they tumbled through her apartment door. Kissed her as they struggled to tear the wet clothes from one another's bodies.

Then lifted her into his arms and carried her to his bed. Where they made love. There was no other way to describe it.

And later, as she lay snoring softly in his arms, he told himself he'd find the right time to tell her about his plans later. Even while he knew that version of later was already nothing but a dream.

The night before the Epic Dream Festival was set to launch, the gang were having a night. The six of them—Adelaid and Ted, Sawyer and Petra, Ronan and Hadley—enjoying mouth-wateringly good bubbly and deliriously delicious antipasto on the gorgeously appointed balcony taking up a good portion of Ronan's floor of the Big Think Tower.

Petra leant on the heavy concrete balustrade, looking out over the river. For Melbourne had really put on a show. A crystal-clear night, stars peppering the inky black above, the city set to let off fireworks due to some other festival Petra hadn't quite caught the name of.

Though they were all there to celebrate *her* success. Apparently Big Think was big on that kind of thing. And, it seemed, since she was with Sawyer, they considered her part of the family too.

While Petra finally felt as if she'd found herself again. She felt as if she was truly living inside her own skin.

Petra turned to see Ronan holding what looked like a small cactus that Adelaid had presented him with on arrival. Ted was holding up his hands, as if miming *Don't blame me!*

Hadley was refilling everyone's drinks, while Sawyer poured chips into a big bowl. He'd ditched his jacket, and the edges of his tattoos caught the light. He looked so big, and strong, and grounded.

It hit her in that moment, with the gentle grace of an autumn leaf fluttering to the ground, that she had fallen in love with him.

Not the crush she'd had as a kid. Or the hots she'd felt as a teen. But love. Big, sweeping, scary, raw love.

She had to tell him. And she would. When the time was right. For things were still new, and precious, all the pieces holding them together stacked like a house of cards.

Once she got through the first day of the festival, and went home, and crawled into his bed, exhausted and happy and spent, she'd tell him then. Maybe.

Hadley came over and gave her a glass. "I can't even look at you."

"What's that, now?"

"The way you are gazing at that lug of a man. I'll need a fire extinguisher by the end of the night."

Petra laughed, but didn't deny it.

"You guys have some fantastical goodbye night planned?" Adelaid asked as she joined them.

Caught watching Adelaid suck up a whole glass of iced water in one go—pregnant with baby number two, apparently cold water was her thing—Petra had to rewind to replay what she'd said.

"Who's saying goodbye?" Petra asked.

Adelaid looked to Hadley, then across to Sawyer, then back again.

Hadley, not one to pull her punches, said, "Sawyer. Thought we'd have him a bit longer this time, considering. But he's off again next week. A month or more, much of it completely off-grid. Prepare yourself-as for Sawyer, this usually means another three months of him faffing about the place, spending the company money on any hard luck story he finds."

"Hadley..." Adelaid chastised, and Petra realised she must look as pale as she suddenly felt.

One time he'd given her a heads-up, and she'd believed he was no longer beholden to whatever used to make him disappear in the first place.

Instead, while she'd been standing there feeling smug about how well she had a handle on things, so much she'd admitted to herself that she loved the guy, Sawyer was making plans to leave. As if their dalliance was a blip on his timeline. As if, when it came down to it, she wasn't enough for him to change his plans. His ways. His heart.

"Excuse me," she said, pressing away from the railing, her body feeling as if it had been wrapped in cotton wool.

Sawyer looked up, his gaze tracking her, as if he had some kind of radar where she was concerned.

Pressing back the very real urge to cry, Petra cocked her head, beckoning him to meet her inside, then walked through the French windows and into Ronan's kitchen.

"Hey," Sawyer said as he joined her. "Everything okay?"

Petra moved around the other side of the bench, out of his reach, not trusting herself not to lean on him, hold him, kiss him in the hope it would break whatever spell meant he couldn't love her the way she loved him.

"So," she said, her voice thick. "I had a thought."

He mirrored her stance and said, "Hit me with it."

"What with the Festival happening tomorrow, I've done what I came here to do. I think this would be a great time for us to...tear off the Band-Aid."

"What Band-Aid?"

"The fake engagement Band-Aid."

Petra saw the moment he realised what she meant. Agony seemed to sweep across his beautiful blue eyes, before the shutters came slamming down.

"You want to do this here?" he asked, his tone crisp and cool. "Now?"

"I think it's best," she lied. Needing it over, before she fell in a heap. "I've had a few feelers come my way—"

"So you said," he shot back, his voice raw.

She had? She didn't remember that. Had *that* played into *his* reason for making plans to leave? Because he thought that was *her* plan? Surely not.

"This was always temporary, Sawyer. A means to an end. And what with your plans to leave next week, the time seems right—"

"What plans?" he said, moving towards her, his expression fierce.

"Hadley mentioned you are going away again. For months. Actually, Adelaid mentioned it first, then Hadley confirmed." Leaving her, as always, the last to know. "While I *did* ask that you give me a heads-up if you made such plans, as it happens your timing is perfect."

His jaw worked so hard she feared he might break a tooth. And a huge part of her hoped that he might fight back. That he might tell her that she was mistaken, that he wasn't going anywhere. That it had never been a ruse. Not for him.

Instead he said, "What do you need me to do?"

Love me back! she thought. And very nearly said it.

Till he said, "Do you need me to go with you and tell them we're over?"

Them? Petra risked a look over Sawyer's shoulder to find the other four had gathered at the far end of the balcony, giving them privacy. As if they already knew what was coming.

Deflating—like an unexpectedly pricked balloon—she figured they'd probably expected it of Sawyer from day one. How mortifying to know she was the only one left surprised.

"You can tell them whatever you like. They're your people."

People she'd come to really like, which was a big thing for her. And now she was losing them too.

She shook her head. "I'm going. I have a huge day tomorrow anyway. And I think it's best you don't come home tonight. It might seem…confusing, to anyone paying attention. Perhaps you could head back to the Elysium till you go. Then we tie our story off with a neat bow."

Sawyer ran both hands over his face, and through his hair, finishing with them gripping the back of his neck. He looked…confused. No, he looked harrowed. And yet he still said, "Okay. If that's what you want."

It's not what I want! a voice screamed in the back of her head. How she kept it there she had no idea. Some last, wobbly thread of self-protection held her together while her insides were shaking apart.

He'd been too good a friend for this to end so badly. So she walked around the bench, put her hand on his chest, right over the pink feather tattoo, and leaned in to press a kiss to his cheek. Closing her eyes, committing to memory the roughness of his skin, his warmth, his strength. As if it wasn't already indelibly marked on her psyche.

When he sucked in a long slow breath she imagined he was doing the same.

But what did it matter? What could she do? Beg him to make another promise he didn't mean?

If *his* issues meant he was afraid to commit, unwilling to change, unable to love her then she was done hoping. Done waiting. She was not going to live the emotional roller coaster of loving him. Not any more.

"Thank you," she said, pulling back and looking him in the eye.

"For what?"

"For putting those pretending skills of yours to good use. I was floundering, and you saved me. Which was all *you* ever wanted."

His jaw clenched. His eyes searched hers. But she didn't want him to see inside her, not any more.

"You know what the funniest thing about all this has been. Finn would have loved seeing us together. But even if he hadn't, it would not have been his choice."

"Petra," Sawyer said, his voice ragged, finally showing emotion, his expression pained.

But she was done. Spent. Wrung out.

If being with him had taught her anything-and after having to put up with the push and pull of her parents' affections her entire childhood-it was that her feelings were valuable. Worthy. That she did not have to accept anything less than whatever it was she wanted.

And if he couldn't give it to her, then it was out of her hands.

"Goodbye, Sawyer," she said. "I hope you find what you're looking for out there."

Then, without looking back, she turned and walked away.

CHAPTER ELEVEN

"AREN'T YOU GONE YET?" Hadley stood in the doorway to the Big Think Founders' Room—which looked more like a university den—glaring at Sawyer as he tried to come in.

"Trying to," he growled, not in the mood for her attitude. "One last meeting then I'm out of here. So please move out of my way, or I will physically move you."

"I'd like to see you try," Ronan's voice called from inside the room. "Get in here."

Sawyer pressed past Hadley, who moved her foot at the last moment, as if about to trip him.

"Seriously?" he barked.

She curled her lip and let him by.

"What's your problem?" Ronan asked.

Sawyer took off his jacket and tossed it over the back of a chair, then sat astride the seat. "My leg," he lied, rubbing the offending spot.

"His leg is *not* his problem," said Ted, while pulling apart a mobile phone and putting it back together again. "That would be Petra. She did not go home with a headache last night. He did something to screw it all up."

Sawyer hadn't told them, in the end, that things were over. He'd made his excuses and left himself soon after, heading to the boat, where he'd slept on sheets that still smelled like her. Because he couldn't believe it himself. In his eyes, in his plans, they were only at the beginning.

"I did not screw anything up. I—" How could he put it without giving Petra away? "I need to take this trip. Check up on those I've helped set up in the past, and hand them over to their new contacts so that I can start my new project."

Ronan picked up a piece of paper he had at hand and read, "The Big Think Centres for Physical Therapy."

"That's the one. I want to start by refurbishing a centre in Darwin. And building a few other rural centres, in consultation with the communities up there."

He waited for Ronan to shut him down. To say it was too narrow a focus. If he did, then Sawyer was ready to walk. Go at it on his own. It felt that important to him. That right. And right now it was the only thing that *did* feel right.

But Ronan only nodded. "Does Petra have something against rehab?"

"She wasn't upset because Sawyer's going, she's upset he didn't tell her he was going," said Ted. Then, noticing the surprised silence that came on top of his rare emotional insight, he added, "At least that's what Adelaid thinks."

"Why the hell didn't you tell her?" Ronan asked.

Because he was only just getting his head around the fact that he could do something for himself. As soon as he told her, she'd know it was because of her. She'd know how much of an impact she made on him. And he might as well prise open his ribs, point to his heart and say, *There, take it, it's yours.*

Complete and utter capitulation, which would negate all the work he'd done to be her support system above all else.

"Harking back to Hadley's earlier point," said Sawyer, attempting to distract them into getting on with the damn meeting so he could get the hell out of there. "I'm leaving asap. So can we get on with the meeting so I can tie up any loose ends before I go?"

"What about Petra?" Ted, Ronan and Hadley spoke at the same time.

Sawyer let his face fall into his hands. Then rubbed it. Hard. He might even have growled before taking the chance to glare at each one of them. "Leave Petra out of this."

"After you," said Ted.

Sawyer glanced Ted's way. "When did you become the foremost expert on...all this?"

"Since I fell in love," said Ted, with not even a hint of irony.

Once again Sawyer looked at the others, intimating, *Can you believe this guy?*

But they were all three looking at him as if *he* needed help.

"You're an idiot," said Hadley, clearly loving this.

While Ronan sat back in his throne, making it clear he was in this now. They were not moving on until the subject was resolved. "Usually I'd be all for you having no life outside of Big Think—you know that, right?"

Sawyer was well aware.

"But the terrible truth is, we are also allowed to live lives outside of this building. This job."

"You don't," Sawyer shot back.

Hadley cleared her throat. Was that a flush rising up her neck when everyone looked her way? "What? I breathed the wrong way."

Ronan looked at her for a long moment before turning back to Sawyer.

"Either way, we are all in agreement. Only a fool would let Petra go."

"I honestly can't believe that this is the room in which decisions are made regarding billions of dollars' worth of funding. And all you want to do is talk about my love life?"

"He loves her." That was Hadley. "I *knew* it."

Then, in a last-ditch effort to put this thing to bed, Sawyer found himself saying, "It was fake!"

"What do you mean, fake?" Ronan asked.

Sawyer knew he could trust the people in this room. With

his life. He'd already done so for years. Still, it took him a few beats longer to feel sure he could trust them with Petra's.

"The thing with Petra. It wasn't real."

He went on to explain. "That scene in the club, it was a kind of in joke gone wrong. When the video came out, she didn't need the negative press that would come with a denial so we rolled with it. Then, when the time seemed appropriate, we 'broke up'."

He added air quotes. Though they were half-hearted. Every move he'd made since that night at Ronan's had felt half-hearted. As if when she'd left she'd taken a big part of him with her. The part of him that had always been hers.

He blinked to find them all watching him. No humour, no reproof, just…pity.

Sawyer pushed himself to standing, grabbed his jacket and began to slide his arms through the holes.

"You love her," Hadley said, matter-of-fact.

"Of course I bloody love her!"

Sawyer's words echoed around the room, inside his head, his heart. And he sat back down, his jacket half on, half off.

He loved her. He was in love with Petra. Madly, completely, insanely. To the point that he couldn't see straight where she was concerned, and never had.

"Then go get her," Ronan said.

Go get her. As if it was that simple.

Only, wasn't it?

She'd asked him once to trust her. Trust her to make her own choices, make her own mistakes. If he didn't tell her how he felt, explain why he'd made the choices he had, then he'd be denying her that.

And he didn't want to deny her anything.

Sawyer shot out of the chair, into the lift, through the lobby and outside. Onto the street. Where he pulled out his battered old phone and pulled up Petra's number.

What to tell her?

That he finally knew what he wanted? Finally knew where his passions lay?

On the couch with her, her feet on his lap as she melted over nineties French cinema. Following her down garden paths, his shirt scooped ready to carry anything she found. Tucked up beside her in bed, even when her feet were cold.

Imagining the real possibility of that life being his for ever, he made the call.

She'd done it. Petra had done what she'd set out to do.

The Epic Dream Festival had taken over the forecourt of the Gallery of Melbourne, transforming the space into a maze of wonder and delight. From the fairy floss stands to the beautiful vintage merry-go-round that pealed haunting music up into the sky, the pale pink velvet ropes herding people past pop-up stands filled with the most eclectic to the new façade of the gallery itself, it was nothing short of wondrous.

It wasn't exactly within the purview that she'd been given, but the gallery was back on the map, had money in the bank, and Petra had done it her way.

While the press, in the end, had been a boon. The memes, as well as the rapport she'd built with the regulars who followed her, three questions ready to go every day, had shone an unexpected light over her plight.

And the people had come, as she'd absolutely known they would. They'd bought tickets, and food, and pieces from the amazing, prolific young artists who'd rallied to her cry.

And even while her eyes felt gritty and small behind her big dark sunglasses, even while her heart felt like a shrivelled-up prune, and even while her parents still might not understand her approach, she felt proud of what she'd achieved.

It was called multi-tasking.

"This is amazing!"

Dredging up a smile, Petra glanced over at Deena, who'd stopped in front of a life-sized nude sculpture with a chocolate wrapper in place of a fig leaf.

"Put in a bid." Petra nudged her. "Think of it as a tax deductible talking point for your firm."

Deena waved over her shoulder. She was on it.

"Hey, boss," said Mimi, who was wandering the place dressed as a fairy, on stilts, her tutu torn, her pointed ears covered with rings.

"What's up?"

"I've had a couple of press asking when Sawyer will be here. Shall I give them an ETA, or keep distracting them with the popcorn stand that's not real popcorn?"

"Distract," Petra said with a smile. "They'll figure out soon enough that the art is the star here today."

They both looked across the forecourt right as Daisy, who was chatting with a camera crew about her installation, looked up and gave them a huge smile.

Mimi nodded. "Do you need me for anything else?"

"No, just carry on doing what you're doing," Petra said.

Mimi grinned, checked her earpiece, then stalked off to make sure everything ran smooth as silk.

Leaving Petra to sigh gustily. Her head was fuzzy, as if she was listening to the conversations around her while her head was underwater. Because, wonderful as the event was, she wished Sawyer was there to see it. Not for the press. Or good PR. But because he'd been a part of this too.

Just because she'd been brave, and strong, in saying *no* to having her heart completely smashed, didn't mean she could just switch it off. Forget all of the lovely moments they'd experienced together over the past weeks.

It didn't mean she could just fall out of love.

Maybe that was her true curse. Doomed to love him for the rest of time.

Sighing again, Petra stared up at the façade of the gallery, which a week before had been dirty old brick in need of a clean. It was now covered in the most beautiful graffiti. Splashes of pink and bronze and white and silver. Beautiful literary quotes, written in chunky block script, each one about the transformative nature of art, the very centre of which sported a sweet daisy tag.

"It's rather a lot, don't you think?"

Petra turned to find her mother standing beside her, looking up at the graffiti art with a discerning eye. "Mum!"

"Darling," Josephine said, leaning in for an air kiss. "Your father is off somewhere bobbing for candy apples. I tried telling him the last thing his heart needs at his age is that much sugar, but alas, he stopped listening to me some time ago."

"You're here," Petra said, her sloshy brain taking a while to catch up with her eyes.

"Of course I'm here. I am on the board."

Josephine's gaze swept over Petra's pink tulle dress, her aubergine lucky boots and the cropped quilted yellow jacket she'd chosen in the hope it might make her look vibrant and happy, even if she wasn't feeling it.

Her gaze was long-suffering, and yet impressed at the same time, as she met Petra's eyes and said, "Also, my daughter is the curator of this outstanding event."

Petra swallowed. Smiled. Then drew her mother in for a quick hug. "Thank you. Now, shall I introduce you to any of the young artists…help you find something new to put up at the house?" she said, so glad to have something to take her mind off the heaviness in her head.

"Oh, I don't know," said Josephine. "There was a rather dapper-looking clown bust back there. Could pop it in my office, to test the state of my patients' hearts."

Petra sniffed out a laugh, which was about as much as she could muster.

Her mother, an efficient woman who'd done what she'd gone there to do, made to move off, only she stopped and said, "I was hoping you might come over for dinner, you and Sawyer. Some time next week."

Petra held her breath, waiting for the disclaimer. When that seemed to be the extent of her mother's offer, she said, "I'd love to." And meant it. "But it would only be me."

Her mother looked harder. Saw enough to understand.

Petra swallowed. "Would this be for Finn's birthday, Mum?"

"Yes, it would." Then, "I spoke to Sawyer on the phone the other day—did he tell you? No, I can see by your expression he did not. He'd been away and came home to find you not there. He was worried about you. In fact, the dinner was his idea."

Petra shook her head. *What the—? What?*

"He was a big bear of a boy," her mother said. "Only he had the gentlest heart. Much more your kind of person than Finn's. Even then." Another air-kiss. "You've done a wonderful thing here today, darling. You should feel immensely proud of yourself."

Then she was gone. Leaving Petra feeling utterly befuddled.

Sawyer. Calling her mother. Helping her open up about Finn. And taking no credit. Just helping, behind the scenes. Not for the glory, but because it was a kind thing to do.

Sawyer. *Her kind of person...*

She'd pushed Sawyer away, believing that, deep down, he'd not changed. When the truth was he *hadn't* changed. He was the same strong, determined, protective man he'd always been. A man who thought of everyone important in his life before he'd ever consider himself.

If he'd made plans to leave, it wasn't due to a fear of intimacy, or because she was not enough for him; the past weeks *had* proven that. It was because, for some stupid reason, he'd convinced himself that would be best for *her*.

While she, for some other stupid reason, had never told him that *he* was what was best for her. And always had been.

Only now...now it really was too late. Wasn't it?

The event was going brilliantly. She'd done her part, meaning if she wanted to duck away, she most certainly could. She checked her watch, only to find she'd left Do Not Disturb on. Again.

Turning it off, she saw several notifications come flying up on the screen.

The only one that registered was from Sawyer: nothing but an address.

Petra looked from the pin on the map app on her phone to find herself facing a three-storey building, the exterior a stark matte black, even the windows were blacked out.

Only the golden cage-shaped doorknobs on the big shiny double black doors were indicative of what was inside.

Sawyer had asked her to meet him at the Gilded Cage.

Was this some full circle moment? Had she left something in Lost Property? Was he returning to the scene of the crime to say goodbye for ever? Did it matter?

This was her chance to put the record straight. To tell him how she truly felt. To let him know that her heart was his to do with as he pleased, whether he wanted it or not.

She gave the handle a tug, not surprised to find it opened at her touch.

And inside—it looked so different in the daylight. Empty. And gargantuan. Devoid of all the bodies and the loud music, she could really take in the amazing patterns in the floor, the textures in the soft furnishings, the detail in the twirling gilt around the private booths.

Petra didn't spot Sawyer till she reached the bottom of the stairs leading to the dance floor.

He was at the bar. Battered leather jacket on his back, dark curls catching the light from the disco ball above. Standing in the same spot as that first night.

He turned when her boot heels clacked against the dance floor. And her heart, her poor squidgy besotted heart, flipped over in her chest at the sight of him. At the look in his eyes.

For he looked determined. A man on a mission. Not the kind of mission that had sent him off to far-flung lands again and again. The kind that had taken her by the hand and led her to his bed.

She could only hope with all her might that for once their missions did not clash. Or sending them spinning apart. Maybe this time they might finally be in sync.

Nerves zinging, hope riding a roller coaster, Petra lifted her chin, walked across the dancefloor, dumped her handbag on a pink leather stool and looked along the bar.

"Hey," said Sawyer, his voice rough. His eyes were dark and deep, as if he'd slept about as well as she had.

"Hey," she said back.

"So, I heard from Daisy that there's this amazing festival happening down at the Gallery of Melbourne this weekend."

Petra's lungs squeezed as she laughed out a breath. "Heard the same thing."

He smiled. "It's going well?"

"Beyond well," she said.

Then Sawyer breathed deep and slow, his gaze taking her in. Eating her up, as if he'd been starved of her. Till his gaze landed on her collarbone. On the thin rose gold chain, and the pull tab dangling thereon. The necklace she'd not taken off. Even after telling him it was over. Even after walking away.

When his eyes lifted back to hers they were molten. Focused. Ready. "So, I have a question for you."

She swallowed. "Okay."

"New York, or Germany?"

Not the question she'd been expecting. "Sorry?"

"You mentioned, as you twirled in the rain that night, that you'd fielded offers from a gallery in New York and an underground movement of some kind that made no sense to me in Germany. Have you decided which you'll take on?"

She *knew* it. He'd believed she was leaving him. Her chest rose and fell as she said, "I field offers all the time, Sawyer. I'm rather a big name in my world. But I'd not made any plans to take up either. Not without talking to you first."

He took the hit. As if he'd figured it out belatedly too.

Then he said, "After I take this final trip for Big Think, I was thinking I'd like to stay on here. For a bit."

"Final trip?" she asked, only able to focus on one bombshell at a time.

He nodded. "I'm heading all over, South and Central America, North Africa, South Asia, to introduce my contacts overseas to their new Big Think team. After which they'll do the heavy lifting, for I'll officially no longer be the brawn of the operation."

Petra breathed deep. "Wow. That's huge, Sawyer." And maybe even partly her doing, pushing as she had for him to imagine what *his* dreams might be. "If you're not going to be that, what *will* you be?"

"Whatever I want," he said. Then he pushed away from the bar and strolled towards her, till he was right there. Right in front of her. All big strong shoulders and warm skin and those clear blue eyes. "Wherever I want."

"And where's that?" she asked, her voice now a husky whisper.

"I'm thinking I might buy a place. A home, in fact. One I was hoping you'd like to come back to too."

"Sawyer," she said, feeling woozy and wonderful.

He leant against the bar, his gaze roving over her face. "I should have told you all this last night."

"Hell, yes, you should! Why didn't you?"

"According to Hadley, I was an idiot, and I think she was right."

Petra shook her head. "No, you're not. You're considered. And considerate. And you never say things you don't mean. Which means if you're here now, saying these things to me—" She couldn't finish her thought. It was too big to hold onto.

"I have good reason." Then he smiled. Not *the* smile, the one that blinded and distracted and could take out a pair of knees at fifty paces. But the one he seemed to save for only her.

Breathing deep, he lifted a hand and slid it into her hair, cradling her face. His thumb tracing her cheek before his eyes once again found hers.

"I love you, Petra."

The sound that spilled from Petra's lips was half laugh, half sob, pure relief. As if she'd known it for so long, only now she could finally believe it.

"I've pined for you, Petra. From the other side of the world, and the other side of your bed. Leaning into the pain as if it was proof somehow that I loved you despite all the reasons I should not. I don't want to do that any more. I want to…go on adventures, and eat too much, find some fabulous little place with a view and spend the day in bed with you."

His words felt so familiar. Then she remembered—the sweetener she'd used to try to get him to promise to marry her. Because she'd loved him for that long too.

At which point she threw herself into Sawyer's arms with enough gusto he rocked back a step. And another. His arms wrapping around her to catch her, to hold her. To pull her close.

"I love you," she said. "I've always loved you. And I want the adventures and the food and the bed. And the place to come home to. All of it, so long as you're there."

He pulled her closer, murmuring, "And if that isn't just the best news I've had all day…"

"Me too," she said, snuggling closer. Absorbing how real he felt. Not fake, not pretend, but honest and true.

Sawyer pulled back. "One more thing?"

"Sure!" She laughed. "But it's been a hell of a day, and I'm not sure I can take much more."

Smiling at her, all blue-eyed and stubbled and big and beautiful, he said, "The last time we were here I made a complete hash of something. Something important. The next time I tried, I made a hash of it again. No surprise then that it didn't take."

Sawyer slipped away from her then, and slowly dropped to one knee. "I'm hoping third time's the charm."

"Sawyer," she whispered.

Only this time she didn't freak out. Or beg for him to get the hell up. This time she leaned in—to her racing heart and her wild thoughts, and all the feelings filling her up inside.

"Petra Gilpin, you are my best friend. My muse. The reason I've been able to look at my life and make choices that have me feeling excited about the rest of my life. Marry me. Be with me. Put up with me. Travel with me. Tell me when I'm being an ass. Forgive me." He took in a deep breath. "And love me."

Petra took a moment, soaking in every slash of light, every flutter of dust, every glint of colour, imprinting it on her mind's eye. The moment, the most beautiful work of art she'd ever experienced.

"Petra?" Sawyer warned, his voice rough, impatient.

And her focus contracted to find him holding a ring box. Not pretend. Not a place holder. A pink diamond surrounded by petals of white diamonds, on a rose gold band. Turned out Petra was a ring girl after all.

"Yes!" she blurted. "Yes, a thousand times yes."

Sawyer slipped the ring onto her finger, a perfect fit. Then he winced as he pulled himself to standing.

"Your leg!" Petra said, helping to haul him up. Only to

squeak when he grabbed her, twirled her, dipped her and kissed her soundly.

He only broke the kiss to release her laughter, the sound seeming to float up to the ceiling and bounce off the chandelier above.

"So what now?" she asked, tugging on his shirt, tidying it up. Then making it messy again, evidence of their kiss fine with her. "I'm jobless and you're homeless…"

"How do you feel about sleeping in tents and tree houses and tiny backwater hotels with me for a while?"

"I can come? I can come!" Petra had never been to so many of the places Sawyer intended to go. The things she'd see, the culture, the beauty, the art. "How much luggage am I allowed? I have lucky outfits to consider. And then there's Russell—"

Sawyer coughed out a laugh. "Now, hang on a second—"

"He'd not understand if I leave him behind."

Sawyer swore beneath his breath, but his eyes grew dark. "Fine, Russell can come. And can I just say how glad I am to have got to know you all over again, as a grown-up?"

"You may," she said, sliding her hand lower, over his backside. Lifting her leg to tuck it around his calf.

Then they kissed for a very long time. By the time they came up for air Sawyer's curls were mussed, and Petra's clothes didn't look much better.

"Shall we get out of here?" Sawyer asked.

Petra wrapped her arm through his, her head tucked into his shoulder as they made their way across the dance floor. Under the light of the disco ball Sawyer twirled her out to the end of his arm and back again. Only this time she stuck. For good.

Mimi took over Petra's fundraising job at the gallery and did a far better job of that than Petra ever could.

After Finn's birthday dinner at the Gilpin family home, a reserved affair till her mum got into the port, after which things took a quite nice turn, Petra and Sawyer, and a Big Think contingent, set off.

For the next few weeks they travelled everywhere together, before Petra split off to New York for a spell. Back and forth they went, making sure to all be home for the Big Think Ball. Sawyer full to the brim with ideas on how to get the The Big Think Centres for Physical Therapy project underway, and plans to spend time with his family because he wanted to, not because he felt he should.

The first chance they had – between Petra decking out chalets and recording studios and her parents' home with the most wondrous arrays of art—they settled on a beautiful, new, gloriously eclectic hideaway in the Dandenong mountains, where they watched movies on the couch, kept bowls filled with found things on every surface and lived such normal lives, while clearly ridiculously in love.

And those who noticed barely batted an eyelid.

* * * * *

COMING SOON!

We really hope you enjoyed reading this book. If you're looking for more romance be sure to head to the shops when new books are available on

Thursday 8th June

To see which titles are coming soon, please visit

millsandboon.co.uk/nextmonth

MILLS & BOON®

Coming next month

THE BABY SWAP THAT BOUND THEM
Hana Sheik

"Marriage?" Yusra heard herself repeating slowly, enunciating the few syllables, and all while feeling foolish. Because surely, she'd heard him incorrectly.

She didn't want to leave Zaire behind, and like her, Bashir hadn't wanted to let go of AJ. Naturally then, for one brilliant, buoyant second, she had thought he had found a way to fix this.

But Yusra's fleeting hope passed as quickly as it arose.

"Yusra. I'm very seriously proposing this."

"This can't be for real," she whispered as a wave of dizziness swamped her. She was glad she was seated when Bashir had turned her world upside down. Weakly, she protested, "It has to be a joke... Right?"

She would even be willing to forgive him if it were, as cruel as it would be.

"Marriage is serious. It's a life-long commitment." Yusra felt like a hypocrite once she said it. Her marriage hadn't lasted. It also hadn't been full of love and support and reciprocity. And the experience soured the possibility of a second-chance romance for her. Still, it didn't mean she held any less value for the long-standing institution.

"I wouldn't joke about anything that required the level

of trust a marriage demands. I've given this plenty of thought. I wouldn't have proposed it if I hadn't." He then set his jaw firmly, the veins along his temples more pronounced, his brows two furry lines of severity. "Marriage would allow us to live together with the children. It would also present a united front to the hospital. They want to fix their error, and they've already contacted me about having us swap our children and righting the wrong."

"All right, but what made you decide this was the only way? We could co-parent without the ties of marriage."

"It might not seem like it, but I'm traditional," he countered.

"But marriage is complicated. There are things couples discuss and discover even before they consider such an important oath." Even as she spoke, Yusra knew not even a willingness to openly communicate could prevent a marriage from falling apart.

"Then we'll talk and negotiate terms, and outline and sign off on them. I believe it's possible."

Continue reading
THE BABY SWAP THAT BOUND THEM
Hana Sheik

Available next month
www.millsandboon.co.uk

LET'S TALK
Romance

For exclusive extracts, competitions
and special offers, find us online:

- f MillsandBoon
- 𝕏 @MillsandBoon
- 📷 @MillsandBoonUK
- ♪ @MillsandBoonUK

Get in touch on 01413 063 232

MILLS & BOON

THE HEART OF ROMANCE

A ROMANCE FOR EVERY READER

MODERN — Prepare to be swept off your feet by sophisticated, sexy and seductive heroes, in some of the world's most glamourous and romantic locations, where power and passion collide.

HISTORICAL — Escape with historical heroes from time gone by. Whether your passion is for wicked Regency Rakes, muscled Vikings or rugged Highlanders, awaken the romance of the past.

MEDICAL — Set your pulse racing with dedicated, delectable doctors in the high-pressure world of medicine, where emotions run high and passion, comfort and love are the best medicine.

True Love — Celebrate true love with tender stories of heartfelt romance, from the rush of falling in love to the joy a new baby can bring, and a focus on the emotional heart of a relationship.

Desire — Indulge in secrets and scandal, intense drama and sizzling hot action with heroes who have it all: wealth, status, good looks…everything but the right woman.

HEROES — The excitement of a gripping thriller, with intense romance at its heart. Resourceful, true-to-life women and strong, fearless men face danger and desire - a killer combination!

To see which titles are coming soon, please visit

millsandboon.co.uk/nextmonth